C000170550

# DESTINY

*The first installment of The Keeper's Trilogy*

*Dedicated to all those who never
stopped believing in me, even when I
didn't believe in myself*

WRITTEN BY
OLIVIA ALI

# PROLOGUE

"Cry Brethren Cry, for The Betrayer hath cometh!" chants the Interpreter as the hoods watching her listen with anticipation. "The coming of the Third Dawn shall be seen upon the land as the Beginning of the End, as the opening of the Unwritten Times. The Order of the Glyphs shall by touched by the Ancients and the Wretched, and the words of the Glyphs shall unwind."

A low murmur of discussion breaks out among the hooded Keepers below. The Interpreter traces the words she has read, a single frail finger floating across the drying ink. As she finishes, she taps the page making more runes appear suddenly as she looks up towards the crowd of Keepers.

"There is more," her voice is weak and silent, yet heard by the whole room as the Keepers silence themselves and turn to face her. "Our hands will be crippled and we will perish as fools whilst the Wretched One unveils the Bleak Unwritten. Then we will know the face of our Destroyer!"

Silence; the room echoes with it as Keepers turn their heads to each other with anguish on their faces. That anguish turns to panic, and once again the room is in uproar. The Interpreter looks to the First Keeper and he steps up to the podium where she had been. For a moment he surveys his followers, not noticing the books in the shelves surrounding the walls begin to shudder in their places. Clearing his throat, he removes his hood and holds out his hands.

"Silence!" he roars as the room turns to face him, the noise dulling and their faces hoping for salvation. "We must not panic..."

"But First Keeper Felix," interrupts a Keeper below as he too removes his hood. "Surely this prophecy means the end of us all?"

"Brother Percy," he says with a surprisingly calm voice. "I appreciate your concern, but we must remember the balance we have struck. We must not fall apart, lest the rest of the world will follow! We can prevent this prophecy from taking place if only we find a way."

"But how First Keeper?" questions another.

"Brother Basso, we…."

A loud bang sounds from the top end of the room as a book fall from its shelf, the sound echoing on the wood tiled floor. The Keepers watch as a Scribe near the back steps towards the book that has fallen by his feet, the pages bent as it lays open on the floor. He opens, it staring blankly at the white papyrus pages.

"The books," he shouts desperately, a single tear falling from his crystal grey eyes. "They have become…Unwritten!"

Shouts escalate from the hooded crowd and panic erupts like a volcano that has been dormant for centuries. It is an uproar The First Keeper cannot contain and as he surveys his followers once more, he watches as those running to leave the Reading Room stop dead in their tracks. He looks towards the stars that can be seen through the glass ceiling above, the window shattering and the shards raining down upon the screaming crowd.

"Can you not hear the chanting?" someone shouts from within the crowd, many putting their hands to their ears. The First Keeper looks around spotting the perpetrator in a sudden smoke that spreads around the room, enveloping the legs of all the Keepers.

"Father Talus save us from the Shadows that will embrace us in Eternal Darkness!" He prays, and as he finishes other hooded members form within the crowd; their eyes a piercing red inside their non-existent faces, their cloaks showing no evidence of a living form beneath them.

"The Faders are here!" speaks a Keeper Elder as he fades moments later followed by countless others.

The Faders begin to fade too, taking with them the souls of the unafraid Keepers who dared to accept their fate. As they perish, a single tear falls from the blue eyes of The First Keeper and he too fades alongside his followers.

# CHAPTER 1 - THE END OF AN ERA

Sparks flew off the steel as a stone hammer came down hard on the malleable metal, sapping it to a point and tarnishing the natural shine. The arm that wielded the hammer was strong and forceful, his control over his tool shown through every vein that rippled through his flesh. As the shape was completed, he placed the hammer on the floor and removed the mask that protecting his face. As he did so the wisps of blonde brown hair clung to it, the static attracting them. He wiped the sweat from his forehead and admired his handy work, grabbing a cloth from the side of the furnace beside him and wiping the blade clean, bringing back the natural shine once more. He placed the blade into a bucket of cold water which stood on the cobblestoned floor to cool for a moment, hearing a voice coming from the other room.

"Tristan!" Jenni called. "Don't tell me you're still here?" She sighed heavily as Tristan came through from the workroom of the smithy. "You realise you're going to be late?"

"Yes, I know!" Tristan sighed, taking the apron off from around him and placing it on the counter. "Don't worry, no one is going to miss me." He caressed Jenni's face, brushing her deep red hair out of the way. "I bet you will though."

"Of course, I'll miss you," she kissed his hand as it rested upon her face. "But you really should go!"

"Okay, I'm going!"

Tristan leaned forward and kissed her on the lips. It was a longing kiss, a kiss that wanted to last a lifetime. As he broke away, he winked at her, turning on his heel and leaving her alone in the blacksmith's hut.

"Ashes to ashes, dust to dust; may you forever be within our memories, reminding us of your greatness - your reign of gold." chanted the priest as he dropped a handful of dirt onto the ivory coffin that lay in a neatly dug hole in the royal gardens.

Tristan weaved in and out of the crowd of mourning councillors, a few disgruntled glances escaping him as he passed. He joined his father at the head of the procession, bowing his head down as the priest joined them all in a prayer of forever rest for the dead king.

"You're late!" his father whispered harshly, casting Tristan that all too familiar disappointing look.

"I know and I'm sorry but I had work to do." Tristan snapped back, giving his father not one single ounce of respect in his words. In truth he hadn't had to be at work at all today – a public holiday had been commanded throughout the whole city due to the sad event.

"Surely the swords can wait? This is the King's funeral; you should not have missed it!"

A few faces looked around and hushed Theorryn as Tristan smirked at his father's sudden embarrassment. Theorryn sighed heavily as the priest finished the prayer, casting a look of disappointment in their direction, and raised his hands to signal those at the head of the procession to step forward, take a handful of dirt and drop it on the casket. Tristan and Theorryn stepped forward and placed their hands in the bucket of dirt, grabbing a handful and then dropping it in the hole. They stepped away from the crowd, just out of earshot where Tristan hoped their heated discussion would not continue.

"What are your plans for dinner?" asked Theorryn.

"Not sure yet...why?" answered Tristan, suddenly suspicious.

"Well, it's more than likely that I won't be around, I have a council meeting to attend."

"I see, it's alright, I'm sure Jenni will sort me out with something."

"So long as you don't end up going without..."

"I never do!" Theorryn nodded and turned away from Tristan.

"I have to go. I'll see you tonight." He re-joined the procession at the head of the Royal Gardens leaving Tristan to depart and return to the city streets.

Tristan and his father had an awkward relationship; they had ever since Romeo, his older brother had died. He was convinced that his father thought he was to blame for the murder even though he never said so. Three years ago, there had been corruption within the city of Hasaghar where he and his brother were living at the time; becoming Keeper Acolytes. In the chaos, Romeo had been murdered by rioters along with a few other civilians whose names escaped Tristan. He and Jenni had become stronger since; he had begun to rely on her for support in his everyday life, support that should have been given by a father. In total, they had been together about nine years, on and off of course...but no relationship is perfect. For now, Tristan was happy and that was all he wanted.

Tristan left the Royal Gardens, heading back out towards the now quiet city streets. As he passed into the square, he took note of the lowness of the sun and how the moon was just appearing behind the fading clouds. The thought of going back to work did enter his mind momentarily but he thought better of it. Besides, he had more important things to worry about, like the fact that he was already late for his lesson with Merlin.

Merlin had been teaching Tristan about the Keepers and trying to make him remember the time he had spent with them. He has amnesia and there is a period of about six years that he doesn't remember anything about. All he knows is that in this time; he joined the Keepers and progressed to the Acolyte stage, got married and widowed and lost his brother. His father had never mentioned anything of his forgotten past, neither had Jenni, and whenever Tristan asked a question about it, both would try to avoid the subject. The only one to show an interest in Tristan's past was Merlin, but even though he had been teaching him the lessons of his past for just under three years, it wasn't sparking any memories.

The old man lived above the stables. To most, he was thought to be a grumpy old coot who had no manners, but to the children of Az Lagní he was a storyteller and a great one at that. To Tristan however, he was more of a father to him then Theorryn ever had been, even before the Keepers came into his life. Romeo had always been the 'Golden Boy', but he never hated his brother for it, he hated his father.

Tristan knocked loudly on the door of Merlin's residence, stepping back and waiting patiently for him to answer. He could hear footsteps on the other side of the door, meaning someone was definitely in.  The old man answered the door rather briskly, his sideburns becoming even more slanted as his bearded mouth stretched into a smile.

"Tristan!" exclaimed Merlin's gruff voice. "I wasn't expecting you this early. Please, do come in." he was being sarcastic of course.

Merlin turned, opening the door fully so that Tristan could enter. His abode was rather bright today compared to the dullness it usually resembled, the sunlight of the late afternoon catching the patches of baldness on top Merlin's grey head.

"Yes, I thought I'd come a little earlier seeing as there was no point going back to work." replied Tristan with the same sarcasm, stepping straight into the seating area where a fabric couch and a coffee table greeted him to his left. A dining and kitchen area were in front of him with a staircase behind the surfaces leading up to the two bedrooms and washroom.

"So, you decided to go the funeral after all then?" Merlin strolled forward into the kitchen and placed a pot of water on the fire to boil. He pointed to the table, motioning for Tristan to sit.

"To be honest, if I hadn't of gone it would've given my father another excuse to scold me and he has enough already."

"Fair enough I suppose." Merlin sat opposite Tristan, watching the pot on the fire and waiting for it to boil. "How was it?"

"I ah...I arrived late, so I missed most of it."

"And you wonder why your father scolds you so often," Merlin scowled as the water began to boil. He got up and retrieved it from the fire, placing it on a hot plate on the surface and reaching into a cupboard over his head. "What tea do you fancy?"

"What have you got?"

"I have lemongrass, elderflower, and a new berry flavour I thought might be nice."

"Um...I'll try that new one...the berry one."

As Merlin made the tea, Tristan looked around the place, his eyes being caught by the sun setting out the window. He hadn't noticed how late it was until now.

"I have a present for you by the way," Merlin said as he placed the tea on the table, bringing Tristan back to reality. "I'll just go and get it."

As Merlin disappeared upstairs, Tristan stared bemused at the cup of red liquid that had been placed in front of him. It was so red, it almost resembled blood. He sniffed the steam that rose from it, noting the strong smell of rich summer fruits and a blend of honey to sweeten the brew. He was never really a fan of Merlin's tea, especially the elderflower one, but this berry one could be an exception.

"I came across this whilst searching through some of the things you left at Hasaghar. The box this was in was found in your dorms so I thought I'd have a look through." Merlin sat back down and handed a piece of parchment to Tristan. "Here!"

He unfolded the stained parchment to gaze upon a photograph of six men all facing forward. All of them looked rather serious but at the same time relaxed; as though each were in the presence of their brother. He recognised one of them to be Romeo - the details of his death were varied; everyone seemed to have a different version of events. Tristan remembered none of it and it wasn't a particular memory he was looking forward to eventually recollecting. In the photo, Romeo's blonde-brown hair stood up on end, planted scruffily on the top of his head. He wore a smart light green tunic that had a collar up to his neck with tan coloured breaches that disappeared into brown boots. He was a rather tall man, and completely the opposite image to the tall smart man Tristan had known when he remembered him. The men stood around Romeo he did not recognise, however there was something about the man that stood to his left. It was in the blue eyes that stared out from the shaggy blonde brown haircut that was similar to his own just not as scruffy. He wore a brown tunic that left some of the chest bare. His breaches and boots resembled the same colour, only they were slightly darker. If anything, this man looked older than Romeo because of the stubble that stretched around his cheeks and onto his chin.

"That boy there...is you!" said Merlin, pointing to the boy Tristan had just been pondering about.

"That's me?" Tristan asked in disbelief.

"Hard to believe isn't it? You were much more of a rapscallion in those days. I think you are about nineteen in this photo. It was taken not long after you arrived in Dilu actually, to become a Keeper Scribe."

"Who are the others?"

Merlin moved his finger to the man stood next to Tristan, a dark imposing figure who had a regal aura about him, as though he were far better than anybody imagined. He had short black hair that curled around his ears with a middle parting and a rather bony face with fairly tanned skin. His eyes seemed to shine, a stylised beard and slight goatee just touching his chin. He wore a clean white shirt underneath a black leather jacket that had a stitched white design on it. Smart black leggings covered his slim but strong legs and big black boots his feet. A wide belt stretched around his waist with smaller ones that hung off the side so a scabbard could be strung there.

"This is Jacques," Merlin explained. "You and Romeo knew him before the Keepers...you used to call him Jacques Indigo. You three and my boy Thomas were practically inseparable as children."

"I remember Thomas!"

"Jacques' uncle moved him away when he was thirteen, you boys never saw him again...until you became Keepers that was. He was raised in the libraries at Dilu along with the two boys here."

Now Merlin pointed to two very similar looking boys; obviously brothers. The older looking of the two stood at the edge of the left side of the photo, as though they were mirroring Tristan and Romeo stood on the other side. This man was also dark haired like Jacques but his hair was much less groomed than his and a lot curlier. A full beard covered his finely chiselled chin. He too had rather tanned skin like his possible younger brother and Jacques. This man wore a groggy looking white shirt that left his hairy chest bare. This shirt was covered by a patchwork like jacket with different shades of brown. Leather breaches clung to his legs and boots of the same shade of dark brown came to his knees. He was rather cheeky looking, as though there wasn't a serious bone in his body. The one who Tristan assumed to be his younger brother looked a lot more serious than the other, more swarve. He wore a plain red shirt, again leaving the chest bare, with a brown jacket. Dark brown leather leggings covered his legs with boots that came to his knees.

"These two are Ramien and Zhaine," said Merlin at last.

 "Are they brothers?"

"Yes!" Exclaimed Merlin, suddenly feeling hopeful; "Did you remember them?"

"No, they just looked similar to each other."

Merlin's face dropped slightly, the hope disappearing from his face as he hovered his finger above the final boy in the picture. He looked different from the rest of them, an air of naivety and innocence. He seemed younger as well, although in reality he was probably the same age as Tristan was in this photo. He had blonde hair in the same style as Jacques did with a slight beard that was probably more of a stubble really. His skin was rather pale, made paler so by the dark brown jacket he was wearing with its gold patterns and buttons. The jacket draped over a tan shirt and he wore dark brown leather breaches that were covered at the knees by brown boots.

"And this last one is Cedric...Cedric Baldwin, you and him were particularly good friends. There were times you and he were closer than you and Romeo were. Heck you even...."

"I even what?" Tristan asked after a while, looking up from the photo.

"You know I thought a picture might just trigger something." This would have been the first image he had seen into his forgotten past but it had opened no clues to it.

Tristan looked up at Merlin, his eyes as clear as glass. The photo had triggered nothing within his head, no memories, no visions, no nothing. Tristan wiped a single tear from his cheek; both angry and frustrated with himself that he couldn't remember his own brothers. Merlin reached out and placed his hand on Tristan's, comforting him in a kind of fatherly way.

"Give it time Tristan!" reassured Merlin. "It may come eventually. It's clear the picture is making you feel something; you just need to connect with how it is making you feel. We have progress, even if it is only small progress."

Tristan placed the photo on the table so that it faced down and took a sip of his tea. The two men sat in silence for a while, pondering the taste of the berry tea perhaps.

"I'm not sure I like this tea...too strong for my liking," squirmed Merlin, walking over to the window and emptying the contents of it into the street. "I prefer a more dulcet flavour." Tristan sniggered at the sudden poshness of Merlin's voice. "What did you think of it?"

"I quite liked it!" answered Tristan honestly as he downed the rest of his tea.

"You can have it then! Come on," Merlin grabbed his cloak from the back of the front door. "Let's go for some dinner, my treat. I'll wait for you downstairs!"

Tristan rose from his seat, turning the photo over again and looking once more at it. Smiling slightly to himself, he folded it neatly and placed it in a pocket on the inside of his tunic. Then, taking a deep breath he headed down the stairs after Merlin.

# CHAPTER 2 - GLOWING PALMS

The Green Clover Inn was at the centre of the city around a glorious fountain. It was the biggest public house in the whole of Az Lagní, only an inn to those in desperate need, although saying that Tristan had only seen the upstairs bedroom used a couple times by him and the very attractive barmaid coming over to take their order at the bar. This attractive young woman was of course Jennivere Bennett and she was all Tristan's. She wasn't the prettiest girl Tristan had ever seen, that was the woman he dreamt about at night, but she loved him and that was all he could ask; especially after everything he had put her through in the past. Right now, she seemed to be the only person not linked to his Keeper days, and he needed that.

"And what can I get you two fine gentlemen today?" asked Jenni in a cheeky tone of voice, giving Tristan a little wink.

"I don't know about being a gentleman...but I am quite fine!" exclaimed Merlin returning the wink with a cheeky smile. "What's the special?"

"Fish pie with potatoes, peas and carrots."

"My favourite, I'll have that with a brandy." Merlin winked again and removed his pipe from his pocket. Jenni poured him his drink and he strolled over to a quiet table by the fire.

"And what about you," Jenni now turned to Tristan.

"I'll have that red dress off you for starters..." he joked.

"Behave!" she whispered, slapping him on the wrist and smiling blushingly to herself as her cheeks matched the redness of her dress. "What would you like to eat?"

"Well wouldn't you like to know..." he said cheekily, shaking his head and looking her up and down when Jenni raised her eyebrows looking like she was about to say something when...

"Can a man get some service over here?" shouted a deep voice, silencing the whole pub. Jenni looked around, *why had all the bar hands chosen now to disappear?*

"It's okay," reasoned Tristan. "Serve him first; I haven't decided what I want to eat yet anyway."

"Okay," Jenni sighed, slumping off to stand in front of the hooded stranger that stood not far from where Tristan perched at the bar.

He watched as the man pushed down the hood of his cloak revealing a dusty face with a full-length unkempt beard. Long scruffy dark hair draped around his long face like curtains, greasy and greying in areas. An old scar stretched down his left cheek which was shadowed and gaunt, like he had just been involved in a bar brawl elsewhere. Perhaps he had been to one of the other more low-key pubs in Az Lagní and got into a scuffle. Something about him irked at Tristan's curiosity so he planted himself comfortably so he could just about hear the conversation.

"About bloody time too!" The man sounded western, but it wasn't an incredibly strong accent - subtle but enough to tell the direction at least. Perhaps he was well travelled?

"What can I do for you sir?" asked Jenni, putting on her best serious voice.

"Oh, I'm not a sir...aren't you a little young to be a barmaid?" A slight smile crept into the ends of his mouth as he looked down on the wench before him.

"Is there something you want?" the man looked up suddenly at the oversized man who now stood behind Jenni. The landlord's name was Gregory, an imposing stature of a man with wispy blonde hair and a red face framed by a trimmed beard. He looked the opposite of the dishevelled stranger that stood on the other side of the bar.

"I need a place to stay..." he explained rationally.

"We don't offer that kind of service here!" Jenni interjected.

"I was told you do for people in my...predicament."

"I..."

"I'll need to see some sort of identification?" demanded Gregory, startling the already shaken Jenni and flexing his right hand. "Jenni, will you leave us please?"

As Jenni slumped out to the kitchen, the man looked around, forcing Tristan to avert his gaze down at the coaster he was spinning on top the bar. He glanced up slightly, watching as the man removed a black fingerless glove from his right hand. He showed his palm to Gregory, as though there was something upon it. Tristan watched as the lines on his palm formed a shape, a rune within his skin that glowed slightly, emitting a blue light. Whatever this mark meant it was enough proof for Gregory who nodded. As the man began replacing the glove onto his hand, Tristan's own palm began to burn, searing with pain suddenly and causing the coaster he was fiddling with to fling across the underside of the bar. He looked down at his palm, the same mark appearing in the lines as had done on the stranger's. He marvelled at the sight as the glow faded but the mark remained. He looked up in time to see Jenni coming over to him, picking up the coaster from the floor as she did.

"Are you okay?" she asked, a concerned look on her face.

"Yes! Yes I'm fine!" Tristan stammered as he clenched his hand into a fist, sending shooting pains through to his wrist.

"Got a name?" he heard Gregory say.

"Dante Ashdown," answered the man, his face seeming brighter and cleaner than it was.

"Are you sure you're okay?" Jenni asked, turning Tristan's face away from the stranger. "It's just you've gone really pale?"

"I'm fine honestly," Tristan lied his head feeling light all of the sudden. "I'm just hungry!"

"Right, of course," the stranger had unnerved Jenni for some reason; she too had gone rather pale. "How about I ask the chef to fix up your favourite; steak and mushroom pie?"

"Mushroom...yuk!"

"But you love mushrooms? Steak and mushroom is your favourite?"

"No, steak and ale is my favourite!"

"Everything alright old-boy," asked Merlin now standing beside Tristan. "What's taking so long?"

"Sorry," stammered Jenni. "Steak and ale pie and a fish pie coming right up. Can I get you a drink Tristan?"

"A wheat beer will be fine!"

"But you hate wheat beer!" Jenni protested.

"Since when? Jenni what's wrong with you today?"

"Nothing...sorry..." Jenni said eventually when Merlin said nothing. She poured Tristan a wheat beer and handed it to him. "I'll be over with your dinners soon!"

Merlin and Tristan both nodded to her and returned to the table Merlin had selected for them by the kindling fire. As the two sat, Tristan sipped his beer; relishing the taste as though he hadn't had one in rather a while.

"I don't know what's wrong with her today," he started to say as Merlin too sipped from his brandy. "I mean first she suggests a steak and mushroom pie and now she thinks I don't like beer...I love beer!"

"She's right though you know," Merlin said after a while, lighting the candle with a simple flick of his fingers. "Maybe the question we should be asking is what has gotten into you?"

"Excuse me?"

"Tristan, what's wrong?" he stared into Tristan's cloudy blue eyes. "Something has happened, hasn't it?" Tristan shook his head slowly, still trying to get his head round the mark that was still burning on his palm. "You remembered something…"

Merlin looked down at Tristan's still clenched fist, glancing up at his cloudy eyes once more. He gently took the fist into his own relaxed hands and slowly prised open Tristan's fingers, keeping eye contact with him all the whilst. He put up no fight, simply letting Merlin gaze upon the mark that rested on his palm. Merlin studied the mark, a look of what appeared to be relief painted on his gaunt face.

"When did this appear?"

"Just now," Tristan stammered, suddenly quivering where he sat.

"Tristan this is serious…"

"Tristan, you do realise what this mark means right. This might be the connection we were missing…the key to getting you to remember. I don't mean to alarm you, but something has snapped in you. I mean, these past three years all you've drank is ale and you always have a steak and mushroom pie." Tristan stared at Merlin, the colour draining from his face as fear gripped him. "But what can it all mean…why now?"

Merlin looked over at the bar and Tristan followed his gaze back to the stranger who shot a look in their direction. Something in his eyes sparked at Tristan, making him jump up and knock into Jenni who suddenly appeared behind him with their pies all plated up and ready. The plates crashed to the floor, smashing and sending food everywhere, gravy spilling all down her red dress.

"Tristan!" Jenni screamed as she looked down at herself, suddenly very embarrassed.

Tristan starred at the mess he had caused, looking round the pub as everyone stared at him. His head was pounding and he was shaking like a leaf. He shook his head in frustration and stormed out of the inn, Merlin and Jenni both shouting after him.

# CHAPTER 3 - THE SHADOW LANDS

Tristan slumped down on the wooden tiled floor as the front door of his home slammed behind him, his ears ringing. Resting his head in his hands, he tried to quell his headache by massaging his temples and fighting against the visions trying desperately to cloud his mind. His breathing began to slow but he could still feel his hands burning; the tops searing with pain. He stared in bewilderment as two runes etched themselves there, blood dripping from his palms and staining his breaches. He turned them round and glanced at them again, looking in disbelief and confusion. Just then, he felt something harden on his back as the feeling of a thousand needles stabbing him at once met his senses. Jumping up, he raced into the sitting room to stand in front of the mirror above the fireplace, ripping off his tunic and staring at the tattoo forming between his shoulder blades; a blue glyph in the shape of a sigil Tristan knew to be that of the Keepers.

He stared in disbelief at the tattoo, the pain of his new markings subsiding and leaving them to settle within his skin. Shaken, he sunk into the armchair his father would usually sit, again cradling his aching head in his hands, blood still seeping from the wounds. After a while, the pain in his head began to subside and he watched the floor as a dark shadow began to appear before him. Expecting to see his father, he looked up suddenly startled to see another man before him. The man looked exactly like him, only different somehow. He stood there, grinning at Tristan; his stance relaxed slightly and his feet planted firmly on the floor. The man had the same piercing blue eyes that Tristan himself had, looking upon him from behind a blonde brown hairstyle that covered his brow and ears. Tristan ran his hand through his own hair; considerably shorter and neater than his lookalike. A stubble prickled his chin; framing his face and making his high cheekbones stand out. The rugged look had obviously been a thing this double liked...it was probably the only thing differing between the twins. As Tristan continued to stare at himself as though a mirror stood in front of him, he noticed the bare skin on his torso begin to split into symbols and words that seemed to scar his once immaculate form. Tristan gasped, watching as words turned into whole passages that were written as though they belonged to endless prophecies his ears once knew. He clawed at his own torso, looking down to see nothing but old scars from long ago wounds.

He looked back up at his own face as the grin faded and his mouth became stitched together. At the same time, he noticed that although some of the words were too small for him to read, other words he could make out - the word 'listen' was now etched into his forehead. He looked himself up and down, noticing other words; 'secrets' spread across his chest and 'union' just above his midriff. The glyph on his palm rested below the last word, the same glyph Dante shared with him, a word echoing in his head as he studied the glyph.

"Nobility!" the echo came.

The double of him jolted his neck suddenly, the smile stretching back and causing his mouth to bleed as the stitches were ripped out. Tears of blood began to bleed from his eyes, peeling his skin as they spilt down his face and dripped onto his torso. Tristan gasped as the scarred version of himself jumped at him. Flailing, he used his arms to shield himself, his arms absorbed the scars of the man as they became one. Tristan fell to his knees; the immense pain that had just left him gripping him once more. Yelling out in anguish he saw an illuminated figure form in front of him; in the place of where he had seen himself, reaching out with a graceful hand. He reached out to take the hand, begging the glowing silhouette for help, for seldom away from his pain. When their hands touched, he was met by an overwhelming sensation that would only be bought on through torture, a feeling like the bones inside his body were being shattering into a thousand pieces.

Then the figure obliterated, leaving a numb Tristan kneeling on the rug in the middle of the sitting room. Dizzy, he collapsed to the floor.

~~~

A scream sounds in the darkness and for a moment I fear I am not alone. It echoes all around me; causing a ringing in my ears; a sensation which made me feel human for the first time since I became stuck down here. I am still unsure of how long I have been down here – the variations between night and day are much the same; there is no sun or moon, no stars or clouds, just the blackness of the sky above me. The screaming stops, leaving me in silence once more. There is a strange safety in this silence around me, it means I am alone and therefore no one could hurt me...at least that's what it meant down here. There is always danger here. There are cloaked shadows that reside in the Watchtower on the horizon and every so often they come lurking into the darkness and flush out us faded ones from our hiding places. On the surface world, silence is suspicious and makes you feel as though you are being followed or watched...like something bad is about to happen. Here, silence is a sanctity.

I look around suddenly, fearing the screams would arouse the hooded shadows but there was no such movement. The dead trees up above remained still, the blackened grass standing on end, the greying sky...*greying sky*? The sky was usually black, blackest of blacks, but the tone was now changing, a greyness tinging the barrier. It was smoke! The Watchtower on the horizon was beginning to crumble, falling to the ground and enveloping the horizon in smoke. I could hear the crashing and banging of rubble hitting the floor, bringing back the ringing in my ears. As the smoke faded, I noticed a light flickering in its place. It could have been fire but its colour marvelled me. In all the time I had been down here I had never seen colour, even my clothes had become blackened by the dust. The colour was so beautiful...the light bringing me peace as it shone brighter than ever. No way could something that pure be fire. It was like it was calling to me, wanting me to behold it...and I wanted to behold it.

Maybe the light marked the end of my time in darkness; maybe it would take me back to the land of colour and light I used to revel in. I take a deep breath, and before I know it my feet are taking me towards the source of the light. As I begin to leave, I turn and look back at the shadows that cower behind the trees and in the bushes, behind the tall grass and camouflaged within the darkness. Goodbye my brothers, perhaps one day soon, the light will call to you as well!

As I find my way through the trees that have been my solace for so long, a fire begins to burn within me, bringing me courage in these times of darkness. With each step I take, I stand taller, braver and resemble more of the man that I once was on the surface world. The trees are scarce now and I begin to walk through what must be a meadow or a field; my eyes ever vigilant, darting around the sparseness, ready for the shadows that could and would probably jump out at any minute. As I near the edge of the field, a point begins to form at the edge of the horizon, getting bigger and bigger the closer I get. My steps begin to quicken as hope seems to make the fire within me burn stronger and warmer. The point turns into a spire and a spire into a tower, a tower into a building...and a building into a church.

I stop for a moment, marvelling at the sight of it. I feel for a moment as though I recognise it, as though I have been here before. In front of me stands a majestic stone archway with large wooden doors adorned with metal bolts and hinges. The archway stretches up and curves to touch a circular stained-glass window with the paintings of people looking up at a black winged angel. This myth is that of the Amaranth; a tale of a complacent prince who was named a saviour to the people of Asan.

Or perhaps it was God's Sacrifice, the angel that God sent down as a message to us all; the angel God damned. If that was the case, then this was a Hammerite church, and the two arched windows proved this point. These windows had colours red and silver around the silhouette of a hammer. I followed the structure ever higher, finally finding the steeple that had caught my eyes in the first place, its steel cross catching in some hidden light.

My eyes were bought back down to the stone doors and the four guards that stood vigil over it; two on either side. The guards were too made of stone and had crests upon their chests. Another mirrored them forming the centre of the huge doors, something my eyes had missed on the first glance. I continued to step forward, slower this time, still vigilant of the shadows that might jump me at any minute. As I stepped onto the concrete steps that formed the base of the church, the doors opened without a touch and I stepped into the light that seemed to emanate from the building, pausing for a moment before entering the magnificent structure.

I stop just inside the doorway to marvel at the imposing tapestry that stood before me on the wall. Its main colour was blue; a dark indigo background with a much lighter blue figure emblazoned as though the figure were a beacon. But I guess, in a way it was a beacon, a beacon for the Hammerites and their patron Saint Edgar, the father clan. A half-clothed man holding a hammer in the air, light shining from his head like a crown adorned the centre of the tapestry. He had a muscular form and a ring of fire etched around his figure. To the Hammerites, he was a prophet, a speaker for their Lord the Builder. He saved the Hammerites from the accursed Mechanists who betrayed them with their ways of progression as opposed to the means for foundations. The Mechanists had strayed from the path set down by the Builder; the need for the preservation of human life, and instead fought for their advancement and created robotic brains that could power themselves. They had thought they were Gods! And this, St. Edgar could not allow on his oath as a Hammerite. And so, he rose up, for the sake of his beliefs and his God. His strength and valour were truly represented well in this simple yet iconic piece of art.

To both my left and right was a pathway, the way lit up by fiery torches. Assuming they would both lead me to the interior of the church, I picked one at random and pursued its destination along the blue and red patterned carpet that covered the centre of the floor as a runner against the cobblestones. As I followed it around the corridor, I was led into a huge atrium and I realise now that this is no church but a cathedral as told by the level of detail and structure within the room I now occupied. Ahead of me on the far wall was a large circular stained-glass window. Tints of purple and blue formed a mystical background in contrast to the intimidating red of the hammer that lay in the centre of the glass. In front of this window on a podium was a statue of The Builder himself holding a hammer within his hands as though he were presenting it to someone perhaps? Along the pathway towards him were dark wooden pews that stretched up either side towards the podium, the same silver and red carpet forming a pathway between them. I followed the lines up, seeking a pew somewhere near the front to sit and think a while. I sat for a while, thinking and wondering why such a place had suddenly appeared here; a place of worship, a place of colour, beauty and light in a place of decay, darkness and shadow.

I closed my eyes a while, letting the fresh air within the church take me to a place I visited often as teenager in my hometown. The place held significance to me and at a time when I felt very lost, it bought me solace, just as the mystery cathedral I was now in was doing. It felt so strange to feel something warm heat up my core, I felt human for the first time in what must have been years.

Abruptly, I was bought out of my thoughts by a loud tingling sound, as though someone were dragging their hand through a wind chime of some sort. I looked around, having now risen from my pew. I stepped out into the aisle and noticed an open door in the right-hand corner below the stained-glass window. It was something I hadn't noticed before and the design on the door was rather elaborate so you'd think it would be something I would have noticed at first glance. I approached the door slowly, being sure to keep my eyes peeled for movement at any moment. I noticed a pattern forming on the door; it was changing from a plain wooden door with iron ingots to a very macabre image of a hanged man painted on to the door in dark colours. It resonated a strange feeling within me, as though part of me had seen the image before that only that part remembered. The other part seemed to have eradicated it from thought, but the memory of it was still there...somewhere. As I got closer, the image changed again and the door became reinforced with metal; iron crawling over the wood and choking the life out of it, nails wrought themselves in the border and a dove flew into life on the top panel with a golden key in its beak.

I knew then that it was a sign! The Keepers had found me, my brothers had come back for me; this was their sigil and it was showing me the way. A light formed at the end of the corridor the door had revealed and I made hastily for it without a second thought. But the closer I got, the further away it seemed to be, as though it were running away from me as I was running towards it. I stopped suddenly, thinking back to the image that had appeared on the door; the first one of the hanging man. Words from my past slithered into my ears, words a teacher had said to one of my fellow Scribes, who at the time had called Mr Ancient as he looked as though he were over a thousand years old; this was probably an exaggeration though. He had taught us the history of the Keepers and how they were a united religion who believed, like the God lovers, that Noah had sent a dove to find land during the Great Flood but instead of an Olive Branch, the dove instead bought back a gold key. According to legend, the key was a sign from Keeper Rune Mages who had managed to protect their compound and surrounding village against the flooding and rise their land to the surface.

The Keepers split in more recent years into two groups; The Keepers of Time and the Keepers of Secrets. One group concealed the future, the others the past. Talus then came along and he and his brothers united the two once more, however there was a sect of brothers who disagreed with the union and split themselves off and taking on the Dharsi name, becoming a separate brotherhood altogether. The start of their reign had been marked by the hanging of a man, a sacrifice if you like to show their insubordination.

It was then that I realised I had been tricked. I tried to turn back, escape the fate that all this time I had been trying to avoid. As I ran towards the door it grew further away and I knew then my attempt at escape was folly. Now I was theirs! I felt the light behind me turn to shadow as a sudden coldness crept over me sending shivers up my spine. I stopped then and turned, facing the approaching shadows; they would not take me...not without a fight. As it neared closer to me, I closed my eyes and outstretched my arms, letting the light that ran through my veins flow out through my fingers. My light would fight this darkness...

# CHAPTER 4 - THE KING'S DEEPEST REGRET

After he left Tristan to head back to the city, Theorryn came to stand by Ivan as he waited for the rest of the mourners to drop dirt onto the casket. The two waited in an awkward silence. Theorryn preferred it this way though; Ivan was one of many who disagreed heavily with the way he was currently leading his life - right into the nearest pub night after night. Ever since his beloved Mariah had died, a stiff ale had always been the perfect end to his day. It was never just the one though, one followed the other, and another, and so on and so forth. It just made things easier.

As the last of the mourners dropped the dirt, the guards began shovelling more on top of the casket. Ivan turned away, leading the other councillors that had formed around him into the palace and towards the throne room where the Princess Iris would be waiting to receive them. As they walked in silence, Theorryn wondered what the meeting might hold for them. The higher up members had been very secretive as to what it was about and this puzzled him greatly.

"Have you been drinking again?" Theorryn was brought out of his thoughts by Balderick who had been walking next to him.

When Theorryn didn't answer, Balderick shook his head but said nothing. The smell of stale ale was obviously more noticeable than he had realised. But he didn't care – people could think what they wanted so long as they didn't voice their judgements. He followed the others into the throne room and they began filling up the stalls in the sides of the room. Iris was sat at her own throne next to her father's wearing a long black dress almost as dark as her hair and making her pale skin paler still. She had retreated inside after dropping the first lot of dirt onto her father's casket – unable to face the dull affair any longer.

Theorryn took his place next to Hamish in the stalls. Hamish was the mediator with the Keepers – not that his role meant anything anymore as they had all Faded. Theorryn had often wondered what it was about Hamish that had not made him suffer the same fate as his brothers and sisters. Hamish said nothing to Theorryn as he sat, he didn't even acknowledge him with a nod but Theorryn was glad for it – he had never liked the Keepers anyway, not since they caused him to lose both of his sons. He waited patiently as the other members of the council scattered into the stalls – barely filling them out. When everyone had taken their seats, Ivan took to the platform where the thrones sat, Derek the head of the royal guard standing beside him.

"Welcome my friends," Ivan addressed in his heavy eastern accent. He had been a resident in Az Lagní for as long as anyone could remember but his accent was one of the things that had never left him. "I am sorry to ask you here on a day such as today...but as they say...needs must. I have a matter of great importance to inform you all on, but first I would like to introduce you to an esteemed guest." He outstretched a hand and a cloaked figure stepped out of the shadows. "Ladies and gentlemen, Lord Isiah of Nuzùlu!"

Many of the council members gasped, a ripple of whispers and hushed voices suddenly making the throne room rather echoic. Nuzùlu was the hometown of their late Queen Isolde and the Lord Isiah was her brother. *But what matter of Az Lagní would ever concern him?* As the council members quietened again, Isiah removed his hood to reveal long flowing blonde hair, much like that of a woman's. The purple cloak concealed the rest of his body, leaving his attire unto the imagination, but it was probably as regal and girlish as his hair Theorryn thought. They were like that in Nuzùlu. The last time the Lord Isiah had been seen in Az Lagní was at Isolde's and her son Jacques' joint funeral – about sixteen years ago.

"It would appear," Ivan continued with his address. "That we have all been deceived. Now the exact origin of this deceit is unclear but I hope that the Lord Isiah can clear up anything that may be a little unclear. You will all remember how the Queen shared her death with her son Jacques who had been thirteen at the time. He had gone missing in the moments after the poisoning of our Queen at Iris' tenth birthday banquet and the guards had found him dead on the river bank hours after the Queen gave up her fight." The council members, almost in unison muttered a word of memorial for their lost Queen and Prince and now their King, each bowing their heads and placing their right hand over their chests before returning their gaze to Ivan.

"But it would seem that our Prince never died and that he is still alive today."

The rumble of whispers returned to the room only louder this time and more urgent. Many were shaking their heads and clapping their knees in laughter, thinking it were a joke. Theorryn however knew it to be true. He remembered the night well unlike many more recent nights. Isiah had bought a much-tormented Jacques to his door to say goodbye to Romeo and Tristan. He had never explained why he was taking him away, just that it was for the best and that it was time he learnt about his heritage to the Keepers. As far as Theorryn was aware he was then taken to Dilu to become a Keeper but when he heard of the death, he had half believed it until Tristan wrote to him telling him of their reunion on his initiation as a Scribe.

He watched the other members of the council, eagerly awaiting their silence as their rising whispers echoed in his ears causing his head to pulse. He rubbed his temples in annoyance – if he had known this would have been today's event, he would not have had that ale with his breakfast. As he let his eyes wonder, he spied Daniel leaning against the stalls opposite him, a very worried look on his face. Daniel had been the King's advisor – could it have been that he knew the untold story of the true events of Jacques' disappearance? You'd think someone of his stature would after all.

"My friends, please hold your tongues!" pleaded Ivan, raising his voice slightly. "The Lord Isiah will now explain the events of that night as he remembers them." He nodded his head to Isiah as he took to the centre of the platform.

"As Ivan has already stated, many of you will remember that night...some of you through word of mouth and others of you deny the true events in favour of the account just given for reasons of loyalty to your king." Isiah had a very commanding voice, an aura or sheer dominance and masculinity about him despite his contrasting appearance. "I ask you to join with me now in recounting the events as I saw them...as some of you saw them.

"Jacques had been late on attendance to the Princess' banquet so on the request of my sister I went to find him in the courtyard with two young boys. Upon cajoling him, I bade him in, telling him to fetch his mother a glass of wine from the kitchens on his way up. Upon my return to the hall, Jacques was with his mother handing her the wine only for her to hours later be coughing and spurting it back up with blood. Many of you will remember the king's outburst at his son for serving his wife a poisoned brew, how he accused his own son of murder and betrayal. But he was ill-advised on his own part and cast his son out without listening to reason, he had only given the glass to his mother...he had not poured it...we all know the outcome of that story." The poisoning of the Queen had been linked back to the cook Claire who had been given the concoction by a trader from an unknown land with the intention of setting up a rift between the Queen and her brother. Their plan had of course failed when she was arrested and sentenced to death for betrayal to the crown, the trader however was never caught. The only thing they had succeeded in was Isolde's death.

"To save the further humiliation of my nephew I took him away in the hope the King would come to his senses. He stayed with a friend of mine whilst I tried to calm the situation, informing the King that there was no way Jacques would poison his own mother. He chose to inform the people of his son's disappearance and then on his apparent death. So, I took Jacques away and yes, I confess to having harboured him all these years away from you but alas, what else was I to do. Up until now I had been constantly writing to Rubuen, begging him to see the error of his ways. But he never saw things the same way as I, and the reason I am before you now is not to contest your King but to simply do right by my nephew and give him the chance his father never did." As Isiah finished his story he took a step back, giving the floor back to Ivan who addressed the council members once more.

"As you all know the king has been rather ill for the past few months," many of the council members were whispering amongst themselves as Ivan spoke, but he chose to ignore their insolence and continue with what he was saying. "Yesterday evening before the king took his final breath, he admitted to me that his son Jacques was still alive and told me the same story that Isaiah has just told all of you. If any of you contest that story, I suggest you speak up now!" he raised his voice, silencing the council once more.

Theorryn let a snigger escape his lips, unheard by the others – Ivan was not an intimidating man but quite obviously a man that the rest were rather afraid of. He watched as Ivan looked over the members in the stalls, still not saying a word, a stern look painted upon his bony face. He was obviously pausing for effect – seeing if anyone would dare to contest not just himself but the Lord Isiah. Once he saw that he now had control of the room once more, he stepped to the side, addressing the council as he paced the platform where Iris sat at her throne. Theorryn was surprised at how silent she had been – had she too known all this time that her brother was alive? The fresh tears on her face told him otherwise though, she was obviously too overcome with emotion and grief that she couldn't utter a single word.

"The king had me decree that I would endeavour to find his son and bring him home. I do not know whether it was so that he could rule without being contested as our Princess might be due to her being a woman; or whether it was out of remorse for the actions he committed against his son. But what is clear is that he wanted Jacques bought back here...returned home and safe." He paused again – *Ivan liked this pausing for effect thing* Theorryn thought. "I would now like the opportunity to illustrate the importance of honesty within our council. Who among you knew the story Isiah told to be true? Who among you will speak up now and say that when the act was passed that Jacques was dead...you knew it to be false?"

No one rose! It was obvious they were afraid – technically it would be considered an act of treason to say the prince was not dead all this time. Theorryn on the other hand was not afraid, probably due to the amount of ale currently within in his system, and he was the first to rise from his seat. Many gasped upon his doing so and he gulped as he looked around at his fellow council members. Then, next to him Hamish rose from his seat. It was obvious he knew because he taught Tristan for a while when he and his brothers from the Keeperage became Acolytes. Next to rise was Balderick but his standing puzzled Theorryn; he hadn't been at the banquet – but then perhaps Tristan had told him. Three others on the opposite side rose also; Barron Selmy, Lord Crotus and Lord Lancel. They were among Rubuen's most trusted council members and would have definitely been at the banquet. The last to rise was Daniel, Rubuen's advisor – again to be expected.

A few moments passed but no others stood from those already standing. When it seemed no others would, Isiah took the podium once more and looked towards Daniel, addressing him.

"Daniel..." he was questioning for his full name.

"Fullhorn my Lord," answered Daniel, his voice quivering slightly almost as if he knew the onslaught he was about to receive.

"Daniel Fullhorn – the Royal Advisor...correct?"

"That is correct my Lord."

"You knew of Jacques' whereabouts and the king's actions the whole time did you not?"

"I..."

"Speak up man!"

"My Lord I did know that the prince was not dead..."

"And as an advisor to the crown...how did you advise his actions?"

Daniel did not answer straight away. His grey eyes darted up and around at his fellow risen councilmen, almost pleading with them to back him. Isiah's question to him was more of an accusation suggesting that the lies told by Rubuen were down to Daniel – that Daniel advised the outcome of the situation. Whether or not the accusation was true, Theorryn knew not – Daniel had always been a weasel; worming his way in and out of situations. He was very secretive and what's more, he was a Keeper and Theorryn hated the Keepers.

"Well?" Isiah was now pushing for an answer as he looked down on Daniel whose eyes were down, letting his shoulder-length dark hair cloud his face from site.

"I know what you imply my Lord but forgive my slander..." he looked up at Isiah through the gap his parting made in his hairline. His eyes were cold and hard – betrayed by his fellow councilmen. "You are wrong! Yes – I admit that I knew Jacques was not really dead and yes – I admit that I lied to the people about what happened to him...but the lies were not my doing." His voice was forceful now as opposed to quivering with fear. He knew what the outcome of this would be for him, but even so he wasn't going to go down without a fight.

"So you admit to treason?"

"No!" All blame was now falling to Daniel as he stepped forward to the platform. "The king told me to lie…I advised him…I begged him not to make me lie about what happened. I only did as I was asked which is no less or more than any of you others standing here did." He circled the floor where he stood, looking at each of those standing in turn, expecting at least one of them to speak for him, to stand up for him. It was clear that Isiah wanted a scapegoat for all this and Ivan was saying nothing to contest it.

"Of all the King's adversaries it should have been down to you to do what was right. Your duty as a Royal Advisor is to the realm, to advise the king on behalf of the good of the realm and if they fail to do what is right your duty is to report it to the council and for the council to then overrule the king. For the good of the realm!"

There was a long moment of silence before any more words were said. Daniel stared up at Isiah from where he stood in the middle of the stalls; his shoulders broad and wide, his chest heaving heavily as he breathed deeply. His bearded face had turned harsh now and a single tear falling from his eyes. His demeanour came across as the sort of man who was used to being betrayed, used to being pinned as a scapegoat for the wrong doings of others.

"Are you really going to let this outsider speak for you?"

"How dare you…"

"Are you?" Daniel turned to Ivan and watched as Isiah's face grew red with anger. He had been disrespected and he obviously did not take kindly to people doing so. "My princess this is your realm now by right…you are Queen!"

"The princess Iris is now the Queen by regent!" Ivan retorted, putting Daniel in his place. "She has no right to decide what happens to you without approval from the council."

"Unbelievable! So you're going to let a ruler from another land dictate what I should have done."

"Of course not, I am going to let the council decide what happens to you, right here…right now."

"I have a right to trial…"

"Your rights to anything disintegrated the moment Isiah accused you of treason. You have no rights!"

"This is preposterous!" Daniel turned his back on the council.

"Councilmen, you are called to pass judgement on this allegation. Daniel Fullhorn is accused of treason...stand now if you agree that he is guilty."

Daniel did not turn straight away, instead he sniggered to himself, shaking his head as he did so. He honestly did not believe the others would stand against him with a man who had no right to accuse him of anything – that was until he turned around to see each and every single one of the councilmen on their feet. The only ones not standing were Hamish, Balderick and Theorryn, the latter of the three he had not expected to side with him. His face turned to that of a man scorned and his sniggering turned to anguish, tormented with pain and betrayal.

"Guards, arrest him!"

Theorryn watched as Daniel stood tall, the guards stepping forward and taking him by the arms, binding his hands behind his back. He could just about see the tears beginning to leak from his eyes but no remorse was shown towards him.

"Do you have anything to say for yourself Daniel?" asked Ivan.

"Just that if you are going to let an outsider speak for you then the war truly has begun."

"War?" Ivan questioned, a snigger touching his voice slightly.

"The line between Light and Dark is beginning to blur and only time will tell which will overpower the other. The war has indeed begun!"

Ivan and others looked on in confusion as Daniel looked down at the floor. He began to mutter quietly to himself, but no one, not even the guards could interpret what he was saying. It was like he was talking in a different language, repeating the same phrase of words over and over again, louder and louder. Finally, he looked up at Ivan and Isiah, saying the phrase one last time before vanishing from site; the rope that was used to bind his hands falling to the floor.

# CHAPTER 5 - A STRANGER IN THE BAR

Pain! Excruciating pain was all Tristan felt when he woke from his deep sleep. He had woken with such a jolt that he had rolled from his bed, hitting his head on the wooden bedside table. The next feeling that entered his mind was confusion – the last thing he remembered was collapsing in the sitting room and by the state his hands were in he didn't get up here himself. His father must have bought him up! The young blacksmith rose to his feet, trying his best to catch his bearings as he felt where he had hit his head, feeling a prominent bump. He had been lucky. Seemingly drunken, he staggered over to the bowl of water that rested on his chest of drawers with a washcloth dangling over the edge. Examining the blood-stained bandages, he began to remove them from his hands, slowly unravelling them layer by layer. As the bandages fell away, he could not find an outlet for them; all he saw were burn marks on the tops of his hands in the shape of glyphs. As he turned them over to face his palms, more glyphs shone with a blue light that seemed to join up the lines as the light faded. He thought it strange that these marks suddenly appeared on his hands and stranger the next image that appeared in his mind – the image of himself covered in words that were drawn in his own blood. As he rested his hands in the water, he took note of the glyphs once more, feeling a sense of familiarity strike him. The hooded stranger in the bar who had called himself Dante Ashdown had the same markings which meant one thing – they were one in the same! There his answers would be found.

The town, he noticed was oddly quiet – but then what did he expect; the sun had only just risen in the now bluing sky. As Tristan walked towards the square, he watched as the foreign traders set up their wares for the Exotic Market. Smells of rose and lavender reached his nose as he passed the incense stand. Opposite a man with a turban round his head was setting up some plates covered in floury jelly squares that were different colours – yellows, pinks, greens. He remembered how they had been in town once before and Jenni had forced him to try one…they actually were surprisingly tasty. He hoped Jenni would not be there as he reached the door of the pub, especially after his episode in front of her yesterday. He wasn't avoiding her of course – his head was just all over the place at the moment and he needed some space.

"You're too early, we aren't open yet!" exclaimed a gruff western voice as Tristan pushed open the unlocked pub door. It wasn't a voice he knew though; not that of Ernie or Iain or Ned or any of the men that worked at the inn. As he stepped into the light, he recognised the man behind the bar to be the very man he was looking for.

"How are you now…" he started to stammer in response, unable to finish as Dante looked up and cut him off; cursing the air.

"Are you fuckin' deaf?" I said we're not open yet!" he said slowly, quite clearly mocking Tristan. Usually, he would have ignored a comment like that, but something new was boiling deep inside of him; as though an entirely new character was coming to the surface and overriding his senses and reactions. This new character was perhaps an old form of himself, maybe part of the young Keeper he had once been and this young Keeper did not take kindly to being spoken to so rudely.

"I don't like your tone!" replied Tristan, folding his arms across his chest in a smarmy sort of fashion.

"Oh, well I do apologise," he mocked again, his accent becoming stronger as his aggression rose. "Allow me to say it more politely!" he leant back against a barrel that stood behind him obviously waiting to be changed. "We are closed!" he exclaimed, now being serious.

"Okay," Tristan turned on his heel quickly, the essence of him now disappearing slightly and letting his more recent self take control once more.

"Wait a moment," Dante called, stopping Tristan where he stood. The two characters within him were now fighting for dominance, for control over the body they were trapped inside. "Turn around." Tristan did as he was told, spinning around; half anticipating what was to come and half relishing the confrontation that seemed to be approaching the situation. "Now I recognise you," smiled Dante, waving his finger in the air as though his mind had just been blown. "You're the one who had the crazy yesterday afternoon. Man, I have to compliment you on the improvement you made to that wench's dress." He clapped his hands; it was clear that he was talking about Jenni and also that he probably wasn't her biggest fan. Tristan, rather than defending the woman he often professed to love, just laughed along with Dante, knocking the stranger's confidence and silencing him as Tristan took a seat at the bar.

"Did I say you could sit down?" Dante asked rhetorically, again resorting to mocking Tristan.

"I don't recall asking your permission," smirked Tristan, a slight smile touching the ends of his lips.

"I'd watch myself if I were you boy...you attract too much attention to yourself. You're gonna get yourself into trouble one of these days."

"Could say the same about you! The last man who called me 'boy' ended up in the Land of the Faded." Now, Dante looked scared, the unprovoked threat had clearly hit a nerve, even if Tristan actually had no idea what he was actually threatening him with or who he was talking about.

"What do you want?" He launched himself forward and slammed his fists upon the bar, his hair now obscuring the fear that was clouding his eyes.

"I want answers!" demanded Tristan as he rose to his feet, now looking down on the slumped stranger that hunched before him. But the man did not stay down, he too rose up, looking Tristan right in the eyes.

"Answers to what? You haven't asked any questions."

Tristan's demeanour now changed again and this time, Dante noticed. This time though, it wasn't a shift in character, it was a feeling the old him would always put to the back of his mind – using his smart smarmy nature as a defence for his real feelings. This hidden character was scared of the destiny that awaited him, the pain that would inevitably fill him with guilt and resentment for those that had wronged him. In response to Dante's demand, he showed up his hands, letting the marks on his hands catch the light coming in from the windows up above. Now it was Dante's demeanour that changed as he looked around hastily, grabbing Tristan's hands and slamming them onto the bar.

"You can't just go around showing those things off!" he exclaimed, half trying to whisper. "You could get yourself killed!"

"But you did yesterday..." started Tristan.

"Are you really going to be so childish? One rule for one a different rule for the other? Not my style! This place is a sanctuary for people like us...do you even understand the kind of trouble that showing these off could get you in?"

"No, I don't! That's why I came here...answers!"

Dante paused for a while, releasing his grip on Tristan's hands and standing back from the bar.

"Do you even know what those marks mean?"

"No."

"But...surely you do...you're a Keeper..."

"I was."

"I don't understand, what do you mean 'You was'?"

"I mean, I don't remember...I was a Keeper yes...but I don't remember when I was. There's a gap of about three years in my mind, three years that I don't remember anything about."

"So, you were attacked by Faders then?"

"I don't know...I don't even know what Faders or the Land of the Faded is."

"Then why did you threaten it with me?"

"I don't know where that threat came from, I'm not in control of myself. It's like I'm changing and not even realising it."

"You're returning...back to your old self by the sounds of it. When did you start to experience these *changes*?"

"Um, about a month now!"

"Strange...I've been back a month now," Dante looked down at the ground, speaking in an undertone hoping Tristan would not hear him.

"Back from where?" Dante looked up suddenly – he had been too loud as per usual.

"I..."

"Have you changed that barrel yet Dante?" yelled a voice from upstairs somewhere. It sounded like that of Ernie.

"Shit!" he cursed, again a little too loud. "I mean...I'm working on it!"

Dante launched himself over the bar and grabbed Tristan by the collar, leading him to the door. He didn't let go though, instead he leaned in close to Tristan whispering something in his ear.

"You need to leave now, but meet me later tonight by the fountain in the square and I will answer all your questions I promise. But you have to promise something to me!"

Tristan nodded slowly; "Firstly, you cannot tell anyone about these marks that have appeared on your hands...no one you hear me..." Tristan tried to say something but the grasp Dante had on his collar tightened, forcing him to remain silent. "Secondly, you cover up those hands of yours. Do you understand me Tristan?"

"Yes," Tristan gulped, wondering how it was Dante had known his name when he himself had not uttered it to him.

"Good, now be off with you before Ernie skins me alive for not getting this shit hole ready to open."

Dante opened the door and almost threw Tristan into the now bustling square, slamming the door behind him for added effect. It was clear to Tristan that Dante Ashdown was all bark and no bite.

# CHAPTER 6 – BREAKDOWN

It was amazing how much busier the square had got in what must have been only half an hour. Tristan worked his way through the crowds of people, thinking he might as well head to work early as he was already half way there – there was no point going back home now. After all, an extra hour meant more money at the end of the day. He skirted down one of the approaching side streets as he often did when the square was this busy, rushing up some steps and heading through the herb garret before getting to the Smithy opposite the old mill. He came through the front door, only to bump into his boss Lionel, the swords he was holding in his hands crashing to the floor and making a loud clanging noise.

"I am so sorry Lionel," Tristan stammered, lowering to his knees and helping him gather up the swords.

"It's fine, it's fine!" Lionel had a gruff accent that seemed to match his 'built like a brick shit house' stamina. "I am actually glad you're hear early, just a minute and I'll explain why."

Tristan handed Lionel the rest of the swords and followed him out back into the yard, watching as he loaded them onto the back of a wagon.

"Are you making a delivery?" Tristan asked, raking his brain wondering how he had managed to get ahold of so many swords so quickly.

"Not exactly…start passing me those shields down there." Lionel pointed to a pile of plain crested shields that were leaning up against the wall.

"Are we going to war?"

"We aren't, but someone is. Not exactly sure who has made this order to be honest with you."

"What do you mean?"

As the order was finished being loaded into the wagon, Lionel looked around and folded his arms, standing close to Tristan.

"I got a message from Ivan telling me that I had to take the swords that weren't being used by the Infantry and any others that I had in my stock room to the forest of Az Landen as soon as possible. He never said why, just that it had to be quick and to be quiet about it. I don't think he wants people to worry."

"So Az Landen are going to war?" Tristan's uncles lived in the forest and his thoughts turned to them. One of them was married to a princess there so no doubt would be fighting in this supposed war. His father never really spoke of his uncles; he hadn't done so in years.

"I'm not too sure, but somebody is. I'll be gone for a couple of weeks, but not to worry I've roped Digg and Freddie into helping out here and take it in turns to cover your days off. Of course, I had to promise to pay them to actually get them to agree to helping me. So much for helping family out huh?"

"I guess so."

"Oh and one more thing before I go; there's a package slipped behind the helmets in the stock room on the fourth shelf down for a Mr Baldwin. He'll probably come in about mid-day and ask for it so make sure he gets it, it's very important." He turned away and readied himself upon the wagon, grasping the reins of the horses tightly in his hands. "Oh and one last thing," Tristan laughed slightly as he came to stand by the horses, wondering if Lionel would ever leave. "A man was in here looking for you yesterday, said he needed to talk to you about something but didn't say what. I told him you were on your day off so he said he'd come back today and try and catch you."

*Yesterday?* Tristan thought to himself, he didn't even remember having his day off. Whatever happened to him had caused him to sleep through it he assumed. He was going to have to do something about his obsession with this place, especially as he hadn't even noticed it would've been his day off.

"Did he give you a name?"

"John Basso he said his name was."

"Never heard of him!" Tristan answered truthfully, curious to the identity of yet another stranger in town.

"Oh well, he might not pop in then, you never know. I'll see you soon Tristan." He exclaimed as he led the horses away out into the fields and onto the road that headed north.

"See you soon Lionel!" Tristan called after him, waving as he did so.

Back inside, Tristan set about cleaning up the mess Lionel had left in the stock room, scanning his eyes over the helmets a he did so and spotting the parcel he had mentioned. Curiosity getting the better of him, he reached for the brown papered box, shaking it slightly to hear no rattle. He shrugged his shoulders, replacing it back on the shelf and heading to the front door to open up. It was strange how in one week, three absolute strangers had walked into town and somehow, Tristan would come into contact with all three. Coincidence maybe, but in Tristan's mind; nothing was ever coincidence.

The slamming of the front door bought Tristan out of his thoughts and he noticed for the first time that passing hour, what he was actually doing – there was practically nothing left of the smelted iron he had been hammering. Laughing to himself, he threw it in the scrap pile and made his way into the front room to see what the cause of the slamming was. In the space before the door stood a tall, dark haired man with his back to Tristan. He was wearing a long leather coat that almost reached his ankles.

"Can I help you?" asked Tristan, part of him feeling immediately cautious.

The man turned around slowly, casting his eyes over to Tristan. His eyes were a stark brown with a slight tinge of red perhaps to them. His greasy looking short black hair curved across his brow, sweeping around his head like a bowl hair cut only more stylish. The collar of his leather coat almost touched his chin which was covered by a beard that framed around his sublime mouth. Underneath his coat was a dark brown shirt that was tucked into a pair of black leather breaches. The black was tarnished though, looking greyer than anything as they descended into heavy black boots with whitish silver patterns on the back of the heel. They gave off a regal impression, as though this man was a figure of class.

"I was looking for Tristan Romano..." the man had a quiet voice that perhaps once had been commanding but had over the years lost its confidence in speaking in front of others. Somewhere along the lines, this man had been wronged, scared by someone who had overpowered him once before.

"That's me! What is it you want? A sword, armour?"

"Nothing of that kind no," he was well spoken this stranger, Tristan had already assumed he was the man in here looking for him the day before; John Basso.

"Then what? Do you require my services or what?"

"I 'require'...your forgiveness..."

"Forgiveness?" Tristan repeated, confused as to what the man meant. When he did not say anything more, his face turned stern and he uncrossed his arms, resting fists by his side. "Who are you?"

"So it's true then..."

"What's true?"

"You have...forgotten!" Tristan thought he saw a smile turn up the ends of his mouth but only slightly. The man rose his head, turning to face Tristan fully. Now, his confidence had returned, as though the fact that Tristan did not remember him made him less scared of whatever it was he was scared of.

"Who are you?" Tristan asked again, shaken by the man's sudden change in demeanour.

"My name is John Basso," he spoke louder now; his confidence had definitely returned to him now. "I used to teach you when you were a Keeper...you have nothing to fear from me dear boy." Again, the smile touched his lips, it was a wry smile, almost menacing as though it hid a much darker intention.

"Teach me?"

"I taught you magic Tristan, the ability to command and manipulate the Glyphs." As he spoke, he strode slowly towards Tristan, almost circling him as a lion would his prey. As he did so, he turned a gloved hand wrapping his fingers around to form a fist with a blue light shining above it in the shape of some form of rune. Tristan recognised it to be the sigil of the Keepers - that much Merlin had taught him.

"If you were one of my teachers, why is it you desire my forgiveness?"

"I don't know if you know or not, but me and you had a...dispute," he stopped less than a foot away from Tristan, the smile still creeping onto his face, tainting his good intentions. Inside, Tristan felt compelled not to trust him, keep him close like you should someone you wish to keep an eye on. "I didn't approve of your marriage to Dagnen..."

"Why not?"

"It's probably best that you remember for yourself, isn't it? What with her being dead and all!" When Tristan's face hardened, he smirked again. "How tragic it was." He spoke with thought, as though he was pretending to remember at the same time. His tone threw images into Tristan's mind. No one had ever told him how Dagnen had died but it was like it was all coming back to him now. "I do apologise dear boy," Tristan looked back up at Basso, catching himself on the counter as his knees almost gave way. "I had no idea you were this bad." Although the smile seemed to linger, his eyes were full of anguish. Whatever he had done to Tristan all those years ago he seemed very sorry about and he really did want forgiveness. But how could Tristan give that to him if he didn't know what it was for.

"Tell you what, I'm just going to go, and leave you with a couple of words," Basso walked towards the door before turning and saying words filled with grief and agony, the smirk completely gone. "I truly am sorry for everything I did to you and your brothers all those years ago. And I hope one day, when you remember it all, you find it in your heart to forgive me my sins. I am sorry she is dead, I never meant to cause the two of you the harm I did." He watched Tristan stand there motionless, swaying slightly as he held on to the edge of the counter trying to remain standing. It was like he wasn't hearing the words Basso was speaking though, as though he had gone numb from feeling. "If you ever need me Tristan, you can find me in the Mountain pub at Ragnur, whatever it is you need; I will endeavour myself to help you always." Tristan looked up, catching Basso's eyes as he left the Smithy, shutting the door behind him.

No sooner had he left, Tristan's knees finally gave up on him and he found himself falling to the ground. He grabbed the archway and swung himself into the back room to cradle himself and come to terms what he had just heard. As he uttered her name aloud, a face flashed in his mind, but he didn't catch the image long enough to determine any features. Wiping his hands across his face, he thought about shutting up the shop and seeking out his father or Merlin. Someone would explain to him what Basso had said; now once again, he wanted answers. From somewhere within him, a sudden strength took over and he pulled himself to his feet to walk back into the front of the shop where another man stood in the doorway.

At first, Tristan thought it was Basso but then that was impossible seeing as this man looked completely different. He too stood like a man of class, but he wasn't as dark and secretive as Basso. He was more outward about his regal attire and took a more glamourous aura. The man was shorter than John and had blonde wavy hair that stretched below his ears to the base of his neck. It had been groomed neatly, curling inwards at the ends of the layers. His eyes were a taunt blue, as though in his life he had seen many a horror and sadness. His face was framed by a well-trimmed beard that made him look slightly more masculine than he appeared to be. He wore a brown leather jacket that was cut off at his waist with tarnished gold patterns that outlined the seam and buttons down one side. Underneath he wore a tan shirt; similar to the one Basso had worn, that was tucked into brown breaches descending into simple looking dark boots that clicked the floor as he stepped forward. Again, a slight smile touched his lips, as though he were happy to see Tristan for whatever reason that may be.

"Can I help you sir?" Tristan asked, bucking up hidden courage and standing tall behind the counter.

"Yes, you can," the stranger said after a while, the smile disappearing from his face at the sound of the word sir. "I'm here to pick up a package."

"You are?" Tristan tested, there was no way he was going to just hand it over to any man that walked in claiming a parcel.

"Yes, Lionel left it for me. My name is Cedric Baldwin, you have a package for me am I correct?"

"Yes that's right I do, I just wanted to make sure I had the right person before me."

Cedric nodded as Tristan turned away, trying to think where he had heard the name before. He raked his brains as he reached for the package between the helmets on the fourth shelf, Cedric's disappointed face flashing through his mind as though he expected Tristan to know him. What was it with all these strangers turning up in town being linked to Tristan somehow?

"Here you are!" Tristan said, stepping out from the back room and placing the package on the counter.

"Thank you," Cedric stepped forward, picking up the package and turning to leave the way he had come in.

As he opened the door, something dropped from his pocket, almost intentionally. Tristan sprang forward, picking it up from the floor and reaching out to give it back to Cedric.

"Wait," Cedric turned. "I think this belongs to you."

"Nope, sorry. I must be off!" Cedric replied honestly before leaving the shop.

Curious, Tristan turned away from the door unfolding the piece of paper Cedric had dropped. As he straightened out the creases, he noticed it was a photograph and it took him a while to recognise the man in which was himself. He gasped, noting the woman that stood beside him, holding a baby upright in her arms. If it wasn't for the vision Tristan had had back at his house of himself covered in scarred words, he would not have recognised the man in the photo as himself. He was smiling in the picture, a smile that could not possibly be wiped from existence. His eyes looked towards the woman and the baby whom he helped to hold up. His eyes doted on them, on the brown-haired woman that laughed to herself as though Tristan had said something funny at the time. Her face was well defined, high cheekbones flushing a tinge of pink against her green eyes. She bit back her bottom lip, as though trying to stop herself from laughing and the smile took notice away from her tired looking eyes. The baby they were holding couldn't have been more than about four months old. Tristan assumed it to be a girl by the yellow dress that adorned her small figure. The baby was laughing, her blue eyes twinkling and dimples forming in her cheeks like Tristan's own did when he laughed.

He turned over the photo to see writing etched into the back scribing 'Me, Dagnen and our daughter…' There was a smudge next to it where a name might have been. The word 'daughter' struck him like a heavy blow, making his breath short in his chest. No one had ever told him he had a…

He practically fell through the front door as he ran into the street, grabbing ahold of the nearest person he could find. He held up the photo, asking if he had seen the woman and child in the photo, feeling in his mind as though he had lost them and needed to find them somewhere quick…almost as though they were in danger. When the man he had collared shook his head and told him no he let go and grabbed the next person. Again, they shook their head, a woman giving Tristan a strange look as he burst into a run for the square looking to a guard for help. It was like he had gone crazy, like he wasn't in control of what he was doing. Something much deeper than anything controlled him now and it was grief, the kind of grief you feel when you try to deny the truth to yourself. You tell yourself it never happened, try to convince yourself it was all a lie until eventually you believe it.

He stopped in the square, grabbing people by the arms and begging them to look at the photo, to tell him whether or not they had seen his wife and daughter. As he ran around in circles, grief stricken by the people that were ignoring him, he caught Cedric's face in the crowd. He tried to make a break for him, but he was pulled back as a man restrained him round his middle holding him steady and saying calming words Tristan could not hear over his own shouts of Cedric's name. And then someone shouted his name, but it wasn't the man that was clutching his midriff, it was a woman who suddenly fell into his arms. He was somewhere else in his mind, in a dark street beside a fountain very similar to the one he raved near in reality. The woman that lay in his arms was bleeding at her stomach which she clutched; her face torn with pain.

"Dagnen, please don't die!" he found himself saying, almost begging the woman in his arms.

Then the vision changed, as though flashing back into the past a couple of months before to himself and the dying woman once more resting in his own arms holding a new-born baby. No sooner had it appeared though the vision changed again and he found himself standing in front of a grave with the child now in his arms. The name on the headstone reading 'Dagnen Romano'.

Back in reality the now fully conscious Tristan screamed, tears pouring from his eyes. People all around stared at his anguish, at his pain as it fell to the floor with the rain that suddenly plagued the mid summers day. As he writhed and twisted in the man's grip Tristan picked out faces in the crowd around him; Merlin, his father...and Dante stood in front of Jenni, with Cedric lurking in the backdraft. The look of guilt on both his father's and Jenni's faces made him angry, as though they knew they were partly to blame for his breakdown. It gave him strength, strength to break out of the man's grasp and run until he could not run any further.

# CHAPTER 7 - FATE AND DESTINY

*It's the same old story these days; the only people who seem to think you've changed are always those who mean the most to you. Most of the time they're right and you really have changed, but other times you haven't changed at all – they're the ones who has changed. Some people change for the better; they change their appearance, their attitudes...some even change their name. These people have a choice about whether or not they change, however some do not have a choice but to change, whether it be for their own safety – like suddenly changing sides on a battlefield, or even for some other reason. There are even those who do not even realise they have changed – they just wake up one morning and everything is different. Sometimes there are those who change without realising as the result of an accident...because they have forgotten the person they once were. To go from being someone who was so sure of themselves in every action they do to being someone who is the complete opposite...it's unexplainable. The people they know may go as far as to say they have changed for the better – they can start again, wipe the slate clean and just ignore what might or might not have happened in the new gap in your mind. For some, it's just not that easy to begin again. But for others their forgetfulness comes from a certain situation that changed everything – flipped their life upside down. They make an attempt to change things back and then bang...suddenly everything is new...you don't even remember what you were trying to fix in the first place.*

*I don't remember what happened that moment everything went dark and I don't remember what came in the light before the darkness – the actions that lead to me being found in the rubble of the Keeper Compound in Hasaghar. All I remember is waking up in the infirmary with Merlin by my side. I remember the look on his face when I asked where I was or where my father and Romeo were. He simply replied to me 'Tristan you are in Hasaghar...Romeo is dead...do you not remember?' I remember thinking I was dreaming, banging my head against the wall to try and wake myself up. Merlin had tried to restrain me and I jumped up running from the building and into the streets. Somehow, I found myself at a graveyard stood in front of two headstones quite close together. I read the names on them; 'Romeo Romano' and 'Dagnen Romano'. At the time I never realised the importance of the second headstone. I remember still thinking I was dreaming and throwing myself to the floor shouting 'Wake up!' A man came over to me as I crouched on the ground, I didn't know who he was, not even now. He picked me off my knees and stood me tall. 'Do not weep for the dead my dear boy,' he said to me. 'They are in a better place than this Hell. They are beside us always, though not seen by the naked eye. The dead never leave those they love!' In his hands he held two flowers, one being some form of grass root that he placed by Romeo's headstone. The second was a white rose which he placed before Dagnen's. 'A wreath for the return of a fallen soldier and a rose for the maiden who died protecting those she loved. Both taken before their time, and no sweeter was blood ever spilt as innocent as these two souls.' With those words lingering in my head, I watched him leave the graveyard and join another man who, now that I think about it; I recognise now – his shoulder length blonde hair shining out against the grey sky. This other man was holding what looked like a bundle of rags and cloths in his arm, but he held them carefully; as though cradling a new born to make it stay sleeping in a moment of disturbance.*

*I don't remember much about the trip home either, I just remember Merlin trying endlessly to jog my memory by mentioning certain names or events I may or may not have been involved in. Now that I look at it, I wonder why Merlin let me walk away from Hasaghar without my daughter. Was it because he did not know where she was? But surely that would not have stopped him telling me about her. But then maybe the situation was out of his hands and he had no choice but to keep her a secret from me. Whatever the reason, I wish he would have told me! And what about my father? What was his reason for keeping her a secret? After all, she would have been his first grandchild. Perhaps he didn't even know she existed...but surely, I would have told him about something such as that...*

For the first time since he had broken away from the grip that was restraining him back in the square, he looked up ahead of him – to see exactly what it was he was running towards. It was then that Tristan realised he was heading towards a cliff beyond the trees and he found himself unable to stop, launching over the edge in line with the gushing waterfall down to meet the river below. It wasn't long before he managed to get his head above the water but his feet wouldn't touch the bottom as he tried to gain stability. But he felt as though he was drowning as the waves dragged him ever deeper. As they flashed past his eyes, he thought he saw something on the riverbank – *a woman perhaps.* As each wave passed him by, she changed, her white dress gleaming as her face became more and more beautiful. But then she changed again, as though she was dying before his very eyes; her dress becoming dirty and her face scarred as she slipped out of sight, enveloped by the water. He tried again to gain stability, flapping his arms about and trying to turn away from the current. But he is only dragged deeper until his face was no longer on the surface of the river. He lost his breath as the water held him in its clutches, the darkness in his mind suddenly becoming all he could see as he drifted along to the current of the river.

"Tristan!" shouted a voice as its owner pounded down on the unconscious chest that lay before him, dripping wet by the side of the river. "Come on Tristan, for fuck's sake breathe!" he pounded his chest again, this time slightly harder. It had the desired effect though and Tristan shot upright, spurting water everywhere, luckily just missing his rescuer. As he choked out the rest, he turned around to see his saviour...Dante.

"'Bout bloody time too, was almost gonna give up on you."

"How did you even find me?" asked Tristan, thumping his chest to bring up the rest of the water in his lungs.

"Oh yes, why thank you Dante for rescuing me and stopping me from drowning. Oh it's okay Tristan don't mention it…it was my pleasure." It was almost as though his accent strengthened when he mocked people making Tristan come to the decision it was something he enjoyed doing…either that or he just expected people to treat him differently, or it could even be a cover up for his tarnished ego.

"Sorry, um thank you," Tristan uttered as he choked up yet more water.

"Don't thank me yet, I haven't worked out what you owe me in return…"

"But you just said…"

"Actually, scratch that, you owe me a new pair of boots. Just look at the state of them!" Tristan looked over at Dante's boots. To be fair they looked as ancient as the trees around them so it probably wasn't Tristan's fault that they now needed replacing.

"So how did you find me then?" Tristan asked again, determined to get some answers this time.

"Sort of figured out you would end up needing help the state you were in and I didn't see anyone else running after you when you broke away from Balderick…"

"Balderick? I didn't even realise it was him pulling me back."

"You were pretty upset, what happened to make you like that?"

"I don't even know what came over me."

"Did you remember something?"

"I think so…why do you care anyway?"

"You know," Dante said casually as he leant back against the tree behind him. "You remind me a lot of myself when I was your age and let's just say that it's not exactly the safest way to live. The edge may feel great but…" he sighed heavily as though filled with regret. "You never know when you're gonna fall off."

"How old even are you?"

"Excuse me…how rude of you…"

"You see there you go again," he had stopped coughing now, his lungs finally clear of water but his chest sore from heaving. "You speak like you're from a different world…a different age almost. Like this place is far too new for you…like your old fashioned or something."

"Would you like to know a secret Tristan Romano?" asked Dante after a while, now being entirely serious as he leaned forward resting his arms on his knees. "In all honesty you're right; I'm not of this time! In fact, I don't even know how old I am I've jumped so far forward."

"What do you mean?"

"For as long as I can remember I've been walking through the World of the Faded - you see over a century ago, I, like you, was a Brother of Union. That mark on your palm makes us the same...I too am Nobility of the Brothers of Union. I was part of the fifth generation and I've no idea what one you're part of..."

"The fiftieth!" Tristan answered, no sooner had he spoke it though he wondered how he had known that as the answer had sprung from nowhere.

"Bloody hell I am old! I can't even do the math...if there are fifty years between each generation and we are now at the fiftieth that makes me..."

"Almost as old as Linford..." Tristan laughed, pushing his luck and half not knowing where his witty remark had come from.

"Oye, I'm nowhere near as old as him!" Dante scorned as he leant forward and clipped Tristan round the ear. "You know me and you have a lot in common."

"Certainly not the age..." Tristan sniggered, trying to say it under his breath but he was unable to contain his laughter.

"Hey, you're pushing your luck matey! I mean in the sense that we are almost alike in every aspect. I mean you have a wife and daughter out there somewhere and when I faded, I had a betrothed. It's crazy to think that out there somewhere could be my descendants, I might have already even bumped into them and not even know."

"Do you even know why your back...no offense of course."

"None taken! I think I do..."

"Why?"

"You!" Tristan looked over at Dante's still serious face. "I am back to make you remember...because I have a second chance at completing my destiny!"

"Make me remember?"

"Yes Tristan! And I know how this must sound to you but I am telling you the truth, I really am here to help you, at least that's what I believe."

"But why? Apart from the fact that I have a daughter out there somewhere I can't think of anything else that was significant in my past."

"Unfinished business perhaps?" Tristan remained silent, looking away from Dante who took it upon himself to give Tristan some answers whether they were the ones he was looking for or not. "As a Brother of Union it is first your duty to destroy your sworn enemies; The Brothers of Dharsi and second to keep the union of the Keepers together. You see before our great Father Talus came along, the Keeperhood was split in two; The

Keepers of Secrets and the Keepers of Time. They appeared out of nowhere, both to protect the townsfolk from supernatural entities; that was the one thing that united them. Over time their purpose changed, bringing Talus and his four brothers to unite them as the Keeperhood. As a result, he and his brothers were known as the first generation of the Brothers of Union. However, not all the Keepers were in favour of the union and ninety-nine of the brothers from both sides came together to form the Brotherhood of Dharsi, to oppose Talus and the new High Order that had been created. One of their brothers betrayed them though, to the third generation of Union and they were quickly disbanded and banished to the Land of the Faded where they were bound by time itself. However, not all of them were punished...some managed to escape; eight I believe not including the one who betrayed them in the first place. They changed their appearance using dark magic and since, as far as I'm aware, only one of them has been put to justice; Montifon...the Pretend Leader. Me and my brothers exposed him!"

"What has all this got to do with me and my so-called unfinished business?" Tristan was tired of story time now, especially as most of this was what Merlin had already told him.

"Don't you get it?" Dante grabbed ahold of Tristan's hand and showed the palm up to face him. "You are Nobility...a Brother of Union. And from what I understand, you and your brotherhood started a war against the remaining Brothers of Dharsi...a war which you must now finish."

"Why me? Can't they do it on their own?"

"Do you even know what Union means? You, and I mean *you* started this war when you named Herasin; the leader...the father. When you name a Brother of Dharsi you sentence them to banishment...to death even; with the intention of carrying out that sentence. The one who passes the sentence must carry out the sentence and you apparently named two brothers which means you must end two of them!"

"But I don't even remember any of that so how am I supposed to finish something I don't even remember starting?"

"By remembering, which in time I'm sure you will."

"Merlin has been trying to get me to remember for nearly four years now and nothing."

"Until now!" Dante finished, looking at Tristan with concern. "I have a different approach though."

Tristan sniggered mockingly to himself. As if he would know how to help him remember when he didn't even know him. He shook his head, turning away from Dante for a moment.

"Come with me!" Dante said after a while.

"Come with you where?"

"To Dilu. There's an old Keeper Compound there that may have some answers."

"Merlin says that's where I became a Scribe."

"I think that a more physical method will help jog your memory."

Tristan went silent for a while, his mind racing with thoughts of the visions he had seen in the square, wondering what onlookers must have thought of him. Perhaps a break away was what he needed to clear his head...but his daughter. Somewhere out there was a young girl who did not know her father because some brotherhood had wanted to end him and that made him angry – the thought that someone else had taken his own destiny into their hands. He clenched his fists; his decision was made.

"When do we leave?" he asked finally.

"End of the week."

"Not sooner?" Tristan scorned, sighing heavily.

"What and just leave things the way they are?"

"I'm not going back to my father, not after today...and I'm not ready to hear what Merlin has to say just yet..."

"I hope you don't think those are the only ones who have lied to you all these years?"

"Who else is there? And anyway, how is it you know more about me than I do?" Dante sniggered slyly at that, and Tristan shot him a look.

"That is for you to discover for yourself." Dante said as he rose to his feet, his boots squelching as he did so. He held out a hand to Tristan who paused before taking it, still unsure of whether or not he could trust Dante. "If I were you, I'd head back and pack up some necessities from home and then find yourself somewhere to stay. I'll look in on you later, but for now I need to get back to work before Ernie fires my sorry arse." Smiling reassuringly at Tristan, he jogged on ahead into the trees and disappearing into the creeping mist, leaving Tristan to make his own way back to town.

# CHAPTER 8 - AN ANCIENT BROTHERHOOD

As the city gates took form on the horizon Tristan paused for a moment; no doubt his father would be at home waiting for him, tracing his non-existent goatee and running has large worn hands through his short blonde hair. He'd then place his hands on his skinny waist and continue to pace the room, anger levels rising at the same pace as his worry. Since Romeo's death, Theorryn had really let himself go. He relied on the drink even more than he usually did and the only time he was sober was at council meetings, although more recently not even then. He didn't seem to care much for Tristan either, so long as he was keeping his nose out of trouble. *Some things never change,* he thought to himself as visions of his father slating his character came crawling back to him. They were faint in the back of his mind, and he couldn't make out much except seeing himself sat with his head in his hands on the couch and his father pacing back and forth berating him with harsh words. That event was all too common back when he was younger and happened far less once he had become a Keeper. Despite his father never agreeing to them joining the Keepers, he had never been prouder of him then with the feats he performed during his training.

Taking a deep breath, he braced himself; if he was going to face his father, he should better get on with it. *Just one last deep breath!* He made his way up the hill towards their cottage by the vegetable patches on the outside of the city walls. As he reached the front door he dared a look through the window, spotting his father doing exactly as he knew he would be; pacing up and down the living room with his hands on his hips. There was something he didn't expect though and that was the flagon of ale on the table in front of the couch...*trust him!* The sight of this fuelled Tristan's anger even more; if it wasn't for Dante, Tristan would be dead more than likely, and there his father was...looking for answers at the bottom of a flagon, drinking his thoughts into oblivion rather than out looking for him. Then again, Tristan had always been a disappointment to his father, so he expected nothing less.

There was something lying next to the flagon though, something he couldn't make out from his current location but it looked like a photograph; probably the one the stranger had dropped back in the Smithy, the one of his wife and daughter alongside himself. He must have dropped it as he struggled with Balderick and then somehow his father got ahold of it. Taking yet another deep breath he pushed forward on the front door, calmly making his way into the sitting room to face Theorryn the witty younger Tristan was now out for good and he was going to give his father everything he had inside him so that he knew just what he thought of him.

"Tristan...you're back?" Theorryn exclaimed, finally noticing his own son standing in the doorway watching him pace, his eyes all spacey as though he couldn't seem to focus them.

"No thanks to you!" scorned Tristan, looking down on his father.

"Where were you?" Theorryn ignored the comment, deciding to take the responsible parent tone which was next to impossible with the smell of ale lingering in his words.

"I threw myself off a cliff," Tristan smirked confidently, a touch of arrogance to his tone.

"You never take anything seriously, do you? You're just a boy...you are no man..."

"I mean it father," Tristan shouted. "I threw myself off a cliff and who fished me out of the river...not you, not Merlin...the bartender at the inn. Where were you, drowning your sorrows no doubt." He pointed his hand towards the flagon, noticing that it really was empty.

"I had no idea..."

"Do not lie to me! I saw you in the square with Merlin, watching as I struggled in Balderick's grip so don't you dare tell me you didn't know what happened to me." In his father's silence, he took the opportunity to pick up the photograph on the table. He decided to take a different approach this time, mock his father almost, and show him the extent of his new found madness. "Amazing isn't it; how of all the things the glyphs can do the Keepers find a way to preserve a single moment on a piece of parchment. Shall I tell you how it's done?" he began to circle the room, his words taking a patronising tone. "They use a glyph, looks like a square inside a square and then they draw it in the air with their right hand, holding a piece of parchment in the other. The subjects of the photograph stand in front of them a couple of feet away, just acting natural and then their image; their moment of happiness as it were, is preserved in a single image. Fascinating!" He threw the photograph down onto the table so that it land facing his father who scanned a quick look at the image. "Did you know I had a family, a wife...a daughter?"

"I swear I did not..."

"Do not lie!"

Tristan launched himself up the stairs, causing his father to follow. He raced into his bedroom, throwing open the doors of his wardrobe and reaching for something hidden in the darkness of the top shelf; something that he was only half sure was even there.

"Tristan?" his father yelled as he span round the corner to find Tristan on the floor with the contents of small ornate wooden box spread around him. The contents appeared to be more photographs like the one downstairs – dozens of them. "Where did you get these?"

"I've had them ever since I came back from Hasaghar...something you didn't manage to hide from me!"

His father gasped, struggling to come to terms with the words coming out of Tristan's mouth. After all these years, he was finally remembering and this was Theorryn's worst nightmare as the lies he had told to keep his son close began to unravel before him. As more photographs littered the floor Tristan stopped, finally finding the one he was looking for. He rose to his feet and pushed the photograph into Theorryn's chest, knocking him back slightly. Grimacing, he grabbed at Tristan's arm, ripping the parchment from his clutches and staring at the image upon it. He recognised himself and Tristan along with Romeo too. There was a woman also, all draped in white looking radiant on the gorgeous spring day. She held a bouquet of white and yellow roses, the only other colour on her being her brown locks and her green eyes.

"You were there," Tristan exclaimed, cursing as he did so. "You were at my wedding. You congratulated me on the 'catch' I had made. For the first time in my entire life, you were proud of me!" his father remained silent but his eyes spoke a thousand words as they stared at the photograph; a thousand lies unravelling in one single image. After a while he looked up at Tristan, the anger on his son's face almost unbearable for him to face.

"I have always been proud of you..."

"For the last time father, do not lie to me! Growing up, I was nothing to you. Romeo was the golden child, the one who did everything right and there was me – constantly living in his shadow...the black sheep of the family. After all, what was it you used to say, every family has one. Every time I got myself into trouble you would berate me, begging me to be more like Romeo. You were never happy with who I was! Heck, even when Romeo got into trouble too, it would be me you blamed for leading him astray. You couldn't believe that your golden boy wasn't perfect. In fact, the reason he played up was so that you would see it! He hated the way you made me feel which is why I never hated him for the way you treated me…it was you I hated!"

"How dare you…"

"How dare I? How dare you more like! It's one thing to keep my dead wife from me…but my daughter…"

Theorryn was silent. Now his lies were literally crumbling right in front of him, and he didn't even know how to recover the situation. He ran his hands through his hair, turning his back on Tristan in shame.

"You literally have nothing to say? The ale has probably worn off and can't fuel anymore lies for you to spill. I mean, what else have you been lying to me about? The next thing you'll be telling me is that the Keepers didn't try to kill me and there was something else responsible for my memory loss." Theorryn sighed heavily, turning around to face his son; remorse and guilt filling his eyes in the form of tears that would never spill. "I knew it! And you can't even do me the decency and offer an explanation."

When his father still said nothing, Tristan began gathering up the contents of the box and packed it away, placing it on the bed. He grabbed his pack from the chair by the desk and began stuffing shirts and breaches into it. He then placed the box in there, cushioning it with his shirts.

"What are you doing?" Theorryn asked, a little delayed in his response to the packing Tristan was doing.

"What does it look like I'm doing?" he mocked, pulling on his overcoat and throwing his pack over his shoulder.

"Tristan you can't leave…I mean where will you go?"

"Anywhere is better than here!"

Tristan barged past his father, making his way downstairs and to the front door, ignoring Theorryn's constant yelling of his name as he followed him to the door. But Tristan was done listening to the lies that rolled off his father's tongue easier than counting to three. His father stopped at the door though, realising Tristan was not going to change his mind and watched as Tristan continued walking, heading up the hill and towards the city gates in the waning daylight.

~~~

"Mind if I take a pew?"

Tristan looked up from the photo he had been mindlessly staring at, reality swimming back to him as his thoughts deserted him like darkness flees an approaching light. The man that stood before him was Balderick, his bald head seemingly shinier in the dying light of the night sky. He waved his right hand in the air, reminding Tristan of his question. Tristan nodded to him, so Balderick sat beside him, lighting his pipe and proceeding to smoke it; breathing a sigh of relief as he did so.

"You sound like you needed that," Tristan presumed.

"I most certainly did!" explained Balderick as he leant forward slightly, his long purple cloak stretching across his back, the gold buckle at the shoulder struggling slightly under the tension. Balderick was the head of the city guard and the purple signified this. He was a good man and a close friend of Tristan's too despite the fact that he was twice his age and old enough to be his father.

"I tell you it's been a killer of a day!" Balderick went on. "I mean, even before you lost your nut...no offense of course." Balderick was from the south in Telnar and his dialect had once been alien to Tristan, in fact many, even now, took his words to offense although they were never meant in that way.

"None taken, what else happened today then?"

"Started my shift as usual at sun up and it seemed quite ordinary. But it didn't stay nice and quiet for long no sir it did not. Shortly after midday a protest broke out just outside the castle. Apparently, what was discussed in confidence at the council meeting somehow got out to the masses. Do you remember the king's son, Jacques?"

"How could I forget? He was one of mine and Romeo's best friends along with Merlin's son Thomas. He disappeared the day his mother died forcing many to think he did it. Father told us he died; travellers found him in the mountain pass a week later. He was already dead though!"

"Well young chap; that is where you are wrong...our young prince is actually alive."

"What? But they bought back his body?"

"Apparently not! Ivan wouldn't give me the details but seems pretty shady. They don't want any more information getting out, especially as the city folk have somehow convinced themselves the council are harbouring the prince in an underground prison to keep his survival a secret. I mean, it doesn't help the fact that the King's advisor Daniel was even arrested and branded a traitor. It would appear conspiracy and corruption are rife in the castle at the moment. Crazy times we live in!"

"Indeed," Tristan agreed, his mind full of even more questions than he already had.

"Then of course you lose your nut in front of the whole city and the rest, well...nothing a good ale won't cure anyway."

Balderick tapped out the burnt tobacco into the fountain, letting the water take it away and dissolve it into oblivion. Pocketing his pipe, he rose to his feet and stretched tall – his old bones creaking with fatigue from a hard day's work. He looked at Tristan with hope, noticing how he had pocketed whatever the bit of paper was in his hand. He looked lost, his eyes the most clouded over he had ever seen them, even after he returned from Hasaghar.

"Would you care to join me for a pint or two?" asked Balderick as Tristan looked up at him considering his options. "We don't have to go the Sleepy Warden if you don't want...that is to say if you are still avoiding Jenni?"

"It's her night off tonight actually," replied Tristan, not even denying the point.

"Then it's settled!" Balderick knelt to pick up Tristan's bags, slinging it over his shoulder as he did so. "We shall drop these in with Marcine on the way..."

"Marcine?" Tristan questioned, suddenly confused by his suggestion.

"Yes Marcine...my wife who else would she be?" Tristan still looked confused. "You need a place to stay don't you...and we can't have you swindling away in some inn now can we? Besides, we have that spare room now that our Archibald has gone to the academy in Lakir. I can't see him needing it any time soon." Tristan looked shocked; *how had Balderick known about my predicament?* He thought as he rose to his feet, grabbing his other bag. Balderick lead the way to his house towards the castle and then onto the inn for a pint of ale or two.


Taking a stool each at the bar, the two waited for the bartender to notice them. The place was swamped with people and with only Dante serving, things were rather hectic. He got to them in good time though, making quick work of the customers before them – he certainly had a knack for this. As he came over to them, he winked in Tristan's direction, nodding to Balderick too as though he were an old friend.

"What can I get you gents?" asked Dante, slinging his cloth over his shoulder as he patted down the tarnished white apron around his waist.

"I'll have a nice ale please sir," replied Balderick. "And my friend Tristan will have your best wheat beer. Stick it on my tab!"

"Coming right up!"

"Do you know him," Tristan asked as Dante went about preparing their drinks.

"In a manner of speaking I suppose..."

"There we are gents...Balderick I've put it on your tab," announced Dante as he placed down their drinks carefully.

"Why thank you Dante. Why don't you join us after you finish up here?"

"I certainly will when Francis decides to show his sorry arse!" he turned away and began serving his other customers.

Deciding to remain where they sat, the two sipped their drinks – the fresh aroma hitting the backs of their throats and relaxing their every nerve.

"So tell me Tristan, what caused your little breakdown in the square today?"

"How about I ask you a question Balderick?" answered Tristan. He couldn't really explain to himself even what happened so telling Balderick would be a struggle in itself.

"Sure, fire away!" he replied taking another sip of his ale.

"What do you remember about when I came back from Hasaghar?"

"You were very different that's for sure."

"How so?"

"I don't know how to explain it...so let me put in a bit of context. Before you left for Dilu you were confident...a sarky kind of confidence though...not the sort anyone praises to be honest. You chased after maidens, and boy you were ruthless in your selection. You liked the brunettes...you used to say the darkness of their hair tempted you into doing things you never thought yourself capable of – made it out like they were seducing you when really it was the other way around. Then of course, you ran into that Keeper..."

"What Keeper?" asked Tristan, suddenly realising where his memory loss actually began.

"So that's as far as you go is it? What is the last thing you remember from four years ago? Let me describe the situation...seeing as I was the one chasing you..."

"Chasing...yes that's it! I remember we had snuck into the gardens to see Iris; she didn't even know we were there watching her. Of course, that wasn't the intention..."

"Course it wasn't, how stupid do you think I am?"

"Honest...Jacques..." he froze suddenly, realising just how this was linked to their previous conversation by the fountain. He ignored the coincidence and continued with his excuses. "Romeo was waiting below the wall for us, supposedly keeping a lookout; although I swear blind he was too busy talking up Primrose Marie to notice you coming along and yanking us down from that wall. Of course, we went running, couldn't have father finding out we were in trouble yet again. Ended up in a little alleyway waiting for you to give up and then the rest...the rest is all just a blur."

"I'm sure you'll remember in time, just like the rest of it!" he raised his glass to Dante as he spied a look over. "Stick with Dante here and he'll see to it that you remember everything there is for you to remember." Dante nodded to him, sighing as he began serving yet another endless stream of customers.

"How is it exactly that you know Dante?" asked Tristan, his curiosity still not satisfied.

"Well...technically speaking we were once brothers..."

"Once?" interrupted Dante coming over to lean on the bar opposite them as another barman relieved him of his duties for a short while. "Are we not still brothers then Balderick?"

"We can be if you want to be I suppose..."

"You know what I would really like," asked Dante, a cheeky grin appearing on his face. "I would like to know what happened to all your hair." Dante reached over the bar and shined his knuckles on Balderick's bald head. Balderick looked down at his empty tankard, turning red with slight embarrassment. "I mean I remember a time...hundreds of years ago of course, where your hair must have reached your waist." Tristan grinned at the remark, spying the look on Dante's face.

"You're one to talk! Have you seen the length of your hair right now? Practically touches the floor!"

"Yes, but it suits me," exclaimed Dante as he waved his hair around as though he were a woman showing off her luscious locks. "Completes my handsome rugged look - has all the ladies at me feet." Dante smiled, stroking his seemingly soft beard and winking to a woman sat at a table in the centre of the inn who shied away, looking back out of the corner of her eye.

"As I remember it, Nielson spent most of his time teasing you about your luscious locks and how much of a woman they made you look." Continued Dante.

"Ah yes but Nielson..."

"Nielson?" asked Tristan, the name ringing a bell somewhere in the back of his mind.

"Yes Tristan...Nielson is another of our brothers," explained Dante. "How do you know him?"

"I'm not sure, the name just seems to remind me of…someone…" Tristan tried to explain himself as he scratched the side of his head, trying to remember.

"Like Balderick said, it'll all come back to you in time, speaking of which, my five-minute break is probably up by now. Some of us have to work for a living. Why don't you take him home Balderick?" he nodded towards Tristan. "He looks like he needs some shut eye."

"Actually, he will be staying with me until he goes to Dilu with you." Balderick said as he rose to his feet, patting Tristan on the back to pull him up to his feet.

"Oh right," Dante swung his washcloth over his shoulder once more. "In that case I will pop in on you later."

Dante winked at the two of them as he set about his work again and Balderick and Tristan left the inn.

"So you and Dante…brothers?" asked Tristan just as they reached Balderick's house.

"Yep," Balderick turned to Tristan, showing him the glyph upon his palm. "I was Freedom…"

"Like Jacques was?"

"Yes, well remembered!"

"You weren't banished like Dante and the others?"

"Oh no I was…but someone bought me back. I think it was an ally from one of the other generations of brothers. I never saw his face; he was apprehended by other Keepers shortly after he bought me back. I barely got away myself. It's why I cut off all my hair; so I wouldn't be recognised. I disposed of my key so I couldn't be tracked. Then fifty or so years later I met Marcine and well…you know the rest I'm sure." Tristan nodded. "Shall we," he asked, motioning inside. "I'm sure Marcine has set up Balde's room all ready for you."

# CHAPTER 9 - THE TRUTH AT LAST

The city was a calmer notion in the surprisingly mild afternoon. Tristan observed the stall owners of the Exotic Market as he passed them; how they talked up their wares to potential customers who then attempted to barter down the price. More than likely this bartering would usually fail and the customer would settle on the asking price. As his mind drifted elsewhere, he pictured a younger him dragging a woman through the stalls – a short petite thing in a flowing green dress that was corseted at the waist, her brown hair falling just below the middle of her back in short curls that sprung joyfully around her face as she was pulled along at the hand by Tristan. Both had faces of glee as he took her in his hands, tempting foreign sweets before her eyes before placing them delicately in her mouth to taste.

As an old man knocked into him, he was forced back into reality – unsure of whether what he had seen was a figment of his imagination or a dream of what was once real.

"Sorry my boy!" When Tristan didn't answer, the man gave him a sharp slap on the arm. "Wake up my boy, come back to reality."

"Merlin?" Tristan murmured as his vision came back into focus.

"By all means remember the past lad but do not linger in their world – it's the past for a reason." Tristan nodded warily. "How about you step in for some tea?" he motioned to his accommodation above the stables, a concerned look upon his face.

Tristan hadn't even noticed how close to the square he was, how he had been starring at Jenni as she emptied a bucket of murky looking soapy water into the alley by the inn before heading back to serve the lunchtime rush. He followed Merlin up to his apartment and slumped onto the couch as the storyteller set his affairs in order and placed a pot of water on the fire that ignited no sooner had he placed the pot above it. Whilst he was waiting for the water to boil, he perched himself next to Tristan, a moment of silence passing between them.

"I want to apologise; I admit that I knew about your daughter." Despite what Merlin expected, Tristan remained silent, so he continued. "The reason I never told you was because believe it or not I was under the impression she was dead - to lose both your wife and daughter twice is quite a lot, especially if you do not remember either of them. With the condition you were in, I didn't want to make things worse...my plan was to tell you all in good time...when I thought you were more stable to handle the truth. Part of me was also hopeful that I was wrong about her being dead and that was what I was clinging to. I know now that may have been selfish of me and I should've told you right from the very beginning."

"Why did you believe her to be dead?" Merlin was amazed how patient Tristan was in asking that question.

"After your...accident...I went to the inn where you and Dagnen had been staying to collect her." Tristan could tell that Merlin was being careful not to say her name – it was obviously something he wanted Tristan to remember on his own. "You see after what happened to you happened, most of the Keepers faded and as far as I knew only the Prodicals would be spared. My plan was to fetch her with Myrina, whom you named her godmother, and bring them back to Az Lagní with us when you were well enough to travel. However, when I got there the inn had been set alight and the City Watch guards were stood all around. I pushed my way through the crowd and spoke to one of the guardsmen and he told me three bodies had been found in the upstairs; that of a man, a woman and a baby. Their faces were unrecognisable but certain features were still noticeable such as the woman's blonde hair of which the man shared the same colour. I thought it was...."

The pot on the fire had begun to boil now, water spurting over the edges and provoking the embers below. Merlin jumped up, stopping his words and tending to the pot. As he did so, Tristan thought over everything he had said so far – it was obvious where the story was heading but there was something in his mind that told him that perhaps Merlin's tale had a different ending. He tried desperately to suppress his anxiety, feeling hot tears escape the fences in his eyes – he had only found out about his daughter just yesterday and now he had to come to terms with the possibility that she, like his wife; like his brothers, was dead. The grief inside him began to boil over and he couldn't contain it any longer.

"Is she dead?" Tristan asked, exasperated, his voice breaking slightly. He watched distressed as Merlin appeared to ignore the question, coming over to where Tristan sat and calmly placing a tray with two cups and a teapot in the centre on the table. He spooned a heap of sugar into his cup before pouring in some tea, smells of cinnamon and various other spices masking the aroma of manure from the stables below. "Merlin, answer me!"

"I wonder Tristan," he said, completely ignoring the question. "Have you had any visitors lately...to the shop I mean...people looking for you?" He waited for an answer, blowing his tea to make it cool.

"What do you mean?" asked Tristan, slumping back in his seat frustrated as to why Merlin was changing the subject. The old man obviously meant well though, he wouldn't do it without good reason.

"Has anyone come into the Smithy claiming to know you?"

"No! Wait...yes, there was a man who came by. Said his name was John Basso."

"Basso's back...that's interesting. Who else?" he grazed over the point, frustrated as to why Merlin didn't even bother to explain who this John Basso might be.

"Well, no one!"

"Are you sure? I could've sworn I saw him..."

Merlin went off into a stupor, mumbling to himself in no understandable language. Tristan thought about who Merlin was expecting him to have seen; of all the strangers that had come and gone since he started remembering – Dante, Basso...that mysterious Baldwin character...

"There was another man I met yesterday," Merlin stopped muttering and looked at Tristan straight in the eyes as he placed his tea back on the table. "Lionel told me yesterday that there was a package in the store room for a client who would be coming to pick it up in the afternoon. He told me the collector went by the name of Baldwin." Merlin's eyes twinkled in disbelief as Tristan said the name, but he remained silent, almost as though he was waiting for Tristan to correct himself. "The man came in not long after Basso, picked up his package and left. That was the only other man!"

"What did he look like?" Merlin asked slowly, his voice bereft of any feeling.

"He," Trying to remember him was difficult, it was like the event itself had wiped itself from his memory, like he wasn't meant to remember the man who had come into the Smithy that day by the name of Baldwin. "He wore a rather regal attire, a brown leather jacket with gold trimmings," he tried to focus on the small things that he did remember, hoping that once they were put together, they would form a bigger picture. "He had pale skin and a natural smile almost, but one that seemed secretive and full of sadness despite the nature of it. Blonde hair, cropped around his face at different lengths, locks that sprang as he stepped. A slight stubble framed his mouth, a sublime feature and his eyes…they are green like the trees."

As Tristan described the man, his image appeared in his mind but the vision wasn't from the other day. The man stood before him; his attire slightly shabbier; the leather jacket was to be replaced by a beige canvas kind of top that was tucked into black trousers which were also tucked into even blacker boots. The trousers were belted and his stance relaxed as he stood before Tristan, his hand outstretched ready for a shake. 'My name is Cedric,' he says with a voice that seemed to chuckle as it spoke. 'I live next door with Percy and Trevor. Guess that makes us neighbours!' Tristan takes the hand but his voice is silent as he greets; any reaction that he makes void of sight.

"Ceric Baldwin!" Tristan said aloud, the name seeming to leave him in pain as he clutched at his tunic, feeling for the picture the man had dropped yesterday.

"So he lives!" Merlin said after a while, his eyes facing down at the floor. "As you've probably guessed I thought he died in the fire. I knew that if he didn't fade after the incident that he would go back for her…I thought he was dead…but all this time…" he looked over at Tristan, his face pale and for the first time showing his true age. "Did he say anything to you?" when Tristan didn't answer, he placed a hand atop his which was trembling as they gripped at the knee. As the touch was felt on his skin, Tristan jumped, looking over at Merlin with eyes that spoke a thousand hardships. "Did he say anything to you?"

"No!" he said at last. "But he did drop something."

"What did he drop?"

Tristan reached inside his tunic this time and pulled out the picture, giving it to Merlin. The old man unfolded it, his eyes widening as he gazed at the content. He smiled, handing the picture back to Tristan who took it and stared into it like it was a window to what was; he with his arms around his Dags and a young baby between them barely a few months old. A laugh shared between the two as they looked at each other, the baby none the wiser.

"So if Cedric is alive, does that mean she is too?" Tristan asked quietly, his eyes pleading with Merlin.

"I think so yes! If Cedric got out alive then so did she, he wouldn't leave her in there. He is, after all, her godfather. What on earth is the man playing at though, showing up here and not even saying so much as a word to me or to Theorryn for that matter. I dread to think what he believes about your daughter…"

"Why won't you say her name?"

Merlin wasn't sure how to answer. Of course, he knew why he wasn't letting that slip –
Tristan had to remember on his own but how was he to explain it to him in a way that he
would agree that was what was best?

"Tristan I would love to tell you her name! Heck there are thousands of things I would
love to tell you about your past, your brothers, the Keepers, so many beautiful moments I
watched you and Dagnen share. But you see that's where telling fails, to remember *you*
must step into your past, reconnect with it. You can't just be told about it, you can't just
recall it, you must become a part of, become one with your past."

"I don't understand."

"You won't, not until you remember everything. I mean you can't just forget someone,
once you've met them that's it! You never really forget them...it just takes a while for the
memories to return."

"Tell me how to remember...tell me how I know whether or not my dreams are dreams
or memories of what was. These days I don't know the difference Merlin, these pictures
are all I have. But how do I...connect with them as you say?"

"Who we are as people is made up of what I like to call moments of impact. These
moments make us who we are; they are memories, they are feelings, they are events
which shape our true matter. These moments are what makes our lives memorable,
some of them even make it worthwhile. These moments become our strongest
memories and they are the ones we cling to when we feel lost, empty and alone. Think of
it as though there is a box inside your head and these moments are within the box. All
you need to do to reconnect with them is merely find the key."

"And then what?"

"Well as Felix once said; if you have a key, you must infer that somewhere out there is a
lock that it fits into – perfect partners. Once you've unlocked the box, you'll no longer be
lost, empty...or alone for that matter. The first step is to accept that this is how you are
now; lost, empty, alone! Accept that, and only then will you find your true path to being
found and surrounded by people you love."

"Then I guess I know what I need to do."

"Then you've already taken the first step...now climb those stairs, and you'll remember
her...you will remember them all!"

A smile crept into the ends of Tristan's lips as he placed the picture back inside his tunic
and rose to his feet. He felt a little lighter now, as though a million answers had now

been presented to him, all he needed do now was find the right one and follow it through, find the key and then unlock the box...just like Merlin had said.

"Thank you Merlin!" he said, turning his head as he opened the front door.

"Not a problem my boy, you know where I am if you need me," he replied, taking his tea in his hands once more and sitting back as Tristan left the apartment and headed back into the bustling city streets.

# CHAPTER 10 - SWEET REVENGE

The city was a lot busier now as he came out from the stables, people were moving amongst the stalls buying the many wares of the sellers. Weaving in and out of the people, he made his way towards the fountain in the centre of the square, its water flowing generously into each stone bowl, each a little bigger than the one before. The sound bought Tristan a sense of peace, one that was all too easily disturbed by the sight of Jenni storming out of the inn with a bucket of soapy water in her hand.

He didn't know where this sudden annoyance for her came from, just that it seemed bent on discovering some form of secret she may or may not have been keeping from him. He watched her a while – trying to gage what might have caused her bad mood. Observing her attire, he noted yet another red dress; this one was lighter than her last though, probably more of blush red than the cherry red that had been on her the other day. It hugged her figure rather tightly and touched the floor as she turned on the windows, placing the bucket precariously on the sill. She was mumbling to herself – how he wished he could hear her rants.

He felt a prickling sensation on his left hand, the feeling sending a ringing through his ears as he looked down to observe the mark that disappeared beneath the skin on his palm. It was a strange mark that seemed to form a rather pointed eye shape – he had seen it before, but he couldn't think where from. As he took his attention away from his hand, a voice crept into his ear and he turned around to find the source. But no one was around him, as the voice became clear, he realised it belonged to a woman; Jenni. Looking over at her, he saw her mumbling to herself still – whatever that mark was it somehow had made him an ultimate eavesdropper.

"Why should I have to clean the windows?" she said under her breath. "I'm the barmaid, he's just the hired help. Oh Jenni doesn't mind cleaning the windows, she's a woman she likes to clean. I'll give him likes to clean!"

"I hope you're not talking about me?" asked a man whom Tristan hadn't even notice approach her until he heard his voice in his head just like he did Jenni's. The man's appearance had startled Jenni as she looked up at a hooded man who seemed to have appeared from the alley down the side of the inn. His voice seemed familiar to Tristan, one he had heard all too recently.

"What?" she jumped, her voice rather high pitched. "Oh, it's you." As she stared into the hood, the hidden appearance of the man she recognised seemed to steady her demeanour. "I heard you were back in town."

"Flying visit really." The man's voice was very well pronounced with a twinge of a southern accent.

"What are you doing here? What do you want?"

"Nothing really! Just came to see how things were going with your beloved Tristan."

"Wouldn't you like to know?" she asked sarcastically, crossing her arms across her chest accentuating her cleavage which seemed to complete the otherwise disappointing red dress.

"I heard that he'd gone rather mad. Was raving about another woman, his wife I believe…"

"Dead wife!"

"Oh, touchy subject I take it. You seem intent on making sure she stays that way?"

"Tristan is with me now…" she hesitated. "There's nothing that will come between us."

"Not even his daughter coming back from the dead?"

The phrase shocked Tristan. The hooded man had to be Cedric to say something like that. However, the phrase didn't seem to shock Jenni, not even phase her – she had to have known the whole time that Tristan had a daughter and that she was alive. But how did Cedric slot in with her?

"Because she's alive you know," he continued to taunt. "And it's about time he got to know her."

"Why now and not three years ago?" she piped back. Tristan could feel the anger boiling inside him, she had to have known this whole time but how could she do this to him; the man she was supposed to love above all else.

"Face it Jenni," the man leaned in close to her ear but that didn't stop Tristan from hearing him. "You lost him eight years ago when he left you behind and chose her."

He slid a tender hand down her jawline and Tristan imagined a sly smile touching the ends of the man's lips as a single tear formed in the corner of Jenni's eye. The man let his hand drop and a snigger escaped his hidden lips, hidden like the truths that were now slowly coming to light. The man turned, his hood slipping slightly – almost enough to let Tristan see blonde curls slipping past leafy green eyes that dared to look up at Tristan as he disappeared back down the alley. Jenni wiped her face with the back of her hand as he vanished and she turned to finish cleaning the window.

Tristan watched the space in the alley where the man he assumed was Cedric had gone, debating whether or not he should follow. *How was he going to do this?* It was obvious Jenni had lied to him all this time but he had to find out why. The reason why was probably not a very good one, but he had a right to know all the same. The question was should Tristan play her at her own game or just confront her outright? Perhaps he could even do both. Taking a deep breath, he stood just behind her without her even noticing there was someone behind her – Cedric's visit had obviously shook her so much that her guard had dropped – and Tristan was going to use that to his advantage.

"What was that all about?" he asked before jumping back immediately as the bucket finally lost its balance on the window sill and crashed to the floor, murky soapy water splashing everywhere; mostly on the hem of Jenni's red dress. "Whoops, sorry...I uh seem to be making a habit of ruining your red dresses." He tried to hide the enormous grin now creeping onto his face; although it wasn't his intention to embarrass her further, the look on her face right now was priceless.

"Tristan!" she exclaimed, stretching out the dress to see the full extent of the damage, dampness setting in as far as her knees. She looked up at him – she was not impressed – after all he had ruined yet another of her red dresses and lately, they seemed to be the only dresses she had.

"At this rate you'll have nothing left to wear," he joked, taking a step toward her as he debated toying with her affections for a while.

"It's not funny! What do you want anyway? Can't you see I'm trying to work?"

"Well that doesn't usually bother you..." she turned away before he could finish but instinct told him to grab ahold of her softly and turn her back to face him. "I wanted to apologise."

"Apologise for what?" she pulled her arm away, folding them as she had with Cedric; although this time it was in more of an impatient manner as opposed to the flirtatious notion it had seemed before.

"I uh...I've been avoiding you for reasons that escape me now. And I wanted to apologise; I was just so angry with what he did that I took it out on you and that was wrong." His quickness to blame his father had certainly worked as her shoulders dropped and her face turned softer, more understanding and compassionate – perhaps even guilt ridden with the way she had acted.

"It's okay, you don't have to apologise. I understand…" she reached out for his hand, her touch resonating the quelled anger inside him.

"Oh you do? That's good, it's nice to have someone who understands me for a change…like really at least. Most people at the moment only pretend to – they pretend to care…like my father." He had got her affection that much was clear, now it was time to toy with it before ousting her for the dirty liar she was.

"Theorryn? What's he done?" she was playing dumb; she knew what he had done all too well.

"It turns out he's lied to me all these years…in fact not just him but everyone in this damned city has let me believe that this is my life." He dropped her hand and turned his back on her – trying to play on his own vulnerability.

"Lied to you? Tristan this is your life…here…here is your home…" she came up behind him and he could feel her hands grace his back as she longed to be close to him. Now, she was playing with his affections.

"No!" he broke away from her, making her jump suddenly. "You say you understand, but you don't. Nobody does."

"Then help me to understand." He looked back at her through the corner of his eye.

"These three years, it's like I've been living someone else's life – I don't know whose but it's not mine. My life was in Dilu and Hasaghar…with her…my Dags. My life was never here, not even these last three years." He turned around to face her. "Home is where people love you, care about you…where people don't lie to you…" His eyes stared right into her, their seriousness making hers dart away; he had her right where he wanted her.

"Tristan I…" she begun, although he wasn't sure what she might spin next, he wasn't about to let her try to lie her way out of this.

"What is Cedric to you?"

"Excuse me?"

"Cedric, the man who you were talking to just now…how do you know him?"

"How did you…"

"I'm not as stupid and naïve as I look."

"I never said you were. I met him when he came back with you three years ago…"

"Lie!"

"It's the truth…"

"Up until now, everybody believed Cedric to be dead…"

"But…"

"He's been looking after my daughter…whom people also believed to be dead. But you knew that didn't you?" she didn't answer him, she just stared at him, all the whilst her eyes trying to avoid contact with his. "You, like everybody else here who professes to care about me have been lying to me these past three years. Why would you do that…lie to me…you of all people? You're so supposed to love me!"

"Tristan I…" she drifted off, like she didn't even know how to deny what he was saying. All her lies were unravelling before her and there was nothing she could say to pull this all back in her favour.

"Well, I guess it's a start that you're not denying it. Why Jenni? Why did you lie to me all these years?"

"It was Theorryn," she said after a while. "He made…"

"Don't put the blame on him!" he raised a finger to her – his father had enough to answer for. "My father has enough to apologise for but your actions are not one of them. You've always been a feisty woman Jenni, one who was perfectly in control of her own mind…a law unto herself. No one would ever be able to *make* you do anything." He paused a while, studying her pale face; the look of puzzlement upon her lips and the look of sheer panic in her eyes. To his amazement, there was no guilt, no sorrow – it was like she was past caring, like caring for him, loving him all these years had been more of a chore than a want or a need. "Answer me then! Oh, let me guess…you were jealous…"

"Jealous?" now she was denying it.

"Jealous! I chose her over you…and that made you jealous…I'm surprised you stuck around to be honest; but then maybe I'm not considering she died three years ago. Of course you'd stick around so that you could finally sink your claws into me."

"You think I was jealous?" she asked again, her chestnut eyes now looking right into the blue of his own. She looked angry if anything, outraged that he could accuse her of such a thing.

"Well, you were…it's pretty obvious, isn't it?"

"...yes, I was jealous but that's not why I did this." Tristan could tell she was angry; it was the way in which she referred to them as 'this' and now he had cracked her – now he would get the truth.

"Then why? Humour me." Tristan folded his arms and leant casually against the pole where travellers would tie their horses to stop for a drink in the tavern.

"I did it to get back at you, to show how it made me feel that you chose her."

"You silly girl. Anyone else would tell you to move on, I left you Jenni...I think it was pretty clear..."

"Not to me! When you left for Dilu you left me thinking you would come back to me after your Keeper training, you let me think you would come back to me and we could be together properly."

"Oh come off it! You knew I was leaving to discover myself...I didn't know what I was going to find so I left you in the hope that you would move on."

"That's not how it seemed. Even when you wrote to Theorryn and he would come around the town boasting of how his son was making him proud...how his son had found himself a sweetheart...someone was making an honest man out of him at last. He took great enjoyment in flaunting it in front of me."

"You never were his first choice for me."

"Neither was *she*...not after he found out what she was."

"What do you mean?"

"She was damaged goods Tristan and you deserved more than that. When he found out he came to me, told me how he thought even a bar wench was better than some town whore."

"How dare you!" he stood up tall – he may not have remembered everything about her yet but there was no way he was going to let her drag Dagnen's name through the dirt. But now she was taking her turn to talk and she wasn't going to let him get a word in edgeways.

"How dare I? What, afraid to hear the truth? I took his words and I went to Dilu to see you, to see if you really could've devoted yourself to one woman. I saw you in the streets with Romeo and some other men talking about this masquerade ball that was being held at the estate to celebrate the spring solstice. So, I thought I would tag along and see if I could charm you so to speak. I put on a mask and pretended to be someone else just to see if you could really resist the temptation."

*An elaborately decorated hall opened out around him; filled with people dancing hand in hand – men dressed in smart silk tunics with long coats, leather trousers and sturdy boots; women clothed in intricately stitched exotic dresses that shaped their figures beautifully – masks adorning their eyes. Tristan was stood amongst his brothers, all smartly adorned and masked, each parting the group to meet their partner at the stairs at the head of the room and join the parade of dancers. All his brothers having taken the floor, he sighed heavily – still no Dagnen – and turned to fetch another drink of beer from a flagon on the table behind where he stood.*

*When he turned back around, he faced a woman in a red dress. He wasn't sure whether he recognised her or not, then again, the mask didn't really help the matter. The ruby red dress shaped her figure beautifully; a gold entwining leaf pattern entwining her waist, giving them a rounded appearance as the dress descended covering her feet. The gold seemed to compliment the chain effect necklace. Her dark hair was tied up in a bun at the back of her head and adorned with a beaded band tied loosely around it with a few curls on either side falling beside her high cheek bones. Her brown eyes were adorned by a red and black laced mask with gold beads along the edge. The arms of the dress draped to her knees, making her look somewhat shorter than she actually was just below Tristan's shoulders. Although the look caught Tristan's eye, the woman was far too pale for a red dress, not to mention the fact that her assets were somewhat disappointing in a dress that flaunted them so, especially at the chest where the neckline of the dress clung to the tips of her shoulders and rounded off at her cleavage.*

*The two made small talk for a while though; after all, even though Tristan was determined to make Dagnen his, if he wasn't going to get her this night he might as well entertain his options. But just as he was about to give up all hope and ask the woman to dance, his eyes were caught by an emerald green tint at the top of the staircase. Following the attraction, his eyes were greeted by what was perhaps the most beautiful woman he had ever seen and her showing up here meant she was all his. Dagnen lingered at the stairs a while, waiting until she set her eyes on her waiting partner. Taking the hint, Tristan passed the woman who continued to talk as though she didn't notice him moving away for the first moment. When she finally did though, she turned around to see Tristan was making his way toward the staircase and the woman's face had lit up as she set eyes upon him.*

*As he made his way forward, his eyes remained glued to her, studying her every detail. The dress matched her eyes which twinkled in the light and the glare reflecting off the bead strung mask that decorated her face. The mask itself was further complimented by a gold jewelled necklace which coupled as a choker with matching earrings. Her chest and shoulders were left bare, the dress held in place by sleeves that joined the gold patterned bodice that draped down with a translucent fabric. The skirt of the dress bunched out slightly at the hips before flowing freely down to the floor, dragging gently behind her a little way. Her light brown hair was tied slightly behind her and flowed beautifully down her back – it wasn't particularly long but it competed the look all the same. Despite her face being hidden from him, he knew it was Dagnen for no other gave him that feeling in his heart as though time around him had stopped and it was just them two dancing once again in the rain.*

"Obviously I was wrong!" continued Jenni as Tristan's consciousness reluctantly came back to the present. "You may have entertained the idea of getting to know a stranger, but it was clear when you kissed her hand at the stairs that your heart belonged to *her.*"

"So, the woman in the red dress – that was you?" he asked for reassurance. She nodded – clearly red dresses had always been her trademark however it was a shame they did nothing for such a pale complexion.

"I watched you dance with her all night and I saw in her face how hard she tried to love you better than I ever could." Her words were said with a harshness now as her face turned hard and she spat the words in spite. "I was a fool to believe that a man couldn't change – for the right woman they will I guess." The way she was judging him angered Tristan; first she had the nerve to insult Dagnen and now she was judging him – how dare she? There was no redemption from this, no matter what she said. "As the evening drew to a close, the lights grew brighter and the noise of the music died. You took her away, lead her to the balcony where it could be just you and her. I followed behind you though, I didn't want to believe that I was out of the picture. You didn't see me standing there, but I was in the corner…watching you kiss *her* and it broke me.

"So, I came back here and tried to move on; the only reason I didn't go to Shaznul where my father and brother are is because I couldn't face the 'I told you so's. Then when you came back with *her,* I felt like you were rubbing it in my face – God help the both of you if she'd stuck around. Once she left, I heard Theorryn in the bar saying how he was wrong to have judged her and how he was happy for you and I had to listen to him boast over and over again as you left to become an Acolyte, as you married her and then had a child with her. That should've been me! And then when you came back in the state you were in, I saw my chance. It was never meant to last this long…"

"Oh, will you just stop playing the victim!" Tristan had lost his patience with her now, he could not believe what he was hearing; the venom in the words, the forced vulnerability in her tone – it sickened him to the bone to think that he had loved such a thing. "I can't listen to it anymore!" he turned his back on her, unable to look at her any longer. He didn't even know what to say to her.

"Tristan, don't you get it?" she pleaded. "I couldn't go through with it, I loved you too much."

"Oh please," He rounded back on her. "If you had loved me too much you wouldn't have lied to me all these years, you wouldn't have come up with this ridiculous revenge plot or whatever it is you want to call it. You never loved me!" He was right in her face now and the way he towered over Jenni obviously scared her into silence as she didn't even deny it. "When I leave Az Lagní the day after tomorrow I won't be leaving you behind. In fact, the moment I turn my back on you now I will never think of you again...you won't even be a memory."

He dropped his grip on her hand and stormed past her into the hustle and bustle of the streets, not looking back - even after her distressed calls in his name.

# CHAPTER 11 - AT THE GRAVESIDE

The next morning, Tristan awoke with the sun – it was the first night in a long time he had felt like he had actually slept. It was as though a huge weight had been lifted off his shoulders. Hurrying down the stairs, he accepted Marcine's offer of a bowl of porridge with honey before heading out into the bustling city square. The exotic Market was still in town and would be until the end of the week and as he passed, he admired the wares of each stall in turn – gold and silver jewellery, cloths with elaborate patterns and the sweetest smelling food you could dream of.

He passed the centre of the city down to where the performers from far and wide performed by the front gate to Az Lagní. He watched as dancers blew fire from their mouths, and paraded round each other; a man lifting a woman high into the air and a line of men kicking stocky legs donned in fur boots out into the air in some sort of brotherly performance. Taking one last look behind him as some children sped past him, he left through the city gates and headed for the church atop the hill surrounded by white gravestones. The bright sun was just rising behind it and the glimmering light gave him a sense of beauty as it shone through the stained-glass windows, casting brilliant patterns against the grassy hill.

As he neared the huge open oak doors, song met his ears as the choir boys and girls rehearsed ready for the end of week mass. The church itself was a fairly new construction and religion – in the past five years the people of Halsgar had begun turning away from the Hammerites, Mechanists and Pagans and placing their faith in the One Almighty Lord. Tristan couldn't help but think that if it wasn't for the Keepers fading, this movement would never have happened in the first place. But it bought people peace in a time of uncertainty, and that he supposed was the most important thing.

The song that met his ears bought him to sit at one of the stalls and await its end. The sweet sound bought him comfort as he listened to the children sing of hope and trust and a prosperous land. He wondered if the land they sang of even existed in a world like this where so much was unexplained and unexpected. As the choir finished their song, the co-ordinator gathered them around him and instructed them in a hushed tone.

Tristan took his rise at this point, heading for the candles in the corner; some dancing with a small flame and others remaining unlit. Taking a stick from the pot provided, he let the end of it catch alight and lit a candle in the corner. As he did so, he closed his eyes and whispered in prayer to himself. Today marked the day of his mother's death – fifteen long years she had been gone and this seemed like one of the hardest he had faced without her. As he finished the prayer, he bought the key from around his neck up to his lips, touching them slightly. As he did so, he felt a tingling across them as the glyphs on his hands shone brightly in the light. He let the key drop against his chest and opened his eyes, the glyphs fading into his skin so that they seemed like scars etched upon his hands.

He turned his back on the candles as the choir resumed their singing and proceeded out of the doors towards the gravestones. He made his way down to one at the bottom of the hill near a flowerbed of beautiful bright colours. He knelt beside the grave, scraping away the dust from the white-washed headstone to reveal her name; Mariah Araell Romano. She had died fifteen years ago when an outbreak hit the city, killing many of its women and children. He remembered how in her last days she was so weak and so frail. She spent most of her time in bed and his father spent all his time taking care of her at her vigil constantly. When she died, that vigil turned towards the nearest bar to drink himself silly. But he chose not to think about those times right now, instead he chose the happy moments he and his brother Romeo shared with their mother...and father in their younger years.

"I miss you mum," he said quietly to himself. "I wish you could be here; knock some sense into my father and help me remember my past. I could really do with the support – that's for sure!"

A single tear escaped his fraught eyes and his mind drifted away with the memories within his mind. He was so lost in the visions that he almost didn't notice the small shadow that formed beside him. When he did, he looked up to see a small child, probably no older than three years. She had long blond locks and green eyes that twinkled in the sunlight. She was dressed in a little yellow dress with a daisy chain plaited through her hair. In her hand she held a white rose which she handed to Tristan.

"Thank you!" Tristan said as he took the rose from her, confused by her presence. "What's your name little one?"

When she didn't answer him, he stared into her eyes, almost as if the answer lay within them. After a while of quiet, he sighed heavily, twiddling the rose in his fingers, catching one of them on a thorn as he did so. At this, the little girl seemed to get angry and snatched the rose off of him, startling Tristan. He watched as she placed the rose in front of his mother's headstone before turning and facing Tristan once more. He marvelled at the intelligence of the little girl, staring into those green eyes once more.

"Who are you?" he asked again, not really expecting an answer.

As he stared back at the rose, he remembered the man in the vision he had after falling into the river. He had placed the rose on the grave of his wife. 'A rose for the maiden who died protecting those she loved…' the words came back to him as though they were a melody and he lingered there awhile, clinging to the words and not wanting to let go. He had no choice though, for no sooner had he drifted off, words of sheer panic and horror bought him back to reality.

"Evelyn!" a voice shouted somewhere over the hill. Tristan looked worryingly in the direction it had come from. "Evelyn!" the voice sounded exasperated, panic and desperation tainting the air around him making Tristan feel very conscious of the little girl standing beside him. She was looking down at the ground now, fiddling with her fingers.

"Evelyn," he said to her. "Is that your name?"

Unsurprisingly enough the girl didn't answer, but she did nod slightly however Tristan wasn't sure it was in answer of his question or not. Getting to his feet, he stood behind the child as he saw a man appear on the hillside and begin running over to him.

"Evelyn!" his voice was calmer now that he had seen her once more and he came crashing to the floor in front of her, pulling her into a relieved hug. "Don't you ever wonder off like that again you hear me?" Evelyn did a little nod again, placing her hands behind her back and digging her feet into the ground. The man rose now and turned to Tristan, straightening the hooded cloak that concealed his body and running his hand through his red hair. Tristan didn't recognise the man; he certainly wasn't from around here so he thought him a traveller perhaps.

"My thanks to you good sir," he held out a scarred hand towards Tristan who looked at it strangely, taking the hand and shaking it firmly. "Ced would've killed me if I'd lost her…" he trailed off taking Evelyn by the hand.

"She's not your daughter then?" Tristan asked, feeling suddenly unsure of the man.

"No…she…well…it's complicated. How rude of me, I am Hugo and this child is the god daughter of a friend of mine who is in town on business." The man was very careful not to spill any details; mentioning that a certain 'Ced' would kill him was probably the only decent information he was going to get. But Evelyn seemed willing enough to go with him as he led the child away.

"Thank you again, kind sir," he stammered, looking back to Tristan one last time.

"Not a problem," Tristan replied, waving as he did so. "Mind how you go now."

"Oh trust me, this little one won't be going out of my sight again."

Hugo picked up Evelyn and hoisted her onto his shoulders, an eruption of laughter coming from the little girl as he steadied her there. Tristan watched after them as they headed back over the hill and out of sight. He stared after them awhile, laughing to himself as he thought about his own little girl somewhere out there. He wondered how long it would be before he remembered her but then, just to remember what he and Dagnen had named her was all he felt he needed right about now.

He turned around to head back to the city, but as he did so he noticed a woman standing behind him. He started, wondering where she had come. She was stood by the huge oak tree a little way away from him towards the edge of the graveyard, leaning against it as she stared up the hill after Hugo and Evelyn. Her pale face was forlorn and her green eyes weeping at the corner. She brushed away the tear, finding a strand of her wavy brown hair and twiddling it between two fingers. The tops of her hands were scarred, like Hugo's were only this time he could make out a denser scar in the centre...the Keeper sigil. She pushed herself away from the tree, her attire becoming clear as a plain ivory dress flowed around her when she stepped out of the shadow of the tree. It was then she noticed Tristan was watching her and her green eyes met his as he noticed how transparent she seemed – it was like she wasn't really there – but then how could that be so, he was staring right at her. As he stared into her eyes, he felt like somewhere in that greenness, he should know who she was...but why did he feel the sudden need to know who she was?

A slight smile touched her tinted red lips as she began to turn away and head into the corn rows. She was walking with a sudden rush to her steps, almost as though she was inciting a chase and Tristan felt compelled to follow, a soft melody reaching his ears in her wake. He tried to stay close to her fading form as she weaved in and out of the long sheaves of corn, never quite catching up with her. Every now and then she would look back as if to make sure he was still following and every time she did, the melody in his head would get louder dragging him deeper into the chase. Just then though, she slipped out of sight and Tristan felt panicked as he lost sight of her, his pace quickening into a brisk run. He felt as though he should call to her but what name would he shout? As the melody dulled to a whisper, he felt his foot catch in something and he fell to the soft floor face up towards the brilliant blue cloudless sky.

His chest heaved as he tried to calm himself, letting his face fall to the side as he took in his surroundings. The corn rows stood tall around him leaving him in a clearing with trampled corn making his bed soft. Looking to the other side, he was met once more by those green eyes. A smile beamed upon his face as he felt relief in his heart that he was lying beside her. The happiness filled him with light, making the melody louder still as she smiled back at him. As the warm feeling filled his core, he felt suddenly as though he really did know her.

"Dags?" he asked her for confirmation and her smile only widened, as though she had been waiting years to hear him to call her that.

His smile widened too and he reached out to try and touch her face, his fingers slipping through the barrier that separated their worlds. The feel of her face did not meet his fingers, instead it was as though some force was making it impossible to touch her. So instead, he let his hand fall next to her face and stared into her eyes, finding a sense of peace and belonging. If he could just lay here forever, he would be happy, just lay here with her until the sun went down and all of eternity, just being by her side once again would always be enough for him.

~~~

The cold darkness hit me like a ball thrown at the wall in spite during a game of Switch. My brother and I used to play it as children in the streets with our friends. One of us would throw the ball at the wall and once it bounced, we had to switch places with one of the others so they could catch it when the ball bounced back off the wall. You used to say it was your favourite game brother and you used to say that you wished we could stay out long past bed time and play that game again and again. The way you would laugh when someone would miss the catch, the glee it bought you when we were young.

As the cold reaches every part of my body, I try to cling onto those memories of when we were young, playing ball games on the street. I had been concentrating so hard on those memories that I almost hadn't realised the cold leaving my limbs to be replaced by a sudden warmth. They came to life once more, my arms dropping by my waist and my eyes opening at last. A new site welcomed me now, I was still in the Land of the Faded but I thought maybe a different realm. There was still a heavy layer of darkness around everything but I was no longer in a wasteland and as I looked up at the sky above, I noticed something, it was like there was a certain transparency to this world...making it breakable almost.

The Land of the Faded is for those forgotten by their Keeper brothers and here we stay until we are remembered. But sometimes our time runs out and that is when our brothers are lost to us forever. It's not just us who are here though, there are others too, much worse than even the Faders. They were sent here purposefully, a banishment if you like, to seal them away from the surface world and to protect it from the evil deeds they either had committed or would eventually commit. Many a Keeper traitor lived down here with me in this world I had grown to call home. Most of the time when I saw them, I would hide in wait of their passing. They were a danger to me, just as I was to them, they were the Brothers of Dharsi and I was the Union that would help to destroy them all. Back when Father Talus struck a union between the two sects of Keepers, a new sect formed in Dharsi – ninety-nine brothers and sisters who disagreed with the union. They remained underground for a long time, biding their time until they were strong enough to make their move. But when they did, they were betrayed by one of their own who was also Unity. He betrayed his brothers in an effort to help the greater brotherhood of the Keeperage. The First Keeper at the time agreed to pardon him of any sin and treachery so long as he helped to rid the world of Dharsi before their plans spread beyond the Compound. He agreed and bought his brothers together, however their plan quickly crumbled as Dharsi crippled all but Unity. Only Union can destroy Dharsi but unless there is a complete generation, the power needed to defeat them could not be mustered and so the Keeper Council had no choice but to exile them to the Land of the Faded. They could not afford to wait another fifty years for a new Band of Brothers to be formed and accept their destiny.

So the Keeper Enforcers were enlisted, those bound entirely by Glyphs so much so their faces become crippled with markings. On a dark and stormy night, they dispelled the Brotherhood of Dharsi in their sleep. It was quick. It was painless. But it was not complete. Somehow, eight of them made it out and disappeared never to be seen again, that was to say until my generation. We never chose our destiny – it chose us before we had even initiated as Keeper Scribes. It chose us as the last of Union...the last chance the Keepers had to defeat Dharsi once and for all.

I remember how you had been so ambitious to take up our destiny. Me, I was rather the opposite; cautious and calm as the wind but then some things never change. That cautious and fearful nature had faded away in this Land I now called home and it was replaced by a need to survive, a cunning that was bent on escaping this world whether you remembered me or not. I was determined not to let this home be a permanent residence.

I looked around at this new bare land I seemed to be in, but as I stared tinges of colour tainted the darkness and buildings rose up around me. They formed a street I recognised with stalls all around – the Exotic Market was in town and passing through me like ghosts were people bustling through the streets. But of course, I was the real ghost that no one could see, not even you brother as you too pass straight through me without even looking back or batting an eye lid. Biting my lip, I became confused as to what was going on. Why was I here? Had I been concentrating so hard on my memories that I was still in them, and if so, what memory was this? I may remember the streets but they have aged since I was here last and the town seemed lost like a child who has lost its parent in the crowd. The panic kicks in as they shout relentlessly for their parent to return. But in this case, it didn't look like the parent could hear, not that they cared. They weren't coming back so the child remains lost trying to pick up the pieces left of their life and move on without the parent, alone in a world that cares not for a scruffy looking child.

It is then that I realise where and when exactly I am. It had been common legend that there were two realms to the Land of the Faded. There was the realm I had not long left filled with dying trees, darkness and dense shadows. Then there was this other realm that lay over the surface world, this realm was known as the Land of the Greater Faded and it was filled with flecks of colour and life. But I think it is more painful than the realm I have just left because it is filled with people I love, people who I can see but cannot see me.

I watch you brother as you pass through the gates of the city and up towards the old church on the hill. In my time, it and been a Hammerite parish but now it seemed the Hammers had left the city. The red banners that draped either side of the huge oak doors had been replaced by a white washed wall and the chanting mumbles of the priests was now replaced by the high-pitched hymns of child choirs. I see you enter the church, almost reluctantly, as though you feel you must. I choose to wait outside – the church was not a place for Keepers; we weren't a very religious fold and preferred to stay out of the mechanisms of the city life and only intervene when necessary. You looked so different now brother, that carefree spring in your step was gone and replaced by a timid march. The spark in your eyes that had wrinkled when you were happy was forever gone, but I hoped that was not the case.

The time passed slowly in this world and I began to marvel at the sun, its brilliance shielded by the shadow of this world but amazing all the same. It was certainly a feature I had missed in my time away. It is then that I begin to wonder why exactly you had come here. You had never cared much for religion or worship. You said like the Keepers, your religion was simple – there was no need for temples or churches, no need for complicated philosophy. Your own brain, your own heart was your temple and your philosophy was the good will of good men. I tried to think about what today might have been, but all capacity of time had escaped me and I didn't even know how long I had been gone, let alone the day I had returned on.

After a while you emerge from the huge oak doors and I follow you down the hill towards a gravestone on the edge of the yard by a large overhanging tree. The tree strikes me as odd, not just because of the life that seeped through it but because of its sudden relevance to the location. I remember stories told to us about how our father had strung up a swing to this tree when they first moved here to begin their new life. Back then, there was no church, no headstones, just the tree in the middle of a field and our parents laughing and smiling around a swing strung onto it. Today was the day she had died all those years ago and it all seemed so distant to me now, like the world I had returned from had made me numb to any emotion I should feel. As I look away from where you are kneeling, I notice someone standing by the tree leaning on it slightly. I take a few steps closer and realise it is a woman. She is watching you intently, her eyes focused solely on you. I take a few more steps towards where she is standing, thinking that she must be like me - Greater Faded. I wonder if she can see me like I can see her but she appears not to notice me as I come to stand next to her. I look her up, taking in the creamy tinges to her dress, the red flush in her cheeks, the brown locks of her hair and the greenness of her eyes. As I take in the features of her face, I begin to recognise them but I cannot seem to place a name to the face. I stare deeper into her eyes, searching for an answer and then it hits me. How could I have been so blind? Why did I not see it as soon as I saw her? It was her; my brother's beautiful sweet smile, your rosy cheeked maiden that made you strong and ignited a fire deep within your being. She was yours and you were hers as the saying goes; the one you would gladly lay down your life for. But then there was no need for you to do that because she had done that for you. So why was she here?

My eyes wonder back up to her own and I notice a single tear creeping down her cheek. Wondering if it is something you had seen, I follow her gaze back to where you are kneeling to see a young girl standing with you. I look at the way she stares at the child, so caring and devoted and then I look at the way you look at her with quiet concern blind as to who she is. Unheard to me you say something to the child and she looks back as though someone has called her name. As she looks back to you, it is like someone has yelled her name in my mind and I notice her green eyes and the resemblance they share with your beloved. It is her, the light of your life, the apple of your eye. I can see it! How can you be so blind dear brother, she is your daughter – how could you not see it? I look back to your beloved as another tear slips from her eyes as she longs for her child, to be able to shout out and tell you who she was.

As I look back over at you, I notice someone else now who has come down from the hill with a look of joy on his face at the sight of the girl. His face is yet another which I remember, one from our past with the Keepers. He seems to care for the child, there is no doubt about it and his eyes seem to show a certain sadness, one that is probably there because you do not remember him. He leaves with the child and after a while you turn to face us and a small smile lingers at the end of her lips as she hopes you might see her, the tears from her cheeks now gone. You stare a while as she steps out of the shadow of the tree and I watch as her smile widens, her legs springing into movement as she moves towards the corn rows behind us. You begin to follow her – how was it you could see her but not me? Slowly at first but quickening in pace as she slips out of sight and passing straight through me once again.

I begin to follow you both, you and her only just within my sight is you weave in and out of the corn. When I finally catch up to you, you are lying side by side on the floor in a heap of trampled corn, staring into the eyes of one another. Your closeness now is like you were separated only yesterday and now reunited forevermore. As you stare into her eyes with nothing but undying love and her heart begins to sing with unheard joy. You stretch out your hand to try and touch her face and I realise all her tears are gone, even as your hand passes straight through her face and she remains safe on the other side with no more tears left to cry. So instead, you just stare, your eyes finally open to see her and everything she was. I hope in time I will find the strength to show myself to you dear brother, show you everything that we were and are, to embrace you once again. So as I watch you and her now, I make this promise to you. No matter what, I will not relent from finding a way for you to see me as you see her. I will escape this world whether it be through my own brute force or you remembering me once and for all. Until then, I will remain by your side, watching over you every step you take, to protect you from danger just as brother should do, just as I would do had I been beside you in a physical form. But until then dear brother, be strong and do not falter for I am sure the five of us brothers will be reunited once more sooner or later.

# CHAPTER 12 - THE GIRL IN THE FIELD

Dante paced the deck to the inn once more, looking up at the fading sunlight as day turned into night. He scratched the back of his head – where was that boy? Tristan was meant to meet him outside the Green Clover Inn at least an hour ago when he finished work but he was nowhere to be seen. Despite the regularity of that boy being unpredictable lately, Dante couldn't shake the feeling that something was wrong. He leaned against the wall, staring up once again at the waning sunlight – if Tristan wasn't going to come to him, he was going to have to find him. Stepping down from the decking, he took a brisk walk towards the guard-post by the main gate where he hoped he would find Balderick. As he neared the post, he caught sight of a vibrant purple cloak and a shiny bald head – at least one person was where they were supposed to be. Quickening his pace, he reached Balderick and the other guards in no time as the trio broke into a hefty raucous of laughter.

"What's so funny?" Dante asked as soon as he was in earshot, making Balderick jump as he turned to face his brother. The other guards just stopped laughing immediately, almost as if the joke was a secret never to be told.

"Dante?" he stammered as his face immediately turned serious. "You shouldn't sneak up on people like that, especially at this late hour."

"Sorry, I didn't mean to startle you."

"That's alright!" Dante saw the other guards look at each other as much to say 'I didn't know Balderick had a brother'. They'd probably clicked on it being so when they heard both had the same accents. "What did you want anyway?"

"You haven't seen Tristan, have you?" asked Dante once he had ushered the Captain of the Guard away from his men and out of earshot.

"Not since this morning no! Why do you ask?"

"He was supposed to meet me about an hour ago outside the inn but he hasn't shown up."

"Maybe he's been held up somewhere."

"Well that's what I thought, but I can't shake the feeling something is wrong."

Balderick was silent for a moment. He crossed an arm over his chest and stroked his stubbled chin. He was obviously thinking about where Tristan had got to and a few moments later his facial expression dropped and his eyes widened.

"What is it?" Dante asked, the expression worrying him.

"I've just realised the significance of today," he answered rather ominously as he turned back to his comrades. "Richie, you've been here since sunrise haven't you?"

"Of course I have boss, just like I promised!" piped up the guard, standing to attention. Despite the smart attire of his armour, he was rather gormless sounding; as though he wasn't the brightest bolt in the box.

"Don't worry, this isn't an attendance check."

"Oh well in that case I've been mostly here since sun up cap'an."

"Good! Have you seen Tristan pass through the gate this morning at all?"

"Oh, uh, I don't know. What time roughly?"

"This morning you idiot, like I just said."

"Uh…"

"He left through the front gate this morning after the Exotic Market opened up ser." The other guard answered, this one sounding a lot less common, and sighing at the incompetence of his comrade.

"Thank you, Wallace, at least I can count on one of you!" exclaimed Balderick, shaking his head in Richie's direction. "Has he returned since?"

"Not through this gate boss."

"Answer me this…theoretically Wallace, if you were coming back from the cemetery, which gate would you come through."

"That's obviously the East you'd have to cross the bridge and at the moment that's out of bounds for repairs, and the South would be completely out of the way unless you planned on paying a visit to the herb garret in which case…"

"I don't need a detailed agenda of your life Wallace; I asked a simple question and I expect a simple answer which I guess, in *short,* you've given me." Wallace shrugged, mumbling something under his breath but Balderick ignored the comment giving Dante the impression that he didn't care much for the sly remarks of his men. "I think I know where he might have been last so are you coming?" Dante nodded and Balderick turned to lead them out of the main gates. "Make sure this gate isn't shut until I'm back. Wallace, you're in charge until then, make sure the other gates are closed before night fall." Wallace nodded, a sneaky smile appearing on his face as he silently goading Richie.

Ignoring the silliness of his men once more, he led Dante in the direction of the old Hammerite church on the hill where the Puritans now resided. Dante was curious as to why they were heading this way, but knowing Balderick like he did – all would become clear in the long run. He followed him up and over the hill, past the church and down to a cluster of headstones just at the edge of the forest and cornfields. He came to stand by a grave just underneath a huge oak tree, observing the white rose placed in memorial. As Balderick looked all around, Dante took the opportunity to read the ephigy on the headstone, indicating the grave belonged to Tristan's mother.

"Let's split up, we'll cover more ground that way." suggested Balderick, however Dante got the impression it was more of an order. "I mean he can't have gone far!" He nodded to Dante and then began weaving in and out of the gravestones back up to the church.

"Oh it's okay Balderick, I'll be fine on my own." Dante placed his hands on his hips and shook his head. "It's not like this place ain't somewhere I'm familiar with but no, it's fine you just saunter off on your high horse…" he trailed off in an undertone, sighing heavily.

He didn't even know where to begin with searching for Tristan – it's not as if he was familiar with Az Lagní, let alone the territories surrounding him. As he thought about where to start, a soft breeze took hold of his long hair, making him look in the direction of its origin towards the corn rows. He turned, seeing a figure pass between them which looked to be a man, the dusty trousers signifying this. Curiosity getting the better of him as it always did, he strode along in the same direction through the rows of corn. Weaving in and out, he followed the movement of the figure having lost sight of his form; watching for the shaking of each wreath as it was pushed out of the way of an unseen searcher. After a while the movement stopped and as Dante waded his way through to catch a glimpse, he found himself in a clearing with trampled corn strewn all over the ground. In the centre of the clearing was Tristan and the fading shadow of a woman sitting with his head in her lap. She looked up at Dante moments before she disappeared, green eyes standing out as the only bit of colour on her. Her mouth moved as though she was saying something, but before Dante could catch what she was saying she disappeared, Tristan's head flopping onto the floor.

"Balderick I've got him!" yelled Dante, letting what he had just seen sink in a moment before rushing to his side.

As he waited for Balderick to catch up; that's if he even heard Dante, he knelt by the side of Tristan's motionless body. Placing his hand above his mouth, he breathed a sigh of relief as his warm heavy breath tickled the hairs on the back of the ancient's hand. He moved his hand up to Tristan's cheek to feel it was ice cold and his hair was damp to the touch. Dante couldn't help but wonder how though – they were in the middle of summer and it hadn't rained all day. He also wondered about the shadow of the woman he had seen and those green eyes – somewhere, some when he had seen those eyes before. Being alone for over a thousand years meant he never forgot a face; *when you're alone all you see in your head are the faces of people you know*. His thoughts disappeared as he heard the corn rows being thrown aside as someone stomped to a halt behind Dante.

"Is he okay?" Balderick asked, trying to catch his breath.

"Yes, he's just cold," explained Dante, still trying to figure it all out.

"Did you find him like this?"

"No Balderick, I threw him in a lake and then bought him here, of course this is how I found him."

"Alright don't get angsty with me!" Balderick shrugged his shoulders and glanced up at the darkening skies. "Come on, let's get him back to mine before it gets dark." Balderick walked off up ahead at a slow pace, weaving in and out of the corn rows.

"Well I suppose I'll be the one to carry 'im then!" he exclaimed, hoisting Tristan over his shoulder carefully and rose slowly to his feet. "Gods Tristan you're heavier than I thought." He quickened his pace in order to not lose sight of Balderick for fear of getting lost without a guide, onward through the main gates and through the streets to Balderick's abode.

# CHAPTER 13 - DANTE ASHDOWN

Back at the house, Dante placed Tristan on the couch whilst Balderick fetched some blankets from upstairs. A fire was lit and Dante was left to watch over the young Keeper alone whilst the captain of the guard returned to his watch. Eventually, boredom drove him in search of a bottle among the cupboards, something to take the edge off the day's events. A sudden knock at the door made him stop, his heart beginning to race as though he expected to be set upon. Proceeding to the door, he opened it slowly, only to gaze upon a man whose eyes he appeared to recognise. The man's hair was greying and well-trimmed around his head, the top coming to a short length. His eyes were grey too – ancient and wise like the lines on his forehead. He was dressed in a blue long-sleeved shirt which was tucked neatly into brown cotton trousers and leather gauntlets that stopped just before his elbows. The trousers too were tucked in to smartly shined boots with a cloak swung around his back to complete the look. Dante had seen him in the inn often enough telling stories by the fire to the young children, but he felt as though he was much more than that; a face from his distant past.

"...you're not Balderick!" he said bemused, doing a double take as he looked on.

"Well what makes you say that?" asked Dante in his usual joking tone, almost mocking the old man who shook his head from the confusion.

"Tell me my good fellow, where is Balderick?" The man's voice was well-pronounced, oozing a wise and caring nature.

"He's..." he never got chance to finish, instead he was pushed aside by the man showing unexpected strength as he spied Tristan lying motionless on the couch.

"Tristan?"

"Oh, that's alright, you come straight in...don't mind me."

"You don't exactly own this place, do you?" the old man snapped sarcastically, feeling for a pulse on Tristan's cold-as-ice neck.

"Okay, who are you?" Dante asked, taken aback by the man's all too familiar nature – it was all too similar to his own and that caught him off guard.

"My name is Merlin, I'm the town storyteller. And you are?" Dante didn't answer straight away; his answer would need to be considered as he knew not whether this was a man he could trust. "You know what; never mind! What happened to Tristan?" Dante shrugged his shoulders and huffed as he slumped onto one of the chairs at the dining table.

"We found him like this."

"We?"

"Me and Balderick! He was supposed to meet me this evening and he never showed up so I sought out Balderick and we found him in the corn fields exactly as he is right now."

"And what are you to Tristan...or to Balderick for that matter."

"...a friend..."

"Are you now...Mr Ashdown?" The man rose to his feet and Dante froze, his eyes darting up to look at Merlin; wondering how he knew who he was. It was at that minute that he noticed the blue flame flicker within his eyes. The flame made his heart stop, his head racing to the last time he saw it – staring death in the face. He dared to look to the tops of Merlin's hands, seeing the scared markings of a Keeper Prodical. He gulped heavily, rising from his chair and backing up against the kitchen sides. The Keeper Prodicals were the highest of all the ranks and above all were law bringers. They were the only Keepers with the power to banish a traitor to the faded worlds and not only that, they were a master of the runes and glyphs meaning they could tell a traitor from a mile off.

"I do not mean you any harm!" said Merlin calmly, offering his hands up to show he was unarmed.

"Who are you?" Dante asked, his voice cracking with fear – he had only just escaped the Land of the Faded there he was determined not to go back to...not now, not ever.

"My name is Merlin," he answered, slowly coming to sit at the chair opposite where Dante had been. Dante remained where he stood, managing another gulp and not breaking eye contact with him. "Are you not Dante Ashdown?"

Dante didn't answer, instead he just stared at the man; trying to trace his name, his face, his eyes. Somewhere in his past, Merlin's origins to him lurked but oh how they had crept up on him from a shadow deep and dark.

"I knew your brother...I was...am a good friend of his." Merlin continued.

"You know my brother?"

"Yes, your brother by blood."

"Nielson?"

"Aye!"

"You mean...he's alive!" Dante stepped forward, returning the chair he had been sat on to its upright position and sitting himself down. The fact that he knew his brother had to be a good thing – surely it meant the two were once friends.

"He is very much alive my dear boy," he smiled slightly as he noticed Dante sigh with relief as his eyes welled up with tears. "I haven't heard from him since the fall but I know he is alive."

"The fall?" Dante's fear was now replaced by curiosity and speaking with the old man became easy; as though he were catching up with an old friend.

"I assume you know what happened to Tristan?"

"I know that he lost all memory of his life about three years ago but that's it."

"Then let me elaborate. Three years ago, he was betrayed and someone set the Faders upon him. He forgot everything and everyone from his life as a Keeper. I believe he lost a total of three years and everyone who meant something to him and his journey. Not long after he left there was a prophecy reading that foresaw the coming of the Third Dawn. At the end of the reading the Faders descended upon the room and all the Keepers faded...Scribes and Prodicals alike...even the Interpreter disappeared. I returned to Hasaghar shortly after to find Nielson in the ruins where I tended to his wounds and got him to Keeper allies in Venshá. I left him there on his orders, I know that he is alive...but I do not know where."

"At least I know *he's* alive."

"You say that like you left others behind?" Merlin crossed his fingers, leaning his elbows on the arms of the chair and linking them together.

"You wouldn't know them!" explained Dante, crossing his arms across his chest and breaking his eye contact to look over at Tristan on the couch.

"I'm not sure you've quite remembered who I am."

Dante looked up at Merlin and thought for a minute. It's true – he didn't. He still hadn't placed the eyes, let alone the name. But it did ring a bell that was for sure, he just wasn't sure where in his past it belonged. Even before he Faded, he had lived thirty years at least – he didn't remember how many exactly; thirty something – and achieved many a great deed before his ultimate betrayal.

"I have been gone over a thousand years," he recalled. "Why don't you jog my memory?"

"You've not changed one bit you know that? I on the other hand…well you'd be surprised." Dante cocked his head to the side as though he didn't believe the old man. "I was a doe eyed, sorry faced kiss up of a kid who sucked up to every one of those teachers." Merlin smiled, shaking his head as he realised how embarrassing he was. "I followed Nielson around like a lost puppy, he was more than just my friend; he was my mentor…as good as any older brother…"

"Hold on, I think I remember you now!" pursued Dante, leaning forward on the table and wagging a finger at Merlin. "You were that pale faced, scrawny little weed who followed my brother around like a shadow."

"That's the one!"

"Now I remember you." Dante sat back in his seat and smiled, resting one leg on top the other and fiddling with a lose piece of thread on his boot. An unsettling silence seeped into the already awkward air as Dante tried to pull the thread free.

"So who else did you leave behind?"

Dante didn't say anything at first, his forehead and nose wrinkling as he tugged at the thread. Merlin watched him intently, his eyes darting sideways for a moment as Tristan turned over on the couch. He considered how alike Dante was to the Tristan that had been and gone. He tilted his head to the side slightly, watching the smile smooth out the wrinkles as he finally pulled the thread away from his boot and dropped it to the floor. Then he looked over at Merlin and acted as though he had never heard the question and pursing his lips.

"So…what's your interest in Tristan then?" Merlin asked patiently, his eyes locked on Dante to watch for a response behind the eyes.

"Destiny!" Dante said after a while, looking down once more and spying yet another thread on his boots. "When I came back from the Land of the Faded, I was in this dingy dark room with this man staring right at me. He said his name was Cedar or something like that. Claimed he knew why I was back, why I'd been able to escape."

"Escape?"

"One day I woke up and darkness wasn't the only thing I saw. I saw this light on the hillside and I decided even if it meant my death, I was tired of the darkness…tired of the screams, tired of it all. So, I left my brethren betrayers and found solace in the light and it placed me in a dark room. At first I thought it did nothing until I saw the man."

"What did he say to you?"

"He asked me who I was, so I told him honestly...didn't really consider at that point that people still might want me gone. He told me about this prophecy that had been read foretelling the coming a Bleak Unwritten I think he said. Said that meant someone that had forgotten everything...become unwritten if you like. According to the prophecy, the Wretched One would bring him forth and everyone knows that means my family. It's our curse, for being the first of Union to betray. He told me about Tristan and how three years ago someone very close to him betrayed him and he became Unwritten. According to Cedar, this Tristan needed to be written once again...it was my destiny to help him remember."

"According to this prophecy you say?"

"Not just the prophecy. You see even before he mentioned it, I knew that he was right. Some people say that when perspective Keepers who have a certain *potential* come in, they have special training that tests their current abilities. Such tests were bestowed upon me and my brothers and we faced three tests. In the first; we had to name all the betrayers based on the glyph on their hands...simple case of trial and error I guess except we got it in one. Second test required us to make an object which could hold dark magic, trap it so that it couldn't be accessed by anyone who did not possess the key. In the third and final room...Nielson forgot who he was. All these shadows appeared around us, shadows with cloaks and red lights for eyes. With every passing moment they got closer to us and we tried desperately to get him to remember. Balderick used his mind to project images of our childhood in front of him and we all followed suit. Then the creatures reached out to us and I remember closing my eyes thinking it was all so real. When I opened my eyes, the shadows were gone and Nielson was on the floor. I thought he was dead...so I reached out and touched his shoulder. He got up instantly, he said he had a crazy dream that he didn't remember anything. Said it would be his worst nightmare if it were to come true.

"They say these trials imitate the Keeper's Destiny. And I know it's just a saying...there's no physical proof to it...but surely, I am the proof. We all are! Me and my brothers; we wrote in the Book of Names the final names of Dharsi, we created the hourglass for the Heroic Three to contain Gallow for life...we just never got the chance to do the third bit. And that's why I'm back...to finish my destiny...just like the voice said..."

"Voice?" Dante looked over at Merlin's interruption; his expression had changed now, like he had just had a moment's realisation. Dante wondered if there was more to it but he continued anyway.

"As I got closer to the light...back in the Land of the Faded; this voice spoke to me. It said 'You who have not completed your destiny have been awarded a second chance to do so. Complete it and you will be free...part of the Brotherhood once more. Find the Bleak Unwritten and make it Written.'"

"You remember every word?"

"It's hard to forget your second chance, especially when it's handed to you on a plate."

"Did you ever think about looking for those you left behind?" he asked, changing the subject all too quickly for Dante's liking; but he went along with it anyway.

"I did for a moment," he said after a while, his voice containing a longing. "But then I saw a glyph on the Cedar's palm...Ally! I knew he was Union the moment I saw it so one of the first questions I asked him was what generation he was from. He answered me saying that he was from the fiftieth generation and that his were the last to ever be chosen. Too much time had passed, I very much doubt any of those I left behind are still alive."

"Nielson's still alive."

"That's different! Even though he was only an ally he was still part of the Brotherhood that betrayed and therefore cursed to live forever while those around him died."

"But you left others behind too."

"What's that supposed to mean?"

"You had a wife before you were banished, didn't you?"

"Yes! Ana-Maria...was married to her for five years. But we never had any children so therefore there's no family to curse and seeing as she wasn't blood..."

"That's where you're wrong..."

"The only sibling I ever had was Nielson, I think I'd know if we had a sister..."

"That's not what I meant," Dante looked at Merlin with bleeding eyes, almost as if they were hopeful that somewhere out there was someone waiting for him.

"We were married for five years...and you're telling me that after my betrayal she..."

"Fell pregnant!" he paused, letting the truth sink in for a moment. "She told Nielson the day after you were banished...said she found out the day of your trial but no one would let her see you before your sentence." Dante gasped, tears beginning to fall from his eyes. "He told her to go somewhere she'd be safe, said that his link to his brothers was too dangerous...too close to protect her. So she went to her brother Aled; you remember him? He was a Hammerite Priest and he took her to the Cathedral at Anderon. That's the last I heard of her but when I was reunited with Nielson about eight years ago he told me what happened to her."

"...and..."

"She had a boy, named him Jacob. But there were...complications...unfortunately she didn't make it." Dante let the tears run freely now, unable to stop himself as he stared up at the ceiling. "So Aled raised the boy as his own into the Hammerite faction. He told him all about his parents and the legacy you; his father lead...even the bit about the betrayal. Made sure he understood that it wasn't your fault. Jacob lived a great many years, surviving two wars with the Pagans and outliving nearly all of the Cathedral soldiers. Hundreds of years passed until the Cathedral was attacked by the Mechanists who had grown tired of their placid leader – now was the true Age of Metal and all wood had to be vanquished. Jacob was taken as a prisoner when he refused to join them and they were unable to kill him because of his curse. For years, he was dragged around all of Aberson by them. When they eventually grew tired of torturing him, they left him in a Prisoner of War Camp in the capital. Among the other prisoners there was a woman by the name of Neym who gave him peace when he looked at her...something he considered a gift. She found it odd that he could live forever, helped him heal the wounds the Mechanists had dealt him. And in the time after the war when the Mechanists were finally supressed, he came to forget his vows of celibacy and let himself fall in love with her. He married her and on their wedding night made a killer confession – something he maybe should've told her from the start. He told her that their life together would not be able to include children and when she asked why he told her about the curse, said that he wouldn't want his child to have to live forever and watch all those he loves die like he had to.

"Neym replied by asking him if he knew what a Nym was. As I'm sure you know, marriage and then consummation of the marriage to a Nym breaks any curse on that person. It can't just be a marriage to break the curse...it has to be true. The reason she was telling him this was because she herself was a Nym and therefore capable of breaking any curse placed on his family and those to come. All he had to do was consummate the marriage with her upon the promise that he loved her more than anything in the world. And so, he did; about a year later came a son...three years later came a daughter. Jacob died in the next war to be had when a band of rogue Keepers erupted thought to be followers of Dharsi. Neym moved the children to Anar, a secluded little village she thought would be safe for them. And who should she bump into in the market, none other than Nielson himself who just so happened to recognise the medallion of which the son wore. Jacob had left it to him...it belonged to you. And when the woman confessed that she was Jacob's wife he took them to where he was staying in Anar and they lived with him for about three years. When the girl was eight and the boy eleven, Neym died. She contracted a disease somehow and never really recovered. Once Nielson was sure the children had no symptoms, he moved them to Ashdowns coincidently enough. The children showed great promise having been born with Keeper abilities so he trained them to control their magic.

"When the boy turned twenty-one, he was offered the role of First Keeper…I guess he was as gifted as his grandfather. He accepted the role and the three of them moved to Dilu where they lived out their lives."

"Are they still alive?"

"I'm afraid not! The son was murdered by Dharsi who had enough of living in the dark and the daughter fell in love with a young Keeper who was full of promise. He too had a great Destiny before him and after his Scribe training finished, he took her back to his hometown. After a couple of weeks, she returned to Dilu so that he could put his affairs in order. A year later he travelled to Hasaghar where he was reunited with her upon the start of his training as an Acolyte. They were married by the end of the year, but unfortunately, she did not survive a year of married life. She died protecting him after Dharsi tried to kill him…"

"He was Union!"

"How did you guess?" Dante shrugged; his tear-stained face still full of hope. "But don't worry, all is not lost for he is still alive."

"I don't understand."

"About three months before her death, the daughter had given birth to your great granddaughter who's somewhere out there."

"Really?" he wiped away the tears, managing a smile. Merlin nodded slowly in receipt; his expression still unreadable. "What's her name?"

"I'm not going to tell you that."

"Why not?"

"Because of the man who married your granddaughter…who bore your heir…"

"Why does he matter?"

"Your grandson they named Xavier…and your granddaughter…they named Dagnen after your mother. Dagnen married Tristan and together they had a daughter…and that…that is your legacy…"

# CHAPTER 14 - DUTY AND DESTINY

The words hit Dante like a ton of bricks; somewhere out there his legacy lay in the hands of a tiny young girl who was Tristan's own blood and making the men family. He stared over at him as he lay on the couch, seemingly sleeping peacefully. Gasping, he let a single tear escape his eye – *how could it be so?* In his wildest dreams of being reunited with his family, he had never imagined it would come this close to home. He looked up at Merlin, a sort of pleading in his eyes that almost begged him to turn around and say he was only joking.

"I am sorry Dante...but it is true," Merlin said quietly. "So you see not only is it your destiny to help Tristan...it is your duty."

"And Dagnen...my granddaughter...she is dead?"

"I'm afraid so! She died three years ago when she sacrificed herself to save Tristan. God knows what she was doing there but what is done is done. Your great granddaughter is alive out there somewhere at least."

"You don't know where she is?"

"Unfortunately not. Until rather recently I believed she too was dead. But if he is alive then she must be too."

"Who's he?"

"Cedric." Merlin rose from his chair and headed over to the oak wood dresser next to the couch. He lifted a box from off of it and bought it back over to the table. "He was Tristan's best friend when he was a Keeper – he trusted that man more than his own brother."

Flipping open the lid of the box, Merlin lifted a small pile of photographs and began flicking through them. Oddly enough, the box seemed to be a lot smaller than it looked from the outside but there was something about it that seemed familiar to him. The box itself was made from rosewood, the ripples of the wood giving off a shiny effect. Sculpted feet gave the box some height at the corners and upon the lid was an ornate engraving of a white dove holding a golden key. Along the border was a pattern in two tones that made the dove and the key stand out that little bit more. Something about the dove though made his heart flutter, striking him with fear; but he couldn't be sure why.

As he came back from his thoughts, Merlin slid a photo under his gaze, hovering his finger over a man. Dante followed the notion, noticing a slightly younger Tristan standing amongst five men whom he assumed were his fellow brothers of Union. The man Merlin was indicating wasn't as tall as the others and he seemed younger too. He had long locks that trimmed off at his chin leaving a cleanly shaven face. His eyes gleamed an electric blue that oozed a sort of greatness – like his regal attire told him something of the title of the man in question.

"I know that man!" Dante gasped before Merlin even had chance to say who he was.

"That's Cedric...how do you know him?" asked Merlin, tying his best to be patient.

"That's the same man who I came back to...that is Cedar...I must've misheard his name."

"So you mean to say Cedric was the man who was in the room when you came back from the Faded worlds?"

"Yep, that's him alright. Do you reckon she was there with him...he had to have known my relation to her surely..." he trailed off and began pacing in frustration.

"Well we can add that to the list of questions we have to ask him when we finally catch up to him."

"Well if it helps, he was in Az Landen forest when I appeared to him."

"It would make sense for him to be there, Tristan has family there. But something tells me his family do not know Cedric is there. It gives us a lead all the same."

Merlin pursed his lips as he leant back in his chair, stroking his bearded chin as though he were deep in thought. Dante's eyes trailed back towards the dove on the box lid as he came to a stop by the table once more, his brain racing trying to figure out why the mere image of it made him feel the way it did. Merlin eventually noticed the way he was staring and leant forward, closing the lid and looking at the box in a funny angle. He turned it upside down and saw a metal key in the base and began turning it as though he were winding up a music box of some sort. Once he finished turning the key, Dante watched as the pattern on the lid of the box changed to resemble a glyph he recognised as the glyph of Union. He was marvelled by the change, his eyes widening as Merlin turned the box to face him.

"Only a member of Union can open the secret compartment." he said, a glint sparkling in the old man's eyes.

"How?" The memory of the box seemed to strike a chord somewhere in the back of Dante's mind but he couldn't tie it to an origin.

"Just touch it!"

Looking up at Merlin, Dante outstretched his right hand placing it firmly on the Union glyph. As he did so, a satisfying click broke the silence of the room – a small drawer popping out of the bottom of the box making Dante jump slightly. Merlin nodded to him and he pulled the drawer open as far as it would go. On the inside was another small pile of photographs with a handkerchief next to it which seemed like it held something within it.

"This box belonged to Nielson; he gave it to Dagnen as a wedding present." Merlin explained. "I believe he crafted it himself, but I do not imagine Dags ever found the secret compartment if only a member of Union can open it."

Carefully, Dante lifted out the handkerchief of which he noticed had a sigil embroidered into the centre. He recognised the sigil to be his own family name; the mountain in the centre with the cloud of ash embracing the fire atop it. The material of it was silky smooth and he could feel the cool metal of something concealed within it. Carefully, he unwrapped the hidden object only to gasp when he saw the contents. It was the Onyxum Flambertus; a huge onyx stone encased by a golden wing effect with a chain for it to be worn. The necklace itself was crafted by the third generation of Union when the Faders first came into existence – they used as a way of sealing them in the Faded Lands. However, something in their manufacture went wrong and the pair became a way of summoning the Faders onto the surface world. When the necklaces were reclaimed, they were placed under the protection of the fifth generation. With only one here, Dante had no idea where the other might have been, only that its placement here in this box had to be kept a secret lest it fall into the wrong hands.

He placed the Onyxum back in the handkerchief and replaced it in its place in the drawer. Next he grabbed the small pile of photographs and handed them to Merlin as he took a seat at the table, already knowing that he himself would not know who was in each one. Taking the hint, Merlin turned over the first picture and showed it to Dante, a fond smile upon his face.

"I remember Nielson showing me these photos upon our reunion a few short years ago," he began, hovering the picture in front of Dante's eyes. "He was rather proud of the little family he managed to raise."

Dante stared at the picture before his eyes, recognising the woman instantly – his own Ana-Maria. She, like him, was a lady of high acclaim and in the eyes of class, their match would never have been approved simply because his standing had been lost and her father was a proud man. However, they had gone against everyone's wishes and married anyway, causing Ana-Maria's father to disown her. Her brother was a member of the Hammerite faction and not even he had approved of their relationship. Despite this, he seemed to have done his best to help raise the family Dante had missed out on out of respect for Ana-Maria. Aled was indeed a man with questionable loyalties.

In the picture, his bride was as beautiful as he remembered, her stunning green eyes still striking him with the same warmth and admiration as they had done all those years ago. He even recalled fondly how much he had loved the dress she wore; a green bodice that was cut at the waist by a yellow sash which draped past her knees. The skirt was an overskirt that seemed to cut it at the knees before the same green of the bodice concealed her feet from sight. Her shoulders were left bare, her arms cropped by a yellow shawl which reached the ground. Dark brown locks were covered over by an emerald headdress which was kept in place by a lily at the side of her ear leaving a couple of curls either side to frame her slender face.

Ana-Maria stood gracefully in the arms of her lover as the two cradled one another in the middle of a ballroom. Dante himself certainly looked the part of a courtier – a perhaps worthier match than his actual status – his hair was much shorter and held back into a ponytail. His eyes were brighter too, much happier days were his past but now his eyes were shadowed by the darkness he had lived in for so long. Even his clothes were more colourful, less dusty and certainly completing the look he was obviously aiming for at the time. A green tunic clung tightly to his torso, belted at the waist with beige trimmings that left his chest bare. His leggings matched the colour of the trimmings and knee high black boots which matched the belt. It certainly was an impressive attire and the two together looked the perfect couple.

He smiled fondly, recalling the moment the two of them had shared that night at the election of the new earldom. A ball had been thrown in celebration and of course, Dante's attire was the ultimate disguise and it had done the trick – that night he assumed the title of Lord Ash of Ashdowns. Balderick had called bullshit but that didn't mean that the stupid high-borns had distrusted his title. They believed every lie he spewed!

"I remember this night as though it were yesterday," Dante recalled. "God I miss her!"

"She truly was a beauty," Merlin agreed. "And I'll tell you now, Dagnen was the image of her…but you'll see that for yourself in a moment. Would you like to see your son?"

Dante looked up without hesitation, guilt tainting the happiness in his eyes. Even though his betrayal hadn't exactly been his fault, it didn't help how he felt about the whole ordeal. Silently, Merlin handed him the next picture of a rather exhausted Ana-Maria hunched over with a baby in her arms. The picture only just showed his face and sparkling blue eyes which matched Dante's own. He smiled at the familiarity of him, flinching slightly as Merlin slipped another picture into his hands.

"Ana-Maria passed not long after that picture was taken," Merlin explained. "She went into early labour whilst Aled was escorting them across the border of Aberson. They believe that she must have caught some form of infection somewhere along the line. She died just after they arrived so Aled took it upon himself to raise your son."

Dante took note of the boy stood beside the man he recognised to be Aled clad in the red robes of a Hammerite Priest with a ruby topped staff at his side. His head was covered by a blonde bowl haircut with a cleanly shaved jawline. The boy stood beside him must've been no older than nine or ten. It was a big change from the new-born baby but Dante was glad to see his own eyes looking right back at him. Young Jacob even looked like he did at that age; pale skin that was whiter still against his dark hair which was a messy mop on the top of his head. Another picture was slipped in front of him and Dante watched the boy grow older still, this time to about sixteen. It looked as though he had just been named a novice of the Hammerite faction as he stood there shaking Aled's hand with an excited look on his ambitious face. Again, it was a look Dante recognised as his own, the boy or man as he was now in a new picture, truly was his father's son as he stood about twenty-one fully clad in the armour of a Hammerite soldier.

"That's the most recent picture this collection has of him," Merlin said with reluctance, wishing he could show Dante more. "However, Nielson may have a few in a private collection. I do have a last couple of pictures to show you though, this one of your grandchildren."

A short smile appeared on Dante's face as he set eyes upon the picture of two young children with a woman and a man. The man he recognised as Nielson – he was older, much older but he still had the same dark eyes hidden by a heavy brow. The lines on his face tainted the young picture Dante recalled in his head as they wrinkled his forehead and lined his eyes. He seemed happy, a healthy greying beard clinging to his chin with hair of a matching colour that just scraped his shoulders. The woman in the picture was knelt down in-between the two children. She had a certain look about her, like she was more than the picture made her seem but he wasn't sure why.

"The woman is Neym," Merlin explained, noticing his forehead wrinkle in thought. This picture was done not long before she died I believe. Xavier is about thirteen making Dagnen about eight."

"He's short for a thirteen-year-old!" Dante sniggered.

"So were you."

Dante scowled, looking back down at the picture. It was clear to see that Xavier was every bit the image of his mother; blonde hair gracing his shoulders just as hers whipped freely around her petite jawline, her almost purple eyes again matching his. The girl, Dagnen, on the other hand had a look of otherness about her – like no matter where she went she would always be an outcast. She had dark little curls that drowned her little face with green eyes that were so bright against her pale cheeks that seemed too rosy as she smiled slightly at the touch of her mother.

He watched the children age as another picture was placed in his hands. It looked as though this must have been when Xavier was named first Keeper as he stood by a much older woman Dante guessed as the Interpreter. A man stood the other side of him, a man he recognised but couldn't pinpoint why.

"Xavier was the youngest ever First Keeper, wise beyond his years they said." Merlin recalled fondly. "He was only twenty-one when he was chosen, but I guess he had the advantage that by that time he was already a Rune Mage and taking on the challenges of an Elder and beyond. Dagnen didn't accelerate as quickly but then I think she was just happy following her brother around, I don't think she really cared much for her progression with the Keepers."

"Who is the man stood next to Xavier?" Dante asked, the face of the man eating away at his cool composure – *what was it about this man that made him feel as though he knew him?*

"That is Felix, Xavier named him his Second Keeper as a thank you to the guidance he had shown him along his journey with the Keepers." The name meant nothing to Dante so he chose to ignore it. Perhaps he had one of those faces which you think you know but they mean nothing important.

Xavier stood tall with sweeping green robes, his long blonde hair tied back in a ponytail leaving his blue eyes to outshine the picture. Dagnen seemed to do the opposite though and darken the picture with her 'otherness' and plain faced smile; like it was a shield for the emotions she felt inside – a fake smile if you will. Her hair seemed lighter now as it was held off her face slightly leaving her green eyes to be more obvious. At this age, all he saw in her was his own Ana-Maria. She resembled every aspect of her that he remembered – the flawless face, the calm composure, the hard exterior and those green eyes.

"That's all that is in that little drawer." Merlin said as Dante placed the pictures back in the drawer of the box, locking it shut so that it was no longer visible from the outside. "But I'm sure Tristan has a few more around. Are you going to tell him?"

"Tell him what?" Dante scowled, standing up and staring blankly out of the kitchen window.

"About who you are to him?"

"No! At least, not yet. I don't want him to feel like I have an ulterior motive in all this because that is how it will seem. I need him to think that I genuinely do want to help, because I really do...I'm just not quite ready for him to open my book before he's finished his own."

"That is fair enough, I can understand that."

"Anyway, I hope you don't mind but I really need some air. Would you mind keeping an eye on Tristan, just until Balderick gets back?"

"Of course not, you go ahead. It's a lot to take in everything I've just told you. I'm surprised you didn't walk out ages ago."

Dante sniggered, grabbing his cloak off the chair and swinging it over his shoulders. He smiled to Merlin, patting him on the shoulder as he passed and glancing back one final time to look at Tristan, a thousand thoughts rushing through his head. How did everything suddenly get this deep? Turning away, he made for the door when suddenly Merlin stopped him.

"Why don't you take this one with you?" he suggested, handing Dante a picture and smiling to him. It was the one of Ana-Maria holding their son just hours after being born. He smiled back, nodding in thanks as tears formed behind his eyes, and turning to leave the house.

# CHAPTER 15 - THE FINAL GLYPH

*Oglivy's Treatise on Sentients and Sacred Places*

*Introduction*

*Sentients: Otherwise known as Artefacts, Relics or Soul Stones are extremely powerful objects crafted by the many generations of the Brothers of Union; some for good such as the Horn of Quintus, others for evil such as the Ruby of Sorrow. The latter of these objects possessed a certain power which gave them a consciousness thus the ability to manipulate whomever's power lay on the inside. It is not known how they were created, nor why and efforts to secure them all for study have yet to be completed. The pages that follow list the current known Sentients and their suspected places of whereabouts. Theories say that certain groupings can be made by combining four good relics with one bad and uniting them with their corresponding landmarks. However further study is required before formulating this theory further.*

*1 - Contents of 'Known' Sentients*

i.   *Anvil of St James*
ii.  *Orion's Medallion*
iii. *The Chalice of the Builder*
iv.  *The Crown of the Trickster*

*iv.*    *The Glyph of Unbinding*

*IV.I The Final Glyph*

*The Final Glyph is a grouping of five different artefacts with five glyphs engrained within them to make one final glyph. This Final Glyph was put in place by the High Council of Elders to keep the Brothers of Dharsi from returning from the Faded Worlds. The Glyph is weak though and easily manipulated by those of Dharsi who still remain. If it is modified in any way, the only way to stop its destruction is to destroy the Glyph itself. This can be done by uniting five different Sentients; one of which must be an evil doer in need of containing. The Sentients required depend on the place of its unleashing but the Sentients must be united with their corresponding landmarks. Once the power of the Sentients is unleashed the Final Glyph will answer to its true master but the faction of the Keeperhood will be forever changed. The only ones capable of destroying The Final Glyph are the ones who put it there to begin with; The Brothers of Union – for only Union can destroy what Union created.*

"This is it," a voice said beside Tristan. "This is where it all ends!"

Tristan took a deep breath, checking his belt for the pouch and breathing a sigh of relief. If they somehow lost it after everything that had happened these past few days…well it would be unspeakable. Inside the pouch was a diamond the size of a man's fist known as the Eye of the Storm. It whispered slyly to him and prayed on his darkest thoughts of self-doubt. The Eye had been crafted by an ancient race of Keeper betrayers and over time they had fallen into the hands of Dharsi until Father Talus retrieved it and buried it deep within the doors of The Forgotten Cathedral.

"You know what you have to do right?" asked the voice of Romeo, as he looked back before joining their other brothers in distracting Trevor. Tristan nodded to him as he ran off leaving Tristan alone with The Eye.

"Returned have I in the hands of a different man who has seen time," The Eye spoke to him in a bellowing voice, deep and raspy. It had an eeriness about it that sent shivers down his spine. Try though he might, he could not block out its voice for it bought his own dead and haunting thoughts to life. "Only this man is a much worthier wielder. You don't really want to do this Tristan. You need me!"

*Tristan hid himself by the wall, closing his eyes to what was going on around him. He could hear his brothers shouting to him, alerting him that it was time but he could not move. He was rooted to the spot; but not out of fear or unwillingness but because he needed to block out the Eye. If one ounce of his mind was not focused on the task at hand, all would be lost.*

*"Tell me, did your brethren cry when I chose you? Did they warn you what I would do?"*

*He was talking about Jacques. A little over a year ago they had stolen The Eye from the Cathedral to save the rest of the Keepers. Back then, his brother was the only one who could hear it, the only one who could touch it. Or at least that's what they thought, only it spoke to Tristan too; prayed on his unspoken fears and tried to manipulate him against his brothers. Now, it only spoke to Tristan, and that made Jacques and the others nervous, like they thought he could be swayed, that Tristan could betray.*

*"I suppose they thought I would destroy you...and them. I suppose they were right though; I would destroy you all!"*

*Tristan could hear it laughing at him, mocking his resolve and pitiful attempts at blocking him out. Taking another set of deep breaths, he opened his eyes to the world around him once more, noticing one of his brothers lying on the floor in front of him. It was Cedric; his eyes wide open as though he were dead. Suddenly The Eye was silent again as he ran towards his fallen brother, immediately checking for a pulse. It was there, but it was fading fast. He had to act quickly.*

*"Cry Brethren Cry for the betrayer hath cometh!" The Eye chanted, its voice no more than a whisper in the back of his mind. "I will cripple your hands with my wretched and ancient hands." He rose, ignoring the voice that rang in his head and darting between the flying pieces of rubble that spun around where Trevor stood. "I will spawn a child of ignorance bred from you by fear and anger and with his birth will come the beginning of a Third Dawn and the coming of the Unwritten Times." Tristan recited along with The Eye now, as though he was possessed. But he knew what he was doing, he had to convince it that he would do its biding in order to manipulate it into doing his. "Here cometh the Bleak Unwritten. By my hands his reaping be done! The betrayer hath cometh, and with my words and his wrath the Glyphs will unwind and you will all perish as fools."*

*He had let himself get too carried away; now the Eye really was in control as the rocks rebounded off an invisible shield, crashing into walls. His eyes sparkled as Tristan strode forward in an unnatural way, arms reaching for The Eye as he bent at the foot of the City Square fountain. Where he knelt was a niche in a hexagonal shape where The Eye would fit perfectly; returned to its former place of glory. Placing The Eye into the slot he turned it left, right then left again, pushing it in deeper still. Light beamed from it and Tristan rose to his feet, unable to snap out of his trance. It was like his eyes were a glass and he was watching himself. Banging on the glass, screaming for him to stop, to do anything but listen to The Eye.*

*"Tristan!"*

*Somewhere out there a woman screamed his name. It was a voice is self-conscious recognised and cried out for him to notice. As she screamed again, it screeched of something different. Rather than fear, this time it was pain. This time he heard it...*

*"Tristan!"*

*Immediately, he turned in time to see Dagnen get struck by a bolt of red light. Holding out his arms he only just caught her as she collapsed in his arms. Cradling her head in his arms, Tristan looked up briefly in the direction of the bolt, seeing a flash of red in an alleyway just off from where his brothers fought against their foe. It can't have been Trevor. But who? Tearing himself back to his love, he stared down at her pale face with those striking green eyes the only ounce of life left within her. In that moment, life seemed to stop, slow down to an almost unnoticeable pace. He could feel hot tears bleeding from his eyes and staining her pale face as she tried to say something that seemed to fall upon deaf ears.*

*"What?" Tristan asked, willing her to stay with him as more tears spilt.*

*"I love you!" she croaked, her eyes wincing as the pain of the bolt sunk in. Tristan looked down to her midriff, seeing blood form on the ivory night gown. What the hell was she doing here? She should've been back at the inn with their daughter. "Take care of our..."*

*Those last words were such a struggle for her and she choked as she blurted them out, more blood escaping from the side of her mouth. He knew she was dying. But he didn't want to believe it. He couldn't lose her, not now, not ever.*

*"Dagnen...please...please. Stay with me!" He begged her, willing for her to take hold of what life she had left and prolong it somehow. But destiny had other ideas! And how he hated her for it. "Dags?" she managed a smile as he felt her body shiver in his arms, as though the last bits of her life were escaping through her breath, sending her body into uncontrollable spasms. The smile faded and her head lolled to the side; lifeless.*

*They say in the moments before your death everything is silent. But what they don't say is that it is also silent for those around the person that has died; those who are closest to them. Even their own voice they cannot hear. It's like they are so overcome with that one emotion that everything else just goes out of action. That's what shock feels like. Like even you have died alongside your loved one. It is only once you dare to look away from the face of your love, or go to close their eyes that life comes crashing back to you. The sounds deafen, leaving a ringing in your ears. As the tears fall heavier the vision blurs and* you cry so much that you can barely breathe, coughing and spluttering as the realisation kicks in. You look around and people seem not to notice, not to care; they just continue on with their own mundane lives like no one matters at all.

As the tears began to stop, his grief was replaced by anger; hot boiling anger for whoever it was that took his love away from him. He looked up, just in time to see another of his brothers fall to the floor, his eyes remaining open just as Cedric's had. And as all life came swimming back to him in full speed, he realised he had to do something.

"Cry Brethren Cry!" the voice of The Eye was back. "For your Betrayer hath cometh."

What happened next happened so fast he didn't even stop and think first. Tristan was just so full of rage and hatred that he could barely contain himself. A hammer lay beside him – it was all he could see through the sudden rain that beat down and all he could hear was the voice of The Eye. He let Dagnen slip gently from his arms, closing her eyes over and kissing his fingers before placing them upon her forehead. In a single swift movement, he picked up the hammer and swung it at the Eye, closing his eyes as it smashed into a thousand shards, all breaking further as they hit the cobblestoned floor.

With the voice of The Eye finally gone from his mind, Tristan's knees buckled and he crashed to the floor, falling beside Dagnen's lifeless body. The rebounds of the smash reverberated all around him. But he didn't see the effects that it had on the rest of his brothers, what it did to Trevor as he lost his

source of power. All he could focus on was Dagnen who lay beside him safe on the side of death and there he lay in life, no more tears left to cry.

# CHAPTER 16 – EVELYN

Tristan woke with a start. His breathing came in gasps as he struggled to balance himself on the couch and tumbled onto the floor in a spluttering mess. Merlin knelt suddenly by his side and helped him back up, leaving him to calm down as he went to fetch some water from the kitchen pump. Once Merlin had turned his back, Tristan felt a burning sensation on his left hand, staring in disbelief as another mark crawled beneath his skin. Feeling a knot build up in his throat, he threw himself out into the backyard and spurted the contents of his stomach onto the dry grass. Lowering himself onto a wooden bench Balderick had made for his children when they were young, he took some deep breaths trying desperately to calm himself. All that was going through his head were those last words Dagnen had said to him. The memory had been so clear except for that last word. Try though he might, he could not finish the sentence.

"Take care of our..." echoed over and over again, making his head seer with pangs of pain.

He could hear footsteps on the cobblestones behind him, but they weren't confident footsteps. They were heavy and clumsy as the feet scuffed along the floor.

"I really hope you intend on cleaning that up!" said the voice of Balderick. "Not to mention fixing the wooden coffee table you've now brought to the ground..."

"Coffee table?" Tristan questioned, looking up as the Knight Commander came to sit beside him.

"Wow, your memory is short."

At once, Tristan looked to his right hand which had reached out as he fell from the couch. On his palm were scratches, a couple with splinters sticking out of them and his tunic was torn up his arm. As he fell from the couch, he must have launched himself onto the coffee table without even realising in his state of shock.

"I wasn't even aware that I..." stammered to Tristan.

"It's okay, it was on its last legs anyway..." Balderick sniggered to himself. "Get it...last legs..."

"I get it Balderick it's just a bad joke!" Tristan managed a laugh.

"Well in that case, I'll go wake the children up." Balderick rose to his feet and made his way towards the door back into the house. "At least they appreciate my humour!"

Tristan buried his head in his hands as Balderick disappeared back into the house. The words of Dagnen still echoed in his mind – it was like there was a mental block over that last word...or maybe it was a name...

"Here, drink this."

He looked up again, only this time it was Merlin who was sat beside him, a concerned look upon his face. He handed the young Keeper a glass of water and he took it. Merlin took note of the strained look on his face – it was a look he had seen him pull often in the last three years in their sessions together as he struggled to remember his past.

"What is it you're struggling with my boy?" Merlin asked, leaning back slightly. "Perhaps if you go through it out loud it will come back to you."

"I remembered her death Merlin," he croaked.

"I can't imagine what it must have been like to see that all again."

"I remembered everything...that is to say everything except her last words to me. It's like I just can't remember the last bit."

"What does she say?"

"Take care of our..." he closed his eyes, trying to clear his mind a focus on the memory and only the memory, just as Merlin had taught him. "Take care of what..."

"Think about what she might be talking about. Of all the things she was leaving behind, what would she want you to take care of?"

"I guess..." as he thought about what to say a whisper replaced the words spiralling round in his mind. The whisper belonged to a woman and it motioned the same word over and over again. "Evelyn..." Merlin smiled at the sound of her name. "Evelyn...my daughter's name was Evelyn."

He smiled to himself, proud that he had finally remembered something of the daughter he didn't even know. But that smile was soon replaced by a look of anger. He wasn't sure who he should be directing that anger at but for now it was on Hugo, the man he had seen at his mother's graveside with the young girl he had been looking after for a friend. The girl had been called Evelyn.

"Tristan, what's wrong?" The look of concern appeared once again on his old face.

Tristan hastened to his feet and made his way back into the house, Merlin shouting after him. He rushed into the sitting room and reached for the box he had retrieved from his house. Slamming it onto the table, he opened the lid, rooting around the pile of pictures. Merlin appeared behind him, watching the chaos of his crazed memories open up as he sifted through picture after picture. Finally, he found the one he was looking for and stared at it, turning back to Merlin and thrusting it into his hands.

"Tell me who is in the picture!" he demanded, the look on his face unreadable.

"Why don't you tell me?" Merlin took a seat back at the table and placed the picture on the table, nodding for Tristan to take a seat. Tristan scrunched up his face, almost as if he was angry at Merlin for not making it easy for him. But then what did he expect from the old man. "Come on! Take a seat and tell me who is in the picture and then maybe we can find out who you are so angry at."

Tristan took a deep breath, his face relaxing as he decided it was probably best that he did as the storyteller said. He sighed heavily, slumping into one of the vacant chairs at the table and picking up the picture, staring blankly at it. The picture depicted a crowd of people, all stood in lines. They all beamed with smiles, with older people stood on either side. The younger faces belonged to the Scribes and the older the teachers. Immediately, he spotted his own face surrounded by his brothers both by blood and choice. As he stared for longer, his eyes lingered on a face in the bottom row, the eight brothers of which were seated on wooden chairs. His attention was drawn to the third from the left, a scrawny looking boy with freckles on either side of his abnormally large nose. The colour of them was a little lighter than his hair which sprawled in a mess on the top of his head. Put a few years on him he could easily be Hugo just without the freckles.

"This man here," Tristan pointed to the boy he believed to be Hugo. "Did I know him?"

Merlin sighed, staring at the picture and the man Tristan had pointed to. Merlin himself had initiated him all those years ago, he had initiated them all.

"You knew of him yes," Merlin explained. "He was in the room next to you and your brothers. He shared with the boys either side of him; Cedric and Percy. Also in the room was Trevor."

"What was his name?"

"I think you already know! What about him anyway?"

"Because he was here...and he had my daughter with him."

"Impossible!"

"I saw him just yesterday when I went to see my mother's grave. There was this little girl and this man calling the same name over and over again. I can't believe that I had my daughter right in front of me and I didn't even know."

"How can you be so sure?"

"Because, Hugo mentioned that Ced would kill him if he lost the child he called Evelyn."

"He wouldn't be stupid enough to bring her here though."

"Maybe I was never meant to see her...I'll kill him for this. Whatever his reasoning for keeping my daughter away from me it's not a good one."

"I'm telling you now, you're not the only one who wants some answers." A moment of silence passed between the pair. "What did she look like? Evelyn, I mean."

"She was so small, how old would she be now...three? She had these really messy locks of blonde hair and these striking green eyes...just like Dags. How could I not have known...what kind of father does that make me?"

"Tristan none of this is your fault, you weren't to know."

"I'm going to find them though...and Dante is going to help me."

"Dante?" Merlin's look was the one that was unreadable now, it was like he was confused as to how Dante was supposed to help him.

"It's a long story but basically he's here to help me remember. It's his destiny! He's going to take me to Dilu where I became a Keeper Scribe. He thinks that going to a place that was important to me once will help...in a physical way."

"It's a good theory, but why would he want to help you?"

"Like I said; it's his destiny...you should come Merlin..."

"What...no I'm far too old for another adventure."

"But there's no one here who knows more about my past than you do. At least if you're there, you can help me with anything I don't understand. Please Merlin, please come with us?" Merlin let out a big sigh.

"I suppose at least if I do come, I can keep an eye on Dante."

"You know him?"

"Like you said earlier; long story. Alright, I'll come on one condition...you make things right with your father." Tristan looked away. "I'm not saying forgive him, but hear him out at least. He is your father after all! Don't leave things like this though, you'll regret it forever if something happens."

"So if I at least hear him out, you'll come?"

"I will yes, but don't pretend because trust me I will know whether or not you have seen him."

"Alright I'll do it!"

"Good lad, now I best be off. Things to do, people to see and all that gubbins. When do we leave for Dilu?"

"Tomorrow morning."

"Well, you could've given me more warning lad."

He shook his head playfully, wondering out the front door and into the quiet morning streets of the village. Tristan could hear the children waking upstairs; Tessa's high-pitched voice echoing off the floor boards and making his ears ring once more. Deciding he wasn't quite in the right mind-set to deal with an eleven-year-old and an eight-year-old, he readied himself to leave, pausing for a moment as he rose to his feet and packed away the box once more. *Perhaps I should sort out that table first*, he thought to himself.

# CHAPTER 17 - SINS OF THE FATHER

A strange feeling of déjà vu crept over Tristan as he lingered by the open window to the cottage, he and his father called home. Theorryn was slumped in his chair, his head resting on his hand and a forlorn look on his face. Tristan had never seen him look like this – his face looked so old and wrinkled; stress and concern pouring from his tired eyes. He scanned the table and the floor for any signs of bottles, flagons...anything he could pinpoint to go in a have a judgement about his father already made. But there was nothing. The sitting room, if anything, actually looked tidy for a change. Peering round into the kitchen lead to exactly the same image – an ordered family home. Tristan stepped back in disbelief, half happy for the surprise and half disappointed if anything. However, the disappointed half was slowly fading to become a feeling of pity towards this flaccid old man that sat in the living room awaiting the homecoming of his son. Sighing heavily, Tristan braced himself before entering his once home.

"Tristan?" Theorryn jumped up from his chair at the sound of the front door shutting.

Turning on the spot, his eyes were welcomed by the sight of his son. Somehow, he seemed different; changed for the better. Perhaps him remembering everything he had done was good for him after all. He relaxed his stance slightly, waiting for Tristan to start; say something...say anything for that matter. When he didn't, Theorryn sighed, watching Tristan calmly take up a chair at the table in the kitchen, like he was waiting for his father to tell him his side of the story.

"I am glad at least that you look well," Theorryn began but Tristan said nothing in response. "What have you been up to then?" Still Tristan didn't answer, not that he was expecting him to. "I must say Tristan that I am so sorry for what has happened. I really should've told you everything right from the start." When Tristan still said nothing, he placed his hands impatiently on his hips. "I don't know what else I can say to you. Sorry just...doesn't seem enough." Nothing, not even a muttering of some form. He just stared back at his father saying nothing. "I mean if I could turn back..."

"Stop right there!" Tristan exclaimed, his eyes flashing with sudden anger that he tried desperately to quell. "That's enough of the excuses."

"Right...of course. Let me just say this. Um...how to put it. I really did want to tell you everything but things never seemed to let me tell you. Plus, she's dead you know...you lost a wife and a daughter and I lost a granddaughter...and there was no way I wanted to make you relive it."

There was a long silence. Both father and son stared at each other, the shared stubbornness speaking volumes. Both were determined not to falter, and seemed to be doing very well with the continued silence.

"She's alive!" Tristan said finally, folding his arms across his chest. "My daughter...Evie...is alive."

Theorryn stared in disbelief at his son but the disbelief was shared as well by Tristan as though he wasn't sure whether to believe it or not that his father thought Evelyn was dead.

"Impossible!" Theorryn stammered. "But the fire...and how would you know anyway."

"Because I've seen her. I didn't know who she was but...I've seen her."

"Where...here?" Tristan nodded. "I don't understand."

"The other day I went to see mum's grave and lay some flowers. This little girl appeared out of nowhere. She didn't say anything but there was a man shouting the name Evelyn, He was distraught. I assumed she was his daughter. He finally came to where we stood and he was happy to see her and she him. He said that he was looking after her for a friend and they disappeared again."

"So you're basing this on a little girl who had the same name?"

"Not just that no." Tristan paused for a moment, realising that he was being genuine. "Merlin told me there was a fire at the inn and Cedric, Myrina and Evie were inside. Their bodies were found by the city guards and everyone assumed it to be them. But Cedric he...he came to see me."

"He what?"

"Well not exactly. There was a package at the smithy for him. No idea what was in it but he accepted it and walked out saying nothing to me. I don't know whether he was expecting me to recognise him but he dropped something when he left...he dropped that picture of me Dags and...and Evie."

"Tristan, I had no idea he was here!" Theorryn came to sit beside Tristan at the table, placing his hands in front of him calmly. "This is all such a mess. And you're right...there's no more excuses left to give. What's done is done...it's time to move forward. So I would like to start by saying sorry...again but this time for a different reason." Tristan looked his father in the eye. "I understand I've...I mean since your mother died that I've not exactly been the best father in the world...especially to you. And although I've not really shown it in the best way, I really am proud of the man you are today...and I'm sorry that I don't always show that." Tristan nodded his head in acceptance.

"I guess it runs in the family...I mean I looked my daughter right in the eyes and I didn't even know it was her."

"You can't be to blame for that...if anything I am to blame. You must not think it is your fault."

"But what if it is...what if whatever happened to me was my fault to begin with."

"Tristan...have I ever told you why I never liked the Keepers?" Tristan shook his head.

"I always thought it was because of how Romeo died...not that I remember how he died but I just always assumed the two events were linked."

"It's one of the reasons but not the primary reason. When I was your age, I trained to become a Keeper as well. I was an orphan you see and when I started showing certain...gifts...they took me in and raised me. But they...one of them betrayed me...betrayed me and your uncles. And the, situation, shall we say was never resolved. The Keepers simply acted like it never happened. So...we left and I never forgave them."

"So why did you let me and Romeo join their ranks?"

"Because at the end of the day the choice was yours. It wasn't for me to tell you yes or no you were old enough to make that decision yourselves. And besides, Keeper gifts left untamed are the very reason the betrayers betray so they say. I could not keep you from your destiny."

Tristan looked away and down at the scars upon his hands, tears that would never spill forming in his eyes. Theorryn studied his son, taking note of his brokenness and how in one week...less even, he had seen his son change unbelievably so. He had watched him break and shatter into tiny pieces like a mirror on impact. The shards show distorted images in our reflection, some joining together to make a whole but very rarely is that whole perfect. Its image is never again resolute, it can never again show a true image of the man that looks upon it.

"I have every faith in you Tristan," reassured Theorryn. "One day soon I am sure you will remember everything you achieved..."

"That's why I am leaving Az Lagní tomorrow morning." Tristan stated, his father looking up at him with confused eyes. "I am going to Dilu with Merlin and D...a friend from the past."

"I see…"

"They think a more practical method will help me to remember. After all, haste is important now that I have a daughter out there somewhere." Theorryn nodded in agreement. "I will of course write as often as I can though, let you know how I'm getting on."

"Well, I wish all the luck I have to give. But perhaps I can help…wait right here."

Tristan watched as his father got up from his seat and disappeared out of sight into the sitting room. He could hear the creaking of the stairs and footsteps above him as Theorryn passed the upper floor. He wasn't sure what his father was fetching but he was curious all the same; so he waited patiently for his father to return.

"Merlin gave me a few things when you came back," puffed Theorryn as he dropped something heavy on the table, jolting Tristan suddenly. He seemed to have gone off in a daze slightly, unaware that his father had even come back into the room. Rising from his seat, he watched as Theorryn opened the box, dust enveloping the air as he did so.

"That's a big box for him to have bought back from Hasaghar," observed Tristan.

"Oh, he didn't bring back all the stuff in here, just a couple of bits. The main contents of this box are the letters you and Romeo would write me while you were with the Keeperhood."

"You kept them all?"

"Every last one! Ah here we are."

The table jolted again as a couple of hefty books were slammed onto the table, dust rippling off the hardback covers. As Theorryn dug back into the box, Tristan observed the spines, taking note of the titles; *Annals of Union - L: I* the other two being the same except for their numberings.

"Don't ask me what those books are about," Theorryn ordered, noticing Tristan's curious look. "There's no writing in them…they're just blank." Tristan shrugged his shoulders – if it was indeed about Union then it would make sense that his father couldn't read them for the secrets of Union were only known to themselves, *but even so they shouldn't leave the Shrine…* "Do you remember any of these items? They have no meaning to me but perhaps they might to you."

Tristan watched as Theorryn placed the items atop the book. First, he placed a gold necklace with a large onyx pendant, pausing a few moments to watch for Tristan's reaction. The necklace didn't trigger anything, it just caused a shudder to run up his spine and an image flash before his eyes but it passed too quickly for him to take anything from it. The next item Theorryn took out was one which puzzled Tristan and one that sparked an instant memory in his head – as though someone had simply placed it back where it belonged.

"That was the ring I presented to Dagnen on our wedding," Tristan stammered, trying to figure out why it would be there in the first place. He figured he must've removed them from her hand before she was buried.

"And its partner…"

Theorryn placed another ring beside it and Tristan came to stand beside him, taking them both within his hands. The first ring his father had retrieved from the box was an endless gold band which entwined into a heart shape at the front. There was no tarnishing to the sheen amazingly – it still sparkled as brilliantly as the memory that now lingered in his mind; a memory of him placing the ring on Dagnen's finger in front of all their guests with Merlin at their heads leading the ceremony. The other ring, gold as well, had two gemstones on the front; one pink with greenish tinges and the other a light blue with yellow tinges. Surrounding these was a circle of tiny sparkling crystals Tristan assumed to be some form of diamond. The names of the gems escaped him for the moment but the ring itself he remembered already being on the finger of which he had placed the gold band.

"The rings themselves resemble an ancient Salysman tradition," Theorryn explained, filling in the missing pieces of information within Tristan's memory. "This ring is known as the Today, Tomorrow and Forever ring." He pointed to the gemstone ring first. "Both of these gems would have been mined by the dessert men who burrow deep into the sand to find these gems. Many say they are from the core of the Earth itself but of course if that were true many would die from the pressure before getting that far. Anyway, that's beside the point…the pink gem symbolises today, the blue tomorrow and the endless circle of diamonds forever. The gold band the same; an endless circle of unbreakable love. The idea would be that you ask the father or carer for their blessing and then present the love interest with the Today, Tomorrow and Forever ring and then at the actual ceremony you present them with the gold band to mark the union of the two."

Tristan smiled slightly, his heart fluttering with warmth as he recalled the rings upon her finger on the day of their wedding. The white lacy dress of which she wore with the translucent white veil and the flower crown upon her head. Her green eyes twinkled in the daylight and her petite face stretched into a sweet smile.

"I have no idea what happened to the gold band she gave you on that day," Theorryn said, bringing Tristan back to the present day. "But I'm sure it's lying around somewhere. This is the last item I was left with."

Theorryn reached into the box one final time and lifted out an ornate trinket box of some form. He placed the box within Tristan's hands, the cold tinge of the golden sculpted feet making another shiver run down his spine. He studied the patterns along the eight sides of the octagonal box, the corners and edges of which were wired in this sparkling gold. The patterns upon the box were very eastern in style; paintings with base colours of light blues and lilacs with contrasting butterflies and flowers of pinks and yellows against the backdrops. At the top of the lid was a golden spire which acted as a handle for which to pull the lid open. Admiring the workmanship of the piece, Tristan tried to remember the context of it but the thought failed to retain itself.

"It's a music box," Theorryn explained when Tristan didn't give the reaction he was hoping for. He took it from his hands and flipped it over, turning a key on the bottom before putting it the right way up. "Now lift up the lid, let's see if this practical method works."

Eager to understand what his father was saying, he slowly opened the lid; a sweet lullaby of a tune silencing the demons of doubt within his mind as though they were a cavalry of horsemen chasing away the dark. The tune bought with it a memory which was influenced further by the dancing couple that twirled as the box was opened to its fullness. Theorryn watched in wonderment as his son's eyes sparkled, a smile touching the ends of his lips. He smiled to himself, the tune bringing memories of his own into view as he let Tristan follow the images appearing in his mind.

The images took Tristan to a much more homely version of his own sitting room. There was more colour than there was in the present day; colourful tapestry throws covering the couch and chairs with a rug upon the wood floor. A piano sat in the corner by the stairs, one which was now beyond retuning. A woman sat at the piano with a young boy by her side. He recognised the woman to be his mother, her long blonde hair tied up in a messy bun on the top of her head, a brown smock covering her white under-dress. A smile decorated her face, masking the ill-natured drained look that he, as his older self-recognised. She played a tune to the young boy, who nodded his head in time with it; his head eventually falling onto his mother's shoulder in sleep.

This image soon trickled away though and was replaced by another that swam into view. This time a much older him sat beside a brunette at a similar looking piano in the corner of a quiet public house. Only a few punters were scattered around the converted barrel tables and there in the corner sat he and the brunette. She played he same tune, and he smiled alongside her, occasionally trying his own hand at the keys but he could never get the same gentle tone which she could.

Suddenly the tune was gone and he was back in the kitchen of him and his father's cottage, a sudden sadness gripping him as he longed for the memory to stay a while longer. Noticing the smile slip from his face, Theorryn placed a hand on his shoulder, gripping it tightly and supportively, as he always should've done.

"It is alright my boy," he assured in a compassionate tone. "You will remember her...you will remember them all in time, I am sure."

Tristan nodded, closing the lid of the box after placing the two rings inside it along with the pendant.

"Thank you for showing me all this," Tristan sympathised, shrugging his father's hand off of his shoulder. Listen, there's a couple of us having some drinks tonight what with me leaving tomorrow. Maybe you could join us?"

"You know, I think I'd like that!" Theorryn smiled, the wrinkles on his old face all joining into one. "What time do you leave in the morning?"

"Depends on how much we drink tonight."

"Sounds like a plan!" Theorryn chortled along, clapping a hand on his bony chest as Tristan backed towards the front door.

"I'll see you tonight then."

"That you will my boy, that you will."

Tristan nodded again, a slight smile touching the end of his lips as he left the house. Theorryn on the other hand remained where he stood, picking up a scroll at random from the box and scanning over the words. Part of him was disappointed he had not asked him to join them on their journey to Dilu but he knew this was something Tristan had to do on his own without people who might interfere; a distraction he knew all too well he may provide. As he finished reading over the words once more, he looked up in time to see an eagle flash past the window, a scroll dropping into the washing bowl atop the surface. As the scroll slipped out of view, he caught sight of the royal seal that was waxed to close it tight, fear creeping into his eyes. For now, ignorance was bliss...but that's the problem with 'for now'; there was always an end to it.

# CHAPTER 18 - LAST ORDERS

A raucous of cheers erupted as Tristan entered the Green Clover Inn later that evening, rather surprised at how many people were already there even at this early hour. He smiled brightly, his bad mood already improving. This afternoon had been one filled with errands, the latest of which had been running by the Smithy to tell them that he would not be returning to work for the foreseeable future. You can imagine how that went down with Lionel's sons who would now have to pick up his shifts and work even harder to keep the place tipping over whilst their father was away. Neither were happy with that predicament – they never really cared much for the Smithy; they were too obsessed with their own meaningless lives as Knights of the City Guard. Even Balderick would say they were lazy layabouts.

"Tristan, come sit your arse over 'ere!" demanded Balderick, clapping a hand on the stool next to him over by the bar as Dante placed a fresh beer atop the work surface.

"Tell you what that beer is needed today," Tristan sighed exasperatedly as he came over and took a sip. "You not joining us Dante?"

"Aha, you wish!" Dante winked, leaning on his elbow on the counter for a moment before the rush came on again. "A certain barmaid quit her job today out of the blue. Personally, I'm rather glad to be rid of the wench...but then I found out that it meant I would have to cover her shift until Iain could get in to cover me. So in answer to your question, I will be joining you in approximately one hour."

"I'm going to assume this certain barmaid would be Jenni?"

"Well yes, but that's not what I would call her. According to Gregory she came in this morning like an hour before her shift and said she wouldn't be working it or working here ever again. She didn't even let him say anything in response, she just turned on her heel and left. At first, he didn't think she was serious...of course when she never showed up, we gathered she was being serious. Tell me, you wouldn't have anything to do with her not being here, would you?"

"Unless you count me basically telling her to leave me alone then no."

"I thought as much, excuse me."

Tristan took another sip of his beer as Dante jumped up to serve a couple of people that came over to the bar, one of which was Merlin. Once he had his drink, he joined Balderick and Tristan, listening in on their conversation of the day's events with Dante adding his input whenever he had a spare minute. When he finally joined them, the others were already on their third drink so he had a lot of catching up to do. But he made short work of it and was chatting up one of the other barmaids in no time.

"What?" Tristan asked as he saw Balderick shaking his head, blinking his eyes funnily as the beer started to attempt control of him.

"Oh, it's just amazing how little someone can change in over a thousand years." Balderick explained. "Heck, I can't even believe that it's been that long – it doesn't even feel it. Even more so the fact that most of that time he's spent in the Land of the Faded."

"You were too though, minus fifty years that is."

"But you see the difference is I've changed. I've had to; to ensure my survival. Plus, I've had kids and that always changes you whether you like it or not. But Dante...he has nothing to fear and therefore no reason to change. I mean it's not as if the Keepers will catch up to him...there's none of them left."

"Doesn't mean he's not changed, just because you can't see it I mean..."

"True, very true."

As Balderick gulped down the last of his ale, Tristan looked over as the door to the bar opened and closed once again; another anonymous punter entering the bar and taking a pew. Noticing the darkness outside, he began to accept the fact that his father was probably not going to show up. Swallowing the last of his beer, he felt a sharp hand clap him on the back as an unknown bystander came to stand by his side.

"Care for another?" came the voice of a man, as Tristan turned to look at the owner of the offer. "On me of course!" The voice was that of his father, encouraging a relieved smile upon Tristan's face. "Sorry I'm late...the council meeting overran."

"That's alright father, you're here now." Tristan replied, his voice unevenly pitched due to the amount he had already drank.

"What are you drinking? I'll join you for one and then settle for a softer drink I think."

"Well, if you're offering, I'll have another beer if you please?"

"That's my boy, Samson get this man another beer."

The rest of the evening frolicked on drunkenly giving Tristan, Dante and Merlin the send-off they deserved. But of course, the morning wasn't so jovial or welcoming for that matter. However as far as hangovers went, this one wasn't as bad as it usually was. To his surprise, Tristan awoke in his own room feeling a little worse for wear, his stomach performing somersaults before he'd even had chance to contemplate his surroundings. As he moved himself into a more upright position, he felt his head join the circus acrobatics that were going on underneath his midriff. He gulped heavily, closing his eyes momentarily as a bell rang deep within his mind, the words 'last orders' accompanying it majestically. But not in a gentle majestic way that strikes with a feeling of awe, the heavy sort of majestic that strikes with nothing more than fear and sheer bewilderment. That feeling hit him in the stomach like one of those somersaults where you fall on your bottom as opposed to your feet, and sent him straight into the washroom to hurl the contents of his stomach into the john.

The queasy feeling had subsided slightly by the time he made it down the stairs to slump at the kitchen table, the aroma of whatever his father was cooking sending his stomach into an encore.

"Oh how the mighty have fallen!" Theorryn laughed as he turned to face his pale faced son. "I do not miss that feeling." Taking his pan off the cooking fire, he ladled the brown liquid in to a goblet and placed it in front of Tristan before pouring the last of into one for himself. "Drink that, it will help trust me." He took a sip of his own after letting it simmer, breathing a sigh of relief as the taste turned to a feeling of energy erupting through his body.

Tristan took in a whiff of the brown liquid's aroma. The smell bought with it the all too familiar feeling of drunkenness and how the both his head and stomach needed fixing before his long journey began.

"So, how did I get back here?" Tristan asked as he swirled the liquid around a little before chucking some down his throat, the unknown substance burning his tongue slightly as he swallowed it. A nutty taste welcomed him, embracing him for the strong grainy palate that was followed by a musky aftertaste. He wouldn't have called it a taste he relished, but he certainly savoured the feeling of the hot liquid as it swam through his insides, melting all the queasy and sleepy feelings that remained in his body from his drunken stupor that evening. Nodding his head in appreciation, he took another sip, this time less so as not to burn his tongue further.

"A little after last orders you disappeared," Theorryn explained. "Balderick figured you'd headed back to his so went to check whilst me and Dante searched the surroundings of the inn. Of course, what we found wasn't exactly pleasant but it was heading for the city gates which told me that you were wondering off home sicking up all the way. We found you passed out on your bed."

"And Dante?"

"As far as I'm aware he and Balderick headed back to the inn for a nightcap." Theorryn shock his head, swallowing the last of his goblet and tipping the dregs onto the flowers that sat in the basket on the open kitchen window. "The beauty of coffee; how it manages to pour life and being into that of a human and even prolong the life of a simple flower."

"Coffee?" Tristan questioned, swallowing the last of his too.

"Yep, that's what the Abersonians call it anyway."

"What time is it?" asked Tristan after a while, his thoughts suddenly becoming clear against the dull after-feeling the beer had given him.

"By my guess, a little before mid-morning."

"So much for leaving at mid-morning."

"I guess you better get your rear in gear then."

"I guess I better. One last thing though?"

"Anything my boy!"

"Meet us at the Southern gate in about an hour. It would be nice to have someone to wave us off."

"I'll be there." Theorryn winked to Tristan, picking his goblet off of the table as his son left the comfort of his childhood home.


Tristan stood below the window to the attic room in the Green Clover Inn. He pondered for a moment, wondering if Dante had even welcomed the prospect of waking up. Balderick came to stand by his side; he'd been out when Tristan had returned to clothe and wash himself but it was nice to see someone else looking as falsely fresh faced as he did.

"How's the hangover?" he asked, folding his arms and standing beside Tristan, following his gaze up to the open window.

"Fading," Tristan replied despondently. "What's the betting he's not even awake yet?"

"Why don't we find out?"

Balderick bent over and retrieved a pebble from the side of the cobblestoned pavement. Weighting the pebble in his hand, he took aim and threw it through the open window, the clanging noise telling him he'd most likely overshot the bed slightly and hit the washbasin. Cursing the air, he picked up another, took aim and threw; a smashing sound erupting moments later. An ornament of some sort perhaps? Cursing again, he picked up another stone, this time throwing it harder. The sound that welcomed it this time was not one he was expecting – the scream of a woman. Flinching, both he and Tristan remained reluctantly rooted to the spot. A sharp slap sounded, followed by a disgruntled 'ouch' and the slamming of a door...twice.

A few moments later, the door to the inn burst open and a sheepish looking woman stormed past them, her pink dress torn in places and her blonde hair covering a single red tinged cheek. Another, who could easily have been her twin followed, her attire sweeping behind her in the same fashion. Confused, both the men stared back up at the window to see a stunned Dante looking angrily back at them.

"Alright there brother?" Balderick called, a smile touching his lips as he put two and two together. "Nice catch!"

"Thanks," Dante replied gruffly. "Now will one of you kindly point the finger to which one threw the rocks?" Without even thinking about it, Balderick pointed straight at Tristan, not even giving him a chance to do the same.

"In my defence, it was Balderick's idea." Tristan took the blame boldly. Little did he know he would come to regret it.

"So, if Balderick had an idea that you should jump off a cliff would you do it? Actually, don't answer that."

"Tell me, what caused her to uh…" Balderick pointed to his own cheek, forcing Dante to lift his hand to his face and feel the red-hot mark that was slowly appearing.

"Well, the rock landed right on my forehead." Dante touched his forehead and Tristan noticed a break in his skin. It really was a good shot from the Knight Commander. "Of course, my reaction was to slap it as though it was some bug or something. Let's just say…my aim was a little off."

Both Tristan and Balderick burst into fits of laughter, both clapping each other on the back and shoulders. As soon as they had gained control of themselves, they ushered Dante along, telling him they had to be ready to leave in less than an hour. Of course, he took longer, and a little over an hour later the three travelling companions were all saddled up and ready to leave with Balderick and Theorryn to wave them off.

Before turning his back on the city, he had called home for so long now, Tristan looked over his shoulder one last time, watching as the people of Az Lagní finally rose from their houses and began the day's work; a little later than they should've been but most of them had probably spent the evening drinking alongside Tristan. Next, he looked to the faces of his companions. Merlin looked determined and ready to begin a new adventure, Dante on the other hand was practically falling asleep in his saddle. Those barmaids must've been a good ride. Lastly, he looked to the faces of Balderick and his father whose faces bade a thousand previous goodbyes both had said to their corresponding grievances. Dante clapped his hand on Balderick's shoulder, the two bidding a silent goodbye to the other and a wish to see each other again soon. Theorryn on the other hand stepped forward, patting his hand on the flank of Tristan's horse.

"I've never been one for goodbyes…" his father began.

"Me neither!" Tristan interjected. "So let's leave it at see you soon."

Both nodded to the other, a smile touching their faces as they shock hands. The three made their way towards the rising sun and the southern gates, Tristan knowing that this was only the beginning of everything that was coming his way. Looking back one last time, he caught sight of Jenni loading up a wagon with all her things, her disappointed brother giving her a hand. The image of another woman appeared next to her like a mirage, a mighty smile upon her face as though she were saying 'that's right, get out of here.' The image was that of his Dags and no sooner had the two shared eye contact and a bright smile relit the flame within him, he knew she too awaited him somewhere out there. As she faded like the shadows in the noon sun, he turned back to face forward and follow Dante and Merlin in the direction of the Mountain Pass and onward towards Dilu.

# CHAPTER 19 - A DETOUR

With a final push, the wagon rolled heavily in through the gates of Ragnur. Tristan and Dante had been pushing it since noon when one of the wheels' spokes had snapped, crushing it under the pressure of all their belongings. Merlin had been 'driving the horses' so of course; he was fine. The other two however dropped to the floor; their lungs heaving as they caught their breath.

Ragnur was a rich man's town. High lords and royally clad ladies draped in all their finery paraded around the town, fat coin purses at their belt buckles, practically ready to burst. As one of them walked past, he threw a coin in their direction, laughing heartily when he passed. Tristan shook his head in a cursing manner, jeering at the man as he turned his back on them.

"Pompous git!" Dante swore, pushing himself up off the ground before lending a hand to Tristan and helping him to his feet.

"You know, my rear is so numb from all that travelling," Merlin strained as he stretched himself out. Three days on horseback had given him a stiff back. Tristan and Dante looked to each other and shook their heads. He was being sarcastic of course but that didn't make it any funnier. "Tell you what, why don't you boys head on into that inn and get yourselves a nice drink. I'll find someone who can fix this here wagon."

"Well isn't that nice of you old man," grunted Dante. "Don't count on me getting you one in though."

Warily, Dante made his way towards the inn, Tristan following a little way behind muttering something under his breath. No doubt it was some curse slating Merlin's good name. The inn was quiet on the inside, a low grumble of lunch time punters enjoying the grub. Tristan and Dante slumped into a booth, motioning for the barman to come over.

"What can I get you sirs then? If you're after food we have a nice roast steak with potatoes and veg. How 'bout it?" The man had a gruff voice and scratched his abnormally large belly as he waited for the men to respond. The landlord was perhaps the most unexpected image of a rich man within the whole of Ragnur, in fact this whole bar was the bottom end of the spectrum compared to the grandeur of the rest of the town. "Well? Ya called me over here so tell me what ya want!" This time the man scratched his bald head which wasn't even shiny in the bright lights of the midday sun shining through the window.

"I'll take the steak," sighed Dante. "But well done...I want it literally like charcoal if possible."

"Crazy goof! But I'll see wha' we can do for ya. Anything to drink?"

"Ale...good strong ale."

"Coming up, and yourself sir."

"I'll take the same...only not charcoal," sneered Tristan. "Just burn off all the red bits."

"Both of ya' are crazy. Steak needs to be blue but ah well suit yourself. Drink?"

"Beer please."

"Coming up!"

The drinks arrived promptly in well-polished glasses that contrasted against the sloppy looking joint. Even the plates of steak and vegetables were shined to the brim that not even gravy tainted. The food was just as good, and cheap for the quality of it all. Merlin wondered in a little after they'd finished and slumped down next to Tristan, wiping his finger along the plate for a taste.

"Not bad if I do say so myself," Merlin applauded, licking his lips. "Afraid we're going to have to stop the night. Stable owner is very busy today, said he can't get around to it till much later but it will definitely be done by tomorrow. So I paid the man to board the horses and figured we could get our heads down for a decent sleep for one night at least."

"Tell you what, sounds good to me!" Dante answered without even needing to think twice. Tristan nodded in approval, clapping a hand on his full belly. Dante stretched back, placing his hands behind his head and his stomach moaning in appreciation.

"I'll book the room then?" Merlin stormed, rising to his feet and heading over to the bar.

"Well, we did push the wagon for half a bloody day you lazy swine." sneered Dante in an undertone, Tristan laughing in response.

Tristan watched the dregs of his beer dance around as he swirled the liquid in his tankard, his eyes barely able to stay open. He was tired but there was no way he was going to fall asleep with both Dante and Merlin's snoring. Plus, the reason he'd woken in the first place wasn't particularly something he wanted to keep seeing in his dreams.

He motioned for the barman to give him a refill to which he kindly obliged, looking up as the door swung open and shut again, nodding to the person who walked in. Tristan looked around out the corner of his eye to see a familiar face. It was the man from the Smithy who had wanted Tristan's forgiveness. *What was his name? John Basso?*

As the name recalled in his mind, an image flashed before his eyes with John stood at the head of the room, row upon row of desks facing him as though it were some form of classroom. A blackboard was behind it with something scribbled across it; The Magic of Glyphs.

*"Welcome to The Magic of Glyphs," John addressed. "My name is John Basso but you can all call me Basso; too many Johns in this place anyway. Here you will learn the different Glyphs that surround our world. By the end of this class, you will know how to find and conjure Glyphs and then eventually command and manipulate them. It will be very enjoyable I'm sure!" he didn't sound convinced.*

The sound of a tankard being placed on the bar bought Tristan out of his thoughts, making him jump slightly. He covered it up with taking a sip from his newly poured beer, his eyes wondering over to where Basso now stood.

"Tristan?" he said in disbelief, blinking his eyes hard as though he thought he were imagining him. "What are you doing here?"

"Oh, our wagon needs a new wheel so we're here on a detour," explained Tristan, smiling as he did so. "How've you been then Bass?"

"All the better for hearing you sound like you know me again." That statement was all too hesitant for Tristan to take confidence in it, but he accepted it all the same.

"It's getting there."

"That's a start at least! So, what brings you this way then?"

"We're heading to Dilu…"

"Dilu?"

"Yes! It's where I became a Scribe so Merlin figured it would be better for my memory if I actually went to places that once meant something to me."

"Well I hope it works."

"Me too. What would be helpful though is someone who was actually there with me but I suppose people like that are in short supply at the moment."

"Bloody hell that man can snore!" exclaimed Dante, slumping down in a stool next to Tristan and covering his eyes with his worn hands. The barman came straight over and placed an ale in front of him as Basso stared over – almost like he knew him from somewhere.

"So can you," chuckled Tristan, nudging Dante in the side. "Why do you think I'm down here?" Dante looked down on Tristan imposingly, forcing the young Keeper to stop and continue drinking his beer.

As Dante shook his head, his eyes cast over Basso. Something about him was familiar but he wasn't sure what, not to mention the fact that he didn't get a good feeling about the guy whoever he was.

"Oh, Basso this is D…" Tristan began to explain, noticing the looks the two were exchanging.

"Daxon!" Dante interjected. With how uneasy this man made him feel, he wasn't about to tell him his real name. Tristan looked over at him suddenly, sharing a look that made him realise he needed to play along for the moment.

"This is…Daxon…Daxon this is John Basso." Tristan continued.

"Pleasure…I'll leave you two to it." Basso nodded, standing up and hiding away in a booth in a dark corner of the inn.

"Daxon?" Tristan questioned once Basso was out of earshot.

"I don't want people knowing who I am," exclaimed Dante, waving his hands about as though it were obvious. "Especially when they're Keepers. Who is that guy anyway?"

"He taught me about Glyphs and how to use them when I was an Acolyte. I don't know much else; I just remember his lessons as opposed to anything outside of that."

"Maybe you should ask him to come with us?"

"I didn't think you liked him?"

"I never said that! But you know, maybe it would help to have someone who knew you back then come with us. I mean Merlin's good but...he didn't *know* you."

"Thing is I don't think I trust him myself. I just can't help but think there was something far worse that he did to me that made me want to kill him like I supposedly did."

"Then maybe that's another reason for him to come with us."

Dante guzzled down the last of his ale before rising to his feet and heading for the john, again glaring at Basso as he passed. Tristan took the cue to join Basso in the booth, getting an odd look as he did so. It was almost as if he didn't want him around, like he actually didn't want to be remembered at all and that was the intriguing part. The Brother of Unity wasn't a violent person so for him to threaten to kill someone meant they did something that really hurt him.

"Can I get you another drink?" Tristan asked, motioning to Basso's half empty tankard and instantly regretting the offer as he took another sip from his own.

"I'm alright thank you," replied Basso, replicating the action.

An awkward silence passed between them; both taking sips from their tankards more often than they should. *What was taking Dante so long? Wait, maybe that question didn't need answering...*

"You should come with us," Tristan suggested, causing a strange look from Basso. "To Dilu I mean."

"Oh, why do you say that?" asked Basso, his eyes widening slightly making that red glint stand out all too well and sent a shiver down the length of Tristan's spine

"Funny you should ask that. You see...Daxon..." he'd forgotten the persona Dante had created "thinks it will be a good idea to have someone who knew me back then."

 "Did he not know you back then?"

"He knows me now."

"Right...but Merlin?" He was making excuses. Surely if Basso had wanted Tristan to remember him, he would jump at the offer but the fact that he didn't unsettled him. Why did Basso not want him to remember?

"He knew me but...not as much as you...or any of my teachers for that matter." Basso nodded his head.

"You see I really need to be here...I can't come...I can't return to Dilu. I'm sorry!" Basso rose to his feet and headed for the door.

"But Basso..."

"I'm not coming Tristan...I can't do it!"

Basso turned and left the inn in a huff, the barman flapping his hands – he obviously hadn't paid. Then again, he hadn't even finished it. Tristan slumped back, noticing the angry look on the barman's face as though he expected him to pay for it after upsetting a paying customer. His stare off was interrupted by Dante finally coming out of the john.

"You took your time," Tristan snarled, a hidden joke in there somewhere.

"I wasn't actually...I would never...I was giving you chance to finish your conversation with Basso..." Dante suggested. Tristan threw him a look as if to question his intention. "I did! So where did he go?" Tristan shrugged his shoulders. "Well, I'm going for a walk, got a headache I can't shift."

Dante grabbed his cloak off the hook by the door and headed out into the night air leaving Tristan alone in the inn. He was used to being alone these days, alone with the dreams he slept alongside. Who knew someone would not want to sleep for fear of what they might see...?

# CHAPTER 20 - BRETHREN BETRAYER

Breathing in the night air, Dante looked around the city streets and spied his target immediately. Of course, he wasn't going for a walk to clear his head. There was a reason this John Basso was familiar to him and he wanted to know why. Whether or not that was a good idea was another matter. Pulling his hood up over his head, he followed Basso in the shadows to what looked to be a hostel of some sort on the outskirts of town. The building itself was an abhorrent eyesore; skulky characters leaning against the exterior, hoods up and pipes hanging from their lips. A couple of whores flounced about between them and he watched as Basso passed vacantly by them - as though they hadn't even noticed him pass. This puzzled Dante, but then again, he was a Keeper and therefore if he didn't want to be seen he didn't have to be.

Using the windows as his guide, he watched Basso pass down a corridor to a room right at the end of it, obviously where he was staying, and headed hastily inside. Skirting round the back into an alley, Dante found another window near a back door which apparently led to the room Basso was in. *What was the point in going in the front door when he had a personal door?* Then again maybe he was scoping out the market, Dante knew he'd be doing the same with those girls in their skimpy dresses.

He positioned himself between the open window and the door, peering through the gap as torches were lit inside revealing a man sat at a table in the centre of the room. From the back he didn't look like much, all Dante could make out was the bald head that was shinier than a diamond and a very round body structure clothed in a dirty white shirt that was much too tight and a leather waistcoat that didn't even stretch to his waist. Basso certainly didn't look happy to see the stranger, his pale face going paler still and his thin mouth wrinkling in astonishment under his beard. He imagined the man to by smiling slyly as Basso straightened up, trying to look down on his acquaintance.

"'ello Bass!" exclaimed the man in a low and common sounding voice, a voice that seemed to tug at the marks on Dante's palms. Nobility knew the man that was for sure. "Long time no see."

"What are you doing here?" Basso asked, his voice quivering ever so slightly.

"I...or should I say a mutual friend has an offer for you."

"Offer?"

"Let's just say that the Herasin is in need of your services once more."

"I have no reason to offer my services..."

"Ah but you still have a bargain to wager."

*Bargain?* Dante thought; *perhaps it had something to do with his qualm with Tristan?* Either way the notion intrigued him and the word Herasin had struck fear into his hard heart. Herasin meant father and was the name for the leader of the Brothers of Dharsi. It also meant that Dante was perfectly in his right mind not to trust Basso, his association with whoever this man was obviously meant that he was in with Dharsi. However, he didn't think it meant he was member. The bad feeling wasn't that evil a notion.

"I finished my end of the bargain.  He's out of the way isn't he? Yes, there was collateral damage along the way but what's done is done. It's over!" Basso explained, circling round to lean against a counter opposite where the stranger sat.

"Ah but you see that's where you're wrong. You see, he's remembering which means you didn't do the job properly." He was talking about Tristan, that bit was obvious. It was also obvious now that perhaps Basso was the reason Tristan didn't remember. "Not to mention the fact that people are returning as I'm sure you already know what with you being back. Which reminds me, how did you get back? I'm sure it's not because he remembered you because he'd be here already waiting to kill you."

"Oh he won't remember that, I'll make sure of it."

"Well don't count on it. If people are returning without necessarily being remembered, then we can be sure that it won't be long until his brothers return. And when they do, they'll find him and they'll be out for all our blood." He paused, for effect probably, stroking his chin perhaps - the way his arms stretched across his middle and up to his face. "So, you see it is in both our interests that you join us once again."

"I told you I'm finished with you people. And besides, what would be in it for me?"

"Tell me Basso, why did you join us in the first place?"

"You know why..."

"Yes, but remind me. This thing," He pointed to something on his face; a mark or a scar perhaps. "It halts the memory you see. It's not as good as it was."

"I did what I did for revenge. He deserved everything he got!" Now this puzzled Dante. As far as he was aware, even from what Cedric and Merlin had said, Tristan had done nothing against anyone to have revenge inflicted upon him. Unless it was his legacy meaning Nobility or Union in general could be his excuse for revenge. But that would make him a lot older than he looked, however it would also explain why Dante recognised him. *But surely, he couldn't be that old...*

"That's right! And what did we promise you in return for completing your end of the bargain?"

Basso was silent. His face had gone even paler and it was obvious he didn't want to answer from the way he kept biting the inside of his lip. Perhaps he'd had a change of heart in recent years. Maybe being in the Faded lands had shown him the true meaning of humanity. Either way it was clear he was fighting himself to come to a decision.

"What is your new offer?"

"We offer you...your freedom!" Dante watched as Basso's expression changed yet again, almost as though his heart had left his chest. "We've given you your original prize so to speak, and in time he'll show himself to you.  So now, we offer you the chance to rid yourself of us wretched lot for a small price. Of course, you know what that price is...so pay it and we will set you free...once and for all."

More silence. Dante could tell Basso's forehead was wrinkling under his fringe, again he was fighting himself. *But what were they going to free him from?* Perhaps he was bound to Dharsi, like an ally. Maybe he'd done it decades ago and they'd chosen a ripe moment to use it to their advantage...like a pawn in a game of chess.

"Well Bass, what's your answer?" Basso's response was too quiet for him to hear. It was as though he had to hear himself say it out loud to see what it sounded like, to test out his answer. "What's that, I didn't hear you?"

"I won't do it!" Basso launched himself forward, slamming his hands on the table and making the empty bowl and pitcher shudder in their place. The action didn't seem to faze the stranger at all though, he just cocked his head to the side and stared at him.

"Won't...or can't?" Was the stranger's response as he slowly rose to his feet, circling the table and leaning in next to where Basso stood. The side of his face became visible now, the man was no longer a stranger to the watcher. His face was round and blotched at the cheeks, his eyes bulged from his skull and three chins stretched as he leaned in towards Basso. If it wasn't for the tattoo running down the side of his face, Dante wouldn't even have recognised him. After all, it was Dante who had given him that mark in the first place. The runes for Brethren Betrayer etched in ink upon his face scarring him for life, marked like a pig for the slaughter. Dante on the other hand had never got the chance to follow his threat through and kill the coward that he was.

"I think you need to decide where your loyalties lie," he threatened Basso, the words only just loud enough for Dante to hear.

Basso said nothing in response. He just stayed rooted to the spot, his arms trembling and his breath coming out in ragged huffs. The man; Boris as he'd name had been then and may still have been, smiled sneakily, his eyes flickering red in the light. He turned to leave, but not through the front, through the back and right to where Dante was standing. But he too was a Keeper and he too didn't have to be seen if he didn't want to be.

Leaving Basso to dwell, he followed Boris down the alley a bit, chasing up around the corner and backing the traitor up against the wall. The hood of his cloak slipping to reveal his face as he did so, a look of horror masking the false confidence Boris seemed to have gained whilst threatening Basso.

"Not...it can't be..." he stuttered, his body stiffening as Dante pushed his arm underneath his chin. "You're...you're..."

"What's that Boris?" Dante goaded. "Forgotten my name after all these years?"

"But you..."

"Now I'm back and we have a score to settle." Dante pulled a knife from his belt and put it up to Boris' neck. "After all, I did make you a promise."

"But you can't kill me...not now..."

"And why can't I?"

"'cause you didn't mark me...well not really..."

"I think you're forgetting that I was the one who marked your face like that in the first place...unless you were marked again. Oh, now that would make things interesting." He pushed on the knife slightly, drawing enough blood to make Boris gulp. "Tristan marked you as well didn't he? That's why you want Basso to help you...oh this is priceless." Dante sniggered, a fearful silence being the only sound Boris made in response. "Tell you what I'll leave you scathed for now, at the moment you're all too useful to me." Dante laughed again and sheathed the knife after he noticed a guard approaching them out of the corner of his eye.

"There a problem here sirs?" He asked, pulling the pommel of his sword into the light as a threat.

"No trouble at all," Dante remarked, letting go of Boris. "We were just...reacquainting ourselves." The guard nodded, turning away slightly.

Dante winked to Boris and he straightened up, giving a wry smile as he did so. The guard turned away and continued his watch. Dante turned to Boris, backing away as he did so in the direction of the inn.

"I'll see you soon...Brethren Betrayer!" He chanted, the ends of his lips twisting into a haunting smile. As Boris keeled over in pain, lifting his hands to his face as though his mark was burning him, he lifted the hood of his cloak again and headed back for the inn. *Once a traitor, always a traitor,* he thought to himself.

# CHAPTER 21 – DILU

A week's travel bought them to the pitiful city of Dilu, an unpleasant looking town drenched in poverty. The town itself seemed ghostly to Tristan as he stepped down from the wagon and surveyed the shabby town houses around them and the long-broken water fountain which lay a few feet away. Something about its structure struck him as familiar, then again this town was full of forgotten memories for him so there was going to be a lot of that. A stable boy stepped over towards Merlin and took the horses as he was handed a few coins.

"Pitiful isn't it," Merlin examined. "Compared to what it used to resemble anyway."

Tristan sighed as Merlin and Dante began unloading the wagon onto a smaller wooden trolley, the stable boy leading away the other horse. Once the trolley was loaded, Merlin began walking towards the fountain; leading the way.

"Merlin wait," called Dante. "Don't you think it would be better to let Tristan lead the way?"

The old man nodded, stepping aside for Tristan to take the lead. Dazedly, he stepped forward; his feet seeming to lead his body without any direction from his head. Taking a couple of steps forward he stopped at the fountain, took a left turn and proceeded down the street that opened out before him. He wasn't really sure where he was going, he just had a feeling he was going the right way. After about fifty paces he stopped, suddenly unsure of where to go next. Either side of him was an alleyway, both as dark and dingy as the other. He looked around, trying to clear his mind and focus on something other than the alleys. People passed him where he stood dressed in dirty clothes, unhealed scars covering their cheeks, arms and hands. Deciding ahead of him provided too many distractions he looked up at the sky, noticing the tower towards the east, another mirroring it on the west. The western tower was much more overbearing and perhaps the only feature Tristan did not recognise - it was something that hadn't been there three years ago. His feet began to lead him again, this time forward and out of a gate which hung from its posts at the top of the street between the alleys. An abandoned building rested before him, most of the windows of which were bordered up or shattered. It was a rather big building which was probably rather impressive in its heyday. But even in its current state, the building was rather imposing. The trio stepped up towards the steps to a door which was also bordered up by a couple of wooden beams. A sigil rested above them; a blue background with a key on the forefront. The mark itself was the sign of a Keeper Compound, a sign of where Tristan had learnt everything he currently knew about the Keepers and where he spent two years of his teenage life.

"This is it?" Dante asked, his voice breaking as he did so.

"Yes," answered Merlin. "After the Fall the Compound was abandoned and fell into dissolution under the new Estate of barons and lords. They rule this place with a firm hand and a fine-toothed comb...tyrants in their own right. Not that that's a good thing of course...but yes, this is all that's left."

"Dante help me with these beams will you?" Tristan commanded, taking to the top of the steps.

Dante placed the handle of the trailer on the floor and stepped forward to grab the beam with Tristan and pull it free from its nails. They made quick work of it, carefully easing the doors open to darkness and dust that fell from the non-existent ceiling. Merlin stepped into the room that welcomed them, clapping his hands together once and then parting them to light up the torches that were dotted around.

"If it somehow turns out that that there are Keepers still here, my name is Daxon and I'm from Az Lagní like you." suggested Dante in an undertone, being sure that any lurking in the shadows would not hear him.

Tristan stepped into the centre of the room, taking in his surroundings as Merlin and Dante bought in their possessions and shut the doors. He looked around, watching as blank papyrus pages still fell from opened books on the shelves around the room and those that went up and up at least four floors. Parts of the banisters were missing around the shelves and the once glass ceiling above them was now gone, the shattered pieces littering the white tiled floor. A few tables scattered the atrium they seemed to be in, books open upon them and chairs littered around, some of which were on their backs. Two corridors lay at the ends of the hexagonal room leading off into different sections and a door was closed to his left, the plaque above it reading 'Reading Room'. Another was to his right, the plaque reading 'The Elders Library'.

Tristan jumped suddenly as Dante launched forward striking his sword up at the air. He watched confused, *what had he seen?* Tilting his sword forward a bit more made his sword strike true, a figure suddenly appearing before them with a trickle of blood leaking from a small cut that now appeared on his neck. The figure was that of a man, shoulder length black hair masking a dusty old face that had startling green eyes...*just like Dante's,*

Tristan thought. The man wore a holed blue tunic which was tucked into brown breeches, black boots protecting his worn feet.

"Please, don't hurt me!" He begged, his voice coming out in ragged rasps. "I mean you no harm I swear."

Tristan looked to Dante who had gone very still and pale, his eyes staring into those of the man's, a look of shock washing over his face. He stepped towards his long-haired companion, reaching up to his arm and pushing it down so that he lowered his sword, his eyes focused on the man that stood before them.

"Nielson?" Merlin said aghast at last, the man looking to his old friend and a sigh of relief reawakening the stranger's face. The two embraced each other in a brotherly way, smiles creasing up their old faces. "It is good to see you my brother. You remember Tristan?" Merlin grasped Tristan on the shoulder and the two shook hands, a notion Nielson seemed uncomfortable with, as though he expected a different greeting. Yes, Tristan recognised the man, but anything past that was still a blur.

"Of course I remember him!" Nielson exclaimed as they clasped hands. "It is just a shame he does not me."

"He will in time - that is why we are here. But I'll come onto that later, this man here is..."

"Daxon!" Dante exclaimed before Merlin had the chance to forget. "I'm a friend of Tristan's."

Dante extended a hand to which Nielson took giving a firm shake. The two shared an odd look as though both recognised the other but weren't sure either way. The look itself only confirmed Tristan's own suspicions on Dante's link to him, after all there had to be a deeper reason than Destiny for Dante wanting to help him so much.

"It's nice to meet you," Nielson appreciated, releasing Dante's hand and stepping back. "So what are you all doing here in Dilu?"

Whatever Merlin went onto say was lost to Tristan as he felt himself collapse under the force of unseen pressure. His knees buckled and he crashed to the floor, hearing only Dante's voice shout his name as all three of them tried to catch him in his fall. As he hit the floor, his vision blurred to black, darkness embracing him and lulling him into an unwilling sleep filled with dreams of unknown faces.

~~~

It is a unique world the land of dreams. Sometimes you are in complete control of what is going on, other times everything confuses you and there is no making sense of it all. And then there are those dreams that are so real you just can't break free of them – like you're there on the other side of your eyes banging on the glass and begging someone to wake you up. But no one can hear you; they just stare over you and watch your eyes blankly as though they believe there is nothing they can do except let you sleep.

That is exactly the sort of dream you dear brother are experiencing right now. You want to wake up but you just cannot, all you can do is relive those memories over and over again with no one being able to do anything to help you out of it. Not even me. All I can do is watch you dream, watch as Dante and Merlin carry you down the left side corridor towards the dorms where you and I and the rest of our brothers spent two years training as Keepers.

Slowly, I begin to follow them and you, down the corridor, up two flights of stairs and into a room right at the end of the corridor. They place you on the bed by the window, the same bed you slept in back then...despite the fact it was already claimed when we got here. That didn't bother you – but then you always did get your own way one way or another. Reluctantly, they leave you to sleep. They probably think all the familiarity was too much for you and that you just couldn't process it in your mind. It probably doesn't help that you haven't slept in days for fear of what you might see but you must see it my brother or you will never remember.

I, above anyone else, know just how hard this is for you. I, before all of our brothers know the struggles you went through and the secrets you kept. I may not know the secrets themselves but I know the pain they put you through and the promises they made you break. It's a sad state of affairs really, how you felt you could never share these secrets with anyone, not even the one person you should...and all because of that bloody mark...

Suddenly you jerk in your sleep, your hands clenching into fists as the marks burn red on the tops of your hands. I step slowly over to you – do you even have the mark anymore – I wonder. Does it still plague you so? Part of me thinks it has yet to make its dent on you again, it always had a bad habit of only revealing itself when you stumbled across something you shouldn't. It made you think you were a traitor. But I guess that's where The Eye dug its foot in, it too played its part in making you believe you were a Brethren Betrayer. I continue to watch as your face scrunches up and writhes in pain. It is as though your head is about to burst into a million pieces, like the pressure has once again become too much for you to handle.

It isn't long before you relax again and fall back into a softer sleep. I wonder if your dreaming of her, the her that is standing right next to me looking just as worried as I. She sits by your side, reaching a hand out and resting it above your face, unable to touch you as she longs to. I wonder if, like me, she is as much a part of your world as she is mine...or is she just part of my world where she must remain forever. She is of course dead in body but if her soul didn't die and she remained here then perhaps there was a chance that...no at least not in this world. Things would be simpler if she stayed dead at least, at least then she would be safe from all the heartbreak of our world, so much of which she had already endured in her life before death.

A weird sensation swamped me as Dante walked straight through me, stopping just before your bed. Having someone pass straight through me was an odd feeling, it was like being sick only the feeling itself was short lived. One minute the urge to hurl is there and the next it's gone, like it was never there in the first place. It was cold and hazy...but then I suppose I wasn't part of their world yet.

I watched as she rose back up from the chair and Dante took it over. He looked over you with concerned eyes, cocking his head to the side as though he were looking right at her. Next, he looked to me, staring into my very soul. Could he see us? It wasn't surprising if he could – after all he had been a part of our world for so long he probably still had some form of connection.

"I feel your pain," he said, still looking right at me. "The sorrow of having to watch those you love without them taking a second glance at you. But it won't be long now, you'll be here again soon."

Looking back at you, he rose to his feet again and promptly left the room. She remained by your side, but I was still shocked at how someone from your world could see us, could connect with us. But was he right, would we soon return to your world? I could only hope and pray, for part of me feared that the call of the shadows was too strong and soon I would be back in that dead world of rotting flesh and darkness.

# CHAPTER 22 - VOICES IN THE DARK

Ash spurted from the ground like a geyser, fumes enveloping the grey around him. Tristan was crouched on the floor next to a crater that had opened in the ground where the ash rained down from. He looked up, a stinging sensation itching his eyes as he did so and making the hairs on the back of his neck stand on end. Struggling to his feet, he noticed a dark figure through the smoke. Squinting slightly, he could just about make out a man; about his height and with short hair. Something about him was familiar though, it was in the way he stood tall and proud, that way he held himself so majestically like a leader watching over his troops on the battlefield as the enemy rallies its troops on the horizon.

Taking his eyes off the stranger for a moment, Tristan surveyed his surroundings, noting the sheer deadness of everything; from the spindly trees that rose above him to the hay like grassland which he stood on. Even the birds that flew overhead were skeletal in their being and were like no birds he had ever seen before. Something stirred behind him and he looked back to see a black cloak of some form disappear behind a tree. Looking back towards the figure he saw him brace himself before diving into the geyser like it were some form of escape. The action itself startled Tristan, unsettling him greatly - so much so he almost didn't notice the Fader that was stood right behind him reaching out to touch...

Turning just in time to see its ghastly shadow, Tristan jumped back away from the Fader, it's snarling sending a ringing noise through his ears. It grabbed again, forcing Tristan closer to the edge of the crater, his foot balancing right on the edge. Now he saw why the figure jumped, because there was no escape and death was the only escape at the bottom of that crater. But then if this was a Fader before him then he was in a place worse than death. He didn't have time to consider his options as the Fader grabbed at him again. This time though his balance wasn't enough to save him and he fell clumsily into the crater, the smoke enveloping him.

The wooden flooring hit hard as Tristan collided with the floor. It had felt like he had been falling forever; the rush of it all had begun to feel boring and despite the tough landing he was rather glad to be back on the ground. Stiffly, he rose to his feet, scratching sawdust from his hair as he did so. He wasn't sure where he was, it wasn't a place he recognised in the slightest; it was just a square wooden room with five beds sprawled around with some desks and a bookshelf. Deciding it was probably irrelevant anyway, he headed for the door, surprised to find that he passed straight through it as though he were a ghost. It was rather a satisfying feeling. It made him feel on top of the world; but that too showed his immaturity. Pushing that thought to the back of his mind, he pressed on down the corridor he now found himself in. As he seemed to near the end of it, he could hear shouts and cries. The air around him began to feel hot and sticky making it hard to breathe. His vision became hazy, a reddish tinge eating away at the colour. Pressing on forwards, he came to an atrium covered in smoke which surprisingly didn't obscure him further. Then again, his presence in this world was more ghostly than real so it was no surprise. People were running about everywhere, some passing right through Tristan and others disappearing on the spot. And then, someone appeared at the head of the room. Amid people running to escape it seemed strange for someone to be coming into the building, especially when that person was him.

A younger him that is, maybe by about three years. He was little more rugged round the edges but was no different from what you'd expect. There was something different about his demeanour though, it was the way he walking through the smoke recklessly, like he had nothing left to lose. He followed himself down another corridor and past the faces of many a fading Keeper. They walked past without fear, his own mission already clear to him as he turned and stopped before a door, the plaque above it identifying it as 'The Reading Room'.

And then it struck him, he was in the Keeper Compound at Hasaghar, watching his own fall from grace come flying back to him with brute force. He tried to shout to himself, warning him not to go any further; to turn back and go back to his daughter. But his shouting fell upon deaf ears and all he could do was watch himself enter the room and fall once more.


*The room that opened out before them was circular in shape, giant pillars stretching up to the top of the room to a glass ceiling which was probably on the verge of smashing into a million pieces. Arches stretched out from the columns forming platforms where the Keepers would stand to hear the prophecies be read at the podium which stood opposite them, a man stood behind it staring menacingly at them. Without even knowing who he was, the man seemed to strike fear into Tristan's very core. He stood tall and imposing, a striking figure with dark hair that was swept back to the base of his neck. His face was well chiselled and cleanly shaven with eyes that were almost red in colour. A green robe covered his stocky body and flowed behind him as he stepped down from the podium to face Tristan.*

*"I was beginning to think you would not come!" The man observed, looking down on Tristan through slitted eyes. "Tell me, does the destruction enthral you?" His voice was*

*well pronounced and had an air of greatness to it, as though a great many men respected him.*

*"You son of a bitch!" Tristan heard himself say, standing tall and strong against his foe.*

*"You'll never win Charles, not whilst Union stands strong."*

*"But alas, Romeo is dead so Union is broken. How are you supposed to take Dharsi down without your fellow Brothers?"*

*"And for that you will pay!"*

*Tristan launched himself forward, striking his sword in Charles' direction who parried the blow pulling his own sword out of nowhere. A series of blows followed, sparks flying as metal clashed with metal, neither seeming to gain the upper hand. It was clear to see neither were good swordsmen but they were trying none the less. But Tristan wasn't exactly your conventional fighter and finding his advantage he forced himself against Charles, pushing him up against the wall and causing him to lose the grip on his sword.*

*The rest of what happened seem to play out in slow motion in which Tristan watched himself gain the upper hand, throwing Charles to the floor and standing over him, his sword poised high above his head ready to strike down into his heart. But if you think that Tristan is the winner here then that's where this story disappoints. You see in this story good does not always prevail for evil is just around the corner. Light will never beat dark, instead they face an endless chase in which neither will win. When Light gets to dark, it is already running, darkness is always out of reach and at the end of Light, Darkness envelopes all.*

*Tristan watched as he saw himself stop in mid strike, the look on his face turning to one of torment and pain. The grip on his sword relented and it fell to the ground, clanging as it landed. Tristan fell with it, something invisible striking him to the floor in a sprawled mess of tangled limps. His eyes didn't even close as he lost his fight with whatever struck him and Charles rose to stand over him. A darkened figure came to stand beside him. It wasn't darkened in the sense that there was no light to see him clearly, it was darkened as though the figure itself had been removed from his mind, erased almost. The most he could tell was a man, and a man that he felt was familiar. As the vision faded the last words of the men stuck in his mind, even the voice of this other man seemed blurry; unidentifiable almost.*

*"Took your time, didn't you?" Goaded Charles.*

*"So many things to do...so little time," the man said. "Patience, great father, is a virtue."*

The words 'great father' stood out in Tristan's mind as he fell back into the bed in the dorms he was staying in. They weren't parental in the term, it was more like it was a title, an epithet that gave his name meaning. From what he remembered about Dharsi their leader was known as the Herasin or the father and if he was to take the figure's words literally it meant Charles was the father; the leader of Dharsi. What was also clear was that Charles was not the reason he did not remember. He may have been part of it but he wasn't the sole reason and perhaps that was why the figure was darkened. The darkened figure was who he had to remember for all of it to make sense, for all of it to come back.

# CHAPTER 23 - DANCING IN THE RAIN

Tristan awoke with a start, his heart thudding in his chest and his breathing coming in rasps. He calmed himself, taking in his surroundings.  The room he found himself in was like the one in his dream only with a slightly different layout. Getting to his feet, he straightened up and headed for the door once he saw that no one else was there with him. He headed through the corridor and down the stairs back into the atrium. He wasn't sure where he was going, he was just following his feet just as he always seemed to do these days. Proceeding down the opposite corridor to the bottom he came to another room. Torches emblazoned the room he came to filled with books so alive they made every mahogany shelf sparkle and the parquet flooring shine. Of all the places within this Compound, the Library must have been the only place Nielson maintained over the years. Then again, what was a Keeper Scriberium without its books?

The library truly was a magnificent sight to behold. Even the scattered strewn books on the desks ahead of him seemed to have a purpose and place in their blankness. A staircase spiralled upwards, leading to three further floors filled with more books and desks of which to study them at. Stepping up to the table, he flicked through a couple of the pages, each displaying the same emptiness.

"They have become unwritten," sighed a voice. Tristan looked up to see its owner descend from the gleaming stairs above in the shape of Dante. "The worst fears the Keepers ever had took place right before their eyes. I can't imagine the fear they must have felt."

"I can't either," Tristan replied, his eyes still in awe of the library as though he were looking upon it for the first time.

"How are you feeling?"

"Good, just a little hazy."

"Shouldn't drink so much then!"

"Very funny!"

Pulling up a chair, Dante sat with the back facing forward so that he could rest his head on the top of his arms.

"What's the matter?" Tristan asked, taking note of his disheartened stance. Something was definitely bothering him but he wasn't sure what.

"What do you mean?" answered Dante, shrugging off the question. "Nothing's wrong with me it's just..."

"Just what?"

"Tristan, I have to tell you something. Come take a seat."

Tristan took a seat on the opposite side of the table noting how Dante's face seemed to be fighting with his thoughts over something. Half of him suspected he knew what he was about to say but the other half was still doubtful and remained utterly clueless.

"Tristan I uh...there's something I've been meaning to tell you but I just could never find the words. I can't do that now to be honest..."

"Dante just say it!"

"Okay...it's about Dagnen...she's uh..."

"Your granddaughter?"

Dante was silent but his eyes were wide like a deer when it realises the hunter has found it hiding behind its bush.

"How did you know?" he said at last, his voice aghast.

"Nielson...he used to talk about you all the time. Well not you but this brother that he lost, he never actually used your name but that's not the point. When he found out who we were he told us that we had to be there for each other at all times. He said he'd learnt that the hard way, he let his brother down and lost him forever. He never gave us the details. Not to mention the fact that you and Dagnen, before she married me, both have the same last name and what with Nielson being her uncle."

"Clever!"

"Simple really."

"I guess so. So, it doesn't change anything then?"

"Well no! You're family aren't you technically...so it changes nothing? If anything, it gives you more of a reason to be on this journey with me."

"...thank you I guess..."

"Don't worry about it."

A moments silence passed.

"You should tell him...tell Nielson that you're not this idiot Daxon..."

"Idiot?"

"You tell me...I don't know anyone called Daxon."

The two shared a hearty chuckle and Dante seemed to relax for the first time since he'd met Tristan.

"He didn't even recognise me." Dante sighed as the moment passed.

"He did, I could see it in his eyes." Tristan reassured, tilting his head to one side.

"You reckon?"

As Tristan nodded, a loud bang erupted from outside of the library. Both of them jumped up from their seats and ran from the library to see what all the commotion was about. Rushing into the atrium, they saw a shadow tumbling over a chair which was now on its back on the floor. Bringing light into the room with a single flick of his fingers, Dante rounded on the intruder clutching at the knife that rested in his belt. Tristan followed behind a few paces, bracing himself. As the man looked up though he realised he had nothing to fear.

"Basso?" Tristan exclaimed in disbelief.

"Tristan," He sounded in as much disbelief as Tristan in truth.

"What are you doing here?"

"I decided you were right; I should be here."

"John Basso!" exclaimed another voice as Merlin and Nielson came into the room.

"Nielson Ashdown my old friend."

Basso embraced him in a brotherly grasp the two laughing as they did so. Merlin greeted him in the same way, it was a greeting Dante would probably have been jealous of and wished it was the kind of greeting he had shared with his brother by blood. Tristan looked to him now to notice he had turned away from them, remorse coating his eyes in a fine liquid ready to leak. He nodded before making his way to the doors and out of the Compound.

Once the formalities were over, Basso turned to Tristan and shook his hand, smiling as he did so.

"Where'd your friend go?" he asked, Tristan turning to where Dante had been standing. "I swear he was just stood there."

"Oh, you mean Daxon," answered Tristan, trying to come up with something to say as to his whereabouts.

"Yes, where did Daxon go?" Asked Nielson, Merlin widening his eyes behind him. A look of concern tainted the suspicious look on Nielson's face, making Tristan believe he had an ulterior motive for wanting to know.

"He umm...he lost his brother recently," it was mostly true. "It's partly why he's here with me, to get some space."

"'tis a hard thing to lose a brother," Nielson consoled. "It is best just to leave him to it; he will come round eventually."

Tristan nodded, following Nielson as he let them all into the dining hall near the barracks. Hours later; long after Merlin and the others had finished catching up and decided to bed down for the night, Tristan had finally found Dante lurking in a public house near the fountain in the centre of town. Truth be told, it should've been the first place to look as opposed to the vast open spaces around town he had been searching. Dante, as expected was sat at the bar hunched over a full tankard of ale. A couple of other people were scattered around a table in the corner but it was nothing to warrant a second barman. The only barman in sight was a much older man who leant against the back wall next to the entrance to the cellar twiddling a piece of barley between his fingers.

The bar itself was a dingy affair, a shabby old thing that was probably quite cosy in its time but was now a place the poor people of this town had forgotten, hence why the only table of punters were city guards. In one corner of the room was a podium where metal stands stood which probably at one point or another held musical instruments of some sort. Just down from there was something covered in a large sheet coated in a thick layer of dust. He wasn't sure what was underneath it but it was probably nothing worth him worrying about. Something that was worrying him was how ghostly this public house seemed, it was like someone was trying to tell him something about this place but they were talking so loudly their echoes were reverberating off the wooden walls making it impossible for him to hear what they were saying. He came to sit beside Dante, clapping him on the shoulder as he did so.

"What'll it be my friend?" The barman offered, the piece of barley now hanging from his mouth.

"A beer please sir." Tristan requested, flipping a gold coin onto the table.

"Coming right up." The barman turned away down into the cellar. Obviously, a wheat beer wasn't something that was commonly ordered here.

"You okay?" he turned to Dante.

"I'm fine I just..." Dante sighed.

"Just what?"

"I just couldn't stand that Basso getting the greeting I should have. I told you he doesn't even recognise me! What did you tell them anyway?"

"Tell them?"

"You're telling me they didn't even notice I was gone?"

"Oh, Basso did and then Nielson asked where you'd gone. I told him you'd lost a brother recently...it's kind of true I guess."

"Here we are, one wheat beer for ya!" exclaimed the barman, pouring some of a flagon into a tankard in front of Tristan. "Sorry about the wait, it don't get ordered as much here now there's no Keepers. In fact, you guys are the first Keepers I've seen in these here parts in over three years."

"Really?" questioned Dante, half wondering how he could tell they were Keepers.

"Well yeah! About three years ago there was this...uh...to be honest, I don't know what happened but they all disappeared and that Compound just crumbled. I mean there's probably still some of them there. I've seen those lights that come on at night in there every now and then."

"What do you think happened to them?"

"Oh, I don't know, I know what they tell the children here."

"What like ghost stories?"

"Precisely. You see, this here town is ruled by a Baron called Hagen..."

"Hagen?" Tristan questioned; the name sounded familiar to him but he couldn't figure out why.

"Yes! They say he is a Keeper but they say that he ain't a good one."

"So, he's a traitor?" Dante confirmed.

"So they say. Anyway, when the Keepers disappeared, he was all too quick to step up to the plate. Some folk said that he was the one that sent them all away with scary shadows that had no faces just these red beady eyes. Now if that don't sound scary, I don't know what does."

"So, this Baron, he's the reason this town has hit the shit?"

"Precisely, I mean you're new here my friend so you won't know but Tristan here..."

"What?" Tristan spurted, confused suddenly as to how the man knew who he was.

"You remember what this place was like surely. It was full of free spirits, fine wine and high-end fashion. Folk did what they wanted when they wanted. They enjoyed their jobs and they were happy. The Keepers dealt with all the political stuff and hey, that was life and it was bliss. The problem was, or is for that matter, that we've lived so long with the Keepers we've forgotten how to live without them. We've relied on them all these years and now we have to rely on ourselves. That's why folk left this here place...they left to find the Keepers."

"And did they?" asked Dante, taking a sip of his ale.

"They must've done, they never came back. Those that stayed here are those who have families too old to move. There are even some folk here that believe one day the Keepers will return to Dilu. I guess we were right!"

"Hey Frankie, any chance of some drinks around here?" shouted one of the guards at the table. "Any more waiting we'll have to serve ourselves!"

One of the other guards muttered something unheard to them but whatever it was it made the others laugh loudly. It was probably some snide remark of some sort. Frankie sighed heavily, apologising to Tristan and Dante as he poured some more drinks for the guards.

"Do you know him then?" Dante asked once Frankie was out of earshot.

"I don't know," Tristan said bemused. "I must do I just don't remember."

"Must do."

"Sorry about that gents, but I can't afford to turn away the custom." apologised Frankie as he came over to join them once again.

"It's okay, we understand." Dante consoled as he topped up their drinks.

"Frankie, could you tell me something?" Tristan asked.

"Of course, anything."

"This Hagen character, what's his propose for being here in Dilu? I mean why Dilu?"

"Well, some say what with him being a Keeper and all, that he was here before."

"Before?"

"You know when you were here as a Scribe. Going on nearly five, maybe six years now maybe more. I don't know if it is the same man but it could be."

"And where does he...rule this place from?" Dante asked, curiosity getting the better of him.

"There's an estate with a tower just outside of town. He lives there with his lady and all his servants. God knows what they see in him. Then again, I hear he pays well and that's probably the reason they all stick around. I reckon if he died, they'd all just fade into the backdrop."

A man came to the bar and Frankie went over to him, their conversation just out of earshot of Tristan and Dante. Tristan wasn't concerned with the other conversation though; he was concerned with whoever was arguing with themselves behind him. Looking behind him out of the corner of his eye, he saw no one except the guards at the table and they were nowhere near close enough to hear.

"A woman?" the voice said. "She wouldn't have gone with him she wouldn't!" He must have been referring to this lady who resided with Hagen. But either way, whoever she was, why did it matter?

"Thanks for that Monty," Frankie said coming back to the bar. "See ya later!"

"Frankie who is this lady that lives with Hagen?" Tristan asked when he came back over.

"I don't think she's there out of choice to be honest with ya. We never really see her unless it's at events like the seasonal formals and folk like us can't afford that. All I knows is her name...Myrina; means sacred in Salysman."

*Myrina.* The name niggled somewhere in his mind making his head pang with pain. He could hear Dante and Frankie talking amongst themselves, distracting his attention from focusing on whatever was niggling at his mind. Shaking the thought from his head his eyes were caught by a woman standing by the podium. She was just stood there staring at him and when she noticed he was staring back she looked to whatever the sheet was covering next to her. Looking her up and down, he realised who she was; Dagnen - which probably answered for why her appearance there seemed ghostly. Her brown hair was parted at the sides of her ears, a green and brown smock dress clothing her. It wasn't a dress she'd been wearing in any of the photos Tristan had found of her and them together so he couldn't associate the way she looked with a memory. *But she kept looking at the sheet...*

"What's under that sheet?" he asked without turning back to look at Frankie or Dante.

"Oh that, it's just a piano," shrugged Frankie. "It's not been played in years but I just can't bring myself to sell it like everything else that were in here."

"Why not?" as he asked, Tristan rose from his seat to walk over to where she was standing.

"There used to be a girl who would play it, Dagnen her name was you should remember. Anyway, she used to play at it, the locals loved her music. The place was always so calm and happy when she would play that I just couldn't get rid of it."

Pulling at the sheet, a cloud of dust shrouded the room as the fine organ was revealed, the veneer finish shining beautifully. The sight marvelled Tristan and he watched as Dagnen sat at the cushioned stool. No dust settled on the keys or anywhere on the piano so he sat beside her and lifted the cover that protected the keys. The white and black keys seem to speak to him and tell him the tune to play as did her hands as she motioned the movements he should make. Starting a few keys down, he began to mirror her movements, a sweet lullaby of a tune radiating from his fingers as he pressed down gently on the keys. He smiled as he went, realising it was the same tune the music box played.

Dante too felt peace in the melody he was playing, staring into his ale as though all of his problems were drowning within it. He almost didn't notice Tristan walking out of the bar in a daze almost and staring out at the sudden outburst of rain.

"Well what 'ya know, I ant seen rain in these here parts in as long as I ant seen the Keepers."

Frankie's words bought him away from his thoughts long enough to notice Tristan standing on the deck outside. By the time he got up to stand with him Tristan was already prancing around in the rain as though he were dancing with an invisible maiden.

"Tristan," he called out, remaining under the shelter of the deck. "What are you doing?"

"Dancing in the rain!" Was his reply, the glee in his voice seeming to block out the darkness.

"But why?"

"That's life...learning to dance in the rain..."

Shaking his head in wonderment, Dante watched him prance in happiness. In that single moment, he saw Tristan differently and the life he was remembering. It was a life filled with happiness and simple pleasures, a life he once shared with his own sweetheart. Tristan was right, life wasn't about waiting for the storm to pass, it was about learning to dance in the rain.

# CHAPTER 24 - THE SHRINE OF UNITY

The next morning Tristan woke in an elated mood, however Dante didn't look like he had slept much. The two nodded to each other as Tristan washed and dressed before they headed down to the Dining Hall for some breakfast. "Tristan I've been thinking," Nielson said after they had all finished eating.

"Merlin's told me about some of the lessons he's been giving you about your past, is that correct?"

"Yes," replied Tristan. "He's been teaching me about the History of the Keepers, just like you used to."

"No magic then?" Basso questioned, chewing on the pulp of an orange.

"No, my marks only came back a few weeks ago so that would probably have been a bit premature."

"Well, I was your teacher in magical Glyphs and Runes so why don't we have a few lessons? See if we can get that old brain of yours ticking?"

"Okay, sounds good!"

"Shall we say noon in that old classroom then? Gives me chance to spruce it up a little that way. Merlin can join in if he wishes and your welcome too...Daxon."

"I think I'll pass!" replied Dante, shrugging off the offer.

"Suit yourself. I'll see you there Tristan."

Getting up from the table, Basso left the dining hall as Merlin and Nielson began cleaning up the plates.

"I'm surprised he didn't try to convince you to join in," joked Tristan to Dante.

"To be honest I don't think he has a good feeling about me," Dante said perplexed. "Then again I suppose the feeling's mutual."

The two of them shared a look. Why Dante didn't trust him Tristan had no idea. All he knew was that when he shared eye contact with Basso, his head filled with screams and a shiver ran down his spine as though the man struck him with instant fear. If there was one thing his father had taught him it was to always go with his gut and his gut did not like Basso as harmless as he seemed to be.

"After your lesson meet me in our dormitory," Dante ordered. "There's something I have to show you."

Another look was shared, despite the vast age gap and personality differences, the two always seemed to be on the same level when it came to understanding each other without the need for words. Dante brushed himself down and then left the dining hall, probably to spend the morning in a pub somewhere no doubt.

Later that day, as agreed, Tristan met with Basso in the classroom just opposite the library. He was thankful to see Nielson also in the room as well, not trusting the man this was a welcome relief. The classroom had definitely seen better days, especially with the state of the scratched chalkboard. It was clear Basso had done his best to put the room into some order but even with the desks all pushed to the sides of the room and a longer one placed in front of the board, it wasn't a vast improvement to the room.

"Good to see you Tristan," Basso said, taking him by the hand briefly. "I hope you don't mind but Nielson has decided to sit in on this session?"

"No, that's fine." Tristan shrugged, pulling up a chair and taking a seat.

"Okay, then we'll begin. We'll start with some basics..."

"I hope you don't mind Basso," Nielson interrupted causing a certain hacked off look on Basso's face but he nodded in approval anyway. "How about we see what Tristan remembers about Glyphs and how we use them."

Again Basso nodded, shrugging his shoulders and leaning against the table, probably feeling a little useless now. Feeling the pressure, Tristan sat back - truth be told he didn't remember that much at all about the Glyphs, just how to use them. He gulped, peering up at Nielson who winked at him hoping to reassure him not to worry.

"To be honest I don't remember much at all," Tristan begun, making Basso smirk. "But I do remember the start of your first ever lesson."

"Well let's start with that!" inclined Nielson, seeming to take more of an interest in Tristan's current memory than Basso.

"I remember Basso saying the Glyphs are all around us. They are what make the world the way it is. They control everything from the direction in which the wind blows to the colours of the flowers in the Spring. They are essentially nature!"

"Excellent!" exclaimed Basso, a little surprised if anything. "Almost as though those were my exact words..."

"Guess it proves how much I'm remembering." Tristan could sense his tone and it wasn't a nice one so his response was with the same likeness.

"Alright then Mr Cocky, how about you show us how much you really remember?"

"Alright then!" Tristan was mocking him now - Dante would've loved to have seen what he was about to do.

Tristan stood up from his chair, making it move aside without even touching it. Clearly, he was showing off and it was clear as crystal that Basso was seething underneath his cool composure. Nielson on the other hand, grinned shaking his head as though he expected nothing less.

"I remember something Nielson told me," Tristan explained. "Just because it's happening up here," He pointed to his head, "Doesn't mean it can't happen out there."

"Show me fire," Basso demanded, ignoring his sarky comment.

Smiling cheekily, Tristan held his fists out before him. With his right hand, he pointed up with his index finger, a flicker of flame sprouting from it. His left hand he opened out and spread his fingers wide, a vast flame roaring from the centre of his palm.

"Which would you prefer?" he asked rhetorically, a devilish smile bringing life to his face. Truth be told he didn't know where any of this magic was coming from but it was certainly having the desired effect on Basso.

"Show me water." came Basso's demands again; clearly he wasn't going to give up seeing whether Tristan would fail anytime soon.

Again, Tristan obliged, in the same attitude he had done with the fire. Tracing along with his finger, he drew water in a line. Time and time again he made Basso even angrier, displaying the rest of the elements along with a couple of moving objects for added effect. When at last it seemed that Basso had had enough, he stormed from the room without saying a word, an almost worried look on his face.

"What did I do?" asked Tristan, coming down from his showing off high all of the sudden.

"I'm not too sure to be honest with you," Nielson was indeed confused by his behaviour too. "But if you don't mind, I wish to do a little demonstration. Pull up a chair at the desk and take a seat Tristan."

Nielson took the vase of the windowsill; it was nothing special just a plain porcelain vase of no colour worth noting. He placed it on the desk in front of Tristan.

"Break the vase," Nielson ordered. "And then put it back together again."

Tristan nodded, focusing on the vase. Within seconds, he had caused it to smash to pieces. A couple more passed and he put it back together again; piece by piece so that it didn't even look like it had broken in the first place.

"Excellent, now tell me how you did it." Nielson commanded, a commendable smile upon his face.

"I don't know," Tristan was telling the truth, he honestly didn't know how he did it. "I just pictured it happening and then it happened, I can't explain it."

"Wrong, that is what you can do." Noting Tristan's confused look he decided to fill in the blanks himself. "As a Keeper you passed through three of our stages. You started as a Scribe, progressed to become an Acolyte and then you became what you are now; a Runebound. There are other stages but I'm sure Merlin covered that much. Anyway, a Scribe does not learn how to use the Glyphs but they learn that they are there. An Acolyte learns how to call upon the Glyphs in their hour of need and a Runebound can manipulate and make the Glyphs work for them to their advantage. The difference between an Acolyte and a Runebound is the latter of the two doesn't have to find and draw upon the symbol they need...they simply picture it in their mind and it is there.

"When you were first inducted as a Runebound this would've been the first trick you learnt. You would've learnt to sense the Glyphs around the vase, put them to one side and then find the cracks within the vase and force the Glyphs into the cracks so that it smashes. In doing so you would have changed the purpose of whatever Glyphs are around you to do what you want them to do. You do the same to put it back together again."

"It sounds pretty amazing when you put it like that."

"Well as a Keeper, it is important that we remember that it is not the Glyphs that control us but we who control the Glyphs. If we do not remember that I guess we already forgot because the worst has happened in what you see around you."

"I see!" Tristan's head was beginning to feel heavy with exertion and Nielson could tell.

"I think that's enough for today, don't you? Why don't you go get some rest?"

Tristan nodded, rising from his feet and bidding Nielson good day, leaving the classroom to head back to the dormitory where Dante would probably be waiting for him.


Back in the dormitory, Tristan found Dante dosing on his bed against the wall by the bookcase. The slamming of the door bought him around and he sat up, leaning against the wall and yawning.

"How did it go?" he asked, only half interested but it was the courtesy really.

"I put Basso in his place," smirked Tristan. "He stormed out of the room after I did every trick he asked of me and more."

"That's my boy!" Getting up from the bed, he clasped Tristan tightly on the shoulder in congratulations.

As Dante let go, a light flashed across Tristan's vision over by the bookcase. He pursed his lips, a pang of suspicion suddenly taking over his senses. He strolled over to the bookcase and glanced at the spines of the books. Tristan wondered if they were unwritten like those in the library but one in particular seemed different. He pulled on the book, but it didn't leave its place on the shelf, instead part of the wall near the window began to move aside to reveal a small alcove with a staircase.

"After you," Dante motioned with his hand for Tristan to lead and he followed behind as though he had been waiting for him to reveal the passageway the whole time.

At the bottom of the passage that opened in front of them of them was a dark oak staircase which they descended into a dark hallway with no apparent source of light. Wishing he had bought a torch down with them, Tristan took a few tentative steps into the unknown, not even sure whether Dante was still following. After a couple of steps, a strange noise filled the darkness and suddenly flame torches emblazoned along a wood floored pathway that led in between several rows of bookcases.

"What is this place?" Tristan asked, suddenly very confused as to how he got here.

"Tristan," Dante said, stepping into the lead and presenting the sight before them. "I give you The Shrine of Union. The place itself is enigmatic meaning it can be accessed from any Compound. How you ask, by the Scribe passages; a series of passages created by the second generation who were the ones who built the Shrine in the first place. The passages were sealed away after every generation was disbanded but each new one has managed to reopen them."

"That's impressive!"

"And now that we're here..." Dante headed down the centre passageway and then to the left side bookcases around the blue flame. Coming to the last shelf, he sat on the floor at the end of the row, following with his finger across the numeric titles on the spines. "Now it's pretty clear that we can't act out and make you remember everything that you did as a Keeper and that is where these handy little books come in."

"Little?"

"You see the ally doesn't just help the Brothers of Union on their way," Dante continued ignoring the comment. "They compile the annals of that generation so that their legacy is preserved long after they are gone. I thought maybe they would help fill in the blanks. At least I would...but they're not fucking here!"

"What are you looking for?"

"Your Annals...they would have been written by your ally."

"Cedric?"

"Yes. They tell of your legacy as a Brother of Union."

"I have those!"

Dante stood and turned slowly, a puzzled look on his face.

"How do you have them; I mean those books can't leave this library?"

"Well they did. They were in a box of things that came back to Az Lagní with me. My father gave them to me before we left."

Dropping his arms against his side in annoyance, he sighed. His brilliant idea had turned out not so brilliant after all.

"Written in those books," explained Dante as he finally came over to him - "Is everything you and your brothers did as Keepers, well everything you did that Cedric knows about anyway. They should help and that was what I was going to show you!"

"I guess it's the thought that counts."

Tristan shrugged and took a seat at one of the desks, an open book upon it. Dante had looked over in time to see Tristan go very pale. When he called out to him, no answer came, instead his eyes just widened like a wild rabid dog's. A burning sensation in his left hand, causing his head to pang with pain. Staring at his palm, a strange mark appeared before becoming part of his skin, concealing itself within the lines on his palm. The mark itself was one Tristan recognised instantly, the word 'Betrayer' echoing in his mind. His heart began to thud in his chest, his breathing heaving as he struggled to catch it. As he looked away from his palm, a figure appeared near the blue flame. The figure resembled the scarred version of himself he had seen back at his house. Once again, the scars were less than before but this time they seemed to resonate around a symbol which was scratched into his chest, the same symbol of Betrayal which had appeared on his own palm.

Concerned now, Dante came back to stand in front of Tristan to see his eyes fall into the back of his skull leaving only the whites visible. Slipping from the chair, he hit the floor and began to fit in a seizure of pain and breathlessness. The sight shocked Dante and pained him too as he could not do anything except try to stop him hurting himself in his twisted torment. As he held Tristan steady, he whispered words of encouragement, begging him to come back into the light, a single tear leaking from his worried eyes. Eventually, the fitting subsided and Tristan lay still, his eyes slowly closing as his heartbeat steadied. Dante sat with him, waiting for him to wake, hoping to God that whatever he was remembering was an easy memory and not something that would rip out his soul, especially after the struggle he had just witnessed him experience.

# CHAPTER 25 - THE BEARER OF SECRETS

When at last Tristan awoke it was like he had stepped out of his body, every effort to lift himself from the ground feeling weightless and almost ghostly. He wasn't sure where he was; it was a courtyard of some sort of which was overlooked by an ornate balcony connected to a large building. The room beyond the balcony was well lit, the flames of the torches visible in their dancing shadows and Tristan could just about make out dark wood bookcases as he rose to his feet. Looking down on himself as he brushed away invisible dust, he thought he seemed grey; his once brown tunic and leggings now a dusky colour. Even his skin seemed dull in the lack of light but then maybe that suggested that whatever world he was in he was just passing through. The world around him seemed so full of colour it felt odd to contrast against it as he did. As he scanned his eyes over the greenery and hedgerow with its surrounding masonry wall draped in climbing ivy, voices fluttered to his ears. For a split moment he thought he should hide, but considering how familiar and ghostly this world seemed, he decided to remain where he stood. The voices themselves sounded worried and scared. A man was shouting and another was trying to calm him down.

"Why can't we move now?" exclaimed the more scared voice. "I swear they're onto me by now."

"You need to stop worrying brother," the other voice cajoled.

The other voice seemed to be consoling him, and Tristan could just see him hushing his brother, dragging him into a corner where they would not be overheard. He took a couple of steps forward to hear what they were saying and get a better look. The figures seemed familiar to him; the first he saw was a very round man with a white tunic making him look fatter still. A leather waistcoat clung to his shoulders and barely reached the middle of his back with a large belt rested around his large middle and brown trousers covered his stocky legs with cloth soled shoes. His head was bald and his face chubby. The other man was exactly the opposite of him; an image of pure class. Thin and tall he stood with an air of glamour about him. How the two could potentially be brothers was beyond Tristan. This other man was dressed in a long black and grey robe that was split at the middle leaving black leggings visible, boots of a matching colour reaching his knees. His short hair was a dark grey and a stylised beard and moustache framed his chiselled jaw.

"But what if they find out what I did," the fat man kept shouting. "What if they catch us out before we even get to do it?"

"Boris..." *Boris?* "You need to calm down, I'm sure Herasin has everything in order. But you need to keep your voice down, someone might hear us..."

"Hagen is right!" *Hagen?* "We wouldn't want anybody to know what we were up to now would we?" The question was quite obviously rhetorical and spoken by a man Tristan had seen all too recently stepping into view. It was Charles, the man from his most recent memory of his own fall. "Now will you please pipe down, there is someone I would like to...reintroduce you to..."

"Meet our newest recruit!" Charles stated.

Through the gap in the banisters, Tristan could just about make out a shadow stepping forward. He couldn't make out much of its appearance, however he could tell the man was tall and stood as though people bowed down to him wherever he went. The word pompous came to mind.

"Hello gentlemen!" The voice was deep and raspy; one of those that women find insanely seductive and attractive, well pronounced and defined.

"You?" Boris cursed, spitting as he did so as though of all people, he least expected it to be who it was.

"Don't tell me you don't recognise me?" Said the voice again. "My brother was a good...friend of yours."

"How is he supposed to help us?" asked Hagen exasperated.

"Perhaps you might remember him as our pawn in the shadows...our light in the dark. My brothers this is how we win our war." Charles explained.


As the vision began to fade, his left palm tingled but he wasn't sure why. A new image formed, now he was in a narrow corridor standing beside...himself. He watched himself in colour, listening. He looked more tired than usual, dark circles under his eyes and a bandage wrapped around his left hand. He braced himself all of the sudden, two men shoving each other into the wall next to where he stood. Strangely, they seemed not to notice Tristan at all...unless the Brothers of Union had a way for concealing themselves from other Keepers.

"I said hush!" The two men grappled with each other, the thinner of the two was pushed up against the wall by a shadowed figure indescribable in features due to the darkness. It was much like the figure that had stood beside Charles when Tristan lost his memory. The man he held up was Hagen and he didn't look happy with him. "How dare you question my methods?" he yelled, again his voice unidentifiable.

"All I said was..." Hagen squirmed in his grasp.

"I don't care what you said...if Herasin trusts me then so should you. My methods are my methods and I won't have you question them. I will have my revenge whether the Herasin wants it or not. And if you stand in my way...you will only join them in time."

Again, his hand prickled as the vision faded only this time it was more painful and caused a ringing in his ears. He shut his eyes tight, the scene around him changing again. The pain became unbearable and he crumbled to the floor, clasping his hands over his ears as the ringing deafened him further. He screamed out, his knees landing hard on a wood surface floor as his head hit the deck, the pain and ringing subsiding momentarily. In its absence he looked up, looking around to find himself in a brilliantly coloured cathedral. Echoes of a voice reached him where he crouched making the ringing come back.

Through his scrunched-up vision, he saw a group of five men appear in the centre of the atrium looking up to the top of a huge hammer statue with something that glinted on the top. As the echoes of the voice cleared, he could hear what it was saying.

"Comes a man to rescue me," it chanted in a deep bellowing voice. "Comes a man who thinks himself worthy of me."

He could see one of the figures reach up and touch their head as though something pained them, one of them turning to him to see if he were okay. It was then that he realised the figures were him and his brothers but what they were doing here in this cathedral was unknown to him.

"Comes my vessel, my own storm." Came the chanting again. "Cry Brethren Cry, for the Betrayer hath cometh!"

As the chanting stopped, the pain became even worse, his head literally feeling like it was going to burst. The chanting began to echo in his mind until through the gaps in his eyelashes he could see a blinding light.

"Tell me, will your brethren cry," the chanting came again as the pain became excruciating. "Will they cry out for you to stop? I guess they think I will destroy you...and they are right for in time, I will destroy you all."

Yelling out, unable to control the pain any longer he began to surrender, letting it overwhelm him. The light began to fade and he felt as though he were falling, a strange symbol of Betrayal appearing on his left hand. But perhaps it wasn't Betrayal at all that had marked him but something completely different. A few of the features were different, dots in different places. Tristan, in the past, had a lot of secrets that he kept only to himself - he didn't even tell Cedric most of them. Perhaps the symbol was representative of those secrets; making him some sort of Bearer of Secrets. He felt himself land softly and once again he seemed peaceful, sleep befalling him as he rested his aching head, the mark remaining burnt into his left hand for all to see.

# CHAPTER 26 - THE CITY OF GHOSTS

Tristan's head collided with the desk as he shook himself awake, a sharp pain now greeting his forehead. As he rubbed it to soothe the pain, he realised this was becoming a habit of his and he needed to make it stop, else he might not have a head to bang.

"Honestly, I leave you alone for ten minutes whilst I'm in the john and you try killing yourself." Dante came dashing back into view from the entrance to the Shrine, holding out his left hand for Tristan to take. Receiving it also with his left hand, Tristan got to his feet warily. No sooner had he rose though, Dante snatched back his hand as though his touch had burnt it.

"Are you okay?" Tristan asked, feeling a burning sensation itch his palm.

He watched as Dante dared to look at his left hand before quickly recovering himself and smiling briefly.

"Everything's fine," he replied half-heartedly. "What did you see anyway?"

"That's depends on what's wrong with your hand."

Tristan already had an inkling he knew - perhaps this mark of his pained his own Betrayal mark...but then surely it was the wrong hand. Dante shook his head, biting his lip hard enough to draw blood. He was obviously nervous about showing it to him, so Tristan made the first move. Calmly, he held his left-hand palm up to show Dante the mark that had appeared. As Dante's eyes widened, he realised he had got the reaction he had expected.

"Where the bloody hell did you get that?" Dante gulped, his voice breaking slightly.

"I'm not sure how and I'm not even sure why. I just know that it's got something to do with the secrets I kept." Tristan explained, worry building within him as he started to doubt his suspicion.

"How do you know that?"

"Well in my memories, whenever it appeared I was overhearing or watching conspiracies of Dharsi. It always seemed to appear when I was stumbling across a secret I may have kept."

"Like?"

"Like the fact that Charles was the Herasin." Dante looked oddly at Tristan, he didn't know who Charles was and Tristan hadn't remembered enough to be able to tell him, so he changed the subject slightly. "There's this figure that I keep seeing too. He seemed to be part of Dharsi's plans but he's so shadowy I can't even make out what he looks like. It's like he's wiped himself from my memory so that I won't remember."

"A figure huh. When did you see him?"

"When I forgot! I think he's the reason I did."

"I have something I need to show you."

Without hesitating any longer, he showed his left palm to Tristan, revealing the same mark they now shared. Now it was Tristan's eyes who widened; it was like he was showing his hand to a mirror.

"How do you have it too?" He asked, not even sure what to say.

"I've always had it. It appeared not long after I stumbled upon my own secrets. Like you probably did, I thought it meant that I was a traitor. I wrote myself off so and that's why I eventually did betray. However, I discovered that wasn't what it meant all too recently thanks to Cedric."

"Cedric?"

"When I appeared before him, it was one of the first things he noticed about me. He told me the mark meant I was the Bearer of Secrets, which is simply what it says it is. Out of all the Brothers of Union you have more secrets to hold because of the mark. Because of the mark you doubt whether you should tell your brothers about what you know. It's like the mark punishes you for keeping secrets from your brotherhood. Yes, it is very similar to the mark of Betrayal but I suppose by keeping things from your brotherhood you are betraying them. You're supposed to be united and how can you be if you keep secrets from them."

"So I'm not a traitor then?" Dante shook his head, his eyes filled with compassion and relief, probably to know that he wasn't alone with this mark that they now shared. "Are there others like us?"

"As far as I'm aware you and I are the only ones. And even if there are more there aren't many because everything that was ever written about them is through theories interpreted from prophecy. Nothing is known for certain about them at all."

"I wonder if I told anyone about my mark."

"I know I didn't, so if you did then you obviously had some inclination as to what the mark meant."

Dante was right, if he had told someone it would be Cedric most probably seeing as he knew what it was. He shook his head, bewildered as to why he felt the need to keep all the secrets he did.

"You know I think I need some fresh air," Tristan suggested with a tone that perhaps meant he wanted to be alone.

"You're telling me," Dante laughed. "If you don't mind, I'll walk out with you but I think I'll find a nice pub to relax in."

Tristan nodded and the two departed the Shrine together before parting ways outside the Compound. Dante headed in the direction of Frankie's pub, Tristan on the other hand remained where he stood observing the town in the darkness. But as they say, at night is when the city comes alive.

As Dante faded into the night air, Tristan looked around at the town that surrounded him. Many of the old town houses were bordered up, a few faint lights in the windows of those that were occupied. Sighing heavily, he closed his eyes; trying desperately to clear his mind of everything that made it want to burst. As the pain begun to subside, he eased his eyes open, the town before him seemed to change. He was marvelled by the sight. Night turned to day; barren and abandoned houses to a town filled with life and laughter.

Despite the clarity to the scene though, the edges had a slight shimmer indicating that perhaps what he was seeing wasn't really happening at that moment. Day turned back to night and still the hustle and bustle continued as though it were showing Tristan what Dilu was like when he was a Scribe; that carefree life that Frankie spoken of. Taking a few steps forward, he marvelled at the sight, his eyes truly overwhelmed by the spectacle.

As he stepped out of the vicinity of the Compound, a woman appeared a few steps away from him. At first, she had her back to him, long brown curls that reached the small of her back, the top layer of which was stretched into a plaited crown leaving the rest to hang free. The skirt of her dress was red and flowed around her hidden feet, sweeping the ground as she turned to face him, a sweet smile gracing her face. Her cheeks blushed for a moment, a sparkle shimmering in her green eyes. They seemed to blend in well with her golden corset that framed her bodice, giving the dress a sense of glamour that left the arms bare.

"Dags!" he yelled, hoping she would linger a while longer. To his delight, she did and she inclined her head as though she wanted him to follow her.

Obliging with a smile, he followed her into the square by the fountain which seemed to burst with life as water shot out from the top and disappeared into the ground through tiny holes. Rain began to fall from the dark sky just like it had the other night, and he watched as Dagnen turned to the doors of the Mason Tavern where Frankie worked as they opened to a figure stood by a woman on the deck. He recognised the pair to be he and Dagnen and from where he stood, he could just about hear their conversation.

"Tristan it's raining," Dagnen complained, pulling him back by his hands to the doors of the Tavern. "We'll wait till it stops and then we'll go back."

"Oh, come on Dags, where's your sense of adventure?" Tristan goaded, looking over at her with a cheeky smirk. "Besides, we'd miss curfew and we don't need to give Charles anymore ammunition against me."

"Well you go then, I'll wait right here."

"I'm not going anywhere without you."

"Then I guess we're staying."

"Don't tell me you're afraid of a bit of rain?"

"No, I just don't wish to get wet thank you very much."

"Oh don't you now?" Clearly his cheeky remarks towards women hadn't changed. And clearly their blushed faces hadn't either.

"You act like you've never seen rain before."

"Az Lagní has been suffering a dry spout. I haven't seen rain in over a year, maybe longer." He was joking clearly. Dazedly, Tristan stepped off the deck and into the rain, splashed a puddle as his foot hit the ground. He laughed as water splattered around, Dagnen flinching slightly as she feared it would land near her. "The feel of the rain on your skin...there's nothing like it."

Facing up at the rain, he held out his arms and it wasn't long before his clothes were drenched through, his hair now sticking to his face. Dagnen watched him in amazement, shaking her head as though she were watching a small child play amongst the raindrops.

"Come dance in the rain with me Dags." Tristan held out a hand to her, but she did not take it. Instead, she just stared, as though part of her wanted to but sensibility told her otherwise.

"There's no music..." was her reply.

"And everyone stared at those who danced when there was no music to be heard." He watched Dagnen's vacant expression, noting the sense of longing in her eyes. "Life isn't about dodging the storm Dags, it's about learning to dance in the rain." He held his hand out once more to her. "Do you trust me?"

"My mother told me to never trust someone who says trust me."

"That's why I didn't say it. I simply asked if you did."

Reaching out further forward, he held his hand steady and watched as she unfolded her arms, reluctantly taking his hand. Gently, he pulled her into the rain, the coldness trickling down her back and sending shivers through her as she embraced the frivolities of what she was doing. A smile eventually touched her face as Tristan let go of her hand and the pair swept along the fountain, water splashing around everywhere. They laughed together, causing shouts from an open window of a man who was trying to sleep. But when he saw the pair, dancing in the rain as they were, he simply smiled and closed his window to return to sleep. Young love!

As Tristan watched them dance towards the Compound, darkness became light once more and a new scene welcomed him as the town bustled with life. Looking around, he lost sight of Dagnen for a moment; panic setting within him. Luckily, he caught sight of her again moving between the people towards the building that was now the Barron's estate. He hurried to follow her through the crowds realising, as she was, that he was passing straight through them. As they neared the estate, it began to look completely different. The masonry seemed brighter and the domed brick central roof was now a glass facade with glittering colours that shone brilliantly in the sunshine.

But it wasn't the estate that she was heading for. Just to the right of the entrance was a flower patch that surrounded a wooden gazebo, roses of different colours entwined around the pillars. The wood itself has been painted white and within the gazebo appeared another scene from Tristan's past. Now, a woman stood with her back to a long queue of men who each stepped up to her, bowed before waiting a moment and then leaving towards the estate entrance as though a proposal of some form had been rejected. In their wake another would step up to the plate only to suffer the same dismissal.

Stepping up one of the four entrances onto the gazebo, Tristan came to face the woman in the centre; Dagnen who quietly shook her head to each that stepped up, her sublime shoulder line quivering after each one made the salmon pink dress shudder with her. It was as though she was uncomfortable in the dress, like she thought it was beyond her plain - Jane appearance - at least that's what she used to call it anyway.

Looking towards the ever-shortening queue, Tristan spotted his Dagnen again, watching him from the side-lines as a support for him remembering almost. Near the end of the line, he spotted his brothers along with himself all eagerly awaiting their turn...actually it looked more like they were all mocking Tristan about how he would get rejected by the woman he was slowly falling for. Each of his brothers stepped up to her but none such made it to take her arm leaving only Tristan and...Charles.

"Good day my lady," Tristan announced as he stepped up beside her, Dagnen's brother Xavier overseeing the possible match. Xavier was a tall man and stocky. He had brown hair that framed his forehead, a slight stubble upon his chin. He wore robes of gold and green that split at the waist with a brown belt and black leggings with boots covering his feet. Tristan glowered as he stepped up, of course he was going to try a lot harder than his fellow Keepers.

"Good day," she said without even smiling. This must have been before they danced in the rain because part of her still seemed broken; more broken than she had ever been.

"Tell me, would you be so kind as to accompany me to this here dance?" She didn't answer him, but it looked like a slight smile was beginning to pinch the ends of her lips. "Fine suit yourself..." Xavier cleared his throat; an indication that either he was not meant to be stalling like this or because his comment was inappropriate. He was right to judge, the man was the First Keeper after all. "But if you don't dance with me...well...you'll have to dance with Charles..."

Her eyebrows rose and she turned around quickly causing a sniggering smile from Xavier. As Dagnen heard it her smile came into full bloom as she realised she had been duped. Yes, if she didn't accept Tristan she would have to dance with Charles, but it was the fact that he used her discontent for him against her without even knowing it existed. Collecting herself quickly, she took his hand, watching through the corner of her eye as Charles stormed into the estate with Xavier leading the newly matched pair close behind.

Just as those before, the scene soon faded too and once again light changed to dark, bringing with it the rain from before. Looking back towards his Dags, he followed her back through the town and towards the gate of the Compound which stood tall and proud over the town of Dilu. Stopping behind her, he watched as a pair danced in the rain towards the shelter of a nearby alley. Taking a step closer, he saw himself take his chance and kiss the girl, breaking away quickly.

"I'm sorry," he blushed, something he didn't even know he was capable of doing. "I don't know..."

Before he could finish his excuse, she kissed him back; a longer more heartfelt kiss than his, her hands resting upon his neck as his took to her hips. It was then that he realised it was one of those moments of impact Merlin had spoken of when they first discussed him remembering his past. All his defining moments with her would be the impact that he needed; the will and motivation to remember.

A tear slipped down his cheek and he watched as his Dags faded before his eyes, the tears too falling from her own. He watched the couple as they continued to kiss, smiles beaming across their faces. As the rain cleared, they disappeared and the sun began to rise over the present. Tristan spied a ladder that led to the roof of one of the houses. Climbing it to the top, he came and sat a while to watch the sun rise on the horizon near the new Estate. A sense of completion reached him then and he thought about the last three years and what he had spent them doing. Right then, everything looked so strange to him; as if he didn't belong even here in Dilu. Like back home; something was out of place and the worst thing was that he felt that there was somewhere where he did belong but he just couldn't find it. All he could hope for was that he soon would find that place alongside his daughter wherever she may be.

Tristan watched intently as the colour of the sky changed before his eyes; the dusky purple becoming lighter and lighter the higher the sun rose over the horizon to the right of him. The beauty of the sight warmed the young Keeper and bought him a sense of temporary peace as he tried to put the thoughts that clouded his mind at the back of his worries. Successfully managing to clear his mind, he became aware of someone climbing the ladder - it was probably Dante finally leaving the Tavern so he relaxed a little as not to cause a worry.

"Mind if I take a pew?" Came a voice that wasn't Dante's. Turning around, he was shocked to see that it was no other than Basso.

"Bass," Tristan said in disbelief.

"I take it you weren't expecting me?"

"Honestly...no..."

"Well I suppose after my attitude earlier...do you mind?"

Tristan shook his head and Basso slumped next to him. The man was only in his forties yet his bones creaked as though he were much older.

"I want to apologise for my very childish behaviour. I don't think I expected you to become the same as you were then so quickly."

"I don't understand?" he spoke honestly, Basso really wasn't making a lot of sense.

"Back when you were...well...yourself; you were an arrogant little shit." Tristan sniggered. "You were! So cocky and full of attitude...like you thought you were better than everybody else."

"Surely Percy was worse?" Shortly after saying the comment, he pulled a pulled a face - he didn't even know who Percy was yet the comment had been made anyway, causing a similar snigger from Basso as though he were right.

"Ah Percy; that good for nothing know it all. I suppose you're right but he was more subtle than you. You were very outspoken and had an answer for everything...even if it wasn't necessarily the right one. Of course, that kind of attitude didn't go down well with me and as you can imagine I'm sure, I spent a lot of time and energy trying to drag you down a peg or two. But by the looks of it...it didn't pay off so to be honest I should've quit whilst I was ahead."

"That bad, was I?"

"It's not a bad thing to be confident Tristan. I just think there is a difference between being confident and acting like an arrogant pig. But I suppose that's where our views differ I'm afraid. The reason I walked out was because I didn't want to start all that berating again especially when you are as unstable as I have been told."

"I'm not unstable I'm just...unpredictable..."

"Why?"

"I doubt myself..."

"You...doubt...please?"

"Yes, all the time. It's like there's this whole new character trying to break out from inside of me. And even though I know I need to let it free because it's who I am...it's like I'm afraid to and I don't know why...but I am."

"Fear isn't something to be ashamed of Tristan. Fear is what makes us human...it's what gives us a purpose to be better than we are. So therefore, we must find the courage to overcome our fears and beat them to the ground. I learnt that the hard way!"

"How?"

"You might not know this Tristan but I have a brother. He's not a very nice man...wasn't even."

"He's dead?"

"Yes...but don't apologise...like I said, he wasn't a very nice man. He dishonoured my father, who; as you should know, was a First Keeper in his time and a man highly looked up to by the Keeperhood. When he died, I lost all guidance, and I was so young that I was afraid I would turn out just like my brother. So I didn't live so to speak, I just plodded along as though I didn't have a choice in the matter."

As heartfelt as Basso's little story seemed to be, it only sounded half true. It was like he had rehearsed it a thousand times for a play at the theatre or even a lie to tell as a sob story for the pity of others. "Don't make the same mistake...don't die inside when you should live."

There was a long silence between the two after he'd finished his lecture, but it was more awkward than sentimental. Tristan didn't really know what to say in response to him especially as he didn't believe a single word of it. He'd definitely been working on that speech; surely?

"Right," sighed Tristan, a bemused look on his face. "I best get back to the Compound; Daxon will be wondering where I am." He got to his feet and patted down his clothes as though there was dust on them.

"That Daxon, he's a good friend isn't he?" Basso assumed, turning to face him.

"Well yeah, these days he's practically family." To be fair, that was true.

"How do you know him?" Dante was right - perhaps Basso was onto him.

"I know him from the Smithy, he worked with me there."

"And he's with you why?"

"His brother died, so I suggested he should come and get some space from it all. Besides, he knows me how I am now and that's kind of helpful."

"I guess so."

"Anyway, I'll see you back at the Compound later?"

"You sure will!"

Smiling vacantly, Tristan headed for the ladder and returned to the ground. Looking back briefly, he turned in the direction of the Compound still going over the story Basso had told him. Surely, someone can't simply put those words together on the spot like that? He had been telling that story for years no doubt and whether or not parts of it were true he did not know. In fact, whatever part was the truth had probably changed so much in each version to increase the amount of pity that it was no longer true. Pushing the thought to join the others at the back of his mind, he pressed on with Basso watching after him...not that he knew his old teacher was watching, there was too much on his mind to focus on what was going on around him.

# CHAPTER 27 – LIGHT PINCHED DARKNESS

"Sorry there lad!" Grunted a man who collided with Tristan as he walked into him like he hadn't even seen him coming.

Tristan looked up, immediately taking a step back from the abnormally large stranger.

"You okay there mate?"

The two made eye contact and it was like the man was suddenly very afraid, his near invisible eyes coming into sight as they widened in shock. The dark eyes of the man seemed to strike right into Tristan, the scar down the man's right side of his face twitched causing a burning sensation in his left hand before spreading all over his body. The scar seemed to spell out a word in runes Tristan had never seen before, either that or he just couldn't read them. The man shook his head and walked away, mumbling something under his breath as he did so. The man left Tristan with an unsettled feeling, his stomach somersaulting making him want to wretch. His throat went dry and his ears began to ring. Whoever this man was, he certainly had an effect on him. Trying to forget about him, Tristan closed his eyes; if he'd known the man, he would've recognised him...surely...but then there was something about that scar on his face...

"I'll see you later Frankie!" Dante yelled as he stepped onto the deck in the early morning light, catching a glimpse of Tristan standing by what looked to be an old thatcher's mill with an odd look on his face. His skin was pale and his eyes wide, as though something had scared him silly. "Tristan?" He called out, but no answer came. He didn't even acknowledge his name being shouted. What on earth was up with that boy?

As he called out again, all life seemed to drain from Tristan's face and his body went limp. In one swift movement, he crumbled to the ground as his eyes rolled into the back of his skull, something Dante was beginning to see all too often. Rushing over, he slapped his face a couple times, trying to wake his friend to no avail. In all the commotion, Dante almost didn't notice Frankie running over with another man to see what was going on.

"Quick, bring him inside!" The other man urged, looking around as though to make sure no one else was around. Gathering him into his arms, Dante followed the man with Frankie close behind.

"Lay him down in the booth over there!" The man was certainly very authoritative for such a weedy looking figure. As Dante laid him down in the back corner on some leather corner seats, the man disappeared into the back room that lead to the cellar.

"Who is that?" Dante asked Francis in an undertone.

"That is my son; Warrick," answered Frankie, thankfully not taking offense to the question. "He was the town healer before the Keepers left but now, he...moonlights shall we say. The guards make him charge the people but they can't afford it...and apparently, he needs some form of license or something. All codswallop if you ask me though."

"I hope you weren't talking about my medicine father!"

Warrick came back into the room now with a bowl of water and a fresh cloth, the cork head of a vial sticking out of his waistcoat pocket. As he set to work checking Tristan over, Dante sat back with Frankie watching him work. He couldn't help but wonder what was going on in Tristan's head to cause him to pass out such as he did.

~~~

*Light pinched at the darkness that shrouded his sight. All around me I could hear raised voices of panic and footsteps thudding against the ground. As lights turned to colours, colours turned to figures and figures into people, my sight came back to me. I looked down, catching sight of my brothers own body fall to the floor*

*Trying to concentrate on anything but the possibility that you were in trouble, I focused on the faces of the panicked voices; noticing Dante lift your body and carry it off with Frankie and another man I didn't recognise. Basso was still on the rooftop of the thatcher's mill, watching but not making himself known to anyone. How strange? Choosing to ignore that for now though, I looked around, fearing I was being watched. Surely someone couldn't see me? I was Greater Faded now! Looking over his shoulder to the pathway that led down the side of the walled gate of the Keeper Compound I saw another figure stood in full view as though he had taken great enjoyment in watching what he had just witnessed.*

*The man was familiar to me, but the name of the man escaped me for the moment. Instead of thinking of the name, I took in the man's appearance. If he was someone I did indeed know, I got the sense they looked different from how I remembered him, like his whole appearance had changed since the last time we had met. The man was rather stocky and looked as though he'd lost a lot of weight over the last couple of years his midriff seeming more baggy than stocky. The cheeks of his face were flabby as well, his tanned skin seeming to droop down. His eyes were a dark brown, in fact they were more of a maroon in colour, a red spark just glinting in the early morning light. He sported a spiked-up hair do that was a mousy brown colour, his eyebrows heavy and dark casting shadows over his worn eyes. The attire of the man was somewhat slumpy, a patchy jacket covering a dark blue shirt with ties at the chest leaving a couple of hairs bare. The shirt was messily tucked into brown breaches that clutched at his waist as though they were far too tight. On his feet were thick black boots that gave off a pirate impression. I pictured him making a good first mate with a green parrot sitting on his shoulder but perhaps even the role of a pirate was too law abiding for the man.*

*Apart from old scar upon his face as the only identifiable feature, there was nothing individual about the man - but then even the scar from this distance didn't seem all that distinctive. He seemed the sort to be dealing with dodgy people in dark undercurrents of the cities...like a pawn shop owner maybe.*

*The ends of the man's lips tilted upwards as he sniggered at the way Tristan's body was being carried off and spat on the floor before turning on his heel and sauntering off down the way. You'll be okay with them brother!*

*I decided to take advantage of my new found freedom in this world of colour, and follow the man into a darkened passageway and a small building in between two seemingly abandoned town houses. Like the man, the hut was rather shabby looking and had a barely visible red handprint on the door that was so worn by now it might as well be part of the door. Fiddling around with some keys, the man heaved open the door, which looked to be heavy, and disappeared inside of it.*

*Half expecting it not to work, I stepped up the wooden steps to the shack and held my breath, easing myself through the door as though I were a ghost; the feeling of transparency unsettling me a little and sending butterflies fluttering about my stomach. I shook the feeling off, and turned to see the man had stopped dead in his tracks and was staring at the darkness towards the back of the hut by a staircase. He looked suspiciously at the gloom as though he expected someone to be stood there. But as I stared into the same space, I realised there was a figure there and as he stepped out my mouth fell open aghast.*

*"Whoever's there I'll have you know I'm highly skilled in...dismembering people..." The man wasn't very good at making threats and was just making it up on the spot.*

*"You don't even know what that means!"*

*A voice glowered as it came into light, the torches suddenly sparking as the scared man clicked his fingers revealing a cloak underneath the staircase that looked to lead to some sleeping quarters. The room we were in now came into view, revealing a counter just in front of the staircase with a marble top. The walls of the room were rather bare as were the many shelves on the back wall as though the place hadn't been occupied long. It wasn't much of a house so to speak and was more of an establishment of business.*

*"I demand you reveal yourself immediately foul trespasser!" Threatened the scarred man again as he straightened up trying to make himself seem more fearful but obviously it was not working, a quiet snigger sounded from the stranger.*

*"Now now, I don't think that's how you greet an old friend now do you...or should I say brother?" The trespasser's voice was slightly high-pitched for a man but was also unreadable in terms of tone, as though the man underneath the hood gave nothing away leaving everything to the imagination.*

*"Hagen?" At the utterance of his name, my blood boiled. If only my presence in the world were more physical.*

*"Hello Boris!"*

*Hagen removed his hood revealing greying hair that framed his squared forehead in symmetry with a well-trimmed bearded chin. The man's attire was not visible under his black cloak, but considering he was the Baron of this town he imagined it was glamorous and regal. He held his posture proudly - tall and high as though he looked down his nose at everyone he passed.*

*The two brothers smiled to each other and they embraced as though they hadn't seen the other in a long time, smiles upon they're ancient faces. The scar on Boris' face was now in full view and as I picked out the runes spelling out the word traitor, I remembered how you brother had been the one to give it to him.*

*As the realisation began to sink in, a sickness began to take over the fading butterflies and I felt as though I was falling. The scene around me slipped from his sight as the colours blackened into one in a sort of ripple effect. The fall itself seemed to last forever, the blackness being all he could see until finally the colour began to pinch at the sides once more. I prayed to God I wouldn't end up back in the shadow.*

<div align="center">~~~</div>

Tristan opened his eyes, a foggy world now formed around him with figures stood all around. Their shadows glittering as they moved to form a crowd behind two kneeling brothers Tristan recognised to be he and Romeo. They knelt before an elderly woman whom he assumed to be the Interpreter Cadica. The voice she spoke with was uninterpretable, just an echo that seemed to soothe his soul deep within. Without having any control, he and his brother turned to face a line of hooded Elders that stood behind them. His eyes were caught by two men stood behind the row; Hagen and Boris.

In an instant, the vision changed. For some reason, rather than watching each memory play out before him like usual, he was a part of the memory doing exactly as he had done all those years ago. The new scene that glittered in gold before him was one he had seen before as he crouched by the banister of a balcony, watching three men he knew and the head of another conspiring amongst themselves. Again, their voices melded into one making an echo sound over the words as though there weren't any to be spoken because he already knew them.

The glitter figures burst, reforming to show another familiar vision of two men wrestling with each other, Boris being shoved against the wall by the other. Tristan didn't know what was going on, why was he seeing things he already remembered...unless, like Merlin said, he had become part of the memory just as he should aim to do. Again, the glitter burst but this time what came back into view was full colour; the echoes stopping and every ounce of glitter disintegrating before him.

This time, he held Boris by the collar up against the wall; anger making his insides heat up with rage. As Boris squirmed in his grasp he managed a smile - he wasn't at all scared of Tristan and laughed in his face.

"What are you laughing at?" Tristan demanded through gritted teeth. "You killed him!"

"So what if I did?" Boris choked, the smile not leaving his face. "What are you going to do, kill me?"

"Worse, I'll make you wish I killed you; Tabacious!"

At the utterance of his true name, Boris yelled out causing Tristan to drop him to the floor and back away to watch him squirm for real this time. Tristan watched as Boris crouched on the floor yelling out in pain and clutching the right side of his face as though something was burning it. He stood tall as Boris stopped yelling, struggling to his feet with his hands still covering the right side of his face.

"How did you know my name?" Boris begged.

"Wouldn't you like to know?" Tristan answered, a snigger escaping his lips.

In his shock at the arrogance of Tristan, Boris' hand slipped away from his face revealing a word in runes etched into his face, steam still oozing from the fresh scar. The runes spelt out a word in Ancient Keeper; Betrayer. Marvelled at the sheer extent of his naming of Boris, Tristan turned and left the room. He would eventually kill Boris; that was why he named him - marked him for death. He didn't intend to mark him in such a way but maybe that was what happened.  At least now, the whole Keeperhood would see him for what he was.

Just like before, the vision soon faded to be replaced by another again with Boris being held up against the wall by Romeo and still he managed to keep a smile on his face.

"How are you alive?" Not the words Tristan expected to hear himself say but seeing how the last time he saw Boris they were all inside a mountain that was imploding on itself. "Well?"

"Good question...I wish I knew," Boris squelched, his sarcasm only making Romeo tighten the grip he had.

"Where is he?"

"He...who's he?" His grip tightened again and Boris felt a burning sensation in his mark. "Oh, you mean Sarisus...yeah he's dead."

"And the Eye?"

"I don't know...I never found it again."

"You better be telling the truth!"

Romeo released his grip and Boris fell to the floor gasping for breath.

"You're not going to kill me?" He called after Tristan as they began to walk away.

"Don't worry I'll kill you eventually. You might still be useful to me."

For the last time the vision changed and the blackness returned, the pinches of light having more of an effect and sending spasms of light across his vision. As he was forced to disconnect himself from the world, he had just been a part of, a dampness formed on his forehead. It made him realise that he was coming back to reality but that wasn't something he wanted to be permanent. In order to remember, he had to remain part of both worlds and as he tried to focus on that a smell greeted his senses, a smell that was incredibly distracting.

# CHAPTER 28 – TABACIOUS

Warrick placed a damp cloth over Tristan's forehead to relieve the warmness he felt radiating off of it. Once he had cooled a little, he took out the vial from his pocket and unscrewed the cork stopper, a potent smell filling the whole tavern. Dante looked over at the source of the smell, spying the blue crystals within the vial. He watched as Warrick held the vial beneath Tristan's nose, smiling as his nose wrinkled at the smell until finally he came too, coughing and spluttering.

"Works every time!" Warrick exclaimed, quickly sealing the vial over again and supporting Tristan as he sat unsteadily upright.

Once he was steady and the coughing had stopped, Warrick took a step back and pocketing the vial once more before removing the cloth from Tristan's head. Dante got up to stand by his side, relieved when Tristan looked up with a smile on his face at the sight of him.

"You had us all worried for a minute there," Dante said, the concern lifting from his voice.

"Just for a minute huh?" Tristan joked.

Dante shook his head and Frankie got to his feet.

"Right, now that the panic is over," Frankie assumed. "Who's for some breakfast?"

"Yes please!" Dante and Tristan both exclaimed in unison as Frankie disappeared into the back room with Warrick close behind.

"Want to tell me what happened then?" Dante asked after a while, not making eye contact with Tristan.

"I don't know if I'm honest with you," Tristan explained quietly. "One minute I walked into this man and the next..."

"Man? What did he look like?"

"Why is that important?"

"Tristan, do I need to explain to you where you are? It might not be someone you were...friendly with back then."

"Well I don't know, it's all a little...foggy..."

"Come on there has to be something identifiable?"

"How long was I out for?"

"Maybe a couple of minutes but I can't seem to think why that is important. What did the man look like?"

"I only saw his face...but just for a minute. All I remember is the scar on his right side..."

Dante didn't wait for him to finish before he clambered to his feet and ran out the door with Tristan calling out after him, he already knew who it was Tristan had seen. As he reached the gates to the Compound, Dante keeled over struggling for breath. He knew there was something not quite right when he'd seen the faint outline of a red handprint on the wall of the gates just the other day, and if the man Tristan saw was who he thought it was then that would be all the answers he would need. However, it could also spell disaster for Tristan if he didn't remember everything quickly.

Once he'd caught his breath, he looked for the handprint again, spying it by the gatepost. It was rather faded, so much so it might as well not have been there at all. It was just about noticeable though, a red left handprint on its side like it was pointing. Back in Dante's time, a red handprint had stood for safe places in the time of the repression however he had a feeling it meant something completely different in this generation. Following the wall down to the left, he spotted another handprint on a dead-root covered wooden signpost that tilted down a dark passageway between two long abandoned townhouses. Darting down the passageway he spied a small hut in a cluster of other odd shacks and lean toos as though it once resembled a market of some sort. Creeping up towards the darkened window, he peeked inside to see his old friend Boris talking with a man he did not recognise. He couldn't hear what they were saying but he could tell the men were somehow linked by the way they laughed and embraced towards the end of their conversation. As the door opened, Dante darted under the wooden steps that lead to the shack. Watching above, he saw the other man walk down the steps, pulling his hood up as he went. He obviously didn't want to be recognised out in the streets and that told Dante that perhaps he was one of the well to do men that resided up in the estate. Springing up to the steps, he caught the door just before it shut and eased inside, keeping close to the shadows. He watched as Boris took a step behind the counter and ran his hands over the varnished counter, smiling as though he were admiring the place.

"Hagen Hagen Hagen," he sang in an undertone, gratitude leaking from his lips as he spoke. "What would I do without you?"

"Why don't we find out?" shouted a voice that wasn't Dante's...or was it? Not even he knew whether the words were his or not, he had after all intended on saying something right at that minute but it seemed someone had beaten him to it.

"Who's there?" called Boris, his voice breaking slightly with awkward laughter. "Hagen don't be messing with me now."

"I wonder what Tabacious would be without someone pulling his strings."

Dante watched as Boris' eyes widened and his whole body began to quake in fear at the mention of his true name. Dante wondered for a moment if it could be Tristan but...*no...surely not.* It had to be one of his fellow brothers of Union perhaps.

"What do you want?"

"Something simple I promise. Don't worry I won't kill you, it's not my job after all."

*Definitely not Tristan, but who?* Almost in answer to his question, a man stepped out from the shadows who towered over Boris. He was in imposing man, even in his dust caked clothing - a clear sign that he hadn't long got back from the Land of the Faded. Dark hair was combed back with curls at the base of his neck. His eyes too were dark underneath his heavy brow which completed his long face and pointed bearded chin. Despite the dust on his clothes, he could tell they were at one point well put together; a brown leather jacket covering a red shirt that was neatly tucked into dark leather breaches and a pair of black boots. From the look Boris gave him though, it was clear they knew each other but he didn't get the impression it was for a good reason.

"Zhaine?" Boris croaked. "But how?"

"It's not like I was dead, the Land of the Faded is easy really." The man smirked.

"So Tristan, he's remembering then?'

"I couldn't tell you even if I wanted to. However, there is something you can tell me." Boris gulped. "I did have something else in mind for you, but after what I just heard I can't just sit back and let you and Hagen do what you do best. I have to finish what we all started!"

"But how can you, you didn't name me so you can't..." Whatever he was going to say was cut short as he cried out in pain, clutching at the right side of his face as his scar seared with pain. "I may not have named you and I may not be able to kill you...but I can still do an awful lot of damage."

"Alright alright! Stop! I'll tell you anything you want."

In an instant the pain stopped and Zhaine half smiled.

"Okay, then we'll start with Hagen."

"Hagen is the Barron here, this town answers to him now."

"And Myrina, what is she doing with him?"

"That I don't know. I mean I ain't gonna lie to you but we both know that even though Romeo is dead she still wouldn't choose him willingly. I don't know why she's there."

"For once I think you might be telling the truth."

"You're not going to do anything are you?"

"Not yet! How do I get a look at the both of them?"

"Come on Zhaine don't put me in this position."

"I just want to talk to her."

"That better be it because if you endanger my brother in any way you realise I will be in a very difficult position where you are concerned. It's not just my name I am bound to you know?"

"I am aware of that Boris and I swear, on this occasion; I just want to talk to her."

"There's a formal event at the end of the week. Marks the Autumn Solstice and there's a big party. You're going to have to look the part though, only rich people get in."

"I have to pay?"

"Not exactly, you have to make an offering to his treasury...like gold or something...something valuable."

"I can work with that."

"You might wanna find yourself some nicer clothes too, your attire's...well...a little shabby if I'm honest. They'll never let you in looking like that."

"Thanks for the tip Boris but I could say the same to you."

"I'm family so it doesn't count where I'm concerned."

"What about a name?"

"Any name should be fine, of course not your own. Try something like Colinson or Adamson. And put a Ser before your name, no one will ever believe you're a lord unless you can prove it."

"Should be easy pickings. Pleasure doing business with you old friend. See you soon!"

In an instant Zhaine disappeared right before their eyes in a puff of dust. Taking that as his cue to leave, Dante dashed through the door and made his way back to the tavern where no doubt Tristan would be very confused awaiting his return. The eavesdropping had proved useful though he wasn't sure how fruitful for the moment.

"Where'd you disappear off to?" Demanded Frankie as Dante came back through the door of the tavern to a fresh aroma of a full cooked breakfast.

"I had something to do," Dante stammered, winking at Tristan. "Anything left for me?"

"Sure, sit yourself down, I'll get you a platter."

Dante took a seat next to Tristan and smirked at Warrick who had a curious look on his face. He assumed he wasn't the type to attract a lot of trust so he didn't let the look bother him too much.

"Where did you go?" Tristan asked him with a mouthful of unchewed food.

"I'll tell you later," he stated, clapping Tristan on the back and causing him to choke. "Don't talk with a mouthful, it's highly unbecoming of you."

Frankie placed a full plate of breakfast in front of Dante and went back to eating his own meal. The meat smelt so succulent and fresh he wondered how they got hold of it in a place like this. Then again, in a town such as this there had to be a Black Market of some sort.

"Say Frankie," Dante gulped as he finished a gulp of his juice half way through his meal. "If I were looking for a place to get some well to do clothes, where could I go?"

"Why, what do you have in mind?" Frankie answered as he cleared his throat with a sip of his own juice.

"That Autumn Solstice at the end of the week."

"You've got your hopes set high ain't ya? Well put it this way you can't get any such round 'ere..."

"There is a place actually," Warrick interjected causing a surprised look from his father. "The Black Market of course, where do you think I get all my medicines father?" Frankie didn't answer him. "If you follow the red handprints, they lead to a cluster of old houses that come alive in the afternoon with stalls from all around. It's always when the guards are on lunch; security is lax then. It only comes round once a week at the end of the week. They have everything a common old town person might want and for good prices too. If you're going to find something to wear it'll be there. But don't forget your offering of gold to the Baron's treasury when you go to the festival and trust me, they'll know if it's a fake."

"Thank you Warrick, I'll remember that."

Tristan gave Dante an odd look; he suspected something but he didn't say anything. Instead, he continued to eat his breakfast and they all followed suit, the rest of the meal taking place with the odd funny comment.

"So why did you disappear off like that?" questioned Tristan as they headed back to the Compound later that morning. He had to admit he was fairly curious but he was also afraid that it may have been something he had said at the time - not that he could think what.

"I had to go see someone..." Dante answered quickly without looking at him.

"Dante please tell me the truth?" Tristan begged as he stopped dead in his tracks.

"Why do you care so much?"

"The man I saw, he wasn't friendly with me back then."

Dante stopped, that was what he had been waiting for - for Tristan to be honest with both of them.

"Who was he?" Dante turned to face Tristan as he asked the question.

"His name was Boris...I named him...Tabacious"

"Named him?"

"Don't pretend like you don't know what it means you named him first." Backtracking, he couldn't believe the words that had come out of his mouth; how had he even known that?

"How did you know that?"

"I don't know. I just do..."

"This Tabacious, what did he do to you to make you name him?"

"He killed someone, the First Keeper at the time to be precise so I named him in a fit of rage."

"Why did you never kill him?"

"Because I couldn't do it...I couldn't kill someone in cold blood."

"But he killed someone. Tristan, you do realise that you are going to have to kill him...you named him, that's the way it goes."

A silence passed between the pair. Dante watched Tristan as he scuffed at the dirt on the floor.

"So, this formal event," Dante said after a while. "Do you fancy accompanying me there?"

"Why is it even important?"

"I just want to see if it sparks anything for you. You should know some of the guests, perhaps we can have some fun with that."

"You realise before we go there's going to need to be a lot of work done..." Tristan nodded to Dante, a cheeky smirk on his face.

"What this classic look? I think it will pass, don't you?"

Tristan didn't say anything, he just sniggered along with Dante who motioned to him and they headed back to the Compound together still joking amongst themselves.

# CHAPTER 29 - THE BLACK MARKET

The end of the week approached all too quickly and the morning of the Autumn formal was finally upon them. Of course, neither of them had spruced themselves up enough to get past the front gate of the estate, but it was a working progress none the less. A little after noon they both headed out in the direction of the Black Market Warrick had told them about. Following the red hand prints just as instructed, they came to the cluster of huts to a hive of action. The old lean toos and stalls that seemed shabby the other day had been brightened up by the beautiful colours of glittering fabrics and the smell of the manure masked by exotic delicacies and pricey perfumes. Tristan imagined frivolities like this to be a luxury for the common old town's person as Warrick had referred to them as. The sights marvelled them both, they had never seen a sight so full of life, not even the exotic market, but then maybe that was because of the small proximity they were in. Admittedly there weren't many people around admiring the luxuries but the hum of oncoming people every now and then did make up for that. Suppose they couldn't draw too much attention to an illegal market right under the guards' noses.

"So, where do we start?" Dante asked, hoping Tristan would know something more about this then he did. Tristan said nothing to begin with, his eyes wondering around the faces that peered around the stalls. Next, he noted the faces of those who owned the stalls, a flashback coming to his mind at the sight of a man with a turban around his head. A name sprang to mind along with a thousand memories, most of which resulted in him buying priceless pieces of jewellery from this man, just like those that that were currently on his wooden stall.

"Wait here a minute," Tristan stated, weaving through the people towards the man he had spotted.

He looked just like he did in his memories; the purple turban sealed with an amulet at the centre, the heavily wrinkled face and greying sideburns that lead into a goatee. Not to mention the beige and purple robes that swept past his knees and sandy coloured boots that curved up and around at the toe.

"Sekhmet," Tristan called out, catching the attention of the man in the turban. "Long time no see."

"Tristan, my favourite customer. It's been a while." Sekhmet had a snake like voice that slithered out of his lips, but not in a sneaky or sly sort of way, more of a charming way - like a snake charmer. "Where have you been all this time?"

"I've been around. Listen, I need a favour."

"Of course, anything for you my friend."

"Me and my friend over there," He nodded to Dante, "We need to get into the Autumn formal tonight."

"Who him?" Tristan nodded. "What the guy with the straggly hair and tanned skin." He nodded again. "You've got to be kidding me, haven't you?"

"Please tell me there is something you can do?"

"No no no, there is nothing I can do for him. You may pass for a ser but him...there's a lot of work to be done. I can however sort you out with some offerings and I have a friend who can help you sort the rest."

"Thank the gods."

"Wait here a minute. Gladys!"

Tristan looked towards the blonde bombshell who turned around in acknowledgement of the name. In all honesty she looked like one of those hussies who would hang around in the taverns to fulfil the needs and desires of all men who requested it. Her blonde hair was curled in tight ringlets and tied up neatly on the top of her head. A pale face was plastered in makeup, her cheeks forced to blush so pink it matched her low-cut puffy gown. Tristan couldn't hear what they were saying but he did understand Gladys' looks of dissatisfaction in Dante's direction.

"You want me to work on 'im?" she asked coming over to Tristan and pointing in Dante's direction in a disgusted manner. She had a rather common sounding voice that pitched at the ends of her words, making her sound rather patronising.

"Yes," Tristan replied calmly, finding it funny how they were all so obsessed with Dante's look. "I understand that there's a lot of work to be done..."

"Darlin' I'm gonna need a miracle to make him look the part of a ser let alone a lord."

"Luckily for you we just need the ser part."

"Luckily..."

"Gladys," Sekhmet intervened. "The man is an old friend..."

"Sekhmet that man is too shabby for even your circle of friends."

"I'll make it worth your while?"

Gladys stared at him a while before looking over at Dante and then over at Tristan. After a while she sighed heavily making a weird noise as though she weren't happy about what she was about to do.

"Fine, but you owe me big time Sekhmet!" Gladys stormed off out of the cluster of stalls towards Dante.

"You better follow her," Sekhmet urged, winking to Tristan. "I'll be along later with your offerings."

Tristan nodded to him and chucked him a large bag of coins.

"Keep the change."

"May Saracen bless you my friend!"

Tristan went at a jog after Gladys slowing as she reached Dante, looking him up and down and smirking disgracefully. "And you are?" She asked, folding her arms across her chest and extenuating her cleavage. "Who wants to know?" Dante asked struggling to keep his eyes on her face.

"This is Daxon," Tristan answered in his place, deciding to keep up the pretence of his fake name for the moment.

"Daxon? I sure hope you plan on changing your name."

"How about Dante?" Dante quizzed, a cynical look on his face.

"Do be serious, that's even worse."

Dante made a face as though he were about to slander her back only causing a giggle to escape Tristan's lungs.

"Now come with me, we have a lot to do."

She led them in the direction of one of the huts that surrounded the stalls. Fiddling with some keys as she unlocked the door to an emporium of glamorous clothes all different colours and fabrics. A stool sat in the middle to which she motioned for Dante to sit at.

He did so without hesitating. Tristan sat at the bench to the side and watched her survey the work she had to do. Every now and then she'd let out a sigh as if she didn't believe she could do it, but she seemed determined all the same. Tristan had a feeling he was going to enjoy this, even with Dante scowling at him every time he got the chance.

When it seemed like Gladys had finished envisioning her masterpiece, she stepped back a little, a big smile beaming upon her face. She practically skipped over to a chest of drawers and opened the top drawer, pulling out a cloth which looked to contain a variety of tools. She set the bag on another stool which she pulled over from the side of the chest and pulled out her first instrument; a sort of bladed prong which looked like no razor Tristan had ever seen before. He gulped, watching as Dante did exactly the same thing, his eyes shooting up as he felt her pull on the tie that held a layer of his hair up.

"What are you doing?" Dante croaked, fear tainting the arrogant tone he was trying and failing to get across.

"Just giving it a little snip," she replied, a mischievous grin upon her face.

"With what?"

"Just some scissors. Trust me, you're in good hands."

"More like blades!"

Dante had tried to say that without her hearing but obviously he failed as her eyebrows arched even more as she snipped at least three inches off the length in a rather vicious manner. Tristan held in a laugh as he saw Dante mouth the word 'bitch'. Once she'd finished hacking at the length, she combed it through and worked on the shape, curving the edges so that they framed his shoulders from the front.

When finally she was happy with the cut, she went back over to the chest and pulled a box out of the top drawer, setting it down on the stool with the bag. Opening it she took out some circular whalebone instruments with little splinters that looked more deliberate than simple wear and tear. Combing a section of his hair, she threaded the cylindrical objects into it and then clipped them in place at the base of his neck.

"What are those?" Tristan asked, intrigued but at the same time wanting to embarrass Dante further.

"Curlers." she answered simply as she continued to thread the rest of his hair through them.

Dante pulled an alarmed face at her answer, a look that said 'you have got to be joking'. *Balderick would be having so much fun watching this*, Tristan thought. Once all the curlers were set, she took the scissors back from the cloth bag and came to his front, now paying attention to his beard. Carefully, her eyes full of concentration, she snipped off the straggly hairs so that it had no real length to it. Even by taking off the length, Tristan could see a big difference in the impression it gave; from grotty tavern frequenter to strapping upper class lord. After she'd finished the length, she separated the blades by unscrewing something small and round from the centre. She held the blade steady in her hand – looking more like a razor now - and began scraping it over the hairs and taking away the thickness.

"Don't speak or you may die!" She asserted as she felt Dante about to say something and potentially break her concentration. "Don't worry though, you will still have a beard when I'm finished with you."

A little while later she smiled making Tristan assume she was done with his beard and placing down her tools, she stood up and began sifting through the clothes on all the racks. Grabbing what she needed, she placed them in a room at the back of the hut and came back to Dante.

"Right, I've put some clothes in that room over there," she motioned, pursing her lips. "They should fit you. Please try not to disrupt the curlers whilst you're changing into them." Dante nodded and rose to his feet, sheepishly moving towards the room and shutting the curtain behind him as though he were too afraid to say anything against her and embarrass himself further. "Right, it's your turn," she pointed to Tristan and motioned for him to sit on the stool. "Luckily you just need a bit of a tidy up so it will be much easier."

Tristan sat and Gladys went about clipping and reshaping his hair so that there were no straggly bits and then shaped his stubble a little more evenly. She finished just as Dante came back into the room, sporting a white shirt under a royal blue overcoat with gold trimmings that stretched down to his knees. Black cloth trousers tucked themselves neatly into polished boots that reached his knees. Smiling at the result, Gladys selected some clothes and shoved them at Tristan, motioning for him to go and change. Grabbing hold of Dante, she sat him down and began taking out the curlers and tying his hair neatly into a lose ponytail that rested along his back, the curls giving it a more regal feeling.

"How are we getting on?" asked the voice of Sekhmet as he stepped into the room from the approaching night outside, his eyes widening at the sight of Dante. "Well stand up then and give us a twirl." Dante rose to his feet and slowly turned, lifting his arms slightly as he did so. "Now that certainly is an improvement. Do we have a name to go along with the attire?"

Dante shrugged as Tristan came out of the back room, flexing his shoulders as though he were trying to stretch out the leather brown coat he was wearing over a black shirt and leather trousers, that were tucked into polished boots. To be honest, he didn't look all that different just a little more polished around the edges.

"How come he gets the leather?" Dante scorned.

"Well, I have actually been thinking of some names for them." Gladys explained, ignoring the comment and coming to stand by Sekhmet to admire her handiwork as Tristan stood beside Dante.

"Oh really," Sekhmet intrigued. "Let's hear them then."

"For tall, dark and handsome over there I was thinking Balthier Ashdown..."

"Ashdown?" Dante exclaimed, astonished that she'd managed to come up with his actual last name without even knowing it. "How did you come up with that?"

"I noticed the mountain tattoo on your shoulder when I was cutting your hair and it made me think of the sigil for the long-lost Ashdown family. And Balthier...it just had a nice ring to it." She certainly impressed Dante there, after all he still regarded common women as not knowing an awful lot about the world around them and its history.

"What about for young Tristan here then?" Sekhmet asked, nudging Gladys.

"For him, Baldor Runcorn."

"Why Runcorn?" Tristan asked, curiosity getting the better of him.

"It just popped into me head and I liked the sound it had."

"Brilliant Gladys my darling," Sekhmet honoured, kissing her on the cheek. "Now we just need a backstory...how about associates? Both of you trained at a warrior's academy in Nuzulu and you became good friends so you just kept in contact after you left. The rest is as they say...well in this case bullshit!"

A low murmur of laughter enveloped the room at Sekhmet's joke, which was also the truth in all fairness, settled. Once the joke had subsided, Sekhmet pulled out their offerings of gold of which they would give to the treasury; there was nothing special about them but they certainly looked the part. As they prepared to leave, Gladys gave them a final brush down before bidding them good night and wishing them luck. Sekhmet led them to the streets once more and from there they marched in the direction of the estate, breathing in the cool night air that was slowly settling on the horizon.

# CHAPTER 30 - THE ESTATE OF DILU

The estate towered above them in the darkness making a shiver run up Tristan's spine as he stared up at its malevolence with glittering lights that flickered in the windows. Dante sighed next to him, pulling him forward towards the main gates and onwards into the Estate courtyard where already lords, ladies and sers from all around were waiting to get into the venue. Each had a cloth bag at their side, most likely containing the mandatory offering to the Barron Hagen's treasury. The queue was already so long it made Tristan wonder how full it must be if an offering had to be given at every festival celebration.

He looked towards the doors, trying desperately to calm himself before he'd even come face to face whatever he seemed so afraid of. The place seemed to echo familiarity at him, but his ears were ringing so loud he could hear the sound. A face seemed to call out to him near the head of the queue. The face belonged to a man at the with brown hair that was wax combed back, the ends of which curled at the base of his neck. His face was pointed towards his chin which was covered by a neatly shaven beard that framed his face well with his hairline. His attire was much to be desired; he didn't look all that high-class but then maybe that was the point. Maybe, like them, he was trying to pass as someone he wasn't.

Dante spotted the man too, although his reason for finding the man familiar was probably different from Tristan's because he was the man he had seen threatening Boris just the other day. Interesting though it would be to see what he wanted here, it made him apprehensive to say the least. Not to mention what might happen to Tristan if the man was who he thought he was, he could even blow their cover...they could blow his without even meaning to.

When it came to Tristan and Dante's places in the queue, they handed their offerings over to the guards who weighted them in their hands before chucking them carelessly into a sack by the door which was already half full. Once through the door, another guard stepped forward holding a scroll and a quill.

"Names and titles please?" he said in a gruff voice.

"I am the Lord Balthier Ashdown and this is my associate ser Baldor Runcorn." Dante answered.

"Coat of arms?" Dante gulped, *idiot! Why did I say Lord?*

"Just a moment!"

An idea came to mind and he pulled out his medallion from underneath his tunic showing it to the guard who nodded approvingly, a relieved look washing over Tristan's face as the panic faded. Both breathing a sigh of relief, they proceeded down the walkway, armoured suits lining the corridor towards a glorious staircase with a red central carpet. Tristan only hoped that the suits were as ornamental as they looked. At the top of the stairs, they were met by another guard who again asked for their names as they set eyes on the ballroom below.

The ballroom was a magnificent sight; a huge circular room with a domed glass roof. The floor was tiled, colours reflecting off the high polished tiles and hitting back at the glass ceiling. Long tables of food were across one side with musicians playing on a stage at the head of the room, dancers parading around the centre of the ballroom. The figures themselves seemed ghostly to Tristan as the whole room seemed to speak to him, like a voice from the past almost.

"The Lord Balthier Ashdown and Ser Baldor Runcorn." The guard bellowed as they glided down the stairs, trying their best to seem as magnificent as they sounded; one arm behind their backs the other across their chest, straight backs and heads held high.

A man stood at the bottom of the staircase, a blonde woman stood to his left with her head to the floor as though she didn't want to be seen or looked at, unless of course that's how she was meant to stand. The man she stood with was jabbering away to himself, probably to her but she wasn't listening. As they neared the bottom of the stairs, he noticed the look on her face was more quizzical, like she had just seen someone she didn't intent on seeing...a face from her past perhaps.

"Hello there," The man held out a hand, stopping mid-sentence and addressing Tristan and Dante. "I am the Barron Hagen."

"Well, I hope you don't mean that literally," Dante joked and Hagen chuckled along; seemingly genuine, clapping him on the shoulder as he shook his hand. "Balthier Ashdown."

"Pleasure Balthier, I knew the Ashdown family well once if you're the same kin that is."

"I've always been told that I'm a direct descendant of some exiled king in the time of the Auks and I'm not going to dispute it if you catch my meaning."

"I don't blame you. Well met my friend well met. And your associate?"

Dante looked to Tristan who had his eyes glued to a man somewhere amongst the crowds of the ballroom. He gave him a subtle nudge, making Tristan look at the Barron Hagen for the first time since entering the estate. Just as with Boris, he got the sense that he knew the man but that he had changed his appearance since the last time they saw each other. He wasn't necessarily a tall man but an imposing one none the less, at least that was the impression he gave but his eyes were guarded as though he gave nothing about his personality away. His greying hair gave the impression he might have been quite old, but his face was seamless as though there wasn't a single wrinkle in sight. His attire certainly spoke for itself, a black robe that was patterned and studded at the hems, belted at the waist. Black leggings covered his legs which were visible through slits in the sides of the robe and black boots with silver stitching covered his feet.

"Baldor Runcorn," Tristan announced, extending his hand for a shake.

"Well met again," Hagen didn't appear to recognise Tristan thankfully, that's if he was the same Hagen from Tristan's past he had heard about, but his eyes did linger on him for a moment longer before turning them to the woman who stood by his side. "This is my...the Lady Myrina." It sounded as though he was going to call her his wife for a moment but changed his mind.

"Charmed," the woman said vacantly not even bothering to glance up at them.

"Don't be rude now Myrina, they are esteemed guests."

Myrina sighed passively, looking up at them both properly with startling blue eyes that widened at the sight of Tristan. Those blue eyes sparked something within Tristan, something that bought him a sense of warmth and home. She certainly had the look of a lady so to speak but it was as though even she thought it were too high a title to belong to her. She was a beauty though; long lustrous blonde hair that was plaited round her face so that it rested on her left shoulder. A finely detailed face with a petite figure that was clothed in a turquoise valour one sleeved dress, that left her right arm bear with a gold bracelet that rested around her upper arm, a matching one at her wrist. A strap held the dress in place on her right shoulder and a long sweeping sleeve covering her left arm.

A roped tiara was tied around her forehead and a teardrop necklace was around her neck, the colour of which matched her dress but it didn't seem to suit her.

"Myrina, this is Baldor and Balthier," Hagen informed, glowering at her.

"How do?" Reluctantly and shakenly, Myrina extended her hand, both Dante and Tristan taking it in turn and kissing it gently. It was clear she recognised Tristan, but she knew well enough not to blow his cover for whatever reason he was here. *It probably wasn't for her anyway.*

"Myrina!" A voice said behind Tristan, causing him to dart around to find no one stood there. "It is you." The voice said again, almost gasping in disbelief. *Who did it belong to?* It wasn't Dante, he was far too busy talking to Hagen as though they were old friends. "But why..."

Tristan rolled his eyes, almost wishing the voice to belong to Dante so that he could put it to the back of his worries. The next thing he knew though, Dante was pulling him away towards the food table, glaring at him as he did so.

"What was that all about?" Dante piped through gritted teeth.

"I don't know..." Tristan sighed impatiently, still trying to comprehend what had just happened and the fact that he could still hear the man mumbling to himself about why Myrina would be with Hagen.

"Of don't give me that bullocks..."

"It's the truth! I literally don't know what's going on!"

Tristan shook his head and stormed off in the direction of the drinks table, the muttering still echoing in his head. Picking up a flagon and pouring himself a beer, he nodded to the squire who stood behind the table and looked out onto the ballroom at the ghostly faces that were moving around the room, the muttering obscuring the music that was being played.

"I mean why, would she do that," the voice ranted. "She hated him so why would she do it?"

"Why don't you ask her?" Tristan mumbled through gritted teeth in response trying to make sure no one would hear and think he was going crazy.

The voice stopped though as soon as Tristan had said it, almost as though he didn't realise that anyone could hear him. Even so he didn't speak again, either that or it was his own imagination.

"Admiring the view?" A voice said in his ear, again it was a familiar voice, making Tristan look around to face a man by his side; the same man that had caught his eye earlier when they were waiting to get into the estate.

"Excuse me?" Tristan started, jumping slightly.

"Alana," the man pointed to a red head stood with Myrina who, not that he realised, Tristan had been staring straight at. "I used to know her way back when and let's just say...she hasn't changed one bit." To be fair to him, the red head was also a beauty, a natural flirt by the looks of it, clothed in a red dress with gold trimmings. Even she seemed familiar to Tristan but he couldn't think where from. "I'm Brandon by the way, Brandon Balchus."

"Baldor Runcorn." The men shook hands, something about the man shouting out in his mind that he knew him, a chanting repeating in his head but he couldn't make out the words due to the echoing.

"Well met my friend. This room it brings back a lot of memories."

"Funny you should say that, it does for me too."

"How strange, were you here before the estate then?"

"Yes, I trained in the academy here at the time," Tristan explained deliberately choosing not to say the Keeperhood.

"So did I, but I don't recall your name. You look familiar though, then again there were so many of us there you've probably just got one of those faces."

"Maybe."

A silence passed between them and Tristan's eyes swept over the room, resting on Myrina for a second before looking for Dante and then straying back to her. He sighed heavily, trying to stop his head from racing around in circles.

"How do gents, how do?" Dante had come to stand over with them, a glass of some dark brown liquor in his hand, it didn't look like anything he'd ever seen him drink. Obviously, he was playing on his character.

"Well thanks and you?" Brandon answered, extending a hand towards Dante. "Brandon Balchus."

"Balthier Ashdown my good sir."

"Ashdown you say?"

Tristan watched the face of Brandon change at the mention of Ashdown to a look of panic and fear as though his own name had been uttered. Tristan looked over at Dante, seeing a delighted and intrigued look upon his face in reaction to the panic on Brandon's face as though he were pleased at the reaction. Brandon seemed to shrug it off quickly though and smiled once more before nodding to them both and leaving across the other side of the room.

"Well isn't that interesting?" Dante said sarcastically.

"Do you know him or something?" Tristan asked calmly, the face of the man spinning around in his mind as though he was trying to place it somewhere in his past.

"No...but I think you do."

"What makes you think that?"

"Actually, I have a confession to make. I know Boris..."

"Yes, we've talked about this..."

"Give me a minute okay. The other day when you mentioned this man with the scar, I had a feeling it was him so I went looking for him. Found him getting threatened by that man only he wasn't called Brandon; Boris called him Zhaine."

"Zhaine?"

Dante nodded, still watching the man as he weaved between the crowds and not even noticing Tristan walk off holding his head in his hand as the name overtook his head with pain and memories that made him feel as though he were about to pass out. Finding his way into a courtyard, he took in the fresh air, leaning on a column that held a balcony up from the floor above somewhere. Once the headache had passed, he looked out upon the beautiful courtyard with plants of all sorts of colours growing in patches. A high bush-wall stood a few feet away, the night sky twinkling above it. Tristan watched as the stars blinked back at him, the simplicity of it all bringing a calmness to him and a sense of peace.

"Beautiful isn't it?" The voice of a woman said beside him.

It was a sweet voice, a calm one that seemed to sing without her even meaning it to. Tristan looked to the side of him to see Myrina standing there, a glass of wine dangling in her hand. When she saw that Tristan had seen her, she motioned for him to come with her and he followed her round the section of bushes that was in front of them to a glorious stone fountain that spurted water through several orifices before falling gracefully onto a pool beneath that was walled with facets of engraved patterns. The sight of it made Tristan smile at the beauty of it.

"Beautiful isn't it," she acknowledged, sitting down on a bench that was in front of it.

"So how did a woman like you come to be here then?" Tristan asked, continuing to sip from his tankard as he sat beside her.

"Why do you want to know that?" she answered more out of intrigue than spite or worry.

"Call me observant or whatever...but I happened to pick up on your nature."

"Nature?"

"Your mood I mean, you're very...how do I put it...it doesn't look like you want to be here."

"That's because I don't, I hate events like this."

"Why's that?"

"Because I have to stand there and greet all the guests, but the moment they've all been in he palms me off to Alana or one of my other maidens so he can go socialise."

"What and you want him to pay attention to you?"

"No but...wait you knew I would say that didn't you...just like you supposedly picked up on my mood." Myrina stood up and looked down on Tristan with an almost accusatory look. "I mean who even are you?" Tristan didn't answer her straight away, he just stared at her knowingly. "Well?"

"She's not changed one bit!" The voice said next to him only this time he didn't look around, it was like he expected the voice to say something about her.

"My name is Baldor, we met earlier." Tristan reasoned, trying to ignore the fact that he obviously recognised him but not enough to be confident about it.

"You see I don't think you look like a Baldor to me. Baldor is a strong name and while you may look the part but you don't seem it."

"What's that supposed to mean?"

"I don't know, you just seem...sensitive, compared to most men I mean."

"More like soft!" The voice snarled in his ear. Whoever it was was now taking full advantage of their position, but surely by that comment it meant he had to know whoever it was.

"So you really had no other choice over Hagen then?" Tristan asked, changing the subject.

"Nope! My father died when our tavern went up in flames..."

*Flames?* So the fire at the tavern where Evie had been in Hasaghar really had caught fire. It wasn't a fake. But did that mean Cedric chose Evie over the others and left them to die?

"Then my betrothed was murdered and his brother who vowed to take care of me..he just disappeared and I never saw him again. He looked rather similar to you actually now that I come to think of it."

"Well you didn't have the best run of luck then did you?"

Myrina shook her head in response, seemingly remaining silent as she thought back on her life, her eyes darting back at him every now and then. Tristan on the other hand shook his head - the pain had returned and bought whispers back with it that echoed within his ears making his vision obscured and pinched. He didn't even notice the strange look Myrina was giving him as though just then everything had just become clear and she had realised just who he was.

"Snap out of it brother!" The voice urged, trying to bring him back into the real world. "Get up and get out!"

Tristan rose to his feet dazedly, noting the way Myrina was looking at him as his vision began to blur once more. Dropping his empty tankard to the floor, he stumbled back towards the edge of the bushes.

"Wait," Myrina called out as she rose to her feet. "Please don't leave me again?"

She'd worked it out, she knew it was him. Tristan stopped momentarily, but didn't linger. He began stumbling again and he thought he heard her say his name as he walked straight into Brandon, bringing his attention back to the forefront. Their eyes met, locking on each other for a moment sending shock waves all over Tristan's body as two faces flashed into his mind, one belonging to the man that stood in front of him and the other to a similar looking man.

*"I'm Zhaine,"* the face of Brandon said, the voice echoing in his head. *"And this is my brother Ramien."*

Brandon's face went pale and his eyes wide - surely he must've heard Myrina shout his name. Feeling his stomach begin to somersault, Tristan pushed past Brandon, apologising as he did so and making his way back into the ballroom, up the stairs and into a quiet alcove of pure darkness, his heart racing and his blood boiling over as his head surged with pain. His hands feeling like they were burning as his marks reappeared scarring his hands permanently on both sides. Burying his head in his hands, he felt fresh blood begin to trickle down his back, visions flashing before his eyes and sending a ringing through his ears. Writhing, he swung his head back, feeling a hard thud against the back of his head as it collided with the wall.

~~~

*Darkness and emptiness are the two feeling often coupled with the coldness of one's actions, the coldness of events that take place around you. For Tristan, it was the feeling that amounted after the deaths of his Dags, of Romeo...the blackness that came after he was struck down moments from ending the cycle of hate. His brotherhood had been broken by that cycle and as the darkness greeted him, he let himself think about that moment it all happened now. It was an all too easy thing to do when weakness was all you felt, when strength was a hard action to muster.*

*A scene began to piece itself together before him, colour surrounding him as glittered figures too form. They seemed to be on top of a tower; all that could be seen for miles around was the black lightning struck sky the stars crying as rain beat down on him where he found himself cowering below a blackened figure. Perhaps he hadn't yet remembered this man it seemed, like they had blanked themselves from his memory so that only the action remained. The face was just a blur. All he felt was fear despite the dreamlike state he was in. The fear crippled him, made him unable to move and sick to the core.*

*"I will have my revenge!" the figure echoed in a booming voice that seemed to screech in a distorted manner.*

*He tried to speak but words were lost to him now as he looked up at the figure, any sort of expression that might've been there lost to the blackness of its shadow. He reached to his side and unsheathed a dagger its true purpose unclear as he seemed to just hold it there.*

*"You all thought I was the weak link," he went on to say, like he had confused Tristan's identity with someone else. The voice seemed crazed almost, like he was possessed. For whatever reason he felt the way he did, it obviously wasn't an easy feeling for him to burden himself with. "Well I will show you, I'll show you all. It is me who is strong and you who is weak. Do you remember what you called me? Let me show you just what it means."*

*Whatever the figure was going to do next was lost in the next few moments as a flash of blonde hair shoved into the figure. Recoiling suddenly, the face became visible – it was Romeo and he clutched at his midriff, blood spilling from his mouth as he stumbled backwards. Tristan looked to the figure who watched helplessly, like he hadn't intended to use the dagger at all and now he was stunned at the circumstance of it all. He stumbled to his feet and shouted out to Romeo as his feet got too close to the edge and he lost his footing. Launching himself forward over the edge of the tower he just caught a grip on his brother's hand, the sight of the rapids and jagged rocks below tightening his hold.*

*"Hold on Romeo!" Tristan yelled, feeling his hands became sweaty. "Please, don't let go."*

*Tristan hadn't long lost his wife; he wasn't about to lose his brother too. He grappled with Romeo's hand, their eyes meeting as he looked up towards Tristan. They looked so drained. As though his life was fading from him. He was dying. And unless Tristan could pull him up now, he was going to fall. Romeo's grip faltered. Tristan wasn't strong enough to keep ahold of his hand for long and he slipped from his grasp. He didn't even yell as he fell, his figure fading as a wave from the ocean below rose up to take him with it. As the waves crashed back down the vision before him faded to black leaving him once again with that emptiness and cold. He felt fresh tears on his face and all the pain he had felt back then. To lose someone once was traumatic enough, but to lose them twice...it was unthinkable.*

# CHAPTER 31 – DHARSTAN

Your arrival at Dilu had bought back a lot of memories for you brother, and it will continue to bring the rest of them back too. Some won't be very pleasant and some will make you wonder why you even started this journey in the first place. But I hope there are those that will make you think about all the happy times and the times where your heart was so full of love it could easily burst. I've been watching you relive those memories for about a week now and you've changed so much since then. You're more confident in yourself, surer of the world that is forming around you. In time I'm sure you'll remember it all, you've just got to be patient with it all.

I have to admit though brother, I've never seen you as nervous as you are now as you await your arrival into the estate where a lavish celebration is being held in honour of some Autumn Solstice. I remember these events from when we were Keeper Scribes here. They were quite the affair. Beautiful maidens all around just waiting to be paraded around a glittering ballroom.  The Keepers certainly knew how to throw a ball that's for sure.

I see something to catch my eye, just as it seems it has caught yours too. There is a man stood at the doors now and looking closely I realise it is a brother of ours. A fellow returned. You look curiously at him but seem to shrug it off quickly. I can see the torment it causes you though; how it makes you more nervous and sends thoughts sparking through your mind. It sends shivers up my spine let alone what it will be doing to you. I follow you into the estate and down the steps into the ballroom where I lay my eyes on a sight of beauty worth my attention. I had always had a thing for blondes, they seemed feistier than most women and more outgoing too. I like a woman who can speak for herself. This blonde is different from most though, her eyes are down to the ground and her brow furrowed as though she had seen someone she didn't like the look of. Perhaps she had recognised our brother, even with his basic disguise. He clearly didn't try very hard, but what did he want here, with you?

After a berating from her companion, she looks up properly and my eyes are scarred. She was mine, my dear Myrina, my love so pure in all her effervescent beauty. To be honest I think I'd forgotten just how beautiful she was. Our romance had blossomed beautifully in the first few months to a year, it was like a whirlwind and everything happened so fast. I had proposed by eight months of courting but by ten we had been ripped apart by a jealous party and she had thrown the ring at my head. Heck if it wasn't for you dear brother, I probably would've killed the man who caused it. Strangely enough, that was the man she was stood with now. Hagen was the very man that had torn us apart. His constant taunting of me and her was what had fuelled my rage. I never had been very good at controlling my anger. It was that fit of rage that made me name him by his true name; Dharstan brother of Tabacious by blood. He hadn't changed one bit now that I looked at him, his hair was greyer yes and his face was now bearded but I still saw the red glint. He was still the black hearted evil bastard he had always been. Just then, I became aware that you my brother were looking straight at me and then all around. I must've been speaking out loud my thoughts without even realising, my anger obscuring my control. But then, how is it that you could hear me. Your companion doesn't seem to be able to. And I have spoken around you several times and you've never even turned your head so much as once. But now...I didn't understand it. I remained silent as you tried to shut me out of your mind, I didn't want to unsettle you further especially when you were trying to keep your cover perfect.

As the night progressed onwards, I stayed by your side, my eyes focused on my sweet Myrina. It is then that I sense your unease and look over to see you talking with Zhaine. Does he even recognise you? Or is that why he is talking to you - he must know what happened and is perhaps trying to get you to remember him. But then why is he even back if you don't yet remember him? As Dante comes over, you make a break for the courtyard and I follow having lost sight of Myrina. When I finally catch up to you, she is there with you and you are talking about how she came to be here in this place. I don't know if I believe her reasons though.  Even if Hagen was the last man on earth and she didn't detest him she would never go with him anywhere. She wouldn't make herself dependable on any man.

As I decide to focus on your conversation, I notice the way she looks to you, like she recognises you but can't place the face. Or maybe she was even doubting who she thought you were. I see the look on your face too, how pale it suddenly goes as your head begins to lull to the side. Something is happening and I needed to help you, motivate you to help yourself.

"Get up and get out!" I leant in close to your ear and whispered, begging you to hear me.

You snap back into focus; it appears to have worked and as you leave, she calls after you and I am sure Zhaine hears your name as he rounds the corner hitting straight into you. But luckily you do as I say and storm off to find somewhere safe to sort yourself out. I chose to stay though, watch how things progress with Myrina. A big part of me wanted to stay with you and make sure you were okay but I realise that even if I were to be part of your world there would be nothing I could do to help you. No. I had to get to the bottom of why Myrina was here and what Zhaine wanted with her.

"Do you know who I am?" Zhaine asks, half expected her not to recognise him. I watch as Myrina pulls a face as if she thinks he is being stupid.

"Of course I know who you are Zhaine, you've not changed that much over the years."

She folded her arms across her chest and stared at Zhaine waiting for his response. She truly was as feisty as I remember her being, if not then more so.

"Well you never know, I mean you didn't recognise Tristan."

"So it is him then?" Zhaine nodded. "It can't be, I mean he didn't even recognise me so I think you are mistaken."

"You don't know what happened to him do you?" A confused look appeared on her face. "He forgot everything. The Keepers, us, Dagnen...even Evie."

"But how?"

"I don't know, no one really does. When they found him in the wreckage, they took him to the infirmary. When he woke up, he didn't remember anything."

"So does he even know that Evie is dead?" Zhaine shrugged his shoulders. It seems the elaborate story that Cedric had let everyone believe about both of them was credible enough even those closest to him believed it. "None of that explains what you are doing here though."

"That's the funny thing about the Land of the Faded, apparently it's easier to escape it than you think."

"So Tristan has remembered you?" Again he shrugged - his casual attitude hadn't changed one bit.

"When I came back, whispers told me you were here with Hagen of all people so I figured where better to go..."

"If you've come here to rescue me..."

"Oh no I wouldn't dare! I know you could quite easily get yourself out of here without any help from anyone. You're good like that." That comment made her smile. "I just came to talk and help out if that's what you wanted."

"Well aren't you chivalrous."

"I do try!" A moments silence passed. "So anyway, why are you here? And don't give me that I had no choice crap because we all know its bullshit."

"You dirty little eavesdropper! If you must know I really didn't have a choice and that was my own fault."

"I'm not sure I follow."

"I made Hagen a promise. After Tristan ran into the Compound Hagen appeared. He didn't realise I'd seen him and went to go in after him but I made him tell me what was going to happen. I made him promise that he would keep Tristan alive and in return I would go with him wherever he went as a companion. He never asked anymore of me, just my company. I swore on Romeo's grave that's what I'd do and so I've done just that."

"Fair enough." Zhaine nodded vacantly. "Of course you know Romeo doesn't have a grave don't you?"

"If you're trying to be clever then don't bother. It's obvious he doesn't technically have a grave; his body was never found.  He's just got a memorial."

"Oh no that's not what I mean."

"Then what do you mean?"

"If I tell you, you won't believe me...but if someone else does..." Myrina looked at Zhaine quizzically. Not even I knew who he was talking about and was very intrigued as to where this was all going. "In the dungeons of the estate you'll find a Keeper and he will tell you everything you need to know."

"A Keeper? Why would Hagen have a Keeper in the dungeons, we don't even have dungeons in the estate."

"Of course there are dungeons Myrina. Hagen is not as harmless as you think, he's a vile human being - why do you think Romeo hated him so much? He's Dharsi Myrina, our sworn enemy and don't play dumb with me I know Romeo told you all about us. It kind of came with the territory the mess you got us out of half the time."

"Romeo never told me that Hagen was Dharsi."

"Well, he should have. Hagen is a dangerous sort, he and his brothers."

"Even if what you're saying is true how do I get into the dungeons?"

"Give me your hand."

Reluctantly, Myrina placed her hand within his, palm up. What he was about to do I did not know but he was right, I should've told her about Hagen. If I had, none of this would've happened. Closing his eyes, Zhaine began to chant in unheard whispers, a glyph appearing on Myrina's palm as he finished.

"This mark will make you temporarily able to see Keeper glyph doors and I'll bet that estate is littered in them." Zhaine explained.

"Myrina!" A voice began calling over the hedgerow, it had to have been Hagen. Without uttering another word, Zhaine disappeared, even from my sight leaving a confused look on Myrina's face.

"Ah, there you are my lady," Hagen came round the corner, a sly smile appearing on his face. It made the anger within me boil. I felt the rage build up until I was unable to contain it, if it wasn't for the fact that there was nothing I could do to him he'd be more than dead by now. "Who were you talking to my sweet?"

"Just myself," Myrina stuttered. I saw the fear that built up in her eyes as though she'd suddenly seen Hagen for what he was. "You know how I get on this stuff." She shook her wine glass as if to indicate she was tipsy. She was quick thinking like that but he seemed to fall for it.

"The guests are starting to leave now so I thought it would be nice to bid them adieu together." Myrina nodded and Hagen took her by the hand. "Maybe leave this here though." He took the wine glass from her hand and left it on the bench, leading her back into the ballroom to say goodbye to their guests.

Looking around, I could not see Zhaine anywhere. The best thing for me to do was to follow Myrina and Hagen. I didn't even know where you were brother, so the choice of what to do next was pretty obvious. And so I watch and follow as she vacantly said goodbye to the guests with him. A passive smile masked his face and my sweet hung from his arm as though it were a chore, a responsibility. After all the guests had left, I follow behind you both as he escorts her, leaving her at her room with a guard remaining by the door. I wait a while before passing through the wall, figuring she'll probably change first and although she wouldn't see me it would be wrong to pry. You dear brother would probably think differently but then she wasn't yours to hold.

After a while I stepped through the wall to see Myrina brushing her hair at a walnut veneer vanity table with a large mirror. Sprawled across the table were various combs, powder pots and perfumes. Up against the other wall was a four-poster bed of the same wood with pink thick sheets and an animal fur blanket at the bottom. A large wardrobe stood by the door and a clock rack on the other side of it. Ahead of me was a doorway with golden handles that lead out into a balcony that overlooked the courtyard we had been in earlier.

A humming reached my ears and I look back over at her as she brushes out the knots in her long blonde hair. She had draped herself in a green smock dress ready for bed with a beige shawl wrapped around her arms. She was humming a tune I recognised, a sweet tune like a lullaby. I remember she would hum it to Evie to get her to sleep while we were staying at the Tavern her and her father owned back in Hasaghar. She continued to hum as she placed her brush down on the dresser, catching sight of the mark on her hand. She stared at it thoughtfully as she rose from her stool and wondered over to the bed, slumping herself down on it. Her gaze remained in the mark and she frowned at the brilliance of it.

She was probably wondering if it would even work but of course it was working. There are Keeper doors all over the estate, she just had to look beyond what was there. If only there were some way I could help her do that. Perhaps if I could gather the strength, I could make myself visible or even physically part of her world in some way. I just had to figure out how? But first I had to find the door. Looking around the room I focused on what was there, trying to see beyond it somehow. I admit I was a little rusty, it was a lot harder than I remembered. Perhaps all I needed to do was make it simpler for myself. There was something about the wall on the other side of the bed, like it called out to me; something was beyond it and I saw it appear on the wall - a Keeper port key.

Now I just had to make her see it as clearly as I could. Wondering over to the other side of the bed, I tried to touch things as I walked past, my hand sweeping right through the bed posts as I went. I was going to have to try harder if she was going to notice the door. Then, an idea struck me as clear as the daylight sun. Focusing on the door handle to the balcony, I reached out, my fingers gracing the smooth surface as I grabbed it and pulled it down, the door swinging open. The sudden breeze stirred Myrina and she turned to see the open door, a confused look on her face. She got up and came and shut the door, sighing and shaking her head as she did so. The moment she had turned around, I opened it again. This time when she turned, she didn't shut the door again straight away, she just stared around trying to see something or someone that wasn't really there. "Look beyond what is there!" I heard myself yelling and a smile graced her lips as though a memory of words I had once said to her settled in her mind. It must've been nothing more than a whisper to her so I repeated the words, this time with a bit more feeling.

Closing the balcony door, she looked to the wall I was stood by, a focused look sprawled across her face. She recited the phrase over and over again to herself until her eyes lit up and she saw the mark for herself. Using the hand on which Zhaine marked her, she reached out to touch the mark, placing her palm firmly on it making the key shine ever brighter. Shielding her eyes with her other hand, she kept her touch true as the wall began to part ways; each individual brick subsiding in its place to reveal a doorway. The feeling of the wall behind her hand disappeared leaving just the air before her as the mark itself disappeared too.

A dark passageway formed before us and she reached for a torch from the wall, holding it before her so that she could see into the passageway. Warily, she stepped into the darkness, the torch lighting a couple of steps in front as she walked. Pulling the shawl tighter around her, we followed the passageway a few steps forward before it descended a spiral staircase that seemed to go on forever. We walked the steps, with each turn hoping to reach the bottom but never quite getting there. After what must have been about five minutes, we began to hear voices. But they weren't voices of a calmed nature: a man was shouting and another grimacing in pain as a whip cracked. The sound made Myrina flinch and she stopped in her tracks before a wall, another glyph appearing upon it.

"Stop!" Another voice shouted, this one distinctly sounding like Hagen. "You know this would be far less painful for you if only you told me what you knew." There was silence. "We don't have to do this the hard way," the voice was quieter now, as though he were talking to only the man for which the whip was meant. "All you have to do is tell me what I wish to know. All this can stop! We were friends once..."

"You were a fraud," the man croaked in response. The voice was another which I recognised and as my curiosity got the better of me, I stepped through the wall without my dear Myrina. "You filthy traitor!"

I couldn't believe my eyes. The very man who was knelt before me chained to the walls was my former idol, a man I professed to be as wise as once. This man was a hero to me, an ancestor to my cause.

"So be it then brother. Any last words, I doubt you will last this torture much longer."

"Once a traitor...always a traitor!"

Hagen scowled and left the room, sweeping his cloak behind him as the door slammed shut. The guard continued to strike at Felix, his face in a mad screw as he laughed menacingly, striking down on Felix's bloodstained body only ripping his clothes further and staining them in fresh blood. I squirmed, but I could not leave him here to face this alone so I stood strong. Why wasn't he doing anything? Had he given up? The Felix I knew would be able to stop all this in a matter of seconds with the magic that was in his grasp. He could smite the beater down as though he were an ant but no. He just took it. Perhaps the Felix I had known had changed since the last time. He disappeared from our midst and left Charles to take his position as First Keeper. He abandoned us!

"Do something!" I heard myself yelling.

I wanted answers from him. If he had never have left none of this would have happened. His sweat ridden head looked up as the words left my mouth, even his tormentor paused looking around to see the source of the sound. But he shrugged it off quickly and readied his arm high above himself ready to strike down again and again until his thirst for blood was quenched. But I could not watch this any longer and as I planned to do something he struck, his own force stopping in mid motion. Suddenly he fell back as though carried by some great wind. When he rose from his feet a scared look now rendering his face fearful. Staggering to his feet he fled the room, leaving his whip on the floor where he had fallen.

"You can come out now," Felix sighed heavily. I wasn't sure if he were talking to me or to somebody else, he didn't really make it clear who he wanted to come out of the shadows. Moments later, the wall subsided and Myrina stepped into the dungeon, gasping at the sight of Felix, a single tear running down her pale gentle cheek.

"First Keeper?" she whispered, her voice full of pain and doubt.

"I am no First Keeper...not anymore." Felix's voice was taunt, as though every word was a huge effort for him to muster.

Myrina dropped to the floor for the bowl of water that was in the corner with a ladle to torment Felix further. Carefully, she filled the ladle with the water and helped Felix to drink it.

"What happened to you?" she asked when he finished drinking.

"Dharsi were blackmailing me. Even a First Keeper has his secrets and they wanted to use them against me. But I would not let them so they sealed me away. Even now I do not know where." He paused to take more water and I felt a tear leap from my own eye as my answers were sought. "You must know, it was not my choice to leave. It was never my choice to abandon the Keeperhood."

"I know," Myrina consoled. "But how did you come to be here?"

"I don't know. I woke up chained to these walls about three days ago."

"What does Hagen want to know?"

"He wants to know of Tristan's whereabouts and state of mind. But I will never tell him...never."

"How does he expect you to know that?"

"It is a gift I was born with. That is why I have the keys. I know what they know. The keys never lie."

"And what do they tell you about Tristan?"

"It is not what they say about Tristan that is important for you to know. For he will come for you in time. It is loyalty who seeks you my dear and he is alive."

"I don't understand."

"Yes, you do, you just don't want to believe. Loyalty is alive...the keys never lie."

I knew what he spoke of, I knew he spoke of myself and my appearance in this world. Whether or not she knew I would probably never find out. Footsteps sounded on the other side of the door and two voices fiddled with some keys intending on punishing the First Keeper for hurting the tormentor.

"You must go now!" Felix whispered. "Both of you must leave this place and never look back."

"But Felix I..."

"Go my dear and quick. I do not have long left...but remember that the keys...they never lie." A tear slipped from her eyes and she kissed Felix on his forehead.

"Be strong!" she whispered, pulling herself away reluctantly and heading for the passageway and disappearing up the stairs.

I stared down at the First Keeper now, my face full of remorse. As the keys jangled in the lock, he looked up at me and right into my eyes.

"Free her!" he said simply. I found it odd that he knew my being here, but then he was the First Keeper.

"Free who?" I asked, feeling stupid for doing so.

"The Daughter of the Storm. She lives brother!"

As the door burst open, Felix faded from me and I found myself in a darkness coupled only by you...the Daughter of the Storm, his sweet and beautiful Dags...

# CHAPTER 32 - REACH OUT

When Tristan came too, he was in a little alcove of a long corridor slumped up against a dark wall. He could hear footsteps pacing up and down the corridor, feeling his heart race as they got closer and closer. The guard passed and then passed again a few moments later. He didn't even notice Tristan was there in the shadows. He breathed a sigh of relief, his head resting back on the wall and a sharp pain residing there. Wincing, he reached back to feel where the pain came from to feel a small lump. He must've banged his head pretty hard. Gathering his strength, Tristan rose to his feet and peered around the corner to make sure the guard was nowhere to be seen. Breathing another sigh of relief, he looked up and down the elaborate corridor with sculptures mounted on plinths at intervals, large paintings or tapestries hanging on the walls behind them. The stone floor was covered in a red carpet in the centre that was like a pathway, leading past the doors that lined the corridor around up ahead. He had to have still been in the estate. How much time had passed though, he wasn't sure.

Shrugging his shoulders, he stepped out into the corridor seeing a flash of purple in the corner of his left eye. Darting his eyes to the left, he saw her there - his Dags was stood there staring at him, a quaint smile upon her beautiful face. Tristan gasped, almost unable to believe his eyes; *she looked so real*. Granted there was a shimmer around her figure making her seem ghostly but she was still there. He smiled back at her and she inclined her head as though asking him to come closer. Looking back over his shoulder, he checked to see that the guard was still nowhere to be seen. Calmly, he stepped towards her, tentatively moving one foot in front of the other expecting her to disappear in the blink of an eye. With each step he took it was like her image strengthened, as though she were becoming more and more real. As he got closer, she stepped backwards and led them down into the ballroom below, stopping halfway down the staircase. It looked different without all the pompous buffoons. He could see the ballroom in all its beauty and glamour.

Leaving Dagnen to watch by the stairs, he stepped into the centre of the room, watching as ghostly women appeared around him dancing in colourful dresses with smartly dressed gentlemen. Smiles adorned their faces as their partner paraded them around the floor. Focusing on their faces he picked out Zhaine, dancing with the girl Brandon had called Alana. Not too far from him was Jacques with...*with Gladys unbelievably*. Also were Ramien and Romeo, both dancing with dark haired girls and then there was he; gliding his beautiful Dags around the floor. He smiled at the sight of her as he said words he did not remember at first, words that made her smile.

"You don't strike me as the type of woman who smiles a lot." It was as though someone had said them right in front of him, making him remember the words instantly.

"I've not exactly had many reasons to smile if I'm honest." said the voice of a woman he knew to be hers.

"You've been broken...I get it."

"How did you know that?"

"What can I say? I like broken things...I like to fix them."

"That's...odd..."

"I want to make you a promise...as a friend I mean."

"Well, as a friend - promise me anything."

"I promise to make you smile at least once every day."

Those words echoed in his head as the dancing figures faded away leaving the room empty once more. Turning around slowly, he saw Dagnen on the stairs, her dress changing colour six different times. It went from a purple to a yellow, from a yellow to a pink and from a pink to a dusky red. They were the different dresses she had worn each time she was here with Tristan perhaps. From the red it went to a green and then from a green back to purple.  He got the feeling they weren't in order though but that didn't matter, each was as beautiful as the last.

She nodded to him again and he ran up the stairs to follow her as she led them out of the estate. Stopping by the gazebo for a moment, staring as they kissed in his memories, her green dress wrapping around them both in wind. Following her past the gates to the estate, they walked through the town together watching as his memories played out before them and the town came to life to resemble the greatness that it once had. He saw them walking hand in hand past their other memories, looking through the stalls of the exotic market and trying the countless foreign delicacies, dancing in the rain together and kissing on the street corners like no one was watching. As they watched the memories a sweet lullaby played out loud. It was the tune the music box played and the tune she had played in the tavern they were now stood in front of. Looking over towards where she had been stood, she was suddenly gone and panic filled his heart. The memories around him shattered and he shouted out her name over and over again.

It began to rain and he sought shelter under the deck of the tavern. As he neared the door, he heard the lullaby being played from the other side of the door but it didn't quite sound like a piano or organ. The sound intrigued him and he pushed on the door, entering the light filled tavern and basking in her sight once more as she stood before him in the middle of the inn. She just stared at him as he sighed in relief at her being there standing right in front of him. He felt like he should say something perhaps, but what?

"Happy Birthday Dags!" she smiled as he suddenly remembered what day it was. "I don't have anything to give you except my thanks. That is thank you for making my life back then seem more than perfect. You made me feel loved, wanted, something no one could do at that time." She mouthed something but her words were unheard to him. He imagined her agreeing or telling him that she loved him no matter what. "In time, I will remember everything we shared but right now there's someone out there that's more important...to both of us. I'll remember her too, and I'll found our Evie."

He could feel himself saying goodbye to her as though he had no control over what he was saying or doing. It was as though these were the words he was meant to say but all he wanted was to snap out of it. A tear slipped down his cheek as he felt the closure beginning to build unwantedly. Tears fell from her face too as she knew he was letting go of her for now.

"You don't have to do this brother," a voice said in his ear. "You don't have to say goodbye...not now, not ever." Tristan looked around but no one was there. The only person there was Dagnen, shimmering in the light as tears fell from her green eyes. "You can look but you shall not find me brother."

"Why won't she go?" asked Tristan, his voice breaking. "Why won't she be free?"

The voice didn't answer him and Dagnen only stared, more and more tears pouring down her face. He watched as the tears slipped down her face and hit the floor like she was really there and not just a ghostly figure. *Could it be? Could she really be there?*

"Go on!" The voice said, almost as though it knew what he wanted to do. "Just reach out and touch her. I promise you she won't disappear, not unless you truly want her to."

Reluctantly, he reached out his hand, taking a step or two closer to her. Hesitantly, he reached out to hold his hand by her face, his fingers daring to fall right through her. But they did not. He felt them grace soft skin, a coldness pricking his fingers as he rested them there. Gasping, he let his hand cup her cheek, feeling the tears now upon his hand as they fell from his own eyes too. He could hardly believe it, but it made him so happy he could feel himself warming on the inside. *Was she really there...like she was alive?* Or was this all an illusion; a figment of his imagination?

"Who's there?" A voice yelled from the back room threateningly as Frankie appeared in the doorway. "Tristan, what are you doing here? How did you get in?"

He didn't answer straight away, watching as Dagnen faded before him, a smile residing on her sweet face. Unable to believe that it had happened in the first place, he tried to make it seem like he wasn't crazy or breaking in to the place.

"The door...it was open," he stammered, pointing in the direction of the door. "I was hoping you were open."

"I knew I should never have trusted Warrick to close up. I am sorry dear boy but we are closed this evening."

"That's okay, I'll be off then. Good night!"

"Good night my boy."

Frankie nodded to him and Tristan turned to leave, shutting the door behind him and stepping into the rain. Almost instantly it stopped and the only cold feeling was the sharp point which rested at his neck. Looking out of the corner of his eye, he saw the scarred man; Boris the man he had named Tabacious.

"No sudden moves or I'll have ya!" he ordered, holding his sword steady. But he didn't scare Tristan, he never had.

"Oh will you now?" Tristan called his bluff. "You don't have the guts...you're not a killer Boris."

"How do you know that?"

"I don't, but I know you won't kill me. You don't have the nerve."

"Wanna bet!"

In an instant Tristan knocked the sword from Boris' hand as he backhanded it and knocked it to the floor.

"Is that so Tabacious?"

At the utterance of his true name, Boris fell to the floor grabbing hold of his face in pain. Tristan sniggered in response, turning his back on him and heading for the Compound.

"You're not going to kill me?" Boris called out after him as the pain subsided.

"No, it's not just my responsibility...not anymore." Tristan answered ambiguously.

Without uttering another word, he headed in the direction of the Compound at a run leaving Boris to cower, watching after him. He had to find Dante and tell him what happened, not to mention the fact that if Boris had the nerve to strike he would be doing so rather quickly. He didn't want to give him that chance.

# CHAPTER 33 - FAMOUS LAST WORDS

Dante had been waiting for Tristan back at the Compound for nearly three hours now. It had gone midnight and there was still no sign of him. *For god's sake what was he playing at?* He could've gone out looking for him admittedly but with how frustrated he seemed to be getting at his situation perhaps it was better to let him do it alone, to let him go with the flow of whatever was happening. It would be nice to just know where he was though so he could sleep at least. Why did he care so much? Then again, Tristan was family now. Sighing heavily, he slumped down into a chair and gulped down the last of his ale before throwing the tankard down on the table rather aggressively. This was getting ridiculous!

"Refill?" Dante looked up to see Nielson stood at the other end of the table with a full flagon of ale.

"I think I've had enough don't you?" he replied calmly, realising the frustration that was now building within him.

"That's debatable," he poured some ale into Dante's tankard and leant back in his chair, looking him in the eyes with a knowing look. "My brother would always get like that after a couple."

"Like what?" *So he talks about me then?* That had to mean their past was all water under the bridge. "Towards the end he had a lot of anger build up in him and his drinking only made it worse. I don't blame him though, after everything that happened, I finally see the light."

"Tristan said he betrayed the Keeperhood...is that true?" Dante was prying now – he had to find out what Nielson's feeling were towards him.

"Daxon how much do you know about the Keeperhood?"

"My father only told me the basics if I'm honest with you. I was born a Keeper and neither he nor my mother were so it was a bit of a shock for them if I'm honest." He was surprised at how easy it was to lie to his own brother.

"I see what you mean. Well to put it simply, my brother got involved with the wrong people. They lead him astray, he and his friends. At the last minute they did turn against their corrupted brothers...but it was too little late and the Keeperhood banished them to the Land of the Faded."

"Was it not awkward...you know...sticking with the Keepers after they did that to him...your brother I mean?"

"At the time...I believed they were right to do it," Nielson looked down, trying to avoid direct contact with Dante's watery eyes. "I thought he deserved it!" Dante rose from his feet and stared out the window, sipping from his tankard and trying to hide the traitorous tears that were falling down his cheeks.

"And now?"

"I forgive him."

More tears followed those he wiped away and he felt his heart shatter within him. How long he had waited to hear his brother say those words.

"You know when they banished him, I was asked if I wanted to say anything to him. I told him I would never forgive him and that I was disgusted and ashamed to be his brother...to call him my blood. I remember those words as though I had spoken them only yesterday. Call them what you will; my famous last words. I regret them! And I only wish he knew that."

"He does..." Dante blurted out unintentionally.

"How would you know?"

"The dead are always with us," he replied quickly, trying to keep his voice together for the sake of them both. "They hear everything we think about them. I'm sure he knows if you forgive him or not."

"Oh I forgive him...but I'm afraid the Land of the Faded is not as simple as death. It is a torturous place that would make him always remember what I thought of him."

A silence passed between them, giving Dante the chance to sniff and wipe away the rest of his tears. The relief and happiness he was beginning to feel was replaced by a growing anger against his brother for the way he treated him, for not helping fight what happened to him back then.

"I only wish that I could have a moment with him, you know, to tell him I'm sorry. That I was wrong, and I forgive him."

Dante smiled again at Nielson's words, he had waited an age to hear those words and they made him feel more alive than he ever imagined himself being. It was as though even if he didn't manage to help Tristan remember, his second chance would be worth it if only to hear those words.

"I trust you are the same?"

"Sorry?" Dante swung around, the suggestion catching him with his defences down.

"Your brother? I trust you have plenty of words you wished you'd said to him before he died?"

"Oh yeah..."

Nielson inclined his head as though he wanted to hear the details. Maybe he was on to him? But as much as he wanted to embrace his brother once more, what if his forgiveness was just a pretence to impress Daxon? He couldn't risk it...could he?

"I'd tell him I wished I stopped goading him and paid attention to him more. Maybe that way I'd have had more of an influence on his life and he wouldn't have been such a grass."

Now he spoke the truth, tempting Nielson's recluse with spite in his words to see if it would bring on a rage. A thousand years or so of pent-up rage against his brother had led to the feelings he would now express subtly as his character, to see how far his forgiveness stretched.

"I'm not sure I understand." Nielson pried calmly.

"I was a bit of a rebel when I was younger if I'm honest," Dante came to sit back at the table. "I used to go places I shouldn't, do things I shouldn't and the only reason I got caught half the time was because he grassed me up. So I wasn't exactly very nice to him and if affected our relationship when we were older. We weren't close in the slightest."

"So I guess we both need second chances."

"Sounds like."

"Want to hear something ridiculous?" Dante inclined his head in Nielson's direction. "I had you written off as a fraud...I thought he was covering for you, Tristan I mean."

"Why would he do that?" Dante froze. He wasn't quite sure he was ready to come clean to Nielson yet.

"I'm not too sure...like I said...ridiculous..."

That's it, he couldn't hold back any longer. He was going to tell him. Nielson's eyes twinkled and he felt himself thinking that perhaps he already knew but was waiting for confirmation. Either that or he had tears in his eyes from his earlier confession. As he was about to say something though, who should form in the entrance way - *Tristan of course...fucking Tristan!*

"Tristan?" Dante blurted; half relieved and half wishing he had waited a moment or two longer to make his debut appearance. "Where have you been?"

"Around..." Tristan heaved as he caught his breath.

"This is no laughing matter Tristan," Nielson lectured, rising to his feet. "Daxon here has been waiting up half the night for you, even after you abandoned him. I think you owe him an apology." Tristan looked up at Dante who had folded his arms and was now glowering at him - he was loving this.

"Just let me catch my breath and I'll explain." Tristan came to sit at the table, his breath still coming in ragged chunks. He sat and poured himself a tankard of the ale, gulping it down without a second thought.

"Where did you disappear too then?" Dante asked calmly once he'd finished the tankard.

Responding calmly Tristan told them of the events that had ensued. He told them honestly how his head felt like it would explode if he'd stayed a moment longer but he somehow managed to knock himself out and the rest *well that's a bit blurry apparently.* Dante got the impression he didn't want to say too much in front of Nielson, why though he did not know...unless he was afraid of wandering ears that is. Once Tristan had finished recounting the events, he poured himself another tankard, this time sipping it patiently, his face suddenly realising how little he actually liked ale.

"So you followed her ghost?" Dante assumed vacantly, trying to make sense of the gibberish he had just heard.

"Not exactly," Tristan sighed. "I mean I touched her face so that's got to mean something..."

"Wait a minute...you touched her?" Nielson stammered.

"She was in the tavern, like I said. A voice said to me to reach out and touch her face, so I did."

"Who did the voice belong to?" Dante asked curiously.

"I don't know, no one was there. I've been hearing it all night, I thought I was going crazy...I probably am...but I definitely touched her face and she felt it to."

"You really have lost it." Nielson sighed heavily. "She's dead Tristan face it. The quicker you do the better."

Nielson stormed off out of the atrium and in the direction of the dormitories. Tristan didn't quite understand the reason for his outburst but then again, he did raise her.

"You know you really do pick your timings right don't you?" Dante goaded as he rounded on Tristan once Nielson had disappeared.

"Oh so it's my fault he stormed off?" Tristan mocked, gulping down more ale. He didn't usually like ale, but in his current mood he'd drink anything.

"Please don't tell me I have to explain that to you!" Tristan shrugged. "Look I'm not going to berate you on how you should be acting because to be quite honest you wouldn't listen to me anyway. But you have to remember Tristan that Dagnen was as much a part of him as he was of both you and me only perhaps more so. By saying she's alive like you just did, that's going to dreg up some memories that he'd probably rather not have floating around in his head. Plus, it doesn't help with what we were talking about before you came in."

Tristan didn't answer him straight away, he just stared at the dregs of ale in his tankard thinking quietly to himself.

"What were you talking about then?" he asked after a while, not making eye contact with Dante.

"Well put it this way, I was this close to telling him who I am."

"Then why didn't you?"

"Well you walked in didn't you? And besides, even though he says he forgives me - if push comes to shove...which it will...I doubt he'll stick to his word."

"Dante, what you did...it is forgivable, especially by someone who is related to you."

"You have no idea do you?"

"I'm sure it's not as bad as you make out."

"Tristan, I let myself be manipulated into betraying my brothers. I killed Keepers, thousands of them in a bloodthirsty rage. I nearly killed Nielson."

Tristan didn't remember much about the Annals of Unity he had read as a Scribe and Acolyte. He had read perhaps all of them to make sure he did not make the same mistakes they did but the details all seemed to blur into one now. He knew enough not to pursue Dante further for details especially with the distress it seemed to be causing him.

"What stopped you from killing him?"

"I hesitated and it gave my mind the time it needed to focus away from the influence of what was controlling me. I turned on my Brothers of Union and Balderick and Felicious followed suit. We were all exiled though despite it. That's all there is to it." He looked exasperated and tormented.

"That won't matter..."

"Oh what would you know? Once a traitor always a traitor!"

Dante stormed off in the same direction Nielson had moments earlier. Tristan sighed heavily, it wasn't his fault he betrayed so why was he so bothered. Then again, maybe the fact that he let himself be manipulated was what it came down to. His eyes were drawn to the entrance way as Basso walked in dazedly - he had been drinking. He looked to Tristan and nodded, a large black bruise obscuring the look on his face. He looked like he'd gone ten rounds with a bear, not to mention drank a whole gallon of beer at the same time. The only bar around here was Frankie's though and that place was shut so where had he got himself into this state? Tristan watched after him as he disappeared down the corridor towards the dormitories, stumbling over his own feet. Waiting a while before heading back to his own dormitory which he shared with Dante, he watched Basso disappear behind his own door. Lingering, he listened as bangs sounded and glass shattered. Whatever had happened had obviously hacked him off. Shrugging, he disappeared behind his door, only half surprised that Dante wasn't there in his bed.

# CHAPTER 34 - THE MAW OF CHAOS

*Oglivy's Treatise on Sentients and Sacred Places*

*I) Contents of 'Known' Sentients*

| | |
|---|---|
| i. | *Anvil of St James* |
| ii. | *Orion's Medallion* |
| iii. | *The Chalice of the Builder* |
| iv. | *The Crown of the Trickster* |
| v. | *The Elemental Talismans* |
| vi. | *The Eye of the Storm* |
| vii. | *The First Hammer* |
| viii. | *The Hand of the Jackal* |
| ix. | *The Heart of St Bradshaw* |
| x. | *The Horn of Quintas* |
| xi. | *The Onyxum Flambertus* |
| xii. | *The Ruby of Sorrow* |
| xiii. | *The Skull of St Yora* |
| xiv. | *The Spur of St. Dalnir* |
| xv. | *The Staff of St Elderbine* |
| xvi. | *The Tapestry of St Elian* |

## II) Important Chronicles and Annals

i.    The Book of Days
ii.   The Book of Names
iii.  The Compendium
iv.   The Prophecetus

## III) Places of Power

i.    The Abandoned Compound
ii.   The Forgotten Cathedral
iii.  The Library of St Jenkins
iv.   The Maw of Chaos

## III) Places of Power

### Introduction to Sacred Places

Sacred Places are all around us in reality; each faction sees a Sacred Place in a different context. It can indicate anything from a shrine to a religious complex. In the case of this Treatise, Sacred Places are those abandoned by the other factions and reoccupied by Keeper renegades such as the Brotherhoods of Dharsi and Union. These Sacred Places house great power which is originally bound to the founding faction. When these places are abandoned, the magic remains to be reclaimed and wielded sometimes by the wrong party. The magic within these places is to a point un-tameable as well and can therefore be dangerous to those who are not in full understanding of their own abilities and the Glyphs around them, not to mention the belief that a certain type of magic will only comply to its true master.

### III.V - The Maw of Chaos

Ancient Sacred Burial Ground of the Pagan faction, however has been abandoned in the last millennia. The Pagans abandoned the place, which resembles a Cocoon, when Bloodroots began to grow without the necessary rituals and they therefore referred to the place as an abomination. It is believed that the place was adopted by the Brothers of Dharsi however this remains unproven. The room resembles a circle in which the Cocoon sits in the middle with a sacrificial plinth in the centre. Drawn on the floor is a five-pronged star however its exact purpose is unknown. It is thought to have something to do with the Brotherhood of Unity however the theories that state this are unclassified and uncredited.

The Maw of Chaos is said to be capable in rising immense power for the wielder, power capable of the most heinous atrocities.

Two Sentients which have since been linked to the Maw of Chaos; The Ruby of Sorrow and the Eye of Storm. Theories have suggested that the combination of these two artefacts with the Maw of Chaos is what corrupted the Brotherhood of Unity, however once again the reasoning behind this is unclarified. It is however widely believed among the Prodicals and Elders. The exact details of the ritual are unknown however it is thought that the Brothers of Dharsi were the ones that performed it.

For further information see sections on the Ruby of Sorrow and the Eye of the Storm. For more information on the brotherhoods of Dharsi and Unity see Anselm's Treatise on Brotherhood.

*Tristan wasn't sure how long they had been waiting in the clearing however it was clear that Boris was late. Then again why break the habit of a lifetime? He could sense Cedric in the trees becoming wary as he adjusted his position of stealth. The plan was simple - hand over the Eye and then if an attack did ensue, pretend to die. Cedric would handle the rest. Of course he had faith in their Ally but the fact that their lives were in jeopardy here made them all incredibly nervous. A rustle echoed in the trees and Tristan looked to each of his brothers in turn as they all nodded to him.*

*"Sorry I'm late," Boris grunted. "Got a bit lost a few miles back." He was out of breath; it had obviously been quite a trek but then for one as large and out of shape as he was it really surprising?*

*"We were starting to think you wouldn't show." Tristan piped up trying to be his usual arrogant self.*

*"As if I would do that? Now, do we have the...package?"*

*"You make it sound so sordid." Ramien joked, a smile touching his lips as Zhaine gave him a dirty look. Tristan could hear Cedric sniggering away in his thoughts - simple minds.*

*"Ha-ha very funny. Now hand it over!"*

*"Aren't you forgetting something?" Jacques stepped forward and questioned. Boris looked at him blankly however he was unsure as to whether or not the oaf was toying with him.*

*"We had a deal remember?" Zhaine finished, looking snidely at Boris*

*"Oh yes, that's right," it sounded as though Boris was hoping they'd forget. But they weren't as easily lead as he was, they wouldn't forget their brothers that easily.*

*Boris placed his hands in front of him so that they seemed to form an orb in which colour flowed into forming figures all behind bars. What looked to be Sarisus' men were unlocking the doors and leaving the room, releasing the Keepers from the capture they had been under. Although all of them knew it was fake, they had to play along otherwise they wouldn't be pretending they were dead - they would actually be dead.*

*"As promised," Boris started, making the vision disappear by clapping his hands together. "The Keepers have been freed and Sarisus and my comrades have left the Compound."*

*"And as we promised," Jacques stepped forward and unstrung a cloth bag from his waist. "The Eye of the Storm."*

*Out of the bag he pulled a diamond probably the size of his fist if not bigger, showing it to Boris who nodded intently, his eyes widening with glee and lust. Tristan tried desperately not to make eye contact with the gem out for fear its voice would come to him again. He hadn't told anyone he could hear it as well as Jacques and no one was going to find out either because sooner or later; all this would be over.*

*"Don't think you can hide from me betrayer!" Too late, The Eye had seen him anyway and its voice echoed in his mind. "I will always find you."*

*Placing The Eye back in the bag, Jacques handed it to Boris. The traitorous scum smiled widely and took it with both hands, clutching it to his chest like a mouse with a piece of cheese. Come to think of it he did have rather a mousy shaped face.*

*"Pleasure doing business with you gents," He tied the cloth bag to his belt which clung to his abnormally large waist, patting it as he did so. "Well, I'll be seeing you then brothers."*

*"I wouldn't count on it!" Tristan muttered under his breath.*

*They watched after Boris as he strode away out of sight, waiting for an attack. Each minute that passed seemed to drag and ache past. A branch broke under the foot of an unseen man and arrows flew through the air, whistling in the breeze. In an instant, all five brothers dropped to the floor; arrows seemingly buried deep in their chests. Boris let out a snigger as he signalled to the men that lurked in the trees to leave.*

*A few moments later, Cedric dropped down from the trees above and checked around one last time. Nodding, the arrows fell free of their occupants as though they had only been hovering above them, and his brothers rose to their feet shaking off the magic that had given them momentary death.*

*"Good job," Tristan praised, clapping Cedric on the back.*

*"Thanks!" Cedric replied as the others echoed their appreciation. "Now, we have to get back to the Compound."*

*With a flick of his hand, he drew up a port key which would get them back to the Compound of Dilu in no time. Each stepped through it in turn and stopped and stared in bewilderment around the atrium they now found themselves in. A shadowy figure was there waiting for them and he came over to clap them on the back and greet his brothers; perhaps.*

*"The Keepers are free," the shadow echoed. "Sarisus kept that much of his bargain at least." Why couldn't he remember the man who stood before them?*

*"Well at least that's something, now we've just got to find out what he's doing with The Eye." Jacques pondered, noting the disappointed looks on Keepers as they passed them by. Even though they had saved them all, their deeds had cast a dark shadow over their reputation.*

*"That is no longer a problem. Whilst you lot were off playing dead, I managed to find out what Sarisus wants it for. Have you boys ever heard of the Maw of Chaos?" They all shook their heads, all except Tristan being truthful – he had skimmed across it a couple of weeks ago when they first encountered rumours of The Eyes appearance in their destiny. "The Eye is capable of immense power and it is the Maw of Chaos that will help unleash that*

power upon us all casing immense destruction. But it needs space to commit that damage, conceal it and it will destroy not just Sarisus and the Maw but also itself."

"But how do we do that?" Romeo asked.

"It's simple really. You see the Maw is a five-pointed star in the centre of which is an old Pagan Cocoon of power. Your runes of Unity are upon each point of the star and all you have to do is unleash the glyph upon the floor – The Failsafe Glyph. This glyph will contain the power causing it to combust and destroy all those within it. Simple!"

"Sounds it." Ramien shrugged sarcastically – he didn't believe it was, if anything it sounded incredibly complicated.

"Tristan!" a voice called as Dagnen came running towards him, arms held out ready to embrace him. She must've feared him dead, even if that was partly true. The lovers embraced as happiness filled their faces to be in the arms of one another.


The Maw of Chaos was a dark dwelling but that was to be expected considering it was situated inside the centre of a deep mountain of which the point was only slightly hollowed out; enough to let in a little light. In the centre stood Sarisus, the light just reflecting off his balding head, straggly ends reaching his neck by the ears. His eyes were sunken and heavily blood struck by the strain he was trying to muster. Sweeping ripped robes covered his unhealthily thin stature. Below his gaze was The Eye, colour sparking through its crystal surface.

As the brothers spread around the star finding their marks within the Failsafe Glyph, Tristan could feel the words of The Eye trying to reach him at the back of his consciousness. Trying to block it out, he took his place by the Glyph of Nobility and stood tall and strong, waiting for the right moment. And that right moment came soon enough as The Eye shone with power, lightning and thunder striking outside as a storm ensued. The power connected with Sarisus before striking up through the opening above, giving the brothers their cue to act.

The five of them took their places, calling upon all their inner strength as they all glowed, shining with supremacy. The power conjoined together and formed a dome over the Maw, cutting off the Eye's connection to the storm outside. Sparks flew off its fluorescent centre, hitting the edge of the shield that had formed around them. As the power began to strike off of Sarisus he cried out in pain, trying to knock The Eye from the plinth it stood on and smash into oblivion. The brothers stood strong, their shield containing the magic within in as it shrunk smaller and closed in on Sarisus and The Eye. The smaller it got, the more blinding the lights of power became until finally the shield disappeared taking Sarisus' cries with it as he dropped to the floor.

*The ground began to shake and rocks began to fall from the top of the mountain, crashing to the floor as a pile of rubble. Without saying a word, the brothers disappeared, reappearing outside of the Maw and watching as the mountain caved in on itself and Sarisus. The Eye was gone forever and so was he.*

# CHAPTER 35 - MEET THY MAKER

Footsteps echoed on the cobblestone floor and Tristan looked up from the book he was reading. After failing to fall asleep once again he had retreated to the Shrine as he had most nights in recent days and taken to reading his own Annals of Union. The words on the page however could only do so much and although they didn't spark off any memories, it was nice to know what to expect. He watched a shadow begin to appear at the bottom of a bookcase as he stared from where he sat in the alcove of an old shattered painted glass window which had long been bordered up. The shadow elongated and it wasn't long before it became a man - Dante.

"Couldn't sleep?" he asked, stopping by the row of desks and perching himself against it.

"Nope, you?" Tristan replied casually still annoyed at his outburst from earlier that evening. He was annoyed enough at himself for saying and assuming what he did, let alone how much so everyone else would be.

"I was woken up by uh...something." Tristan nodded, an awkward silence passing between them. "Anyway, I was thinking that maybe I should back off a bit. Last night I'd had way too much to drink and it was wrong of me to jump down your throat like that. I should've just listened to you."

"Are you trying to apologise?" Dante nodded - he obviously wasn't the sort to do so often, then again neither was he. "Well I guess you're forgiven."

"You guess? Cheeky git!" They shared a snigger. "What are you reading anyway?"

"The story of me believe it or not."

"Is it any good?"

"Bit crap really. Starts off well and then...Well bad things just keep happening to him."

"I see! One of those woe is me stories."

"That about sums it up if I'm honest."

Tristan laid the book down and faced forward towards Dante in the alcove. He sighed heavily, a thousand thoughts rushing through his mind as though someone was trying to tell him something. Of course, it was only a coincidence that ever since he'd set foot in the Shrine that evening Dagnen's ghostly image had been watching him from the other side of the room.

"I was wondering if I might ask you something," Dante said after a while, a look of torment on his face. "You don't happen to know if there are any other surviving Brothers of Union within the Keeperhood do you?"

"What you mean besides Nielson and Linford?" Tristan questioned as Dante nodded. "There are couple of them, why do you ask?"

"No reason..." Whatever he was going to ask Tristan next he obviously changed his mind about.

"You know it's funny you should ask because there is another from your generation that lives." Dante's face was aghast as though he had seen a ghost. "After Xavier died, a man named Felix was named First Keeper. In my opinion, he was the best man for the job," Tristan recited as though he had read the words from the book he had just laid down. "I later found out that he was like us...like Ramien, he was Unity..."

"So Felicious, or Felix as we called him...he's alive?"

"As far as I'm aware yes. They bought him back not long after you were banished to help them find some Keepers that were missing. So he created The Keys which tell the living status of every Keeper ever named. They're in this Shrine somewhere actually. Why do you ask anyway?"

"The reason I woke up actually. I uh went to that library on the fifth floor and fell asleep. I woke up with this immense pain in my head and my mark on my hand was burning. It felt like my head were about to explode but behind all the screaming that surged through my ears I heard this cry...as though someone was calling for my help. I don't know if they meant to but, only a Brother from my generation would be able to call out to me like that. I can't think of it being Balderick because it felt like he was so close."

"So you think Felix is here in Dilu?"

"Yes, and he's in trouble. We need to find him if he's here."

"I know someone who will know if he is or not...Boris."

"Tristan you can't trust anything that man says. Once he's told you what you want to know he'll just go running off to Hagen and that's not what we need."

"Not if we kill him!"

"You're serious?"

"Well yes. We both named him therefore we both swore to kill him. We might not have meant it at the time...but that's just the way it goes."

"Are you sure you can kill him Tristan...I mean...you're not a killer you said so yourself."

"It's time I stopped sitting around waiting for it all to come back and do something. He's got it coming to him, it's about time he paid for his sins and it's about time I finished what I started."

"Well what's bought this on then?"

"I just don't feel like I'm making any progress. I'm remembering yes, but that's it. There needs to be more."

"So what's the plan?"

"I'm not sure yet but I know that Boris has to be dealt with."

"And then what?"

"I send Hagen a message somehow."

"What will be the aim of that message?"

"A warning...to both him and Charles that both of them will soon be meeting their makers." Dante smiled like he would at his own protégé. Tristan was finally taking some sort of responsibility for himself for once and even though it should have happened sooner it was better late than never after all.


Later that evening, Dante and Tristan snuck out of the Keeper Compound. Merlin and Nielson had been sat in the atrium catching up on old times so it hadn't made the task any easier. They managed it all the same though, even with Basso skulking in a corner. Walking through the night air, Dante led them back towards the Black-Market alley where Boris' shack was situated. As they neared the alley, a dark shadow appeared outside their destination. It was Hagen.

Stopping in their tracks, Dante and Tristan pulled their hoods further over their heads and pretended to be exchanging goods of some form in an alcove of the alley. Hagen passed them and grunted as he pulled his hood over his head, not even batting an eye lid in their direction. Sighing relief, the pair continued up the market street and passed through the door of the shack with ease.

"How can I help you gentlemen?" Boris asked as he laid eyes on the pair. He was obviously still in business hours, otherwise he wouldn't have addressed them in such a courteous tone.

"We have an item to sell." Dante enquired, Tristan nodding in agreement and playing along mindlessly.

"Might I see this item?"

Dante reached deep inside his cloak and Boris' eyes remained on him as he did so. From the reaches he pulled out a medallion which he placed on the counter between them. Tristan noted the sigil on it; a mountain in the centre with pathway drawn down it. It was Dante's own sigil - that ought to put the coward on edge. Boris picked up the medallion and inspected it against the light before tracing his fingers across the smooth pattern. His face seemed suspicious; it was obvious he recognised the mark but he couldn't quite place it perhaps. He turned it round in his large hands, inspecting the crafters hallmark on the back. As he turned it back around his eyes widened as though he suddenly recognised the piece.

"Tell me gents," he started, his voice a little shaky. "Where exactly did you acquire this...item?"

"Some idiot in the tavern," Tristan replied trying to accent his voice as though he were mocking Boris. "This long-haired girly looking thing," He could sense Dante glaring at him, "started a fight with us. But let's just say we aren't folks you wanna be messing with. So we knocked him down a peg or two and took this from his person." Boris was silent, his expression changing from suspicion to subtle panic. "Looked like it would be worth a penny or two so we decided to make sure the next drink was on him." Boris was still silent, his eyes not leaving the cloaked strangers who stood before him.

"Well tell us what it's worth then?" Dante ordered impatiently.

"Well...uh...this certainly is an interesting piece," Boris stammered finally, clearing his throat as he did so. "Looks to be a sigil of the Ashdown family."

"Ashdown you say," Tristan joked - he was having way too much fun with this pretence. "As in the place Ashdown..."

"That's Ashdowns you buffoon..." Dante interjected, getting a little too frustrated with Tristan's mocking attitude.

"Same thing, right?"

"Of course not..."

"Actually your friend is right!" Both of them looked over at him in surprise. "The Ashdown family were the patrons of Ashdowns hence its namesake. When the Auks attacked the king took those he could and fled the country. Then one day, out of nowhere he comes out of the mist with this huge army and destroyed the Auks. They were never seen in these parts again and the king assumed his throne once more."

"See...what did I tell you?" Tristan mocked; he could tell Dante was cursing highly under the hood.

"Look I didn't ask for the history," Dante stepped beside Boris and folded his arms across his chest, looking down on him with a glowering stare. "I asked for its worth."

"Well that's the thing...it has none. The Ashdown's are nothing now and seeing as this isn't gold or nothing precious...like I said, it's worth nothing."

"Oh, well thanks anyway."

Dante snatched the medallion from Boris' clutches before elbowing him in the side and knocking him against the wall. With his free hand, he pulled him up off the floor and Boris' hands rushed to latch onto Dante's as the life was threatened out of him. In all the commotion his hood slipped and Boris' eyes were filled with fear.

"Dante...old friend..." he stammered, a slight chuckle making him eat his own words.

"Old friend huh? Not me and you, you and him maybe though." Dante nodded over to Tristan who pulled down his own hood, forcing more fear into Boris' already crippled eyes.

"How you doing Boris?" Tristan asked, folding his arms as Dante had, a sly grin on his face.

"Tristan...what can I do for you..." he struggled as Dante tightened his grip. "Oh come on, what have I done now?"

"Where is Felix?" Dante glowered; his face filled with anger.

"Felix why do you...oh I see..."

"Tell me where he is or I swear to god I will rip your face off."

"Don't worry, I believe your threat. But I honestly don't..."

"No lies Boris! You forget there are two of us and one of you. Not to mention, we have leverage."

"Oh come on Dante...I have a wife...kids..."

"You lie! Who would ever lie with you?"

"Someone might..."

Boris lurched forward as Tristan stepped up to pull Dante back. A smile touched his face before he keeled over in pain from the burning of his scar. Tristan kicked him in the face so that he fell on his back and held a dagger to his throat.

"We've been here before Tabacious," he leant in close to his face and said loud enough for Dante to hear. "Only this time I will actually kill you...and you know I will."

Boris looked up into Tristan's eyes as he stopped squirming. He watched as they filled with anger and a lust for blood. Vengeance would be his no matter what Boris was to say so maybe his futile attempts at stalling his own death were as dumb as they seemed.

"Tell me what happened to Felix!" Tristan sneered, a thousand memories rushing through his mind of Keepers all wondering as to Felix's whereabouts; Charles' appointment as the new First Keeper; the trail of blood in Felix's office; his old friend's face passing into a silvery liquid expanse and disappearing forever.

"We cursed him," Boris explained, for the first time in his life being truthful. "We tried to use him to our own benefit and the curse we placed on him is the equivalent of you naming one of us. He tried to resist at first, hence why we had to put the curse into play."

"So you made him disappear?"

"No! That was never meant to happen but...but...someone intervened," He had been trying to say a name but it was like he couldn't. He wanted to, but something was stopping him. Perhaps there was more who he was bound to. "A couple of months ago he came back from wherever it was we put him. He just appeared one day here in the Compound and when he went on the streets he bumped straight into Hagen. He's been imprisoned up at the estate ever since."

"What does Hagen want from him?"

"Information. Felix has a power, that's why they bought him out of exile in the first place. They bought him out to help them locate some missing Scribes. So he created the keys so that he could tell the living status of every Keeper and help track them down."

"So he's using Felix to find someone?"

"You, he's using Felix to help him find you!"

"What does he want with me?"

"Isn't it obvious?"

Tristan got up and stood with his back to Boris and Dante, going over the words in his head over and over again. Dante on the other hand, stepped up once again and dragged Boris up to his feet. He unsheathed his own dagger and buried it deep in Boris' side, causing blood to spill from his mouth. He beckoned to Tristan who came over and looked Boris straight in the eyes.

"Do me a favour Boris," Tristan whispered into his ear. "When you meet thy maker, give him a message from me. You tell him that I will be finishing what I started, one by one, so to make room for all those whose time is up."

Boris managed a smile, as though he thought Tristan's words were wasted on him. It was as though he thought Tristan would not finish him. This new Tristan didn't have half the backbone he'd once had, he could kill anyone. That was where he was wrong though; for Tristan was more himself now than he ever had been. Boris' smile was soon wiped clean from his face as Tristan smiled back in a menacing manner.

"Now to turn you into a message Tabacious." Tristan suggested, tracing the outline of Boris' jaw with his dagger.

"And how do you propose we do that?" Dante asked, a smile now on his face too.

"Use the scar!" A voice commanded in Tristan's ear. He didn't bother to look; he knew he would find no one there so it was pointless really.

Moving his dagger up to where the scar was engraved on Boris' face, he cut deep enough to spill the blood. He traced the dagger around the scar, removing the skin from the right side of his face. Boris screamed out in agony as he felt his flesh burn with pain. As the skin fell away from his face, the flesh seemed to steam as though it actually was burning. Boris clambered in panic, trying to reach up at where his scar had been but Dante kept a strong grip at his neck. Once Tristan was satisfied with his trinket as it were, he turned back to Boris. His dagger dove deep into his chest, causing more blood to spill from his lips. Dante released his grip and he dropped to the floor, blood creating a pool around his lifeless body.

"So what do we do with that now then?" Dante asked, pointing at the skin that now hung from the end of Tristan's dagger.

"Find me something to put it in, like a box." Tristan ordered. "It has to be something Hagen won't suspect to be odd." Dante looked around to find nothing.

Shaking his head, he charged up the stairs to the sleeping quarters and to his delight found a plain wooden box on the dresser. He opened it up to find it empty, just as he expected the whole room would be. Boris was stupid yes, but he wasn't stupid enough to leave anything incriminating lying around where people could easily find it. Shrugging his shoulders, he raced back downstairs to Tristan and opened the box before placing it on the counter. Carefully, Tristan let the skin drop into the box before sealing it tight with an old lock he'd found in a drawer whilst Dante was upstairs.

"When the guards come out tomorrow for the weekly offerings, we are going to hand this over to them discretely." Tristan explained with a devious smirk on his face. It wasn't so much that he was enjoying the torture that he had just inflicted, it was more the sweet taste of justice which his hands had just dealt. "It'll get pulled up when the guards go through it later and handed straight to the Barron. And when he opens it...well the message will be as clear as crystal."

"Not a bad plan," Dante reasoned, looking back over at Boris' corpse. "But how do we ensure that Hagen won't come here between now and tomorrow evening?"

"It doesn't really matter if he does. Boris is dead and the message is ready. Whether he finds him or not makes no difference, he'll soon know what's coming to him."

"That being said, what do you intend to do with Hagen?"

"Well I can't kill him, but I know someone who can."

Dante didn't say anything in response, the look on Tristan's face told him enough that he needn't bother to worry too much about the rest of the plan. He knew by now that he was more of a take it as it comes sort of person. Needless to say he was proud of Tristan in this moment for becoming everything he once was and as they departed the old shack and headed back to the Compound in silence, he was confident that his memory would be intact in no time. More confident than he had ever been.

# CHAPTER 36 – THE KEYS NEVER LIE

The following morning saw Dante and Tristan sneak out of the Compound once again without attracting the attention of Basso, Merlin or Nielson. Although Merlin might agree with their intentions, they weren't so sure he would be as happy with their methods. The back entrance of the Compound found them in a dark alley just a few doors down from the tavern and the town square. The streets themselves were unusually busy, people were everywhere in large crowds, swarms of guards cluttered among them. Deciding they were probably better off keeping a low profile, they lifted their hoods and darted across to the alleyway opposite, making sure no eyes were upon them. Checking their backs, a hooded figure suddenly knocked straight into Tristan, throwing him to the floor with the figure landing on top. As Dante turned to see what all the fuss was about, he noticed the hood slip away to reveal a thick blonde plait. It was a woman, no doubt some whore trying not to be seen by the guards. Sniggering to himself, he extended a hand to her and helped her to her feet before turning back to help Tristan.

The woman began straightening her cloak and brushing the dust from her blue dress. Both Dante and Tristan turned to face her, startled when they realised her identity as the Lady Myrina. She said nothing to them, she simply stared at Tristan as though she now knew who he was.

"So you're not Baldor Runcorn then?" she asked after a while, obviously sick of the silence. Tristan shook his head in response, his eyes focused upon her as they clouded over in thought. "And you, Lord Balthier Ashdown?"

"Not exactly," Dante replied, thinking twice about telling her the truth. "Daxon is my real name."

"It appears we aren't so well met after all."

"Yeah yeah whatever! You want to tell me what you're doing outside of the Estate?"

"What business is it of yours?"

"Well…I…uh…"

The words of their bickering silenced before Tristan as he became unaware of what was going on around them. Around him was filled with spitting rain and howling winds. The street ahead was dark and two figures stood before him, both of which he recognised as Romeo and Myrina. He stood holding her hands within his as the rain beat down upon them. Stepping closer, Tristan tried to hear the words they might have been exchanging, but they were not his to remember and so they fell on deaf ears. Looking up high at the rain, he could see lightning strike the tall tower that stood behind Romeo. It was in that moment he knew the event that was about to occur and he wished it away, closing his eyes tightly. Since remembering the death of his brother not one night had he spent asleep where he hadn't seen it again and again.

He wished hard and suddenly the sound of the wind and rain was silent for a moment and briefly he opened his eyes. Around him, the storm continued only now it was he who stood holding Myrina's hands within his own. Behind him stood the Compound at Hasaghar in wreck and ruin, parts of the structure crumbling away and hitting the ground. He looked back at Myrina and himself, the rain blending in with the tears that were visible on her face through her damp locks of blonde hair. They pleaded with him, silent at first but eventually, the words became heard.

"Please Tristan," she begged, her voice breaking through the sound of the wind. "You don't have to do this. You can come back with me now and we can leave here and never come back."

"I have to avenge them Myrina," Tristan tried to reason in her. Within the Compound he was sure was Charles. Vengeance would definitely be on the cards. "There is no question of it."

"But what about Evie? What happens to her if you don't come back?"

"Why, that's what you and Cedric are for…" he joked, but Myrina didn't seem impressed.

"Don't joke around Tristan, this isn't the time for it." His smile faded and she pleaded again. "Please Tristan, please don't do this."

"Myrina I will come back, I swear it."

She pleaded with him again and again, refusing to let go of his hands and sinking to the floor as he pulled away repeating his promise over and over again.

"I will come back Myrina, I swear it." He repeated, almost as tough he was reciting it as part of a prayer.

Finally, he released himself from Myrina's grip, his already broken promise still emanating from his lips. Without looking back, his legs carried him warily through the crashing rubble and into the darkness of the Compound. Myrina was left to crouch on the ground in the rain, her begging still heard on the streets even through the wind and the rain and the banging of the thunder that time forgot.

Then all at once he was back in the present where Myrina and Dante stood before him bickering about whether or not he had the right to demand why she was here and not in the estate. It was a question which rested on his lips too but he dared not speak it until he had earnt her forgiveness for his broken promise.

"I uh, I have every right in my place as a lord," Dante stated, standing straight with his shoulders back.

"You...a real lord?"

"Yes...I..."

"Oh Dante give it a rest!" Tristan sighed heavily, cursing as he did so.

"Dante?" Myrina questioned. "I thought he said his name was Daxon?" Dante's eyes widened at Tristan, scorning him but he didn't care all too much for the disapproval he was obviously expressing.

"It doesn't really matter what his name is, he's not important." Now Dante looked back and cursed him under his breath, causing a giggle to escape Myrina as a twinkle appeared in her eyes.

"So you're back then?" she asked happily.

"How can you tell?"

"You seem different today. I mean at the ball I didn't even recognise you until two seconds before you disappeared...but today...I don't know how to explain it. You just seem like you I guess."

"Excuse me," Dante interjected becoming impatient with their lack of worry towards the guards that were swarming the streets. "But may I remind you the streets are teeming with guards who are probably searching for you?" he pointed to Myrina in a patronising fashion. "So if I might ask again, what brings you to the streets of Dilu...my lady?"

"Well seeing as you asked so nicely; I have a message...for Tristan." The two nodded in response, neither had expected the answer - perhaps more along the lines that she had escaped Hagen's clutches and was never going back. "A message from the First Keeper."

"From Felix?" Dante questioned, his face filling with remorse. "He's still alive then?"

"Yes, but he's weak. To be honest I don't know how he's still alive with the injuries I've seen on him."

"How did you find him? B...We heard he was being held prisoner."

"He is! Down in the dungeons. But I was led to him by a...a...something through a secret passageway which connected to my chambers." She was choosing her words carefully here but Tristan was unsure as to why.

"So this message," Tristan ushered. "What is it?"

"Hey, there she is!" In that moment a guard appeared at the other end of the alley and ushered to his companions. "Good work you two!" He obviously assumed that Dante and Tristan had cornered her and weren't letting her pass, from their positions against the only other exit it looked likely.

"Out of time!" Dante said in an undertone as Myrina ran towards Tristan who braced her by the arms.

"Tristan listen to me," she panicked. "The keys never lie remember that. Nobility lives!"

"I don't understand..."

"You will in time!" she reached up and kissed him on the cheek, whispering the words in his ear once more.

"I will come back for you Myrina, I swear it!" he said as she was pulled away.

As if out of nowhere the two guards were now upon them and dragging Myrina away. Although she let them take her reluctantly, Tristan could tell by the look on her face that she wasn't happy about it. As she was pulled out of sight and no doubt clambered in some carriage before being taken back to the Estate, Tristan thought over her words as they rang in his head.

"The keys never lie," Myrina's voice echoed over and over again. "Loyalty lives!" What could she have meant?

He felt a sharp hand clap his shoulder and bring him back to life. Dante's face loomed in on his and he signalled to the toll bell sounding to mark the start of the gift giving. They had a job to do! Tristan nodded, pushing the echoes to the back of his mind and followed Dante out into the street. A guard approached them and shook his cloth bag in their direction, prompting Dante to slip the box into it. The guard didn't batter an eye lid, he just continued on his way. Later when they went through their sacks they would notice the blood that now stained the dark box and open it to find that piece of Boris. He could see their faces now, filled with shock and even more so when they would run to his shop and find his body. It bought him a feeling of completeness, like some form of justice had been dealt. In a way, it had for both of them.

When he turned around Tristan was not there, nor was he anywhere to be seen.

"What the fuck?" Dante cursed, looking around. Where had he gone?


Tristan stopped as he neared the Compound, keeling over to catch his breath. Myrina's words still span around his head, they were what spurned him on. It could only mean one thing, but he had to see it for himself and before he knew it, he was running again through the Compound and to the entrance of the Shrine. He still didn't know where his feet were taking him, but he was confident they at least knew. To the fire in the centre of the Shrine and down a passageway to the left which came to a square room. Chests lay up against each wall, chests that had once contained sentient objects which had long been confiscated for fear generations of traitorous brothers of Union would use them for evil. Now they lay empty and the walls above them a ghostly transparency, as though it wasn't really there at all. It shimmered and a plaque appeared to rise through it as though a hand were reaching through to grab him from the other side. The plaque contained a golden key in the centre which shone brightly and a name plate underneath it. According to the engraving the key belonged to him, Tristan Romano - alive and well.

The Keys were created by Felix; it was part of the reason he was bought back from the Faded lands. He always had a gift for being able to connect with other Keepers and see if they were safe. During the time of the tenth generation, many Scribes vanished and some turned up dead a few days after their disappearance, much like they had in Tristan's Acolyte years. Their only choice was to bring Felix back to help them find out the identity of the tenth generation and bring them to justice. His reward would be his freedom, and as much as it pained him to leave his brothers to suffer, he had to accept. He created the keys so that the Keepers would always be able to trace their brothers through the branding marks upon each.

Closing his eyes, he tried to remember how to summon the keys of the desired Keepers, opening them out of frustration again when he failed. But the key changed. No longer was it glowing yellow, now the yellow outlined a smoky key which seemed to ripple between life and death. The key belonged to Romeo - he was in the Land of the Faded...he lived! *But how?* He asked himself out loud. He had watched his brother fall to the ocean below Deaths Toll, how is it this Key said he had faded instead. Myrina was right and through the questions he felt his mouth twist into a smile, perhaps he wasn't so alone after all.

An idea came to mind, and he closed his eyes again thinking of his Dags. How he considered there even a possibility that she lived escaped him but if Romeo was alive then she could be too...surely. Moments later, he opened his eyes and the key remained the same, the name plaque underneath changing to her name. His smile faded and a tear slipped down his suddenly pale face. She too was faded, alive - but how?

He heard footsteps behind him and turned suddenly to see Dante appear in the archway, jumping. He stared at the key in bewilderment. His granddaughter was alive, that much was clear.

"I don't understand," Tristan murmured. "How, I watched them both die..."

"I assume that means Romeo's key was the same?" Tristan nodded dazedly as Dante's voice choked. "The keys never lie Tristan, that much I do know. How is perhaps a question we should be posing to the books in this here Shrine."

"You have a theory?"

"I do, and I think our answers lie with the Eye of the Storm."

Their gaze met and a renewed hope sparked within them. How was going to have to be a question they answered themselves. They keys never lie, and that would be the hope that spurned them on until they found those answers.

# CHAPTER 37 - THE EYE OF THE STORM

It bought such joy to see your face light up at the keys shadowy glow. It brought a certain warmth to my core, something I had not felt in an incredibly long time, so long in fact the feeling itself was alien to me now. I do remember the last time though, clear as crystal. Back then we were all different people, it was the intensity of the situation that made us feel so alive, that constant feeling like life had no plan for us and we could do whatever we wanted. Of course, then fucking destiny got in the way. Destiny is funny like that; it takes away your dreams and uses your nightmares to drag you down and trap you into believing it's all meant to be. Life has many different paths and it is up to us to choose the right one, so how can it be called fate or destiny if we are the one that has a say in the direction we go? I remember you used to say to me the best way to live was to treat every day as though it would be your last and as though you would die the next. A touch of my brother was coming through in you now, you were slowly getting back to your old self, which meant hopefully we would be reunited once again.

A single word brings me out of my thoughts and that is when I see her, standing by one of the chests and leaning against the wall as though she is part of your world. But then I suppose she is, more so than me anyway with all her colour. I watch alongside you as the room begins to shake but we do not feel a thing. The room seems to regain its steadiness and the keys change - even I am shocked to see what they say. That silver was tainted by the red outline and even as I looked over at her, the colour in her faded - she was shadowing and soon she would resemble the black and white which I adorned. But why? For she was most certainly more alive than I ever was. As I looked back at you brother, I saw the hope light up inside of you at the thought of us both being alive. But at the same time I see the confusion and it extends to me. Even I do not know how I live!

I look back at her, almost asking her why, but as usual it's as though she does not see me. Could Cedric have something to do with the way things have gone for her? I see now more than ever that my purpose in this world has shifted and that is perhaps why I am still here. My purpose is not to make you remember, you have plenty of people around you to help you in that; Dante, Merlin, Nielson, heck even Basso to some extent. Perhaps my purpose in this world was to help her, bring her back to you and thus conjoin the two worlds that are separated by our depths of colour. She looked over at me then and we shared the same gaze as a tear slipped from her eyes and they faded from green to grey. She was already dying, but why? I couldn't understand it, you were remembering her; so what was the problem?

Passing straight through me, she led the way back into the shrine and I followed alongside my brother and Dante. As I step into the room again and come to stand next to her by the desks, she looks up at me and points to a book resting upon it. It looks old, it's leather cover bound but scratched at the spine. It had obviously been read a great many times but its importance in this situation didn't yet strike me. It was clear that she wanted my help though, making herself visible to only you was making her weaker than ever. I tried to muster up the strength I needed and for a moment I felt your eyes on me as in the panic I make myself known to you. I feel the power though, just for an instant, and using all the force I have I strike the book to the floor. The sound makes Dante jump out of his skin and you snigger, your eyes still focused on me as I feel the power leave my limbs and I feel I remain invisible once more. You look away longingly, your focus on the book that now lies open on the floor. Dante stares at the open pages, confused as to where he's supposed to be looking. I look over at her and she mouths a word to me that I think I understand 'storm'. Using the magic I once knew, I imagine the pages flicking through, searching for the passages on the Eye of the Storm. Not even I know what she thinks will be there. You go to stand with Dante and pick up the book, reading aloud the words as though you knew them by heart.

*Oglivy's Treatise on 'Known' Sentients*

*I.VI – The Eye of the Storm*

*The Eye of the Storm is a crystal about the size of a man's fist and capable of immense power. In life, the power inside the crystal was a man who had two brothers (see Cesca's Treatise on the Broken Brotherhood). One was born from a Storm, the other of Sorrow and the other of Unity. Storm and Sorrow were ruthless and always jealous of their brother. They tried to plot against him but failed and their* power became trapped inside crystals to contain them (also see section on the Ruby of Sorrow).

The Eye is said to talk to the hearts of men who are most vulnerable, but only those who have seen time can truly possess the Eye, even if just for a short while. The true extent of its power has never been witnessed by a living man and stories of its power I'm sure are heavily exaggerated. When it was seized from the seventh generation of Brothers, the Eye was sealed away in a Cathedral owned by the Hammerites in Camto, Degstan protected by both the living and dead. Such desperate measures must be taken when considering an item of this grandeur (see section on the Forgotten Cathedral).

Despite its short history, there are many legends regarding a crystal of this appearance. All such legends talk of an actual human eye lying in the centre of the crystal that is only visible to those most vulnerable when they hear the words it speaks. Other legends speak of its brother; The Ruby of Sorrow in its most simplistic form, a red crystal. When the two are united within the Maw of Chaos, they are capable of corrupting any generation of souls who are named, cursing them to an eternity of Betrayal and evil. Such a curse if often linked to why The Brothers of Union turned however, there is likely little truth to this myth.

The last legend I would like to mention talks of the crystal having power beyond its own destruction. Supposedly, The Eye is linked to the Faded Lands which would actually make a lot of sense with regards to the soul that lies within it. It is said that when the Eye is destroyed, the place which it is in becomes immediately linked to the Land of the Faded. Therefore any soul that dies within the proximity goes straight there, their body left to rot in the physical world. It is not known how true this is, but given the constant unstableness of the border of the Faded Lands the likelihood of this being plausible is actually rather credible. Whether or not the spirit could be resurrected or not is not known. But I imagine that if a person had been struck by the Bleak Unwritten (see Palus' Treatise on the Unwritten Times) and then remembers the soul they lost to the Eye and to the Faded Lands, it is believable that such a power could be imaginable at least.

As you turn the page to finish the passage, a piece of parchment falls to the floor without you noticing. Dante sees it though and picks it up, placing it before your eyes to read.

*The Eye was thought lost after the fiftieth generation stole it from the Cathedral on a mission from Sarisus. But their intentions were more than they seemed for they wanted to destroy the Eye once it had reached maximum power within the Maw of Chaos. The plan had gone ahead, but somewhere along the line there must have been a hiccup because two years later it turned up in a museum in Hasaghar. Having retrieved it to make the Final Glyph, the fiftieth generation were once again in possession of it. But it had quite a hold over one of them and tempted them into betraying. Resisted though he did, it was difficult. After placing The Eye in the fountain of the southern district, nothing had happened like it was meant to. In a fit of rage, Nobility took a hammer to the Eye, smashing the crystal into a million tiny pieces and summoning the Final Glyph. Only Union can destroy what Union put there so it would seem that perhaps Nobility was the culprit behind the creation of The Eye hence its control over him. It is therefore possible that the legend stated by Oglivy is a repercussion of one member of Union destroying a Sentient without the support of their brothers.*

Those words were my own, and as you finished reading them, I recalled writing them so shortly after Dagnen's death. I had been the only one you told about the voices you were hearing from The Eye and I had helped you work through it. I had told you that Destiny isn't set in stone. Anything can change it meaning anything can happen. Our actions control us, not fate.

I looked up and see your face so full of light and wonderment. The passage itself had answered a lot of questions that I and probably her both had. I remember my death as though it were yesterday, but then it might as well have been. In the Faded Lands the days melted into one but in this world of light and dark the difference was clear and made me miss a physical presence in this world even more. I had even missed the way I had felt when I had died, that feeling of pain and life rushing out of my veins. I didn't feel alive anymore - I was truly dead it seemed - and you my brother would make me alive again eventually.

But first, I had to help you along the way, starting with her. Something was keeping her in this world and therefore making her die and I wasn't sure what. Perhaps there was something in the world of light that she didn't want, that she didn't care for. But again, what? Whatever it was, I would surely find out and before long she would be yours again and we would both join you in this world of light. I watched as you looked over at Dante who looked as though he hadn't believed the words he had just heard. He was confused, you were confused. But if it were all true than we weren't dead, we were alive and had every opportunity to come back to your world of light. And that is something I greatly wanted dear brother. I wanted to feel again, to be felt. I wanted my beloved and I wanted you. I wanted everything this world of light had to offer, even the bastard that sent me here - I wanted to get my hands on him and gut him limb from limb...

Wait...that was it! What if that was what she didn't want? She obviously wanted to be with you and with your daughter, but perhaps she didn't want what put her here and that's what held her to this world. I had to show her that didn't matter, and that all she had to do was make herself reborn. It would be a mighty task, but I fancied my chances I must say. I guess I had you to thank for that; for my witty remarks dear brother, I had you to learn from my whole life, even if it should've have been the other way around.

# CHAPTER 38 - MORE THAN REMEMBERING

As he read the words from the passage, the words of The Eye came creeping back to his ears like some horrible nightmare. Those nightmares that the more you try to desperately wake yourself up from the deeper in you slip. It's one of those nightmares that repeats over and over until you're out of the phase that caused that nightmare, whatever that phase might be. Those kinds of nightmares are the worst, they're the sort where if they came to life, actual life wouldn't be worth living no matter who was in it and what your purpose in it was. Tristan removed them from his mind easy enough for the moment though, that was the difference between then and now. Back then The Eye spoke of him betraying the Keepers and everyone he loved. Those weren't his fears any more though, and they probably never would be again. Now his fears involved losing his daughter.

"So this passage here," Dante began, disturbing the silence. "There's a possibility that both Dagnen and Romeo are alive."

"I think so!" Tristan stammered, trying to make sense of it in his own head before he attempted to explain it to someone else. "I mean if the legends are true then there's an overlap of worlds in Hasaghar. I imagine it's like the faded lands overlap the real world and that the two intermingle with each other. That's why there are so many stories at the moment about that place being like a ghost town, because it literally is."

"Do you reckon that's how I came back?"

"You'd have ended up in Hasaghar if you did. But it might answer why people are coming back before I've even remembered them..."

"Like me I take it." A voice came from the entrance of the Shrine. Both Dante and Tristan turned to find a man stood in between the bookcases. How long he had been standing there they did not know. But then who even was he? He looked familiar but Tristan just couldn't place his face.

"How did you get in here?" Dante blurted out more out of apprehension than actual curiosity.

"Maybe I should be asking you the same thing?"

He stated in a mocking tone which seemed to match his demeanour, like it was just in his nature to do so. Then again, his expression was cheeky looking, like a child who constantly tested the limits of their unwitting parent. Come to think of it his stance even gave away the same casual nonchalant approach; like you could say anything to him, even insult him and it would not faze him.

"Wait a minute," Dante yelled, pointing a finger at the man as though it had just dawned on him who he was - a notable figure maybe. "You're that Ser from the ball the other night. What was your name...Brandon something?"

The man raised his sublime eyebrows and clapped his large hands together twice.

"Well done...but not correct." He folded his arms across his chest and looked down on them as he took a few steps closer to them. "You see I too was faking my identity."

"I knew it!"

"Did you? Did you really?"

"Yes...I mean what kind of name is Brandon anyway."

"You do realise you sound like an idiot?" Dante looked back at Tristan as though to ask him to back his corner, stand up and say 'he's no idiot' like some sort of doting follower.

"He is right you know," Tristan said quietly, not making eye contact with Dante.

There was silence for a while as Dante tried to shake off his moment of humiliation. Tristan on the other hand was desperately trying to place the face of the man that stood before them with the brown hair that curled up at the base of his neck; the green eyes that were not so dis-similar to Dante's - deep set in a mysterious sort of way.

"Zhaine?" Tristan whispered to himself in thought as the name that belonged to the face came swimming back to him. "Zhaine Veres?" The man nodded as the smile turned from one of sarcasm to one of pure happiness.

"Veres?" Dante repeated as the name struck a meaning with him. Veres was he and Nielson's shared middle name, it had been their father's name and meant victory to the lands in the far south of Aberson. *It couldn't be, surely?* It would make sense for Nielson to change his last name, especially after what Dante did.

"The honourable Zhaine Veres I would prefer," the smile was back on his face now and his sarcasm had reached the surface too. "But Zhaine will do I suppose."

"You've not changed one bit, have you?" Tristan joked, sharing the smile as he stepped forward to grasp his brother in a sentimental clinch.

"I never change for anyone you should know that."

"And Ramien?" The two broke away and again the smile faded. Out of all the people he had been reunited with, Zhaine seemed the most broken; like he had been strong all his life but now his resolve was breaking and taking his defences with it.

"Not seen him since it happened. It's not just about remembering anymore though Tristan. You've got to take action!"

"Good job I have then." Tristan turned back to face Zhaine, catching Dante's glance as he did so. The man was lost deep in thought, his eyes filled with doubt as they raced from side to side with theories unknown to Tristan. He decided to leave him to it for now, Zhaine obviously wasn't concerned with who he was and neither was Dante for the moment.

"Don't tell me you're the reason they're screaming murder on the streets? The pawn shop owner was found dead with a chunk of his face missing. Pretty gruesome from what I hear."

"I think you'll find his name was Tabacious."

Zhaine's grin dropped, his face slipping into momentary shock - he had only been joking about Tristan being the reason the streets were rife with guards. He hadn't expected it to be true.

"And we had...unfinished business."

"So that's what it's come to then?"

"I'm finished here Zhaine, it's time to move on to the next bit. But I can't go without tying up these lose ends and I can't leave without Myrina."

"So you've seen her then?"

"Yes! And he has Felix too according to Boris."

"So I've heard. But what's your plan Tristan; by the God's tell me you have a plan."

"I have a baseline but we'll leave it at that for now."

"Just like old times. Anyway, who's your friend?"

"Meet Dante Ashdown!"

The utterance of his own name bought Dante out of his thoughts and suddenly he was nervous. Too many people were beginning to know who he really was and it was worrying him greatly. No way would he go back to the Land of the Faded, he'd rather die. But the significance of who the two were to each other had only just struck Tristan, if he'd realised sooner, he'd have introduced them sooner.

"Not as in my dad's brother Dante Ashdown?"

Zhaine marvelled in disbelief. His father had told him a couple of stories about the fifth generation of brothers after he discovered that he himself was one but he hadn't told him that he was blood related to one of them - Zhaine had worked that much out for himself but never said anything. He could tell by the look in his father's eyes it wasn't a subject he spoke of without pain.

"Apparently so," Dante managed, his voice shaking.

"Don't worry, your secret is safe with me...if you are trying to keep it a secret that is."

"I'm going by Daxon for the moment."

"Daxon - I like it. I assume you never knew you had nephews?"

"Nephews?"

"I've got two older brothers - Rafe is...was the oldest of us all, he was killed while we were Acolytes. Then there's my brother Ramien, there's not much between us, just over a year whereas Rafe is much older. Eight years separated me and him but we don't share the same mother. Dad never spoke much about her to be honest."

"It seems I get more family by the minute. I mean first I find out I've got a great granddaughter and now nephews." Dante sighed heavily, shrinking back and leaning against the desk behind him overwhelmed.

"You know your dad's here," Tristan said after a while.

"He is?" Zhaine gasped. "I was beginning to think he was dead. He never faded like the rest of us."

"Guess you can't fade twice then."

"I imagine it's something like that. So, does he not know you're back then Dante?"

"Nope!" Dante sighed. "Can't bring myself to tell him just yet. Not to mention the fact that I don't want Basso finding out."

"Basso is here too?"

"Yes. I don't trust him though, so he can't find out."

Zhaine nodded and left the subject alone. His uncle puzzled him, surely his father would be made up if he saw him again, but then maybe their relationship was a bit more complicated than either were letting on.

"So you think she's alive then, Dagnen I mean?" Zhaine assumed after a while.

"Yes, I do. I see her everywhere I go, she's always by my side. I don't know how it's possible though, unless she is Greater faded. Have you seen her?"

"I think I saw her back there, I mean it had to be her. I could be wrong though, I only saw her the once and it was from a distance. But I could tell those eyes anywhere..."

"You can't give him flash hope like that!" Dante stated, stepping forward and looking down on Zhaine in a threatening manner.

"Oh and I suppose you know what's best for him do you?"

"I'm not saying that!"

"Then what are you saying?"

"Look the girl is my granddaughter of course I'd want her to be alive but I have to be realistic. Yes, the book said according to legend once the Eye is destroyed the Faded lands will lie over the Land like a blanket and all those that die will transcend to the world above. But that doesn't mean that they can come back from it least of all whether that be alive or dead."

"He can still hope..."

"I'm not saying he can't hope. All I'm saying is he needs to come at this from two approaches. The first being that she could come back but in that same instant she could drop to the floor and die in his arms all over again. She has no body to come back to so she's just a spirit really. Of course, he can think that she lives and that's as far as it can go. Otherwise he's just going to break all over again."

"You don't know him like I do..."

"I am still here you know!" blurted Tristan, sick of neither of them acknowledging his opinion.

Everyone since he had started remembering had been more about what they thought was best for him rather than asking him what he thought. The two were definitely related the way they argued though.

"Neither of you know what's best for me. So I suggest you both just pipe down...okay?"

The two of them nodded, neither having expected his outburst. He shook his head and stormed out of the Shrine and Zhaine cast a look in Dante's direction questioning why he started that.

"Don't start!" he smirked before Zhaine even had chance to open his mouth.

Dante stormed out of the Shrine after Tristan, knocking into Zhaine deliberately as he passed him. The man was actually rather childish for someone who was older than a thousand years. But as he'd been banished at the age of maybe thirty at the eldest perhaps a thousand years of torture didn't leave much room for growing old.

# CHAPTER 39 - THE FIRST KEEPER

Dante hadn't gone after Tristan in the end, he'd grown tired of trying to steer him in the right direction and then picking up the pieces from where he'd failed. The boy was stubborn and arrogant; much like himself actually, but there was no way he was going to admit that. Instead he'd found himself staring up at the estate trying to keep out of view of the guards that littered the city. Pulling his cloak hood up further, he made a move towards the entrance gate. A couple of guards stood at the huge oak doors whilst another two circled the perimeter of the grounds going in opposite rotations. It looked easy enough for a Keeper like him to get past but the risks were too high to go at it like a cocky brat - his magic might not work as well as he assumed, not to mention the fact that some of the guards could be Keepers themselves and then his cover would be blown.

To the left of the gate was a patch of climbing ivy that clung tightly to a gargoyle atop the post, reaching past the ground that Dante stood on. He pulled on it, testing its strength against his weight as it held fast. Gently, he took a hold of the vines and began to climb the wall that encased the estate, reaching forward carefully with each grab and his feet nudging the wall as he tried to steady himself every so often. Once he reached the top, he scouted the direction either side of him to see no guards pacing. Taking his chance, he dropped down from the wall, bending his knees as he landed firmly. Luckily a bush now shielded his watch as the guards loomed into sight on their rounds but they disappeared again quickly enough. He followed the wall to the left, still shielded by bushes, watching the walls of the estate for the entrance he only presumed would be there.

The building itself was a great many centuries old and had once been the original Keeper Compound at Dilu. Any passageways that were there before would therefore remain and that would be his route. Spying a bluish glow, he stopped suddenly, watching the wall as the Keeper Port Key glyph appeared. He smiled to himself, watching the way for the guards before darting out towards it and placing his hand down on the door. The wall broke away and at once he stepped through into a dark narrow passageway.

Darkness shrouded him almost instantly and the only light became the small flame protruding from his index finger which he held before him. Bracing himself, he blew the flame and it jumped forward, splitting and lighting every torch it could find along its way. He smiled to himself, his abilities surprising him greatly. To his left was a staircase that led upwards and to his right the passageway bent around a corner. He took the right and it wasn't long before a wall blocked his progress further. His only option now was the port key that glowed on the wall which would lead him into the main structure of the estate. Reaching out once more, he opened the passageway it shielded and it opened out into a corridor with a red carpet that covered only the centre of the walkway a guard walking it straight past him without even noticing him or the corridor where he stood.

Sighing in relief at his close call he took a quiet step out and darted to the right behind a suit of shiny silver armour which stood in an alcove with its comrades lining the stretch of the corridor. Checking the coast was clear, he reached into his tunic and pulled out the blueprint he'd swiped from Boris' the previous evening. Unrolling it, he traced his own location towards the bottom of the parchment. According to the print, if he continued going right, he would reach the kitchens in which there was a disused stove just after the entrance. Concealed within this stove was a tunnel which led down to the basement and lower levels, at least that's what it said. Assuming that was his next point of call he checked for guards once more before jumping out into the corridor and rushing down its right passage. His eyes darted around for guards at every alcove; there was no way he was going to be caught out by one.

Spying the door just up ahead, he quickened his pace and disappeared behind the door without even a second look back. The kitchen he found himself in was quiet and dark - the servants had obviously long gone to bed before what would be an early start in the morning. In front of him was a stone cast stove which was coated in dust from years of being dormant. Instead of embers on the base was some straw; as to its purpose there though Dante had no clue. Bringing out the blueprint once more, he found the stove once more and tried to see if there was any indication as to where it led - there wasn't. How typical of Boris not to record such a minor detail. Grabbing one of the pots from the table he held it above the strewn straw and braced himself as he let it drop.

"Hey!" Spoke a voice from below in an alarmed manner as the pot made a clanking noise on the ground. "What was that?"

"What was what?" asked another who was either pretending or he really hadn't heard the noise.

"That noise...didn't you hear it?"

"Oh stop scaring yourself. You got to expect these sorts of noises down here, you can't jump at everything."

"Well if you're sure...I just get so nervous. Especially now he's put more guards everywhere after the murder of that man."

"I heard from Elouise the other day that he was the boss' brother."

"Codswallop I say."

"That's what I said to her."

Shrugging off the conversation, Dante looked around the kitchen trying to find some rope of some sort. It was a quick drop for the pot but that wasn't the point. It was the hard and noisy landing he was trying to avoid. Finding none he shook his head; he really should've thought about this before he left. Climbing into the stove, he dipped his legs into the shoot and braced himself, pushing his body into the tunnel and sliding down to the bottom. Darkness enveloped him as he slid, air rushing past his face at an increasing speed. He dared to look down, seeing the light of a cobblestoned floor getting closer. Trying to bend his knees slightly to better his landing he braced himself. As one foot landed firmly on the ground, the other landed on the pot and he felt his ankle bone crunch and break. Tears filled his eyes as he winced at the pain, trying to keep himself from making any noise at all.

Dante fell back against the wall, his ankle throbbing. Out of the corner of his eye he could make out two guards clad in chain mail and a purple tunic that went over it, a silver eagle marking Hagen's crest on the chest and a brown belt holding it in place at their waist. They hadn't seen him or heard him by the looks of things but that didn't ease his panic in the slightest. Painfully and using the wall for balance, he slid into the corner and looked around at his surroundings. Chains hung from the ceiling and bars stood in front of him. He wasn't in a cage exactly as there was an opening between the centre most of the bars where a door would usually be. The room beyond where the guards stood seemed to be where he needed to go but how he wasn't sure especially with his injury. Reaching inside his tunic he found the print once more and found his location. The map indicated a passageway connected this room with the rest of the dungeons. Putting the map away again he looked up at the wall opposite him in time to see the Port Key again.

Wincing, he stumbled to the other corner, using the wall to steady himself again. Placing his palm on the port key, he pressed down and the wall parted ways to reveal a gap just big enough for him to step through. A quick glance at the room beyond told him there were no guards around so he limped into the centre of the room. Ahead of him were several wooden doors with slats in the top panel that were only big enough to peer through. On the walls around him were chains and various torturing apparatus hanging to taunt the prisoners. Behind him he could see the guards through a small slat in the door which mirrored those opposite. As the pain in his ankle eased with his progressing speed, he checked the gaps in each of the doors all of which turned out empty, that is except for the end one in which a thin and bloodstained man with wet long hair that covered his face knelt, his arms hanging in place by some thick rusty chains that clung to the ceiling. Dante's heart skipped a beat as he reached for the door handle to find it unlocked and pushed it open, stumbling through.

"Just get it over with!" The man growled without looking up. Dante frowned, he obviously thought Dante was a guard or even Hagen come back to beat him some more.

"Over with what?" Dante asked tentatively hoping he would look up. Part of him didn't want to believe that this could be his brother by rite and the other was breaking at the seams at the thought of him dying there like this.

"Don't play games now Percy," Percy was obviously the one who did all the damage Dante could see. "We both know that I'm not going to tell you what you want to heat no matter how many times you hit me."

"I'm not going to hit you."

"You're not Percy, are you?" The man said after a while and Dante shook his head, begging him to look up and confirm his fears. And so the man did and a pair of bloodshot grey eyes stared up at him and shock took hold of them. Dante let tears slip from his eyes as he looked upon the scarred and bloody face of his brother.

"Dante?" He croaked in disbelief.

"Hello Felix!" Dante said, his voice shaky with distress.

"But how?"

"It's hard to explain but I was summoned...to help Tristan remember."

"Of course, our third trial. And how is Tristan?"

"He's getting there." Dante choked.

"Do not weep for me brother for I have lived far too long."

"That's not the point."

"Then you know I am gone already? I am just glad I got to see you one last time."

"So you forgive me?"

"I betrayed too. Every day that I was back here without you all I hated, I was jealous of myself in fact but also of you, not having any expectations upon you."

"Why did they bring you back?"

"To create the Keys of course. Apparently, that was my redemption."

"That would explain how you ended up being the First Keeper."

"Actually, I have your grandson to thank for that. He defied the Elders and made me his second. Definitely your blood!"

The two shared a pained grumble as Dante leant back against the wall, his bones in his ankle reminding him they were hindered.

"You are injured brother?" Felix croaked, concerned.

"I think I broke it on my way down." Dante replied talking literally in a way.

"How did you manage that?"

"Funny story actually."

"Isn't it always with you?"

The two chuckled again - clearly no time had been lost between them and they were as close as they had been in their glory days seeking trouble wherever they went. But those times were far from now and they shot back down memory lane as Felix began to choke, drops of blood leaking from his mouth. His brother's pain worried Dante and he grabbed his wineskin from under his cloak, muttering a single word as he did so. In an instant, the chains that were holding Felix snapped and he slumped to the side as Dante caught him in his arms, his ankle burning as he lunged forward. He unstopped the lid on his wineskin and poured some of the mead into Felix's mouth. He knew it would probably have had a better effect if it were water he was using but there was none to hand. The choking subsided and Felix gasped in exhaustion.

"Bet it's been a while since you've experienced that taste?" Dante joked, talking of the mead.

"The first taste yes but the second is all too familiar now." Felix's voice was sorrowful now, like it was scraping along the surface of his dry throat. "There is something I would like to say."

"Don't try too hard."

"I did try to make them bring you back, you and Balderick but perhaps not hard enough..."

"Don't worry about that now. Let's just get you out of here yes?"

"Worry not for me dear brother for we would never make it out alive together. Not with your crippled form."

"We can! It would be just like old times."

"What so you're going to sling me over your shoulder and limp all the way you came?"

"Actually my plan was to erect a port key but yours sounds better." Felix choked a laugh and Dante fed him some more of the mead.

"Alas, at last my light can be blown out and I can join our fellow brothers..." He gasped as though his last and final breaths were not too far away.

"Felix no please...we can make it..."

"Not...not this time. Please take care of the brothers we have left..."

His eyes slipped shut and his light was snuffed out. Dante felt his eyes spill over with tears before taking ahold of the wineskin and guzzled down the last few drops.

"Here's to you brother," He chanted as he heard footsteps echo on the metal floor outside as a heavy door was hefted open. "The one true First Keeper!"

# CHAPTER 40 - FINAL WISHES

Even now I didn't know what compelled me to follow Dante to this place and this time. I felt helpless, unable to do anything as he sat and cradled his brother tears now leaking uncontrollable from his forlorn eyes. The First Keeper was dead and as was a man I had idolised in my early years as a Keeper, a man who in my eyes was the epitome of everything a Keeper should be; honourable, wise and just. Above all things he was a trusted friend and teacher and one of the only ones who knew of mine and my brothers' true identity. I closed my eyes momentarily, whispering my respects to Felix. They say the dead can hear our thoughts and, in this moment, more than ever I hoped it were true.

As I opened them again, I saw a white sliver escape from Felix's mouth to stand before me as a full-figured man. It was the First Keeper himself, stood before me all white and ghostly looking intently. He reached around his neck and removed some form of medallion, dropping it to the floor. I made a move for it instantly, acting on impulse once again. I don't know what compelled me to come to the stage I was at now but what I did know is there had to be a good reason for it which wasn't brilliant justification but sometimes, you just have to go with it.

My hand graced a cold rough surface as I reached out to grasp the medallion. I stared at the effigy of a dove in mid-flight holding a key within its beak. It was a sigil I had seen recently; the discarded emblem of the Keepers, the adopted crest of the Brothers of Dharsi. I gulped, looking up at Felix's ghost with worried eyes. His were calm though; cool and content as he nodded in reassurance. Perhaps this was never the sign of Dharsi but of something more that combined both Dharsi and Union. The only thing that did was the Brotherhood element...wait...there was another element. One of the Brothers of Dharsi was also chosen as Unity in the third generation. He was loyal to both sides, even to the end. He betrayed Dharsi by giving their names to the Keepers so that they could be banished after the rest of his brothers were killed. He'd left out eight of them though although their relation to him I did not know. Why the eight he chose, I never knew and I don't think anyone ever did. Unless Felix did...

A loud crash sounded and I was bought back to the current action as two guards burst through the door of the dungeon to see Dante fade away and soon the prison cell; even to me, was no more than a fading image.

*You told me once that madness was a line, drawn by us to define our actions. But you knew it as a theory! You have never been near that line so to you the madness does not exist. But to me, it is oh so real and I am all too close to tipping over the edge back into a world I tried so hard to escape from. But even now I feel drawn back to it, the madness calling out to me over the ebb of the line. That's the thing about madness. It hangs over you like a shadow, waiting for the right moment to creep up on you and latch on once more. You think it's gone; you think you've escaped its clutches but just when you do it comes back stronger than ever. But we never become wiser to it and every time we are drawn back into the same old trap of falling into the darkness that is the madness. That call is always one I struggle to resist and now it is like you are pushing me towards it, pushing me over that line and into the clutches of a dark and bottomless pit filled with jagged claws that strike at you from the sides.*

<p align="center">~~~</p>

Eyes opening, I find myself lying on the ground facing up at a dark and starless sky, skeletal birds drifting aimlessly across it. I wipe away the ashes from my face, stumbling to my feet pitifully as I realise I am back in the world I loathe, I had returned to the madness. I sigh heavily, wondering why I have returned - there must be some reason for it. Looking up at the hill where the Watchtower used to stand, I see a light that shines brightly; so brightly in fact that if I were closer, it would probably blind the sight. It flickers a moment, like it is beckoning to me. Perhaps that is why I am here - perhaps someone has a message for me. I take a couple of steps forward, watching the shadows for movement as I fear the presence of the Faders nearing. The road to the hill is vast and open, a dead stream leading up to it like a road. Around me are others like me, hiding in the shadows of long dead trees, trying to avoid the dreadful gaze of the Faders. They prey upon my inmates and their screams rattle through my ears as their torture begins. Whilst they are distracted, I will make a break for it but first I take on last look around, seeing their faces once more; the many faces of my forgotten brothers. Give me a reason to stay now, to fight for them and not for you dear brother. Any reason will do, just a reason that means no more lives becoming privy to a constant onslaught of torture. There is no answer though, not even from the thunder that should accompany the lightning that flashes across the sky. I figure it is a sign, pointing me to the ever-glowing light up ahead. I check the distraction one last time and run, reaching the hill in no time at all and not stopping as I began to climb its steep and rocky slope.

Halfway up the hill, the light recedes and is nowhere to be seen. Slightly dismayed, I continue my climb - perhaps it would return and even if it didn't it would be useless to return to a world I no longer belonged to. As I climb higher my feet begin to stumble and something glitters in the dead grass as my footing fails. It is a chain I realise as I pick it up and scrape away the dirt from the medallion that hangs around it. The surface itself is bronze and engraved into it in immense detail is a dove holding a single key. As I scrape away the last of the grime, light begins to reflect off it creating a rainbow effect for my eyes. I look up to the top of the hill and realise that the light has returned and pocketing the medallion I finish my ascent. Once I reach the top the light fades again and instead around me are scattered memories left for me to see. I stare into the glistening vortexes as faces of people flash in between them, people I knew, people from down here. One in particular catches my eye, enchanting it for a moment. I take a few paces closer staring into the face of you dear brother. The face I see before me though lingers in the residue; the face of a man lost in a world he does not know. These abandoned memories are yours dear brother and they are my memories too for the most part. In another is the face of my foe and fear surrounds my heart at the sight of him. And as my eyes gaze upon the rest, I too remember - every loss and very lie that was ever told to us. I was so quick to defend him at first. He was our friend and our brother and he would never betray us so.

I remember every regret and each goodbye, every mistake that was made along the way. I could see it all around me now. And as I stand here now, I hear his voice reach me once more, shouting out in pain and vengeance at the hand dealt to him by the almighty. The shout rings out my name and suddenly I realise that I am no longer alone. The light appeared once more as I rose to my feet, bathing me in its brilliance. The Faders cries broke the peace around me and the memories scattered a little further. But the light grew stronger, highlighting the Final Wishes of my dear brother and although it welcomed me with open arms, I could not leave without them for they were why I was here.

Clutching the medallion in my hand once more, I felt something hit my foot and I looked down to see a memory lying beside me. As I gazed upon its vision, my grasp on the medallion tightened, drawing blood that spilt into the memory and changing its happy image to one of sadness and loss. I knew not what the Final Wishes were but this had to be a sign of some sort. The light beckoned ever louder but it was masked by the screams of the Faders as they set their eyes upon me. The screams push me towards the light, but at the same time, they are what made me reach for a reason to stay. This time the reason would be one that made me not want to wash your memory clean dear brother, not to fill the hole that gapes within your mind, not to fill the gap which lies between our scattered souls. This time there is a response, but it is not one which I expect and like a startling sign a voice creeps to me, silencing the screams once more. The light formed a hand, a hand to help me across the distance and it forms the truth which I must now seek. I pick up the memory by my feet; the Final Wishes which I must present. Embracing the light, I close my eyes as a surge of energy rushes to my head and I feel hard ground beneath my feet once more.

I open my eyes to see a robed seer standing in front of me, a quizzical look just visible on his chin beneath his hood. I smile confidently to myself and hand him the Final Wishes. Looking around quickly I notice the palace of colour we appear to reside in and he smiled back at me, turning for the grand doors which lie ahead. Gulping slightly, I follow into an even grander room. I could not describe the details for the colour marvelled me so. It was a spectacular sight, one which would take me many long years to forget. You stand before us dear brother, your hands outstretched ready to receive your Final Wishes. The seer graces you with them and I place the medallion within your hands. Your time Is now dear brother, let your Final Wishes come true.

*"You vile and worthless traitor!" Tristan burst out of the front door of the inn and into the streets of Hasaghar. "How dare you show your face around here after what you did!"*

*Stood before him was a darkened figure from which no details were identifiable. It was like his image was absent from the memory, like something was blocking his appearance from coming to life. All he could do was imagine the unphased look he might have on his face, how he might be smirking and begging for a fight.*

*"Traitor huh?" his voice was cold and void of all emotion.*

*Tristan stared at the man, feeling his body boil up with anger and rage in hatred of the man who was probably laughing under his breath.*

*"Is that the best you've got?" The man toyed, rounding on Tristan like a lion approaching its defeated prey.*

*"Why are you here...you've won," Tristan pleaded almost. "You've made everyone believe we are the traitors; Felix is gone and we are in hiding. What more could you possibly want?"*

*He could feel tears waiting to spill from his eyes - he and his brothers had been through so much at the hands of the man who stood before him in the past few weeks and it was all beginning to take its toll. But he would not let them spill, not now, not in front of him...he wouldn't give him the satisfaction.*

*"I have come for what is rightfully mine."*

*Tristan didn't know what he meant but he was more concerned by the shouts and screams he could hear coming from back inside the inn. The screams belonged to Dagnen; not too long ago she had gone into labour in the middle of the inn. They'd closed early* and taken her upstairs but Tristan was now running out of time. All he wanted to do was get rid of this man that towered over him and watch his child come into the world.

"You leave her out of this!" he demanded, seeing the man's grey eyes sneer up at the open window as his face flashed in a blur of colour.

"Oh I'm not here for her, I have no interest in women. I demand my vengeance!" The man replied, clenching his fists.

"Vengeance? What for?"

"For the wrongs dealt to me."

"Me and my brothers have never wronged you, it is you who have wronged us."

"Well that is where you are wrong. Technically speaking your brothers are the ones who wronged me."

Tristan frowned, he and his brothers had never done anything but follow and learn from the man who stood before him. But now that man had betrayed him all in the name of vengeance for what his brothers did to him. How that could even be possible though was beyond him. He was bought out of his thoughts by another scream from Dagnen and his face screwed up in frustration.

"Leave!" he yelled at the shadow. "Leave here now and never come back."

"I will," the man replied cunningly. "As soon as I get what I came for."

"Well find it someplace else."

"I'm not going anywhere Tristan," again his face flashed into view but once again it was too quick to pinpoint any details except those vacant grey eyes that pulsed out from his eye sockets.

His frustration getting the better of him, Tristan grabbed hold of the man and held him up against the wall shaking him a little before throwing him to the ground. As the man launched through the air, he collided with an empty bottle, crashing to the floor with a rumble of laughter and snapping wood. The crash bought colour to his clothes; a green tunic with gold trimmings and black leggings that descended into brown boots. The man got to his feet and turned to Tristan; his face still as black as the night sky leaving no feature seen except for those grey eyes. They tainted him, daring him to do things he thought himself not capable of doing so. He pictured himself beating the man until he was covered in blood, no life left within his battered face, his own face screwed up in anger as he swung at him again and again. He heard the scream again and the front door of the inn burst open as footsteps came to a stop behind him. He thought he heard his brother say his name, but couldn't be sure as he landed a punch to the man's face flooring him *once more. The man looked up in shock, a bearded blooded face flashing in place of the shadow momentarily.*

*"If I ever see you again," Tristan threatened. "I swear to God, I will kill you!"*

*The words struck fear into the man's heart. He could tell by the way he froze there for a second longer just staring up at Tristan as the rain beat down on the streets. Getting to his feet, he slowly backed off before running down the streets and out of sight. Tristan turned to see Jacques standing in the doorway, a concerned look on his face, one that soon turned to apprehension.*

*"Tristan Dagnen needs you...now!" Jacques yelled*

*There was a sense of alertness to his voice as he led the way back into the inn and up the stairs to the guest room where Dagnen was screaming as she tried to halt her own natural instinct to push. She wasn't about to give birth without her beloved being by her side. Tristan came to kneel beside her, taking her hand within his and looking into her eyes. For a moment, they locked and everything around them ceased to move. In that space, time stopped and the only motions were shared by their everlasting gaze. But the second was over all too quickly as she began pushing again, silent screams escaping her as she tried to keep her eyes connected with Tristan's. He was good at keeping calm, even in trying situations and that was what gave her strength in that moment. But soon the silence was broken by the cry of a baby and their gaze broke as both looked down to Myrina who held the bloody child within her arms. Tristan looked back to Dagnen and she smiled as Myrina's father cut the cord and wrapped the babe in a clean cloth, wiping the grime from its face. He handed it to Dagnen and Tristan as they both cradled it in their arms.*

*"It is a girl," he said softly as he rose to his feet and backed up towards the door.*

*"Congratulations." Myrina blushed, smiling to the two of them as she joined her father by the door.*

~~~

The scene faded then and it was as though I were looking upon it like it was a picture stopped in time. I saw you my dear brother with your arms around your beloved as she cradled your daughter within her arms. My niece. So small and so beautiful, so weak and so innocent in that one moment of life. As I reflect upon what I have seen, I realise just what your Final Wishes are and I turn away once more to the darkness that consumes me and separated our souls from uniting once more.

I think of where she'll be now and what she'll look like, whether your beloved will be stood beside her or only able to look upon her face as though she were looking through glass, a barrier between their souls. That barrier is a line, human-made; like that between madness and shadow. But in some places, this barrier wears thin and she can just touch her upon the shoulder, just as you almost touched her face in the grounds of the inn where she stood in front of you just on the other side.

# CHAPTER 41 - NO MORE SECRETS

Tristan stared out at the darkened street, counting the candles that were extinguished in the windows as folk turned in for the night. He sighed heavily, wishing for a moment that he could share in their simple lives of mindless routine and never-ending work to pay the taxes and feed countless mouths. It was true Hagen kept a well-oiled machine here in Dilu but the price came at the health and wellbeing of his people, not to mention their disliking for him completely. He wondered what his reaction must've been like when he discovered what had happened to his brother. Oh, the pleasure it bought to Tristan to imagine the look upon Hagen's face when one of his guards presented him with the box. It probably would've confused him at first and then he would've seen the resemblance between the runes on the severed flesh and those scarred on Boris' face. The guards were probably dispatched and it wouldn't have taken them long to discover the bloody mess Tristan and Dante had left for him. Would he have wept in front of his men? Would he even let on that a lowly pawn shop owner was his brother? Especially after he had been murdered in such a brutal way.

Footsteps sounded behind him, bringing Tristan out of his thoughts as he turned to face Zhaine; a mopey look upon his face.

"I uh...apologise," Zhaine, and Ramien for that matter were never very good at apologising. Then again neither was Dante so it must've been something that ran in the family.

"What for?" Tristan inclined, a smirk lingering on the left side of his lips.

"Oh don't make me..." Zhaine cursed under his breath, perhaps Tristan was more himself than he realised. "Fine! I apologise for acting as though I knew what was best for you."

"And?"

"For talking about you like you weren't even there."

"And?"

"For arguing with my uncle less than five minutes after meeting him for the first time. Now can we give it a rest?"

"Gladly."

Tristan smiled to himself, strolling past Zhaine and heading for the stairs down to the entrance way. As he reached the banister, he felt a pulse shoot through his head and his body buckled over, collapsing him to the floor. He could hear footsteps echo as Zhaine came rushing to his side, shouting his name as he did so. But Tristan didn't hear anything else, just the screams of a woman begging a man to stop an onslaught of some kind. His left hand began to burn and his vision blurred as his face became hot and swollen as though someone were punching him repeatedly. But the punches were not meant for him. It was like none of it was really happening, not to him anyway but to someone else. Only somehow, the pain was inflicting on him too, like whoever that person was was calling out for help. Like they were linked.

No sooner had the pain begun it was over again leaving no more than a lingering tingle across the mark on his left palm. He clenched his fist as he felt Zhaine back off a few paces leaving Tristan to get to his feet on his own. He'd obviously seen the mark and was now thinking the worst.

"I know what you're thinking," Tristan said calmly. "But I'm not a traitor."

"Then why do you have that fucking mark on your hand?" Zhaine questioned erratically, his voice quivering slightly in misguided fear.

"It's called the mark of the Bearer of Secrets. I'm not quite sure what it means, but by my understanding it appeared because of the secrets I kept not just from the Keepers but my own brothers. I guess in a way, by keeping the secrets I did I effectively betrayed my Brotherhood...but I never betrayed the Keepers."

"Who else knew about the mark?"

"Cedric. He more or less worked it out for himself actually with those visions he used to have. And then Romeo found out not long after we were out casted as traitors by Charles."

"So you promise, you're not a traitor?"

"I swear it!"

Zhaine nodded to him, the look of fear now slipping from his pale face as he tried to relax his stance.

"So what happened then?" He asked, not sure how to take what he had just witnessed and heard.

"I think someone is in trouble." Tristan explained, choosing his word carefully to ensure his brother would understand. "You see Dante has the same mark and as far as we are aware we are the only two Bearers of Secrets. He said that he knew Felix was in danger because he felt it when we went to see Boris."

"So you think you felt Dante in danger?"

"Potentially. Do you know where he is?"

"No, he stormed off not long after you. I don't know where he went..."Zhaine's voice trailed off as an echo crept into Tristan's ears. It cried out for help from anyone who was listening. This time the pain felt different, like it was dull and lingering. Obviously, the beating had stopped, or maybe it wasn't a beating at all. The pain he felt deep in his heart was familiar and Zhaine seemed to notice as his face became taunt once more. He placed a hand on Tristan's shoulder bringing him back to reality.

"You okay?" He asked his voice full of concern.

"I'm not sure," Tristan wasn't sure how to explain it not even to himself. "It's an odd sort of pain this time."

"Describe it to me, the pain I mean."

"Well the first time it was like I was being punched over and over again and there was like a...it felt like my head might explode. But now, it's dull and part of me feels lifeless. It's hard to explain."

"When you felt the pain, did you feel like a falling sensation - the second time round I mean."

"No but I did the first time. Why what are you thinking?"

"I don't know if you'll remember but when we escaped the Compound in Hasaghar, just after we were branded as traitors. We tried to portal out but every time we did, we ended up just a few feet away from where we had aparated. It's known as the spliesing effect and was actually really dangerous. Basically, Charles had stopped the use of glyph magic in the Compound which we didn't know at the time, meaning it was virtually impossible to get out of there in one piece. In the worst-case scenarios people have lost limbs...but we got out eventually.

"I remember the pain I felt when we finally got out of the Compound. All that spliesing, over and over again, the pain was almost unbearable and we were lucky to be in one piece...all be it bloodied up a bit...well a lot. It felt like I was being ripped in two afterwards, but during it was like someone was throwing rocks at me continuously. It's...an onslaught of pain."

"So could Dante be spliesed?"

"It's possible. I mean if I were Hagen and my brother had just been murdered, I would definitely be placing magical wards to prevent people from using Glyphs within my premises. He may have gone there to see Felix, got caught, tried to portal out and ended up someplace else."

"We need to do something Zhaine. We need to hit that place tonight! It Dante is there and in trouble, there is no time to waste."

"So where do start?"

"First, we need to tell Nielson who Dante really is but Basso can't know. Dante doesn't trust him and strictly speaking neither do I." Zhaine pulled a face but he did not question his brother, he knew better than that especially with that mark now on his palm.

"Well that should be simple enough considering I know for a fact that Basso is in the street right now throwing up outside that old tavern. I saw him there myself just now."

"Well that's perfect. My guess is Nielson is reminiscing with Merlin down in the foyer over a brandy or two."

Zhaine nodded and together they headed down the stairs towards the foyer where they hoped they would find Nielson and Merlin. Nerves began to brew within Zhaine, he had not seen his father in just over three years and the fact that he had no idea where his brother was made him even more nervous about facing him. Not to mention the fact that he would have to explain why in the month he had been back he had not come to find him sooner. Sure enough though Tristan was right and Nielson and Merlin were exactly where he said they'd be sharing a decanter of brandy as they laughed over old times. He looked back at Zhaine and he lingered where he stood, just out of sight from his father and the old man. Taking a big sigh, Tristan paced briskly towards the table and both the men clapped eyes on his serious face, their laughter halting immediately.

"Tristan," Nielson addressed. "What are you still doing up?"

"I couldn't sleep!" Tristan answered, he was half being honest. "Actually I have something to show the both of you."

He rose his voice a little louder towards the end as though to signal to Zhaine to come out. When he didn't appear Tristan sighed heavily as though he should have expected him to do something like this. Merlin and Nielson looked from one to the other wondering what was going on.

"Don't mess around now you idiot," Tristan yelled, clearly getting impatient. His mood wasn't helped by the snigger of laughter that sounded from around the corner, catching both the old men's eyes as they glared at where Zhaine was hiding.

Once the moment had passed, Zhaine stepped out and came face to face with his father who rose to his feet the moment he lay eyes on him.

"Hello father," he said solemnly trying to avoid eye contact as though he were ashamed to be in his presence without his brother.

"My boy!" without even taking a moment to glance at Zhaine he pulled him into a heartfelt clinch, his closed eyes filling with tears. After so long of not seeing either of his sons, he was coming to terms with accepting that they may never come back. He had already lost one son, there was no way he could imagine getting over the loss of all three of them.

"I am so happy to see you," Nielson cajoled as the two break away.

"I'm sorry father, I do not know where Ramien is," Zhaine began to explain himself. "And yes, I've been back a while but I had no idea you were here..."

"None of that matters now. I am just happy you are safe, and here now. I'm sure Ramien will come back in his own time." Zhaine let a smile touch the edges of his lips, tears forming in his eyes; but he would not let them spill; he was too proud for that. With the family reunion over, Tristan needed to bring them back to what mattered - Dante. He knew the revelation would bring Nielson to the edge so a sensitive approach was needed because not only was one of his sons back in the world of light, so was his brother.

"I get the sense that Zhaine isn't your main reason for coming and finding us Tristan?" Merlin questioned - that old man was too wise for his own good sometimes.

"You would be right there Merlin, it's about Daxon." Tristan hinted, his eyes catching Merlin's who gave him a knowing look, nodding his head in approval of what he was about to do.

"What about him?" asked Nielson, returning to his seat as though he felt the need to.

"He's not who he says he is...who we say he is." Tristan signalled between himself and Merlin causing a stern look to echo from Nielson's old face at the deception he was dealt. "His name is Dante Ashdown."

"Impossible! How dare you disgrace his memory by..."

"Nielson, I'm telling the truth. He wanted to tell you but he was afraid you still hated him. Heck, he tried last week, but I walked in at the wrong moment. But I swear to you, I would not lie about this."

Nielson rose to his feet, turning his back on those around him as he tried to come to terms with what he had just heard. Could it be that his own brother by blood had been stood before him these past few months and he hadn't even realised? The truth was that part of him had realised the truth, the other part of him just hadn't wanted to believe it for fear of being right, for fear that he would have to face something he had been hiding from for so long. The truth was he was disgusted with himself for saying the things he did before Dante was banished - first and foremost they were brothers and you should never utter the words he had to family.

"I should've known who he was the moment I saw him but I doubted myself." Nielson sighed, his voice breaking. "After all, it's been so long I could've been wrong. But nothing's changed...he's still my brother and that's all that matters..."

"I'm sorry I never told you," Tristan consoled. "But it wasn't my place to tell no matter how much my loyalty should've been with you. And now the only reason I am telling you is because he is in trouble and I need your help."

"Trouble? What sort of trouble?"

"I'm not sure, I just know that he's in pain, a lot of pain."

"How?"

"I've seen it. Do you remember when I came to you as a Scribe and I showed you something that made me afraid I had done something? I showed you my mark of the Bearer of Secrets which it turns out Dante shares."

"How are you managing to tell me this?"

It was a good question, in fact even Tristan wasn't sure how himself. The marks that bound them to their Brotherhood usually prevented them from telling anything about Unity to others without the presence of each of his brothers from that generation. But then it had always been that way; right from the beginning the brothers had been able to reveal their secret without any detriment - perhaps it was because they were the last and therefore it didn't matter anymore if anybody knew who they were.

"How have I always been able to tell anyone who I am?" Tristan posed, Nielson nodding in truth. "I felt Dante's pain, I think this connects us."

"We think that he went to see Felix."

"Felix? He's here?"

"Worse, Hagen has him, Tristan found out yesterday."

"And why am I only hearing of this now?"

"Because I thought you'd be ashamed," Tristan explained as Nielson inclined his head. "Of what I did to find that out."

"So you and Dante killed Boris?"

Tristan nodded, avoiding Nielson's gaze. Nielson had always seemed like a father figure to Tristan, especially at a time where his own had failed him in so many ways already. He always felt that he could come to him for anything, the fact that he had acted as the father of his own bride at their wedding had nothing to do with it. The last thing he would ever want to do is disappoint him, even before his own father.

"Well I guess someone had to put him out of his misery," Nielson sighed, a slight smile disgracing his mouth.

"I don't understand...I thought..." Tristan looked up at Nielson, his eyes filled with surprise.

"Well you named the man, what was I supposed to expect? Especially as Dante named him too once upon a time."

Tristan let a smile taint him, as he gasped in surprise at Nielson's reaction. Pushing that to the back of his mind though, he now had to focus on Dante and getting him out of the estate - if their suspicions were correct that is.

"Speaking of Dante, what do you think has happened to my brother?" Nielson asked, fear filling his voice.

"I think he's spliesed himself," Zhaine interjected rather confidently.

"Spliesed?" Merlin definitely wasn't aware of the concept and his father shared the expression.

"You remember when we were banished by Charles and we tried to portal out of the Compound unaware he had placed wards so that we couldn't? We ended up only a few feet away from where we had disappeared in the first place and in a lot of pain. I think that Dante went to see Felix but got caught so tried to get out and ended up being spliesed."

"So if he was in the Estate, where is he now."

"Oh he's still there, I'm sure of it." Tristan asserted, eager to get moving now.

"So what's the plan?" queried Merlin, intrigue getting the better of him.

"Well we break in, save Dante and Myrina and potentially kill Hagen."

"Potentially?" questioned Basso as he stumbled into sight.

"Basso..." Zhaine rose to his feet.

"Hello old friend." The two smiled to one another briefly.

"How much did you hear?" Tristan asked, suddenly afraid of how long he had been standing there.

"Long enough to hear the plan."

"Then I guess we don't need to fill you in."

"Just tell me where you need me."

"In the dungeons. You and Zhaine; your job is to get Felix out." Basso and Zhaine nodded in approval of their role. "Nielson and Merlin, you'll need to be ready at the gate with the horses for our escape in case things get ugly. Try canvassing the building as well from there to figure out where exactly Daxon is. Then let whoever's closest know where to go." Again his suggestion was met with nodding. He hadn't thought this plan through fully, most of it was improvised in the moment so the amount of approval he was getting from the others was very reassuring.

"What about you?" asked Zhaine, half expecting an answer that made him out to be the main hero of the night.

"I'll be scaling the balcony and saving the princess."

"Should've known you'd say something like that." he sniggered childishly.

# CHAPTER 42 - INTO DARKNESS

Later that night, the air rang a coldness that bit sharp on the cheeks of the men as they stood and faced the Estate. It seemed to steady their postures as he straightened up, now was not a time for nerves. At this time of night, there wouldn't be a lot of guards around, none that were awake anyway - most would probably be sleeping at their posts. There weren't many lights on either. The only ones available to their sight were at the main entrance to the estate where two guards stood either side of the door, another pacing the entire grounds at a rather slow pace. Another light was lit in the balcony window above where Tristan knew Myrina's room to be. He wondered what she would be doing awake - perhaps Hagen was up there with her? He didn't want to think about that though, the man had always creeped him out in a sort of slimy way.

"Can you sense Daxon anywhere?" Tristan asked Nielson.

"I'm afraid I can't," Nielson replied sadly. He caught Tristan's eye as though he was disappointed that his own brother had warded himself so no Prodical could trace him. Or maybe just those who knew him.

"I may not sense any Keepers," Merlin interrupted, his grey eyes clouding as they searched every corner of the Estate visible to them. "But I do sense two people in the room above the entrance...the one with the balcony."

"Myrina and Hagen?"

"Yes, one of them is a woman but the man I sense is not powerful enough to be Hagen. I think they know that someone has broken in."

"Then we need to move quickly." Zhaine stammered, his heart racing as nerves seared through him. "Where's our entrance?"

"Well seeing as the map is with Daxon..." Tristan began but he was interrupted by Basso.

"What is he even doing in there?" He asked theoretically. "I mean what reason did he have to be there?"

"It was always our intention to bail Myrina out and kill Hagen," Tristan said truthfully. "He probably wanted to scope the place out a little."

"He obviously wasn't careful if he's been caught." Basso smirked as though he was glad Dante had slipped up.

It made Tristan uneasy and feel like he had seen that look before. It was a look that got off on his failure and short comings; a look that liked the fact that someone was suffering due to their own failings.

"Moving on!" Zhaine interjected, sighing heavily at the inappropriateness of Basso's comments. At his age, he should know better.

"From what I remember seeing on the map, there are two secret entrances." Tristan explained. "There's one near the kitchen entrance and another around the bushes somewhere but I can't remember where exactly. The best bet is the kitchens, an old furnace leads down to the dungeons but you're on your own from there."

"I think we can cope with that."

"You may need to come to terms with the fact that Felix may already be dead." Merlin suggested, his voice uneasy. "It worries me that I cannot sense someone as powerful as him, even if his location is underneath the compound itself. I, or Nielson for that matter, would still be able to sense him."

They all sighed heavily at the potential loss of their First Keeper and at the severity of the mission they were about to take on. Zhaine looked to Basso and the two nodded, readying themselves to climb the wall into the courtyard. Just as they did, a bright light shone out from the centre of the courtyard and they all stared in awe at its grandeur. The edges of the beam rippled as it flickered, shining so bright it could probably be seen from miles around. A glyph appeared in the mist of it; a glyph that marked the passing of only a Prodical.

"He's dead!" Nielson sighed, his voice cracking with grief. "Felix is dead!"

The five placed their hands over their hearts as a sign of respect to their former leader, the glyph beginning to fade now and taking the light with it. A single tear slipped from the eyes of each - this changed everything for Tristan and he damned Hagen for being the cause of yet another death in his life. Cursing the air, he swore then to leave Hagen in a way that meant death would be an easy escape.

"Justice will come my brother!" A voice whispered into his ear as his unknown follower made himself known once more. As the light faded, Basso looked to his comrades with a grave face.

"Now what," He asked, his voice as shaky as Nielson's had been.

A pain gripped Tristan's chest as though warning him of the pain that Dante was in, however something was different this time. It was like it was telling him that the pain was yet to come as opposed to it already happening. Was it possible his vision had been of what would happen? Either way he didn't have time to think about that, not know that they all looked to him for guidance.

"This changes nothing," Tristan started, his voice strong above his own mourning. "You retrieve Felix's body. You bring him back so we can bury him properly."

Zhaine and Basso nodded, and with the passing of the light they climbed the wall and began their mission. Tristan waited a while before following, wanting to give them a head-start in case there were more guards than anticipated. He began his climb, nodding to Nielson and Merlin as he disappeared over the other side, pulling himself into the bushes to find an access point to the balcony. The balcony which was attached to Myrina's room was part of a tower which rounded at the corner of the Estate. He imagined it was part of Hagen's plan to keep her from escaping especially after she had done so all too recently. There was no way he'd get to her in a conventional way, not without the map anyway. His eyes searched desperately before landing on a patch of ivy that rested on the tower. It was just short of the balcony but it looked like he might reach with a little stretch and a jump to get him onto it. Ducking down, he waiting for the pacing guard to disappear out of sight before sprinting for the ivy and making a successful grab to pull himself to security.

Once he was sure the guard was making another round, he began his climb at a steady pace, being careful not to rustle the leaves too much for fear of being detected. When he reached the end of his ascent, he stretched one hand towards the wall of the balcony and grabbed it tight. Letting go of the ivy slowly, he hung momentarily before swinging himself over the banister. Catching his breath, Tristan crept towards the glass doors that closed on Myrina's quarters. He couldn't see much, a thin veil rested on the other side of the glass making details impossible to see. What he could make out was a He squinted, just able to make out some shadows as a figure collapsed to the floor and what looked to be a woman racing over to it to. Tristan reached for the handle of the door and eased it open just enough that he could see the two people for who they were. Luckily the door wasn't locked and it moved with ease not making a single sound and allowing him to remain undetected. Peering through the gap, he could make out a few features of the figure who had fallen to the floor. He was also relieved to see that the woman was in fact Myrina.

The figure she crouched by wasn't in in a brilliant way. Its breathing was laboured and harsh, hands bloodied and long black hair tangled and matted. Tristan's eyes rested back towards the hands seeing a glyph fade back into the skin, his worst fears confirmed. It was Dante, there was no mistaking it and even though he expected to find him battered and bruised, that didn't mean he was prepared for it. He gasped, letting his legs drag him into the room and creaking the door further open. The sound made Myrina jump to her feet and swing around to face Tristan with a sigh of relief.

"Is he okay?" Were the only words he could manage as he expected the worst.

"So that's why you're here then," she said solemnly as though she were disappointed and almost as though she didn't mean to say it out loud

"I'm here for you both. I made you a promise Myrina...and I'm going to keep it." A smile fluttered and the edge of her lips and she looked back to Dante, concern filling her soft face.

"He's in a bad way. I don't know what happened, he just appeared out of nowhere. What is he doing here?"

"I wish I knew. Either way I'm going to need help getting him out so I can't very well leave you behind now can I?" Her answer was lost as she jumped at a knock sounding at the door.

"Who is it?" she asked as Tristan reached for Dante and dragged him out into the balcony, pulling the door shut again.

~~~

I chose to stay in the room rather than follow my brother out to the balcony. After all, it's not as though I had to worry about being seen.

"'Tis your lord my dear," came a wry voice that sent shivers pulsing down my back. I watched her reaction as she shook herself, repulsed and unlocked the door. Turning her back on the intruder, she rested her hands on the back of her dressing table chair, her posture turning rigid. "Good evening my dear!" Came the voice as the door opened and shut again silently.

My eyes met with his, not that he knew it, and for a moment I felt electricity fill the space between us, our connection suddenly becoming physical as I felt the hatred boil over within me.

"Good evening my lord," Myrina answered, keeping her back facing him. "What brings you here at this hour?"

"I could be asking you a similar question my dear."

A look of disgust filled her face as Hagen stepped closer to her placing a firm hand on her hip. The touch itself filled me with even more anger, how dare he allow himself to think that sort of movement was even appropriate.

"I was woken by a commotion outside." she answered numbly. "The guards - they are so restless tonight."

"That is because we have an intruder in the dungeons." Myrina froze. "It would appear someone was there outside of *visiting hours*. You wouldn't happen to know who would you?"

"How should I know?"

"No matter."

I watched helplessly as his grip on her hip tightened and he spun her round. She came to a stop before the bed, her legs catching on the post as she lost her balance. Landing on the bed, she came face to face with Hagen who stood over her with his hands behind his back.

"After all," he said with a slight smile pinching his lips. "It would appear that both of us know the intruder...very well."

"I don't know what you're talking about."

"Do not lie to me wench!" His hand flew across her face causing me to snap my eyes shut and wish with all my might there was something I could do.

~~~

Tristan straightened up as he heard Myrina scream. He couldn't hear a lot from his vantage point but if that wasn't a cry for help, he didn't know what was. He glanced over at Dante who was propped up against the balcony barrier, to check he was still breathing - watching a while as his chest expanded filling his lungs with air. He grabbed the dagger from inside his tunic.

Opening the door urgently, he stopped as Hagen looked straight up at him from where he stood over Myrina who lay on the bed. His face aghast and pale, a dagger protruding from the back of his head as he fell forwards just shy of the bed. Tristan looked up at Myrina her face white and partially covered by a shaking hand. Near the door, he thought he saw a shadow that seemed to fade into the wall as it was no more. Gulping heavily, he inclined his head to Myrina.

"I swear it wasn't me!" she stammered, unable to believe what had just happened.

"You think I care?" Tristan sniggered. "Get your things, we're leaving."

"What now?"

"Yes now!"

"What about Hagen?"

"Just leave him there. I doubt he's going anywhere."

"Are you not even worried about who killed him."

"Nope. Good on them I say."

Tristan turned his back on Myrina and went back out onto the balcony, peering over the edge and spying Zhaine and Basso heading for some bushes by the wall, Felix's body supported between them. His heart skipped a beat before he whistled, making Zhaine look up and nod to him. They perched in the bushes there, awaiting his next signal.

"Myrina," he said, turning to see her staring at Hagen's body, her hand still covering her face. "Is there a warning bell that summons the guards?"

"Yes," her voice was shaky as she answered him. "There's one down the hall. They're all connected so if you ring one you ring them all."

"Good!"

Speeding past her, he opened the door out into the hallway a little, looking both ways before sprinting out towards the rope he could see hanging to his right. Glancing up a little at the bell, he tugged on the rope hard, sending a loud bellow throughout the entire estate as the rest of the bells chimed along with it. Charging back towards Myrina's room he closed the door behind him and bolted it.

"Hurry up and get your things together," He commanded as Myrina remained where she sat. "We don't have a lot of time."

At last she stood, walking slowly over to the dresser and rummaging through her jewellery box.

"Did he do that to you?" Tristan asked as he spied the cheek she had been hiding from him; a small breakage in the akin surrounded by redness. She nodded in response, not looking at him but continuing to search through her things. "Then he deserved what he got."

Tristan went back to the balcony and watched as three guards congregated before heading into the estate. He signalled to Zhaine who nodded once more whispering something to Basso who took Felix over his shoulder and headed for the gate where Nielson and Merlin had now emerged. Zhaine sprinted towards them and began climbing the ivy up to the balcony. Lifting Dante, he cursed at how heavy he was before seating him on the edge and turning him to face outwards. Once Zhaine was in place, he eased him forward, his brother catching him on his shoulder and climbing slowly back down to the ground.

"Come on!" Tristan commanded to Myrina.

He turned to see her waiting at the door, a cloak around her shoulders and a necklace he recognised hanging around her neck. It was an amber heart with silver etching, making it seem more like a chestnut, which hung to a silver chain. Romeo had bought that for her and the sight of it bought a smile to his face. She nodded to him and he moved so she could get to the ivy and climb down to where Zhaine was waiting.

The door suddenly swung open, three guards appearing it in its wake and staring open mouthed at Hagen's lifeless body.

"Is he dead?" asked one of them, none of them seeming shocked at the sight.

"Looks like," said another gulping as he tentatively poked Hagen's lifeless hand with his spear. "What do we do now?"

"Ah just leave him there, he was a bastard anyway." said the third, looking mildly smug.

"But who's gonna pay us."

"There are plenty of Lords within this Estate Drew. I say we go the tavern and toast to our freedom."

"But what about the Lady Myrina?"

"Wherever she is it's a better place than here."

The three guards shrugged to each other before disappearing back down the hall and shutting the door behind them. Hagen must've been a horrible commander to have his own men treat his corpse so. Choosing not to think about it, he pulled himself over the edge of the balcony and climbed down the ivy. Once on the ground, he and Myrina sprinted to the gate where Basso was now waiting in place of the elders. Dante was propped onto a horse along with Felix' lifeless body.

"We'll stop over by those trees," Nielson said pointing to the cluster by the mountain side. "Then we'll give Felix the send-off he deserves."

The rest nodded before making their way towards the spot Nielson had pointed out a few yards. Felix was placed on the ground and Nielson indicated that all the Keepers should stand around him in a circle, their heads bowed. He chanted, tears falling from his eyes as he commanded Glyphs to take their First Keeper to his final resting place. And tall they stood mourning their loss. Just the wind and the stars in the night sky to stand over him as his warden, minding him on his way to his eternal resting place. In his own words as a final tribute; *we hardly knew ye.*

The lost Keepers heard hooves in the distance, and it bought them away from their mourning, their First Keeper's body now commemorated to the Earth. Tristan signalled for Myrina to get onto the horse behind Dante and tried to squint through the rolling mist to see what was coming.

"Well don't just stand there you silly fuckers!" Came a ragged voice through the fog as a white horse came into sight. The rider grabbed Zhaine by the hand, forcing him up behind him before riding off again.

"Who the..." Nielson didn't have time to finish his insult though as more hooves sounded.

"Faders!" Basso yelled, as he came running out of the mist for the horses.

Myrina pushed hers forward after the rider as Tristan climbed on behind Basso and Nielson behind Merlin. They raced ahead, pushing the horses beyond breaking point.

"Bas," Tristan called ahead of the noise and commotion. "Try and catch up to the rider."

"Are you kidding me?" Basso alarmed. "He took Zhaine!"

"You failed to realise that Zhaine didn't resist. I think I know who it was."

Tristan hadn't got a good look at the man's face but the fact that Zhaine didn't resist, not even a little was unsettling. Whatever Basso planned on doing next was lost in the face of a Fader suddenly right beside them. It screamed at them, two red lights glowing in the space where it's face should've been. Acting recklessly, Tristan kicked out at it, knocking it from its horse. Reaching from the saddle he pulled himself onto the dark beast, pushing it onwards to catch up with the shadow on the horizon that was the mysterious rider.

The others weren't far behind him and it wasn't long before he was side by side with the rider.

"Caught up, did you?" he joked, a dry smile upon his face.

"You crafty bugger Ramien!" Tristan yelled to him.

"So you do recognise me. I am pleased."

"Yes, well we don't have time for jokes, we need a plan."

"Well I'm all ears."

"So what you're just running from these guys?"

"Pretty much."

A loud bang sounded behind them and Tristan looked back to see Nielson draw another glyph before disparaging it in the direction of the Faders.

"Tristan," Zhaine called. "How do you fancy leaving Dilu permanently?"

"Well it might be advisable considering that's two murders under my belt now." Tristan replied, the past few days catching up with his moral compass. What on earth would his father think?

"New record for you isn't it?" Ramien chuckled as another bang sounded behind them shining light into the night air.

"Shut up you prat!" Tristan cursed his brothers timing - this was no time for sarcasm or jokes, but then that was Ramien all over.

"I hear there's a group of Keepers forming in Az Landen Forest."

"Az Landen it is then."

"Alright, fall back. I'll get us out of here. Let the others know what's happening. I'm gonna put a timer on this portal."

Tristan nodded, pulling his horse back in line with each of the other horses and telling them the plan. He pulled in behind Basso and they all formed a line as Zhaine checked behind him to make sure they were all ready. There was a good distance now between them and the Faders which meant plenty of leeway for a quick getaway. A blue light shone up ahead as Zhaine commanded the correct glyph and shot it out ahead a couple of feet in front of them. Charging forward, they embraced the blue light that quickly began to fade once they were through. Myrina and Dante passed through next, followed by Nielson and Merlin, Basso and Tristan who just made it as the blue light from the portal faded into darkness...

...to be continued

Printed in Great Britain
by Amazon

67809162R00170